The Blue Manuscript

The Blue Manuscript

Sabiha Al Khemir

VERSO
London • New York

First published by Verso 2008
© Sabiha Al Khemir 2008
All rights reserved

The moral rights of the author have been asserted

1 3 5 7 9 10 8 6 4 2

Verso
UK: 6 Meard Street, London W1F 0EG
USA: 20 Jay Street, Suite 1010, Brooklyn, NY 11201
www.versobooks.com

Verso is the imprint of New Left Books

ISBN-13: 978-1-84467-308-7

British Library Cataloguing in Publication Data
A catalogue record for this book is available from the British Library

Library of Congress Cataloging-in-Publication Data
A catalog record for this book is available from the Library of Congress

Typeset by Hewer Text UK Ltd, Edinburgh
Printed in the USA by Maple Vail

For Nacer, who gave me the name Sabiha

Beyond faith, beyond unbelieving,
Beyond doubt, beyond certainty . . .
Rumi

This is a work of fiction. All the events are fictional. However, a 'blue manuscript' from the early medieval period did exist. In the twentieth century its leaves were separated and sold individually and are now in collections of Islamic art all over the world. Individual leaves still turn up on the international market. This novel hopes to pay homage to that medieval manuscript.

I

The café swarmed with words. Words mingled in a shower of chatter that bathed them warmly. Shards of conversations surfaced, but only Zohra, the translator, caught them. The others did not speak Arabic and Mustapha was preoccupied with his calculations. They were stuck to their wooden seats, their bottoms numb. A long-winded song from a gramophone strung the various corners of the space together. The atmosphere was filled with a haze that somehow made everyone feel snug. The glasses were chipped, the tea too sweet, but fingers hugged the misty glasses the way the atmosphere hugged them. Opposite, a young woman with a pharaonic profile complained languidly to a man who seemed unaware of her timeless beauty. An old woman in black smoked a narghile with concentration. Above her hung a mummified crocodile, the texture of its skin still vivid, even under the patina of dust. The ambience was undeniably mysterious, yet there was the feeling all round that it was completely normal. Having arrived in the late afternoon, they had not seen the city of Cairo yet. It was strange to find themselves here. The café was a close-up view out of context.

Donatella roamed in her reflections. Zohra was perplexed. She so much wanted to ask what the Blue Manuscript was. Was it something everyone should know? Donatella showed no sign of surprise when Mark mentioned it. Would Zohra be revealing her ignorance if she asked? Why should she know anything about it anyway? She was simply an intermediary. She knew nothing about the subject, while all the others had come here on the same common mission. Mark had introduced himself as the project manager and seemed to be keen to get things going. Donatella was an archaeologist and had been on excavations in Italy even though this was the first time she would be working in an Arab country, and Mustapha seemed at home and ready to do anything to ensure they would find the Blue Manuscript.

In their uncomfortable seats, Donatella, Mark, Zohra and Mustapha were sinking into the night. The café had spread, filling the alleyway, which was lit by intricate openwork lanterns. There was no separation between external and internal space. The alley and the café building were sewn together by human action, and on such a warm night they quite forgot they were outdoors. The waiter had pushed two tables together to make one large enough for the four of them, though every time Mustapha leaned forward the tables wobbled and a gap opened up between them. The ancient, gigantic mirrors on the inner walls of the café offered no reflections. Between them and reality clung layers of rust, dust and tapestries of stories woven by spiders, suspended in the web they had spun. Customers seemed to gaze into the glass for hours, unable to see anything, and so they travelled in time, the trail of their thoughts taking them where they had never intended to go. Such mirrors told stories about the other side.

A saleswoman appeared from nowhere, ghostlike, a raucous snigger exposing charcoal teeth. Her mouth was a grotto, and in its depth a golden tooth flashed like a lamp in a red-light district. 'She is evil!' Mustapha thought as he watched her caress her melon belly. It was about seven months ripe. 'She is evil!' he muttered. Prostitution, drugs, corruption of all kinds . . . she lived in the street, of the street . . . it was written all over her face. He would not spell it out though. It would defile his tongue to take the shape of those dirty words. Evil held all those things he did not want to touch. Strings of jasmine cascaded between the saleswoman's green hands. The snow-white of the delicate flowers contrasted with her smouldering gaze.

'For the beauty of the moon sitting in front of you, sir,' she pleaded with Mustapha while scrutinizing Donatella's face. Mustapha looked at her tattooed hands and felt disgusted. How could anyone be willing to stain themselves so?

'Go away,' he hissed. 'Haven't you got a home to go to?' To her ears, the words rang: 'Evil, evil.'

She took a step back. Mustapha absent-mindedly flicked the ash of his cigarette on to the floor. There was still no sign of the ashtray he had asked for over an hour earlier. It was an awkward moment. For reasons that escaped him, he found the jasmine-seller disturbing.

Donatella reached for her purse. She took out what looked to Mustapha like a wad of notes and gave it to the saleswoman for a string of jasmine. They had been required to change money at the airport, the regulation fifty pounds before entering the country. Because they had come from London, the amount was multiplied by six and their wallets were crammed. A barrier had been crossed between two worlds, leading to the magical propagation of their money. They felt rich.

Donatella held her blonde locks back. Giggling, she leaned to place the necklace around her ivory neck, exposing an ample bosom. 'Evil!' Mustapha thought and intoned a protective verse under his breath. His fingers worked quickly with the rosary beads, drawing a screen across his thoughts. He looked away. But the memory of Donatella's bosom was revived in the whiteness of her feet, bare over her sandals. Her laughter rang in his head. 'What is it about white skin that makes it look more naked than brown?' he wondered. 'Twenty per cent would make . . . if on the other hand, the commission was smaller . . .' Mustapha tried to push away the thought of evil by immersing himself in his calculations. His heart was ignited.

'It's a superb Quran manuscript! The diacritical marks are painted with wonderful colours. It's like a garden in full bloom.' He paused to take a deep breath as if he knew he would not breathe for the rest of his speech. 'The photographs may not show it but believe me it's signed the name of the famous Ibn Muqla can be deciphered he was *the* calligrapher of his time as you know such manuscripts are very rare selling it to your collectors will save it it'll be conserved and published while if it remains here it'll simply be eaten by worms . . .'

There was no punctuation in Mustapha's speech. It bubbled like washing-up liquid. Mark had to be precise and place his reply the very second Mustapha halted for breath.

'We will consider it, but what we're really after is the Blue Manuscript. The collection is incomplete without it.' Mark massaged his ear thoughtfully. 'The collectors want the Blue Manuscript,' he stressed. 'Without it, the project will be a failure.'

'Why doesn't the bastard listen! I know he is the one who controls the finance even if the paymasters are far away but he is so stubborn.' Mustapha thought to himself. 'I tell him I have a gem of a manuscript for him, he tells me the Blue Manuscript! It's ridiculous! What does it matter, blue, red or green? Son of a bitch!' His lips took the shape of a benign smile. Inside, he felt the urge to chuckle at his own thoughts. He did not really mean it, but the man was getting on his nerves. He reached for Mark's shoulder. 'I'm going to consider it a deal.' They shook hands. What kind of deal? Mark himself was not sure what they were talking about and he was not making any deals. Their dialogue continued without vibration of vocal chords. Neither Zohra nor Donatella could hear anything.

'But the Blue Manuscript is the real deal!' Mark announced. Mustapha dabbed his forehead. He was sweating, although he was wearing short sleeves. He couldn't care less really. For him, as a believer in the Holy Book, it was a text to be read, not pages to be looked at, and he could read the text from any copy. In fact, printed text was easier. The Blue Manuscript did not even have diacritical marks to help with the reading. He admitted that the writing was dexterous, the hand of a master no doubt, but truly these foreigners were out of their minds. Blue Manuscript, my foot!

His manuscript had been wrapped in cloth, in a coffer, tucked under his bed for many years. He was aware of its value and he knew that he had to wait for the right opportunity to sell it. He had been patient for a long time and he was not going to take any risks now. During all those years in the museum, his father had learnt a great deal. Apart from cleaning cases and making coffee, he watched not only the objects behind glass, but also the reactions of visitors from all over the world. Faces told what he could not understand from words and he learnt about what was valuable and what was not.

'More tea?'

Mark's question startled Mustapha, but he regained control of the situation promptly. He ushered the waiter away then turned to everyone around the table and reiterated: 'Welcome, welcome! We're honoured, you have brought light to Egypt!' It was wiser, for the time being, not to reveal any more about what was burning within him. He smiled quietly and went on caressing his handsome moustache.

From the gramophone came the voice of Um Kulthum. 'Aaaaaah!' performed the diva. Then another 'Aaaaaaaaaaaah.' The third was drowned by the listeners' loud chatter.

'What's she saying?' Donatella asked. 'What's that word she keeps repeating?'

' "Ah",' said Mustapha with a sigh, 'expresses pain.'

'Doesn't it also express pleasure?' Zohra asked Mustapha in Arabic.

'Ah!' nodded the waiter who appeared with new embers for the narghile.

'It also means "yes",' added Mustapha. His tongue released tiny bubbles that made his smile shine. The two striped tubes of the narghile were writhing snakes. Mustapha was suddenly serious; he frowned as he sucked at the head wholeheartedly. The mark on the apex of his forehead seemed darker. It looked like a tattoo but it was not. It seemed somehow important by virtue of its prominent position. With every drag he took, the scented water bubbled, cleansing the tobacco smoke. He blew at the embers and the fire flared and spat.

They sat unaware that, in the inner rooms of the café, Naguib Mahfouz was sipping his tea and reflecting on the charged reality close by. He was still enjoying the bliss of anonymity. All this was a few months before Mahfouz was woken up by a call from London, breaking the news that he had won the Nobel Prize. He hung up after telling the journalist: 'Balash hizar yabni! No nonsense my son!' (Or so the story goes.) To him, the news was not yet credible.

They looked at each other, not knowing what to say. There was still no sign of the Professor who was supposed to join them at the café. His plane was to have landed hours earlier. Three other members were due next day.

'The collectors have invested a lot of money in this project. Let's hope we get lucky and find the Blue Manuscript,' declared Mark. 'They got Kodama San, you know? He's coming tomorrow.'

'The Japanese site surveyor?' asked Donatella.

'Yes,' replied Mark, 'there is only one!'

'Do you think Professor O'Brien got lost?' Donatella continued.

'The Professor!' cried Mustapha. '*Mashallah*, he knows Cairo, and especially the old city, like the palm of his hand. And I thought it would be me showing him around when he visited last year! My business, Exclusive Tours, has knowledgeable guides but nothing like the Professor.' Mustapha chuckled and added, 'He is the Fatimid expert after all. He would be perfect for my diplomatic clients!'

'Yes,' Mark laughed, 'the one who will find our Fatimid manuscript, the Blue Manuscript!'

A turbaned man in a brown gallabiya came by, offering shoe-polishing. He looked at Donatella while talking to Mustapha. Something was wrong with his eyes. While Mustapha was trying to get rid of him, a one-armed boy appeared selling sunglasses. Minutes later, a hunchback followed with leather wallets. Mustapha and Mark ended up with sunglasses and a wallet each. The waiter brought new embers but Mustapha had decided to abandon the narghile and reached for the tobacco in his pocket. They watched him heap it in a straight line, roll the cigarette meticulously, light it and take a deep breath. The edge of the paper quivered as it burnt. Mustapha produced another cigarette and offered it to Mark.

'I don't smoke,' said Mark.

But Mustapha pressed him with a glistening smile. 'One won't hurt! Go on.' Mark took it. The smoke from the two cigarettes rose and coiled gently in an enigmatic dialogue.

'Guess,' said Mark unexpectedly, between the coils of smoke, 'guess what just one page from the Blue Manuscript sells for?' Mustapha had no idea what to answer. Mark whispered a figure and Mustapha's ear twitched.

'According to the historical treatise, the buried volume contains over a hundred pages!' Mustapha's eyes opened wide. 'Awesome, isn't it?' added Mark. Mustapha stopped working on his rosary, stretched his malleable body, threw his head back and looked up for a moment. The full moon between the narrow walls of the alleyway came as a startling surprise.

2

They stood amidst the traffic of languages, of nationalities, at the crossing of worlds, within the transient quality of time – the unique atmosphere of airports. 'It's good Alan, Hans and Kodama San are all coming on the same plane,' said the Professor.

'Hans is the German conservator,' said Mustapha.

'And Kodama San is the surveyor. Alan is my best student,' added the Professor. He stepped forward to make himself visible to the newcomers. He was pleased that the plane from London had landed on time, unlike his own the night before, which had been delayed four hours. 'That's Hans!' declared the Professor, pointing at a tall man wearing glasses. A red-haired officer was studying his passport.

'The same officer dealt with us yesterday!' remarked Donatella with a twinkle.

'He's the one who said, "What's all this beauty!" to you,' injected Zohra, whose bland face had not got a second look from the officer.

'That kind of improper remark is how you know you've reached Egypt!' muttered Mustapha. He eyed the officer; the dark shadow around his eyes deepened his scorn.

Hans was obviously tired. He took one look at the waiting crowd and tripped, losing his glasses. Zohra rushed to pick up the frames while Donatella tried to collect the broken glass. '*Danke*,' said Hans.

By the time Donatella looked up, he had produced another pair, identical to those that had broken. She giggled. 'You should be called Mr Glasses!' A shy smile fluttered over his lips.

'Glasses will do, you can drop the Mister!' he heard himself say.

'Here you are, Glasses!' Donatella was friendly as she handed him the shards.

'Pathetic,' she thought, 'pathetic but amusing!'

'This is Hans or shall I say Glasses,' announced the Professor in a formal tone. Everyone laughed. Glasses apologized and clutched his books to his chest before he could shake hands with the Professor, Donatella, Zohra, Mark and Mustapha. The Professor introduced the others who had arrived on the same flight. 'This is Alan and this is Kodama San.' Glasses' handshake was firm, Alan's was limp and Kodama San's was somewhere in between.

Glasses had a feeling that he had seen Donatella before, but he soon dismissed the idea. 'People have their "double", like a resonance. Anyone who crosses worlds knows this. Things get mirrored somewhere else,' he mused.

Mustapha sat next to the driver. His thoughts travelled. He must meet with Jamel Bey. It was fate that he was in Cairo now. Mustapha was confident Jamel Bey trusted his judgement but they would have to act quickly if they were to succeed. Every day counted. 'The later the digging starts the better,' he concluded. He turned back to the others and declared: 'First, a quick visit to the Pyramids, as promised, then lunch.' Nearly all the members of the dig were here now. Most of them did not know each other. The space within the vehicle was filled with silent curiosity. As it drove from the airport, the minibus zoomed through a red traffic light. The team screamed. 'They're shocked you went through a red light,' Mustapha told the driver.

'It wasn't very red!' he retorted. A laughter of complicity drew the two men together. Zohra translated for the others. Kodama San saw no reason to laugh. He sat motionless, his left hand in an elegant pose, the little finger folded at the knuckle.

'What are those trees?' Zohra asked the driver in her not so perfect Egyptian.

'Which trees?'

'The mauve ones!' She pointed, trying to extract an answer before it was too late.

'Maaaauve trees . . . ?!' he reiterated. By then, the trees had already left them.

'Are there *mauve* trees?' the driver asked Mustapha, who whispered something back, and they both chuckled.

'Juha, the king of laughter, must have been Egyptian,' gasped Mustapha in a hoarse voice, slightly choked.

'You think so?' teased the driver.

The two men spoke in Arabic. Only Zohra could understand what they were saying, most of it at least. 'It's amazing,' she thought, not for the first time, 'the number of languages people speak. The wonder of arranging sound in different sequences and creating a code for communication, each language forming a world of its own. If one speaks only one language, only one sequence of sounds makes sense.' For the rest of the group, this was an alien culture and a peculiar language. The meaning of the Arabic words remained invisible to the foreign ears.

They soon reached the Pyramids of Giza, where a restoration project was in progress. 'Great attention is given to Egypt's pharaonic past,' remarked the Professor in a dry tone. A nearby mount provided a view of the three Pyramids. The few tourists scattered around appeared minute in an unlimited sandy expanse. The Pyramids imposed a foreboding silence of eternity. 'Immortality in stone created perhaps more by an obsession with life than death,' commented the Professor. 'The dead simply moved to a new residence, taking their belongings to ensure the standard of life they had been accustomed to!' They laughed. Standing in this world of symmetry and composure, they gazed at the perfection of those lines, timeless time. In the far distance, the vague contours of the city of Cairo could be discerned, the city they were yet to discover.

'Cairo, the capital of Egypt, *Um ed-Duniya*, Mother of the World,' declared Mustapha.

The silver sheen of the Nile, the river of life, was magnetic, but the view from the minibus was blocked by a truck, loaded with cows that returned the passengers' gaze with a fixed look. They were stuck on a bridge. The city's arteries were choked. Lead weighed heavily on its heart. The jagged lines of vehicles stood still. A man on a bicycle freewheeled momentarily, a small ladder balanced on his head. The sound of hooting and shouting was solid, a multitude of sounds which made it difficult for people to hear themselves. In the turmoil of the city, the world of the Pyramids seemed unimaginable. The sun was burning but Cairo overflowed in a cacophony. People were racing, trying to catch up with time. Temporary time. Mustapha commented on people having two or three jobs, living two or three lives in one, in order to survive. 'To have a decent life,' were his words.

There was a feeling of being trapped on all sides. A staggering number of cars, most of them very tired, customized by the struggle of individual lives. But there were also the luxurious cars. Spotless. A gleaming white Mercedes was impatient; it got very close to a battered car in front but an unbridgeable gap separated them. In the middle of the road, two men were gesticulating intensely. A third had got out of his car and was trying to settle the quarrel. From behind glass, the team watched. No one could decipher a word, not even those who understood Arabic. A man with a bald patch, as though he was wearing a cap, was threatening another. Words exploded from his mouth like thorns.

'*Yahudi*. A Jew by nature!' said Mustapha, pointing at the bald man. Both he and the driver laughed heartily. Zohra did not feel the need to translate.

Unexpectedly, the two combatants embraced each other and everyone seemed happy. The vehicles finally moved. The walk symbol at the lights was ignored again. The drivers gave signals to each other, regulating the traffic – a logic which only the locals seemed to understand. It was so hot and the air conditioning of the minibus was not working. Alan took off his jacket.

'We're not far,' Mustapha said reassuringly.

'What are the mauve trees?' asked Zohra, pointing at one in the distance.

'They're just trees. They don't have a name!' Mustapha burst into laughter and the driver joined him. The others started to consider laughter a local disease.

'It must be in the Egyptian genes,' said Donatella. 'There are jokes in pharaonic temples, you know!'

Glasses opened the door for the others. Unfortunately, as Donatella emerged he stepped on Alan's foot and Alan jerked with a suppressed squeal. Glasses' profuse apologies seemed to embarrass Alan even more. Mustapha handed the minibus keys to a man who had rushed towards the vehicle. Words gushed, full of hierarchical reverence, a residue of the Ottoman empire. They were hollow words, emptied of their meaning. Mustapha was a lord of lords. A sense of the grand was evident in the way people spoke, in spite of the hardship of their reality. It all seemed easy. The man rented out space in the street for parking, even though it was not his to rent. Such was the pattern of his life.

Alan stood to the side, wondering how he had torn his jacket, till Mustapha grabbed it and said: 'Don't worry. I'll be back in a minute.' Alan did not see the point of repairing it – it was a large tear – but Mustapha had already disappeared. While they waited for him, the Professor and his team stood admiring a cloth tent, erected nearby. It was decorated with beautiful geometric designs in vibrant colours. They could hear the Quran recited from within; the grave voice imposed itself in spite of the interference of bad recording. Two young women, one veiled and one wearing a miniskirt, high-heeled shoes and heavy make-up, walked arm in arm. They glanced back at the foreigners and giggled. Somehow, Zohra sensed the team should not be near the tent. Mustapha came back, beaming.

'Don't worry,' he reassured Alan, 'the jacket'll be ready by tomorrow, the tailor gave me his word.' He hurried and urged the others to follow. They were surprised when he told them that a funeral ceremony was taking place and explained that colourful tents were used equally for happy and sad occasions. Mark's curiosity made him linger for a moment.

A few minutes later, the team stopped at the sight of a cart piled with a mountain of nuts of a kind they had never seen before. 'What are they?' they asked.

'*Habb 'azeez*,' said the man as he generously offered them a handful. Zohra was embarrassed because she could not translate.

Glasses tried some. 'It doesn't ring any bells. The taste of the unknown!' he said with a smile.

The Professor could not wait to show them the Fatimid monuments of Cairo. But they were famished and Mustapha was taking them to a popular restaurant. Every few steps merchants greeted him. On one occasion he disappeared indoors with the owner. The team's attention was drawn to a shop selling little pyramids of stone, alabaster and metal. An old man sat at the entrance. To his side was a stack of fine wrapping paper of different colours, ready to wrap the merchandise the way different skins cover different people. A lot of haggling was going on over cups of tea. Nothing had a fixed value. 'Perhaps this is closer to the truth,' remarked Glasses pensively, 'the value of something is not one-dimensional.'

The smell of *meshwi* was appetizing. All the tables outside the restaurant were taken. There were no empty seats inside either, and people stood waiting, but a waiter winked at Mustapha and the group was soon seated. It was hectic, though the atmosphere was light-hearted. Glasses piled his books to one side and leaned on the table. Alan was about to place his little rucksack on the floor but changed his mind and returned to the comfort of his reticence. Donatella went to wash her hands. Under the table, cats waited. Zohra, keen to be part of the team, placed the order for everybody. The waiter laughed at her dialect. Every now and then she had to resort to Classical Arabic, which is understood everywhere in the Arab world, instead of her Tunisian dialect, which sometimes came across as a foreign language in this city.

'What are you exactly, Zora?' asked Glasses. 'I mean, where do you come from?'

'I am half English, half Arab . . . Tunisian,' she heard herself answer for the second time that day.

'Which half is which?' teased Mustapha.

The first time she had answered: 'Half Arab, half English.' It obviously depended on who was asking. The two halves were in constant competition. Her name was pronounced differently in different worlds. Mustapha called her 'Zohra'. Glasses and Donatella, 'Zora'. They could not hear the 'h'. Perhaps she should have answered Glasses' question the way she did administrative forms, with 'other'. That was what mixed-race was. Other. That was how she felt. Always in the place of the other.

Glasses turned to Donatella. 'What nationality are you?'

'Italian. And you're German, aren't you?'

Glasses nodded. 'From Munich.' A smile lit his face. 'So how come you've got an American accent?' he probed gently.

'American school!' explained Donatella.

The room was stuffy. The fan only managed to turn the hot air around. Alan was not eating. 'I'm not hungry,' he said politely, but they all thought he found it difficult to see beyond the dirt. The Professor was wolfing down his food with great appetite. A beer would have completed his pleasure, but only Mirinda, the popular soft drink they had discovered earlier that day, was available. Alan cut his meat into small pieces and fed it to the cat. The one-eyed creature, once white and now a dirty grey, started reaching for the plates on the table. To Alan's dismay, the waiter gave it a kick. The cat escaped, perhaps not fast enough. Alan thought it would have certainly wished to disappear like the Cheshire cat in *Alice's Adventures in Wonderland*.

Eating was slowed down by the conversation. The Professor talked about how the Germans had dug in Wadi Hassoun in the seventies but were mainly concerned with Graeco-Roman and Byzantine remains. He explained their digging had come to a halt as a result of the outbreak of Rift Valley fever and how they had lost many of their workers and it was all rather dramatic.

Everyone followed Professor O'Brien intently. Only Mustapha was preoccupied with his thoughts. He must see Jamel Bey tonight, however late, and agree with him a plan of action.

'What a shame,' said Glasses, 'that it took so long for the German archaeology report to be published, especially the paper fragments which changed everything.'

'Now that they have been deciphered,' said the Professor, 'we know for sure that one volume of the Blue Manuscript was buried with the mother of al-Muizz in Cairo and one volume was actually buried with its calligrapher in the Green Pavilion in Wadi Hassoun.'

Mark's eyes shone. He was excited at the prospect and pleased with himself, he had been instrumental in the sponsors' decision to embark on this venture.

'Even though the Germans found lustre pottery,' added Professor O'Brien, 'they never found a kiln or a lustre waster in Wadi Hassoun.'

'What's a lustre waster?' wondered Zohra who had no idea what the Professor was talking about. The quizzical look on her face did not escape the Professor who was a great teacher.

'Lustre pottery is a Muslim invention,' he explained. 'It involves the use of silver and copper oxides suspended in vinegar. And the process requires firing the object twice in a reducing kiln. The result is a metallic effect which reflects the light. The colour of lustre goes from yellow to copper, depending on the percentage of oxides and the firing.' Zohra's eyes widened. 'It's a complex technique. A precise temperature is required and there's no margin for error. Hence, the high percentage of wastage! And so finding lustre wasters will prove lustre was manufactured in Wadi Hassoun,' added the Professor with glee.

'I don't understand,' thought Mark, 'why the sponsors insisted on using Professor O'Brien while they know his heart is in pottery not with manuscripts! All that mattered to them was that he is a well established archaeologist and keen to dig in Wadi Hassoun.'

The team was curious about Wadi Hassoun. Far away from the city of Cairo, another world was waiting for them. Zohra wanted to ask more questions about the excavation site. She wondered about the Blue Manuscript. Mark had mentioned that pages from one volume were known and that they had been separated to be sold. How could anyone have done such a terrible thing? Zohra looked at all these new people and reflected on the objective of their mission, finding the buried volume of the Blue Manuscript. Somehow, she felt this experience was going to be different from her other translating jobs.

'Islamic lustre developed in Iraq,' continued the Professor, 'it was taken a step further in Egypt, where, in reality, it was a revival of an ancient technique. Then it migrated to Iran and Syria and later to Europe.'

In the conference that had delayed his initial arrival in Cairo, the

Professor had put forward his theory that Wadi Hassoun was a great centre for lustre production in the medieval period. It was a theory that would make his name in the field. He based it on stylistic similarities between Egyptian lustre pottery and textiles known to have been produced in Wadi Hassoun.

Once Professor O'Brien started talking about lustre, there was no stopping him.

A boy came with a shoebox filled with pharaonic cats in soapstone. They stood majestically in rows, reminding them that thousands of years ago, cats were sacred. The boy was insisting that his cats were 'authentic copies' when one of the waiters came to shoo him away. Kodama San pointed to a Nefertiti bust amidst the cats.

'How much is the Nofretete?' Glasses asked Zohra.

'Nofretete? You mean Nefertiti!' said Donatella.

' "Nefertiti" is the conventional spelling in English. We call her Nofretete in Germany. No one knows how the Ancient Egyptians sounded in conversation anyway!'

'That's true,' admitted Donatella.

'There's a lot to see in the Egyptian Museum, you know,' remarked the Professor.

'That's interesting,' replied Donatella, surprised. 'With all the pharaonic stuff that the British Museum holds, you'd think there can't be anything left behind.'

'Just as well there is a lot left behind!' said the Professor.

'Well, at least it's well looked after in the British Museum and everyone can benefit,' said Donatella, unaware of a leaf of parsley which had planted itself between her teeth.

'It's extraordinary,' said the Professor, as though speaking to himself. 'Even a civilization as great as that of Ancient Egypt came to an end.'

There was a moment of silence. The Professor went back to his worries. He would have to spend the whole afternoon dealing with bureaucracy while the rest of the team visited the museum. It seemed that they would have to spend the following day, perhaps even longer, in Cairo, rather than travel to their final destination. But he would at least have some time to show the Fatimid monuments to the team.

'Yes,' murmured Glasses, unaware of the passage of time since the Professor's last comment, 'a great civilization which came to an end.' Then he sank into silence, reflecting on the cycle of civilizations.

3

The group tried to keep up with the Professor, not to lose sight of him, but it was hard to cross the street within the force of human tide created, paradoxically, by a population struggling for survival. The team were embraced by the hubbub, a strange combination of closeness and anonymity. 'One would never dream of trying to find a particular person in this opaque crowd,' thought Zohra. People of all sorts surrounded them, from the very ordinary-looking to characters who seemed to come from another era. Alan was befuddled. Somehow he managed to stay separate. For him it was more like a painting by Bosch. He felt fear. Fear of difference, of this alien culture. Donatella was composed but she was careful where she trod. The Professor was leading the way. Even Mustapha was following.

'I tell you, he knows the old city like the palm of his hand!' Mustapha reiterated, his eyes gleaming with admiration. The Professor himself was excited, his love for the city intense.

Zohra lingered behind. Huge billboards were all over the streets, a narrative collage. They were reminiscent of the covers of the cheaply published novels she had seen in her father's room many years before. Those cheap covers were all she knew of her father's culture. The pouting lips of the stars were painted a red which screamed louder than any mouth could. The publicity panels aimed to be more clamorous than the city's commotion. This was before kitsch started to lose its authenticity and posters got replaced by laminated photographs. Dust engulfed everything. Nothing showed its real face. There were many trees but their green was dulled by dust. The shop windows too were overcast and a film of dust covered the stars in the posters.

Perhaps without the dirt, the patina of time, Cairo would lose its sensuality. Sweat made dust cling, and touch was a force that shaped the character of the city. Everything but everything was in intimate contact with everything else, people touched cars touched animals touched people touched walls touched trees, all in an organic modus vivendi. And human existence had a dilatory quality. In spite of having been baked a million times, the people of this land had remained of malleable clay, and their whole life seemed meaningless in the overall scheme of things. To the side of the bridge, Zohra noticed a man climbing a high pole, busily replacing one of the billboard posters. He wore no protective clothing, nor was he an expert acrobat. Perhaps human life was simply worthless.

A traffic of lorries, cars, buses, motorbikes, bicycles, people and animals. Carriages filled with all sorts of products were led by donkeys, mules or people, depending on their size. Men, women, children carried things on their heads such as cages filled with swollen bread, walking with impressive poise. A barber was shaving his clients on the pavement. Women, men and children, mannequins in frozen poses, filled the windows of the endless clothes shops. On the pavement, people crowded around something. Mustapha managed to get a glimpse: a boy had a green basin filled with water, in which a naked doll swam round and round. A few steps further on, a woman in black crouched next to a spread of cigarettes and lighters. Behind her, the façade of a little shop was a window display of nuts. An old man sold sweet potatoes which he cooked on the flames of his mobile fire. Someone was praying on the pavement. A man smoked his narghile. A cart with a mountain of tin containers was being pushed by a little boy. A man was spreading cloth handkerchiefs on a box. Every bit of space was used. Some sellers worked in shifts. A man who had been selling cassettes all morning was being replaced by someone selling cooked beans. A boy with wide-open eyes, steadfast in the face of dust, pushed a cart with a pyramid of tangerines. He cut through the crowd in the smooth way of an expert, his voice clearing the way: '*Yustafendi! Yustafendi!*' Lovers held hands in the anonymous crowd. Touch brought consolation. On the pavement, an old man was repairing clothes on his sewing machine. People swept in front of their shops. Net sacks of oranges and melons hung on the façades of shops that sold fresh juice. Lines of washing, between apartment windows, dried nonchalantly in the dust. A teenager leaned against a tree sipping leisurely from his glass. Nearby, a woman was selling tea which she stewed in great urns on the pavement. Someone provided ironing in his little shop. People had those luxuries. But it was also as though this was regulated by a pact of complicity to give everyone a chance of survival. Rolls of meat turned against flames. Whole chickens turned rhythmically on skewers on their cyclic journey as though they were enjoying it. But there was simply no chance of escaping the flames.

From a small shop, bursting with rope of different thicknesses and colours, a man emerged carrying two huge rolls of copper wire. He handled them effortlessly as though they were an insignificant weight. Glasses asked Zohra to help him buy some string for his spectacles. The others waited outside. Away from Mustapha, Glasses asked Zohra: 'What did Mustapha say about *Yahudi* yesterday?' Zohra was surprised that Glasses still remembered the quarrel on the bridge. She said that he was talking about the man's bald patch, that it resembled the yarmulke that Jews wear. Glasses, however, suspected that Mustapha's remark was in some way derogatory.

The Professor started his tour of Fatimid Cairo with the gate, Bab Zuwayla, dating from the eleventh century. The Salih Tala'i Mosque was surrounded by a murky pool. A few planks were stretched over the water for access. Shoes stood in pairs outside the mosque door. It was prayer time and the team had to wait to go in. There were piles of sheep skins left to dry. Red streaks marked where blood had run in streams. Kodama San's face showed no sign of shock, but shocked he was. The Professor could read the question in his fixed look: 'Why are Fatimid buildings left to rot?' The Professor gave Mustapha a knowing look.

But Mustapha was absorbed by the carcass of an old car in front of the mosque. 'Its owner must have forgotten where he parked it a few years ago!' said Mustapha with a laugh. Inside the old building the atmosphere was surprisingly quiet and cool. No one would have thought that in the throbbing heart of the city there was a corner so peaceful, so serene.

From Bab Zuwayla unfolded a series of clothes shops, as well as carts selling trinkets of all kinds. A mature woman, dressed in black, sat on the ground, smoking from a recycled detergent bottle. Every now and then she interrupted her puffing to berate the men behind the mobile vegetable stall, a cart fastened to a mule. 'There's no doubt, she's the boss,' thought Zohra. The mule lifted its head, shaking its nosebag, trying to catch the last grains. Zohra's attention was drawn to the Arabic calligraphy which decorated the cart. 'Beautiful calligraphy,' she remarked. But Mustapha shrugged.

'I know calligraphers with extraordinarily gifted hands. There's great talent in this city,' he said before he carried on with his rosary. It was true. Beautiful writing with a sure hand was present everywhere, from the façades of shops to publicity posters. Zohra wondered about the calligraphy of the Blue Manuscript.

The team were surprised that buildings of different types mingled. New constructions, many of them unfinished, rubbed shoulders with ruins. Old buildings, hundreds of years old, were close, too close, to blocks of flats that rose pompously fast towards the sky. Zohra had heard that in some cases, they collapsed just as fast, killing large numbers of people – fake cement sold at high prices revealing its true nature. Layers of time were interwoven in intricate chaos. Old stucco carvings appeared when least expected. The past was present everywhere. Timeless devotion had once transformed hard materials into beautiful lace. Now, time was making it crumble into dust. Zohra took a photograph.

'Ruins have their own beauty,' said Donatella.

'Awesome!' said Mark. 'If these buildings were in the US a lot of money would be invested to restore them. There, there's not enough history. Here there just aren't enough dollars!'

'The history of Cairo can be read through the names of its streets,' declared the Professor, pointing at the words inscribed on the wall. 'This street is named after the Fatimid Caliph al-Muizz, who founded the city in AD 972. Al-Muizz Street originally separated two palaces, the Eastern Palace and the Western Palace. Both have been destroyed and the Fatimid ancestors buried here were removed when the market of Khan el-Khalili was built. This is where the mother of al-Muizz was buried with one of the volumes of the Blue Manuscript.'

'And now we know, thanks to the German excavation,' Mark interjected, 'that the other volume was buried with its calligrapher in Wadi Hassoun.'

'The general plan of the city has remained much the same as it was when it was conceived in AD 969,' continued the Professor.

'I thought you said 972,' intervened Donatella.

'Nine sixty-nine was when the General Jawhar conquered Egypt. Three years later, Caliph al-Muizz came from Ifriqiya, present-day Tunisia,' explained the Professor. Then he added: 'The Fatimids ruled in Egypt for over two hundred years until 1171, when they were overthrown by Saladin.'

A strong aroma of pepper drifted by and a man emerged from around the corner, staggering under two immense sacks. Brightly painted pigeon coops looked down from the roofs of the adjacent buildings. Pigeon was a popular dish.

The Professor led them down al-Muizz Street to the Aqmar Mosque then on to the Hakim Mosque and the great northern gate, Bab al-Futuh. They would pass jewellery, spices and perfumes before they reached the piles of onions at the top of the street. The Aqmar Mosque had a dark face. Its delicate shell motifs had survived a hard reality. The Professor drew their attention to the bands of calligraphy carved in stone. 'This is the Kufic script,' he explained. 'It takes its name after the Iraqi town of Kufa, which was a great centre for culture. Here, leaves and flowers spring from the letters for decoration. The so-called "floriated Kufic" developed here in Egypt.' The Professor smiled. He thought of the florid way that people spoke, of their honey-coated words, and it made sense to him that floriated script bloomed in Egypt.

'Is this the script in which the Blue Manuscript is written?' ventured Zohra.

'The Blue Manuscript is written in simple, early Kufic script, with no decoration,' said the Professor.

The Professor's enthusiasm was bubbling. There were many Cairos and Professor O'Brien's Cairo was Fatimid. His comments were spiced with old stories. The group was impressed by his knowledge. But he had to say almost everything twice. Mustapha found it difficult to follow his Irish accent. Zohra was enchanted by the Fatimid monuments, but was saddened by their poor condition. They seemed desolate and she wanted them to be alive with their own reality. She could not comprehend where this wish came from. Also the gap of time created an inexplicable sense of melancholy. Perhaps not all our sadness belongs to us. Near Bab al-Futuh the overspill of onion shops accumulated in large heaps like a lament on the fate of this grand medieval gate. In its heyday, its iron-studded doors were readily shut by its guards at the first hint of danger, and now they had become permanently rooted, wide open. A man lay asleep in the blissful shade.

They ventured across the Fatimid city wall into the cemetery, with its domed little shrines. They came across people who told them that more than two thousand had made the place their home. A teenager covered her mouth as she giggled, exuding a surprising love for life. Her mother, the mother of nine children, held a toddler in her arms. They all lived in one small room but they had a television, a fridge and a cooker. Tombstones held clothes-lines. Some still held lines of paper decorations from a recent religious feast. Mark, Donatella, Glasses, Zohra, Kodama San and Alan, especially Alan, were in disbelief. What kind of hardship would have led people to live among the dead? But Mustapha commented: 'Prophet Muhammad, peace be upon him, said, "Visit graves, for they will remind you of the Hereafter".'

'How interesting,' said Glasses.

Mustapha thought for a moment then added, 'These people live here because they are attracted by the spiritual aspect of the situation.'

'That's a bit far-fetched!' thought Zohra.

The cemetery hosts stood, a bewildered look in their eyes, and in their laughter a bemusement at the visitors' foreignness. A young man revealed that he had buried both parents in the room where he now lived with his wife and baby. 'We never separated,' he added with a joyful grin. Mustapha translated. The team members watched, confused. The entanglement of life and death was both disturbing and intriguing. The clinging to life had persisted from ancient times, a life-force which conferred a magnetic energy on the city. A lust for life and a heavy pollution saturated the air. And the boundaries between life and death were totally erased.

They picked up Alan's jacket and everyone was baffled. There was no trace of the tear. 'And it's not because the daylight's faded!' said Mustapha, holding it to the light. The nimbleness of Egyptian hands was beyond belief.

'Awesome! They've got magic hands!' said Mark. 'In the States, that guy would make a fortune!'

'Let's export him!' said Mustapha. 'We can share the profits.' They both guffawed. A wan smile appeared on Kodama San's face, or perhaps it was an illusion created by the street light which stood crooked, leaning towards him in the twilight. They saw more of Kodama San's silent smiles than they heard his voice. They hardly noticed he was there. Alan, too, was taciturn. He was eager to go to the hotel and freshen up.

The day had started its bow to the evening and the sun was setting quickly. The car ascended. Mustapha had promised them 'a fantastic view' from the Muqattam Hills. The view was indeed extraordinary. Tall minarets, slender like sharpened pencils, seeking the sky and claiming the city as though it were Muslim only. 'A thousand minarets can be seen from here,' said Mustapha, swelling his chest. Surprisingly, at that very moment the minarets released their voices. The overlapping calls to prayer spread from the tips of the minarets, a transparent ink, tracing luminous arabesques in the dark sky.

They contemplated the view silently for some time, totally unaware that under their feet the mighty Muqattam Hills were expelling dust over the city continuously without ever shrinking. From their vantage point, Cairo looked content, a cradle of lights that gave the illusion of the city coming to a standstill. Deceptive. Things were happening, but veiled by the screen of darkness. Only the moon was witness. It hung above them, its soft light diffused.

It was time to go back to the hotel, but Mustapha decided to stay behind, which surprised the others. He did not seem the romantic type. 'I come here often,' he said, 'when I can't sleep. It's such a soothing sight and the air is so fresh. Do you know that Saladin chose the Muqattam Hills to build his citadel because of its healthy air? He tested the atmosphere in different parts of Cairo by hanging pieces of raw meat. The meat rotted after only one day, everywhere' – Mustapha took a deep breath before he continued – 'except here. The meat remained fresh for more than three days here!' His gaze roamed across the view of the city and his hands stopped working on his rosary. '*Ya salaam 'alik ya Salah ed-Din!* The Great Saladin,' he declared, his voice filled with pride.

Tenderness glistened in his eyes. He drew a deep drag and heaved a sigh of smoke. Everyone went silent. But the Professor laughed and said: 'I think Saladin's main concerns were the military advantages of the hill, and its central location. It provided him with a local stronghold!' Mustapha did not decipher everything the Professor said because of his accent, but he did not ask him to repeat what he had just said.

They crossed the Qasr al-Nil Bridge, guarded by its stone lions, to get to their hotel in Zamalek. Alan, the Professor and Kodama San went in and Zohra, Donatella and Glasses decided to go for a stroll. The smell of lavender and honeysuckle overwhelmed the senses. There were lovers in the cars parked along the Nile. The beautiful river had given people a taste for romance. A gift for all. Florists were selling birds of paradise. Shards of moon sparkled on the water. Zohra suddenly felt tired. She changed her mind, as she often did, and went back to the hotel. Donatella was angry but said nothing.

In the hotel room a dancer performed all styles of dancing, from ballet to flamenco, from belly dance to salsa, changing costumes and choreography in split seconds, a phenomenon of extraordinary imitation. Zohra watched intently, not knowing what she was looking for, perhaps the authentic person behind the performance. The cleaner had obviously forgotten to switch off the television. Zohra pressed a button, the dancer vanished and a story emerged from the day's thick layers of events ... a story the Professor had told them earlier that day about Yazuri, minister to the eighth Fatimid Caliph, al-Mustansir, who ruled in Cairo in the eleventh century. Yazuri summoned two painters, an Iraqi and an Egyptian, for a competition. The challenge was to paint a mural of a dancer. The Iraqi artist painted her as though she were coming out of the wall, while the Egyptian painted her as though she were vanishing into it. Zohra reached for her notebook and for no specific reason scribbled: 'Caliph al-Mustansir and his minister Yazuri', perhaps trying to hold on to the day's memories.

She stood on the balcony. The day's heat had lingered long into the night. Air-conditioning boxes jutted from the tall buildings, and roofs bristled with television aerials. One roof was covered by palm-tree branches, long dead. Zohra guessed that they must have come from a nearby tree. Layers were preponderant. Cairo was a city that could never be excavated. Zohra had grown up in London and the only other Arab city she had visited was Tunis, the home of her father, a comparatively transparent city where just a glance reveals all there is, or so it seems. One could never get to know Cairo, however, because of its immense scale. The city itself did not know every nook and cranny within it. Like a gigantic creature, every one of its pores led to a world of its own. Zohra took a deep breath. Cairo was magic. This was the city of mad passion, where ardent fans committed suicide when their favourite stars died. This was once the capital of the Arab world. This was the city where the stories of *The Thousand and One Nights* were born, but it was also where they were recently banned. Was the medieval mentality more open-minded? Or was what needed to be protected less under threat?

A lightness filled the atmosphere. She was tired, or rather the feeling was that of inebriation brought on by the old city. Cairo was a frothing picture of humanity. Humanity with all its joys and sorrows, its misfortunes and successes, its flaws and perfection, from putrid pollution to pure, distilled essence, humanity with its genius and helplessness. It was only later, much later, that Zohra realized that when one is touched but not concerned, one can have before one's eyes the most extraordinary reality yet remain blind to its implications for the people who belong to it. For the moment, her romantic vision of Cairo obscured those implications. In just a few days, the city had triumphed in its seduction. She had lived in London all her life, and the joy of hearing Arabic spoken all around her now, the joy of what she had never had, filled her. She remembered the Professor's words as he quoted the fourteenth-century philosophical historian Ibn Khaldun: 'What one sees is always surpassed by what one can imagine, because of the scope of the imagination, except Cairo, because it surpasses anything one can imagine.'

As the translator, she did not think of herself as an active member of the excavation team. Yet, lying on the bed that night, she was filled by a sense of the past and an anticipation of the mission that awaited them in Wadi Hassoun. As she drifted off to sleep, Zohra wondered about the name of those beautiful trees that wore mauve dresses under a veil of dust. She did not know, when she closed her eyes that night, that she had fallen in love. The city was a remnant of a civilization that had been exhausted. And her being was starved of what this city used to be. She had fallen in love with what had already gone, nothing less tragic than a doomed love.

In his room, the Professor lay down, a cold beer in his hand and his long legs extending beyond the end of the bed. 'It's going to be hell,' he thought. 'To start digging in May is crazy but our sponsors won't take no for an answer. If only we'd started in February as planned.' Another day of bureaucracy and waiting lay ahead. He gazed at the palm of his hand and reflected. He wondered what awaited him in this expedition, which he had dreamt of for such a long time ... 'He knows the old city like the palm of his hand!' Mustapha's words rang in his head. 'This lively city is dying,' he thought. 'It's rising ground-water levels, leaking water pipes and sewers that are making precious monuments crumble. The process has been going on for years. Water penetrates the limestone and rises. It evaporates and the salt crystallizes within the stone; eventually stone crumbles into powder. The heart of the Fatimid city is being devoured.' Professor O'Brien sighed before he let out a sarcastic laugh. 'Of all the bureaucratic departments, perhaps that of sewerage is playing the most decisive role in the fate of the Fatimid city!'

'And Saladin,' said Professor O'Brien loudly to the pink walls of the five-star hotel room, 'Saladin wasn't so great! He burnt the magnificent libraries of the Fatimids!' The Professor took the last sip of his beer and threw the can on the carpet. But there was no sound to be heard.

He lay in silence, his thick brows joined in a frown. He wondered how long he was going to be stranded in Cairo, negotiating his way through the maze of charm. He felt as though he was caught in the grip of the city, a monster that was preventing him from realizing his dream. And he could not wait to start his mission of digging the remote past of the Middle Ages, where lustre wasters would prove his theory right. Eventually, he went to sleep with a strange thought: 'If everything spoke, archaeology would be totally different!'

4

The caravan marched towards the formation of Cairo, the building of a civilization.

Al-Muizz was carrying the past into the future. Through the invisible chinks of the wooden sepulchres came the first rays of dawn. They brought the hope of hundreds of years to the bones of the ancestors, longing to be buried in Egypt, the desire in their marrow still throbbing alive. Here they would finally dissolve, embracing the earth of this land as though they were born in it, setting roots in their final resting place. The camels loaded with the coffins marched in front. Their walk had a kind of lulling rhythm. Ubayd Allah al-Mahdi, al-Qa'im bi-Amr Allah, Ismail al-Mansur, the caravan proceeded in a distinct line, carrying the sepulchres of grandfathers, sons, daughters, grandchildren as well as their descendants, different generations, one dream. Egypt, a great land worthy of great achievements, the step of a caravan on to a road, entry into Egypt, the establishment of a dynasty, the Fatimid dynasty.

With the sepulchres of the ancestors, the caravan carried the riches of the Court. Six hundred camels were loaded with pure gold which came from the palace in Sabra al-Mansuriyya in Ifriqiya. Other camels carried fine brocades, jewels, rock crystals, ivories, luxurious wares and beautifully carved wooden boxes, many of which were made by the gifted artist Ahmed al-Khurasani. Within one of these boxes, the Blue Manuscript was carefully wrapped in silk. But there were not only treasures of artwork. The Court's invaluable craftsmen too, such as the master potters, were brought on this journey. Along with them came the palace musicians, cooks, the sweet-maker Younes, al-Muizz's trusted story-teller, notorious for his prominent nose, and the court chronicler who was recording the events of history as they unfolded.

There were no fewer than five thousand camels. 'Not all those who want to come with me can,' al-Muizz had said to his faithful follower Ibn Ziri, who was staying behind in charge. 'If they do, by the time I reach Alexandria at the head of the caravan, those at the tail will still be in Ifriqiya!'

'*Adlun wa tasaamuh li-'izzin shaamil wa hukmin qa'im,* Justice and tolerance for complete glory and everlasting rule. Words marked the principles of the new dynasty. Arabic letters were pressed into the sand as the caravan advanced. The horses' shoes had been made by a dexterous blacksmith under the instruction of the Court calligrapher. Though heavily loaded with palanquins, the camels and horses never faltered during this long journey. They somehow knew that Cairo was the ultimate aim. They knew their significant role in conquests at this time. The men moved in silence. You would not think this was the happiest occasion in their history. The desert's sand belts crept southwards under the influence of the prevailing wind. The caravan crossed lines of isolated crescent dunes, a challenging task. Ridges of sand rose high in front of them. But al-Muizz's guide was endowed with a rare skill, a kind of sixth sense. He was renowned for his ability to recognize the way wherever he was and in whatever weather conditions. He remembered features, however small, and he was vigilantly aware of deceptive appearances. The desert might seem empty and uniform to others, but to him it was filled with variations. He could read the desert the way others would read a book. His keen sight travelled a great distance and he could see the horizon which was cut off to other travellers.

The cool, cool breeze caressed the pigeon's feathers. It spread its wings in the soft pink light of dawn and flew high. As it crossed the blue expanse over the desert it dreamt of its nest. Its journey was a journey home. It was going back, carrying a message forward. The written word was its cargo. A significant message to General Jawhar on the first day of spring in the year AD 972. Unaware of the news it carried, the pigeon saw the travellers as mere ants, dark dots linking, breaking and joining again in a long, sinuous line. But this was the caravan proceeding in the desert towards Cairo, or what would one day become the great city of Cairo.

Al-Muizz was watching his own and his ancestors' dream to conquer Egypt unfold before his eyes as the desert receded. He noticed that there was no trace of the words pressed into the sand by the horses' shoes, only the desert's eternal waves. He dismounted from his horse, took a handful of earth and savoured its colour. 'A different soil makes different people.' He cast a look around and could see that the light of Egypt had a golden tinge. It had been a few weeks since he had left on this journey. He touched his bay horse's lucky forehead and was filled with peace. He loved this horse, sensible and calm by nature. It lived up to the popular belief that, born by day, a horse brings luck. He caressed the dark spot on its forehead, tracing the spiral of hair, and glanced at the camels. The look in their eyes was deep and weary. The sun was getting hot. Al-Muizz agreed with the guide that it was time to rest.

The guide chose carefully the place to camp. They unloaded the camels. The hair on their humps looked like the desert's sporadic growth and their colour blended with the earth. They were rightly called 'the ships of the desert' – without them this journey would not have been possible. As with every time they halted for rest, servants fed them salt. While up to now they had eaten whatever bushes they encountered, today was different. The camels were given milk and talked to in the recommended friendly tone, preparing them for their last day's work. Al-Muizz fed his horse sesame seeds with his own hands.

And in no time, the barren landscape was magically transformed into a garden fit for a caliph. Cypress trees, fountains and roses sprang up, a magic world of colour unfurled. Such were the gardens depicted on the carpets imported from Andalusia, the courts of the Fatimids' rivals in Islamic Spain.

5

Merry music filled the car. The driver insisted on playing the same tape over and over again. To the ears of most of the excavation team the songs were alien, discordant sounds and rhythms pulsating with strange energy. To Zohra's ears, the rhythms were conjuring memories to the surface. She felt she should know those songs, but she did not. Zohra and Donatella kept looking at Monia, whose fluid eyes swam like fishes as she teased the driver. To their surprise, Monia, the archaeology inspector, mixed very easily with the group although she hardly knew them. They had picked her up less than an hour before from the last town they had passed. Donatella found Monia's swarthy complexion attractive; her own face was so white in contrast.

The Professor stole a quick glance at Monia's kohl-rimmed eyes. They rekindled memories of many years ago, memories of a woman he had been intimate with during his research when exploring Fatimid Cairo as a student. It was someone he had never seen before and never saw again. She had shown him the way to the ruins of an old building and things had happened . . . sometimes, he doubted whether they actually had happened or whether they were figments of his imagination. He tapped gently on his knee to the rhythm. Sitting in the front, he was keeping an eye on the driver, who every now and then increased the volume of the tape and accelerated for no apparent reason, holding the wheel in an intimate grip. Every time the Professor urged him in a heavy foreign accent to go '*shwayya, shwayya*', the driver slowed down as he rolled his rrs saying: 'Sorry, sorry.'

It had taken the Professor an additional six days to obtain the necessary papers before they could leave Cairo. 'And it would have taken even longer without Mustapha's dedicated assistance,' thought the Professor. The delay meant that Mustapha could not come with them right now to Wadi Hassoun, as planned, because he had to attend to his work in Cairo. For the Professor, the anticipation of this trip to the promising site had started more than twenty years earlier, during his doctoral research on Fatimid architecture. It had taken him until now, 1988, to come so close to realizing his dream of digging in Wadi Hassoun. This was the final step. With his hands locked at the back of his neck, he flapped his arms, folded at the elbows, to the rhythm of the music. To Zohra, in the back, he looked as though he had wings.

'This excavation project means a lot to the Professor,' she thought. Yes, Professor O'Brien was finally on the road. A sense of relief spread to every part of his body. A great sense of relief. Professor O'Brien was a large man.

The driver had had the car's air conditioning fixed and the group was enjoying the cool air. The trip was comfortable as they travelled further and further away from Cairo. Farmers were carrying their produce to the capital, others were on their way to the train which would take it to the factory. 'Sugar cane!' said the driver, pointing to a truck loaded with its harvest. 'The more water you give it, the sweeter it'll be,' he volunteered as he looked at the women reflected in the rear-view mirror. Zohra wondered whether she should translate, but her attention was caught by the scenery. The few people on horse-back as well as the palm trees and the mud-brick houses, strung along the river bank, some painted green and yellow, all travelled with them. However, they were soon left behind for fields of cotton, maize, wheat, all out of focus. A group of farmers waved a greeting as they urged on two oxen turning a wheel which scooped water and directed it into the chosen parts of the field. A fisherman who was using a stick to scare fish into a net also waved, and a small boy who stopped his game of throwing stones into the water. He had been watching the expanding ripples, the eddying motion from his last stone, still reverberating.

Glasses put his face against the window and watched, reflecting. The Nile appeared and disappeared, hidden by the thick clusters of reeds that shot out of it. The river, running for thousands of miles, had seen the passage of different civilizations, remaining constant throughout, the giver of life. Without it there would have been no life in the desert. Without it there would have been no Egypt. The reeds suddenly receded to reveal a felucca gliding peacefully. The river seemed still. Perhaps its memory lay below its reflections.

In Donatella's reflections, the Nile was one of the rivers of Paradise. She had first encountered it in the stone sculpture in Piazza Navona in Rome, when she was a child. 'The Nile,' her father's voice whispered in her head, 'the river Nile flowed in Paradise before it flowed on earth.' And Donatella had so much wanted to ask why the river was in the shape of a naked man. Camels carrying huge loads of firewood walked alongside their owners, who gestured hello from afar. A truck filled with people, mainly children clapping and singing, passed by, cheering, and Donatella waved back.

Glasses' eyes were brimming with warmth. He hardly looked at the map on his lap, part of which had spread on to Donatella's. The comfort brought by the jostling companionship came as a surprise to him. Zohra was trying to keep a sense of rhythm as she translated the meaning of the songs. Donatella's vigorous laughter brought more laughter. Even Alan joined in. He moved his head sideways to a rhythm that did not seem to follow the music but one in his own head. The turquoise charm and the rosary hanging from the car's mirror followed the rhythm more closely.

The afternoon spread a sheet of pink muslin on the yellow light, transforming it into a warm peach. Women and children were washing clothes along the riverbank, the bright colours of their dresses making them look like flower beds. Their tremulous reflections transformed the river into a world of dreams.

'The myriad images look as tangible as reality. Reaching out to them would only lead to wakefulness from illusion, not the discovery of an enchanting world within,' thought Zohra.

'We're passing one of the main centres of pottery-making,' said the Professor, pointing to wisps of smoke plaiting away in the distance. As they got closer, the smoke got thicker.

'They are burning rubbish to make pots for flowers!' said the driver between rhythmic guffaws. He leaned forward and turned up the volume of the music.

Mark interspersed tapping on his briefcase with a mechanical opening and closing of its flap. He watched the others enjoying themselves. He half smiled at Donatella. She was an attractive woman but she was not his type. He glanced at his watch and felt satisfied. They had left Cairo early, stopping only briefly to see a rich villa designed by the architect they had met in Cairo, and later to pick up Monia. Things were finally going according to plan. He took a deep breath and adjusted his posture. He was on the brink of a serious mission. 'But who knows what's going to happen?' He quickly dismissed the apprehension of not being in control and tapped steadily on his briefcase.

They were leaving behind more and more signs which marked the names of villages and towns. The wheels turned and the road unfurled, bringing the Western Desert closer.

6

Under the silk tent, al-Muizz reached for the rock-crystal chess piece. His silver ring, with its granulation and filigree work, stood out against his brown skin. He was a handsome man and he knew it. He held his bearded chin and smiled. A twinkle glistened in his honey-coloured eyes. And, with his usual composed stature, he made the victorious move with a precision of gesture which signalled a precision of mind. He proclaimed to his minister who had just lost: 'How do you expect to rule over Egypt if you couldn't rule over a chess board?!'

An attendant brought a jug of water. As he drank the water of the Nile, and felt it quench his thirst, al-Muizz remembered the precious moment when his general Jawhar returned with a fish in a flask of water and declared that he had conquered Sicily. The Nile was a sacred river. Al-Muizz reflected that in pharaonic times a beautiful girl would be thrown into it as a sacrifice when the level of the water was high. He shuddered at the repugnant act of sacrificing girls and recited a verse from the Quran in his heart before he took a deep breath. The musician went on playing the harp, his fingers seeming to reach the depths of a well from which he drew water which then cascaded in melody. Al-Muizz was filled with the joy of this moment in history. For so many long years, his mother had delayed the conquest of Egypt out of courtesy to the governor, al-Ikhshidi. She had felt indebted to his kindness when she crossed Egypt for her yearly pilgrimage to Mecca. Every time, the governor came to see her personally, bringing magnificent gifts and providing her with soldiers for full protection. 'I am not going to repay his generosity with a military attack,' she told her son firmly.

Al-Muizz's troops had long been ready to conquer Egypt. His general Jawhar had been groomed especially for this mission. And for so many years, al-Muizz had had to postpone his plans. It was not until the governor died that al-Muizz was granted his mother's permission to proceed. And now, the bones of his ancestors would at last reach their final resting place.

The musician had left. There was no reply from al-Muizz when his minister asked permission to retire. It was not clear whether the Caliph had ignored him or whether he was simply absorbed in his thoughts. Al-Muizz had been designated Caliph, Commander of the Faithful, while his father was still alive, and the decision had been implemented when his father died. 'The Fatimid rule in Egypt will be marked by tolerance. We will be fair to Copts and Jews as well as Muslims. Didn't I marry a Christian after all? Tolerance,' al-Muizz thought, 'is simply the acceptance of positive differences.'

He was en route to found the future, an individual who was to affect the course of history. 'A single person,' thought al-Muizz, 'can make or break the vision of a civilization.' He was aware of his responsibility. His thoughts spiralled. He dreamt of building the Fatimid library, the first major public library in the world. 'The library will be one of the wonders of the age. It will house manuscripts in every language, many volumes, beautifully illustrated. Initially, the Blue Manuscript will be its benedictory foundation stone. There will be books on astronomy, my favourite subject. I will build schools and mosques. The mosques will be better than anywhere, better than those in Iraq.' His thoughts were arrested by the memory of the Great Mosque in Samarra. He tried to imagine this spiral minaret of which he had heard so much.

'How high is the minaret of the Samarra Mosque?' His enquiry came as no surprise to his minister, who was used to unusual questions springing from the Caliph's thoughts. After answering him, the minister tentatively added: 'Do you know, O Commander of the Faithful, how its design came about?' Al-Muizz gave him that look which usually meant that he could proceed with his account.

'Al-Mutawakkil was sitting in an official meeting to discuss the building of the Great Mosque. He was bored and toyed with a piece of paper, twisting it obliviously over his fingers. At that very moment, one of the officials present asked what it was, with the intention of bringing him back to the serious subject of the meeting. "Oh," said al-Mutawakkil to avoid embarrassment, turning the paper upright, "I think this should be the shape of the minaret." He had inadvertently twisted the paper into a spiral shape.' Al-Muizz laughed wholeheartedly and his white teeth gleamed. The minister knew that anecdotes about the rival Abbasid caliphate in Iraq would please him and tickle his ego.

Al-Muizz told his minister that he too would build a mosque with a spiral minaret. Then he revealed his plan to build a pavilion in the Western Desert of Egypt. 'I'll call it the Green Pavilion,' said the Caliph with a smile, 'because its gardens will be green, not arid like Qayrawan. Thanks to the water of the Nile, we'll explore all irrigation systems to transform the desert and have gardens that compete with the renowned Madinat Ez-Zahra in Spain.'

Al-Muizz was surprised to see a frown on his minister's face. 'Some notorious and rebellious tribes reside in that part of the country! They're troublesome,' warned the minister.

'All the more reason!' replied al-Muizz, still smiling. 'We'll mount an expedition to build the pavilion next year. Far away from Cairo, it'll declare our presence and control of the land.' Then in his reflections, al-Muizz saw the pavilion embellished with elegant calligraphy, designed by Ibn al-Warraq, the Court calligrapher. He signalled to his attendant. 'Bring my calligraphy tools,' he said. 'Like exercise for the body so calligraphy is to my soul,' he added when he perceived a hint of surprise on the attendant's face. Even though they were resting for a short time in the journey, al-Muizz wanted to practise his calligraphy as he always did by writing and rewriting the ninety-nine names of God.

Alone, after his minister left, al-Muizz went back to his thoughts. His general Jawhar had entered Fustat with thousands of soldiers. Jawhar had prepared the Eastern Palace, whose architectural plan al-Muizz himself had dictated. Al-Muizz wondered about the Palace.

He imagined the worthy mausoleum he would build within its enclosure for his ancestors. His reveries moved to his forthcoming rule in Egypt. Tolerance and fairness were more than an ideal dream. They were a promise and a solemn pact. He reminded himself to remain faithful to the meaning of his own name. Suddenly, he became conscious of the twin angels, one on each shoulder. He had been brought up to believe that one angel wrote down his evil deeds and intentions, while the other recorded his good deeds and intentions. As the blessed, the inheritor of the imamate, he who ignites the spark of Truth and makes the source of wisdom flow, he had inherited from the Prophet a spark of divine light, the mantle of perfection, and he had the duty to live up to it. Though he hoped to be worthy of this responsibility, underneath it all, al-Muizz questioned his own perfection. 'After all, isn't compassion one of the most wonderful traits of Islam?' he thought in silent consolation, as his fingers rhythmically sang the praises of God with date kernels, the beads of angels' rosaries.

7

The explosions of laughter were like bubbles, glistening, ringing. By now, the dissonance of the music had become gaily boisterous and the team was humouring the driver's enthusiasm. Every time he glanced at the mirror, he seemed to be looking at the women in the back seats, at Donatella perhaps. He tapped at the wheel and seemed pleased with the chorus in the back. They had started their adventure in party mood. They were taking their cue from him, repeating the same phrase '*ya habibi*' every now and then, when suddenly the car swerved violently to one side. The driver's grip tightened on the wheel in a desperate bid for control. The car lurched to a halt, leaving the tape singing on its own. The Professor felt the frustration rise within him at this delay in reaching Wadi Hassoun and starting his excavations of the Green Pavilion. He got out of the car and Mark followed. 'I wish he would wipe that grin off his face,' Professor O'Brien grumbled as he watched the driver examine the deflated tyre and then open the boot, which was crammed full of luggage. Still grinning, the driver unloaded Glasses' steel box, which itself was heavier than its contents, even though he knew there was no spare wheel in the boot. Mark was shaking his head, his fine brown hair in disarray, muttering to himself. Only the words 'fuck' and 'spare' reached Zohra. As the translator, she was sometimes in the zone where people said things which were not supposed to reach anyone but which reached her, and she never knew what to do with these superfluous words.

The road seemed to stretch endlessly before them and behind them. They were stranded in the middle of a disconcerting sameness. They stood discussing what to do when a speeding car appeared.

They jumped in unison to let it zoom past but it swerved and halted at the side of the road with a screech. A man leaned out of the window and shouted: 'There's a tyre shop a few steps down the road.' The driver went to talk to him. They shook hands and exchanged grins. Contrary to what the others thought, they had never met before. Complicity with a stranger was simply natural here.

Mark, the Professor, the driver and Zohra went to look for the tyre shop. Glasses studied the complex nerves of the map of Egypt with great interest. Now it was satisfactorily stretched against the window of the minibus. His unshaven beard gave him a serious air. Kodama San stood aside, calm and composed. Monia caressed her black curls, which resembled a wig. She stooped as she tried to exchange a few words with Donatella and Alan. She still felt too tall next to them in spite of her flat shoes. Her height had made it difficult for her to meet a suitable man and she so wanted to meet a suitable man.

Although the scouting party had walked some distance, there was no shop in sight. Mark whistled a relaxed tune as he hurried. He held his briefcase close to his chest, his hands pressing firmly on it as though to keep a lid on the pressure. He was in control. Zohra walked with the anticipation of using her translation skills to help. After about five hundred metres – it seemed much longer to the Professor, whose exasperation had distorted his usually accurate sense of distance – they could see the shop. It stood alone on the other side of the road. No one could have missed it. The façade was dotted with tyres and from afar, the black circles looked at them like a multitude of eyes. There was also a spattering of printed hands above the door, a tiny dark entrance from which emerged a man dressed in smeared red overalls. 'Welcome, welcome,' he called, as he drew to his full height.

The Professor leaned against a pile of tyres, sipping his second glass of tea while Mark and Zohra kept their distance from the grease. Mark paced around. He was eager to start the search for the Blue Manuscript and did not appreciate this further delay. They could hear the driver inside the garage shop, talking to the workers. Mark and the Professor wanted to know why it was all taking so long. They were worried that the wheel might turn out to be irreparable. Zohra daringly put her head into the dark mouth of the shop and shouted: 'How is it going?'

'Nearly there, *inshallah*,' boomed a voice from within.

They had not resumed their journey for long when a nail pierced the other tyre, plunging them into deeper exasperation.

There were two people waiting when they went back to the tyre shop. One of them seemed familiar. It was the friendly stranger who had told them about the shop. He greeted their driver warmly and generously gave up his turn, saying he was happy to wait. Looking at them with eyes the colour of curiosity, he produced a packet of seeds. The discarded seed husks landed on his shirt like flies.

The owner of the garage was also accommodating. He told them that as he lived at the back it did not matter to him when he went home. Since he had opened the shop, six months earlier, he would stay open for any client for as long as necessary. Zohra translated the group's concerns to him about being stranded and not reaching their destination before dark. In the awkward pause that followed Zohra's declaration, a mechanic, also in red, emerged from inside, carrying a tray filled with glasses of tea. 'Don't you know,' said the garage owner, as he reached nonchalantly for a glass, 'despair is unfaithfulness against God.'

8

As he licked his orange and purple fingers clean, Younes, the palace sweet-maker, could not wipe the smile of satisfaction off his face. The grin emphasized the layers of his chin where the sweets savoured by his taste buds over the years had collected. His delight was brought about not only by the sweet taste, but as much by the sight of his latest creation. Never had he achieved anything like this, the most adventurous idea in all the years of his service. He had sculpted a huge tree, over two metres high, from which branched a hundred figurines, all made of sugar. There were peacocks, winged horses, human-faced birds, flying fish and other fabulous creatures, all painted in colours vibrant with life. Apart from orange and purple, there were shades of green, yellow, red, blue and brown.

Younes revelled in this masterpiece, the peak of his indulgent achievements, taste and artistry harmoniously combined, before he gave the signal. The handsome attendants, now eclipsed by the fantastic tree, lifted the wooden base and proceeded towards the doors. They moved precisely, with melodious coordination, and such steadiness that one would not imagine they were carrying a heavy load. Their faces showed no trace of strain, only enchantment with the magical creation. Younes watched the tree walk away from him, and from the root of his heart he wished that he were a fly. Not to gorge unnoticed on the sugar, but rather to follow the attendants to the main *iwan* and delight at the expression on the Caliph's face and those of his guests as they admired his sumptuous tree. 'The Caliph's face never reveals what he is really thinking, but such a delectable surprise might break the permanent mask of composure,' Younes reflected, 'and especially on such an auspicious day, the Caliph's first public appearance since his arrival in the new country. He's sure to be in good spirits!'

The kitchen doors closed, screening the tree from his sight, and Younes sucked his little finger in longing. His assistants sat down to rest after days of toil. In addition to the cooks, craftsmen too had worked on this culinary masterpiece, making the wooden moulds for the sugar sculpture.

In the main *iwan* of the palace, the enchanting sugar tree was a vision from paradise. It formed the centrepiece of the festive banquet. Candles burnt and the colours of the carpets shimmered in the soft light. Al-Muizz listened intently to the first songs of victory, verses by his favourite poet Ibn Hani. The Caliph looked majestic, dressed in a linen garment embroidered with gold thread. The Arabic letters that ran in a band on each sleeve read '*al-Mulk lillah*', Sovereignty is to God. Over this garment he wore a sheer green silk robe, so delicate it was difficult to imagine it being made by human hands. The whole robe had been swept through a finger ring to ensure its refinement, as was the custom. Nearby, sat al-Muizz's granddaughter. When he saw how mesmerized she was by the wondrous tree, he whispered to his minister that from that day forward, sugar figurines should be made on the special occasion of the Prophet's birthday and that *Dar al-fitra*, a centre for the production of sweets, should be founded. Al-Muizz teased his granddaughter about the dark beauty spot on her nose. 'It's good to have a third eye! This quince seed sweetens your beauty.' And the four-year-old princess smiled quietly. She knew she had to behave herself in the presence of the Caliph. Her gaze marvelled at his beautifully embroidered shoes, their crimson and gold peeping from under his flowing robe.

Al-Muizz reflected on his plans for the new country, and how he was to follow what his ancestor the Prophet Muhammad had recommended. He would be a fair ruler. How else would he be worthy of his name and lineage? Today, at last, al-Muizz appeared to the people. His turban was encrusted with diamonds and the parade had been carefully choreographed to the last detail. There were at least two thousand horses caparisoned in cloths of brocaded silk, carrying the name of the new Caliph. There were also thousands of colourful banners with embroidered calligraphy. Al-Muizz had remained within the palace for weeks, while the people of Egypt waited for his appearance, their curiosity increasing. Meanwhile, he had sent many emissaries to gather information about the country. While within the palace, he had been eating food that increased his weight, and he had indulged in cosmetic creams which cleared his skin, perfecting his colour. The intention was to make sure he would manifest himself to the people in full glory. 'Commander of the Faithful,' whispered the minister to al-Muizz, 'today's parade was a great triumph. The people of Egypt are awestruck. They believe that during all the period of waiting you were in heaven and that God had lifted you to Him, and they trembled with reverence when they saw you.'

At the back of the Caliph's mind, however, were worries about the new capital. His general Jawhar had called the new city 'al-Mansuriya', after the Fatimid city in Ifriqiya. But when al-Muizz arrived, he changed its name to 'al-Qahirah', the Victorious. But victorious was not what al-Muizz thought its fate would be when Jawhar related to him what had happened during the laying of the city's foundation. 'Before building the surrounding wall to the city, I gathered the Court astrologers and asked them to choose a favourable star for digging the foundation and another for setting its stones. So the astrologers positioned wooden sticks around the space and connected them with a rope that had bells hanging from it. They ordered the builders to throw in whatever cement and stone they had in their hands once they heard the bells ring. The astrologers were waiting for the auspicious moment when a crow landed on one of the wooden sticks and accidentally caused the bells to jingle. The builders thought this was the sign and threw what they had in their hands into the foundations. The astrologers objected but it was too late.'

'Commander of the Faithful,' Jawhar had told al-Muizz, 'my intention had been to choose a star that would make the country fall under the control of the Fatimid dynasty for ever. But what happened was unfortunate.'

Al-Muizz's knowledge of astrology confirmed Jawhar's fears. 'It's a bad omen,' he thought. He agreed with the astrologers' predictions that the Turks would eventually win the country. Did a crow decide the course of history? Before his memory's eye, al-Muizz saw his caravan march into Egypt . . . the horses impressing the principles of the dynasty into the new earth. Then he watched the letters disintegrate and dissolve, erased by the wind before his very eyes . . .

The story-teller brought al-Muizz back to reality, although he intended in fact to take al-Muizz to an imaginary world. In the magical context of the grand *iwan* that evening, it was a challenging task. The story-teller, descendant of a line of story-tellers and a very privileged member of the Court, sat near al-Muizz. He too had heard of the astrologers' mishap and knew that he must be careful not to include crows in his stories. Although he had the habit of observing reality and transforming it, and although he had in the last few weeks witnessed history in the making, he knew that he had to draw inspiration from another source that night if he were to be sensitive to his listeners. 'A story-teller needs his listeners. Without his listeners, a story-teller is nothing,' he thought, warning himself to tread carefully, for fear of upsetting the Caliph. Then he started telling his story.

'Harith the Bedouin and his wife Nefisa lived in the desert. They would pitch their tent wherever they found palm trees and shrubs for their camel or a pool of brackish water. They had led this existence for years, and every day Harith repeated the same tasks; he caught desert rats for their skin, and with the fibres of palm trees he wove ropes to sell to passing caravans. One day, however, to his great surprise, a new spring gushed from the white sands of the desert. Harith brought the water to his lips. We would have found it horribly salty but it seemed to him to be the water of Paradise – it was much less foul than the water he usually drank. "I must give it to someone who will really appreciate its sweetness," thought Harith. He filled two goatskins, one for the Caliph and one for the road, and left for the city of Baghdad and the palace of Harun al-Rashid, only pausing in his long journey to nibble a few dates. After several days, he reached Baghdad and went straight to the palace. The guards listened to his story and, as was the custom, admitted him to the public audience held by the Caliph.

"'Commander of the Faithful,' said Harith, "I am a poor Bedouin and I know all the waters of the desert though I know little else. I have discovered the water of Paradise and as it is worthy of a caliph, I immediately thought of presenting it to you.'"

Al-Muizz's granddaughter would normally have fallen asleep by now, but her eyes were wide open. Her gaze was fixed on the story-teller's nose. She was amazed at how prominent it was.

'The Caliph Harun al-Rashid brought the water to his lips. He paused for a moment then ordered the guards to take the Bedouin and lock him up in the palace until he had reached his decision. "What is nothing to us is everything to him," he told the chief guard. "At nightfall, take him outside the palace, do not let him set eye on the mighty Tigris River, escort him all the way to his tent, never allowing him to taste sweet water. Give him one thousand gold coins and my thanks for his services. Tell him I have appointed him Guardian of the Water of Paradise and that he should offer it to trav-ellers to drink in my name." '

Al-Muizz smiled as he caressed his beard. 'Were the poor Bedouin to taste the water of the Nile, he would be overcome by its sweetness.' The Caliph's remark brought melodious laughter from the assembled guests. 'Harun al-Rashid himself never tasted the water of the Nile!' he added. Indeed, the Abbasids had no access to the Nile now. The river of life was to provide a high level that coming year and the country's crops were to prosper thanks to this bountiful gift. The scarcity of water and all the battles against drought had now been left behind. Al-Muizz drew a breath of satisfaction and murmured thanks to the Creator. His great aspiration was to take over the caliphate in Baghdad. Egypt was a step towards that aim.

Outside, musicians and dancers went in procession around the palace. This too was the start of a new ritual and tradition. The bois-terous tunes they played were to drive away the jinn. In this festive atmosphere, al-Muizz reflected on the cycle of history. He could not drive the crow from his mind. He looked at the moon which was facing him. A full moon lit his beloved city Cairo, for the moment built mainly in his mind, yet its fate had already been determined at its birth by a crow. But this was not to prevent him from projecting what the dynastic city would be like. Building, tolerance, knowledge, an awareness of history were the main principles that marked the Caliph's vision.

A bronze incense-burner in the shape of a large feline stood majestically to the side. The Kufic calligraphy inscribed around its neck read: 'Within me is the fire of Hell but without floats the perfume of Paradise.'

Smoke unfurls from the creature's mouth and from the decorative piercings in its body. The thin wisps of smoke rise, hiding its turquoise-studded eyes, and swirling, thickens until it builds a screen that separates us from the tenth century.

9

When they eventually got on the road again, with patched wheels, the driver was astute enough to keep off the road for a while to avoid further nails. They did not return to it until they were some distance from the tyre shop. He turned on the music again, but surprisingly, it sounded inappropriately loud. So he turned it off. A sign with the name of a small town went by; they left it behind. It was the last one to be seen. They had just gone off the map.

'Could you tell him to go really slowly,' the Professor asked Zohra, concerned about finding the next turning. He was concentrating fully on making out the road and seemed to have forgotten the little Arabic he knew. Every now and then, he struggled to read the time on his watch. Mark was dissatisfied but confident. Zohra was not bothered about the delay, she so much liked being on the road, while Glasses was filled with a sense of arrival rather than of travelling and he was tranquil. Alan was not thinking at all, and Donatella slept. Kodama San stared out into the semi-darkness. Monia had released the leash of her wild dreams.

The Professor broke the silence: 'We will be staying in a school on the outskirts of the village.'

'School?!' Glasses was surprised.

'It's a new building that's not finished yet. The ground level's built and the government's going to add another next year. The part we'll be staying in has been painted though.' The Professor half turned to the others in the back seats. 'It's the best place and the only public place the village could offer.' Zohra had to translate for Monia who, though she spoke some English, like Mustapha, could not follow the

Professor's Irish accent. But Monia knew already what the arrangements were.

'What about the children?' asked Glasses.

'Oh no, it's not functioning as a school yet,' said the Professor, 'though they did open a new hospital next to it last year.'

No one could imagine what the place was going to be like, perhaps not even Monia. They drifted back to their silence. The car throbbed into the obscurity of the night. The Professor was still having great difficulty deciphering the road. He was suddenly aware that his excavation mission had already started. And after miles in the darkness, it felt as if they had left the world of reality for a world where anything was possible.

Everyone's silence was different. The obscurity brought with it a feeling of intimacy and the space in the car changed. It felt warm and cosy. Donatella was still asleep. She was nowhere, for she never dreamt. Her head lolled gently and a strand of her blonde hair, colourless in the dark, strayed over Glasses' shoulder. He felt it come and go and with it a fluttering in his heart, like a little bird trying to fly but only able to hop. Zohra always liked being in a car or a train, perhaps not so much for itself as for the comforting feeling it brought. Of being in-between. That was how she always felt. Half-half. Rarely did people want to know about both halves, about her other half. The other half was always the other, depending on where she was. This feeling of being on the road, and this darkness that veiled the others from her, brought reminiscences to the surface. The feeling that this translating job was going to be different came back to her. She had worked mainly at conferences, once at a film festival. She found herself in all sorts of situations when translating, encountering a strange array of subjects. She hardly remembered the information. Her mind seemed to discard the message soon after playing its role of delivery. But here and there, moments singled themselves out from the layers of memories because they were funny or embarrassing. An incident from the film festival came to her when a colleague misunderstood what had been said. She translated '*Les mères qui attendaient*' as 'expectant mothers' instead of 'mothers who were waiting'. It enraged the film director because everything he said after that was built on the wrong assumption and took on a different meaning.

The role of the intermediary was strange. It had become dissatisfying for Zohra. For years she had dreamt of writing a book of her own. She slept with a dictionary at her side. She savoured words. For her, a word had not only sound but also a taste, a feel. She dreamt of how she would arrange the words by her own will and choice. It would be her statement. She knew the book she wanted to write was within that dictionary beside her. All the words were there, loose. She would have to arrange them, determine their internal relation and construct a world with them. Yet she did not feel she had that ability. She knew translation was a fine art and there had never been any doubt in her mind about what she wanted to do after studying languages at Westminster University in London. After several years working as a translator, however, she longed for a voice of her own. Perhaps she had no story to tell. Perhaps she should remain a go-between. When this translation job for the excavation came up, she had not hesitated to take it in spite of the relatively low pay. She longed for an exciting experience.

They were on their way to discover the past, the crescent moon their only travelling companion. In this immense expanse of nothingness, the moon had an extraordinary presence, a presence that had made so many people worship it in the past. The rest of the world seemed to have been left behind. And now it felt as if all those people on the road who had waved hello to them had in fact waved them goodbye. They had entered a different world.

10

'It's getting dark, you'd better go home now,' said Rayyes Ahmed, projecting his voice so everyone could hear. The villagers exchanged hesitant looks. They had been waiting for the excavation team all afternoon. Some of them stood up but others did not budge. They continued squatting, gazing at the nothingness in front of them, their chins buried in their palms. 'You'd better go home, I said!' stressed Rayyes Ahmed. 'They won't be coming now.' The villagers felt obliged to comply with the foreman's instruction.

'Good night,' reverberated the chorus of men as they dragged their feet reluctantly across the courtyard of the school. A dog barked at the gate as they passed.

Workers had left farmlands to join the excavation because they would be paid five times the amount they received from the farmers. This was the seventh day they had come, and each day they waited for hours. The last few days had seemed like centuries because time is slow for those who wait.

Rayyes Ahmed rolled the translucent paper over the tobacco care-fully and ran the tip of his tongue confidently over its edge. 'It is like the story of the young man and the egg,' said Amm Gaber.

'What young man?' asked Rayyes Ahmed, as he sealed the cigarette, secretly amused by Amm Gaber's Classical Arabic.

'There was once a man,' said Amm Gaber, 'who found an egg. He was hungry and thought about boiling it. But then he put it in front of him and started thinking of the many ways this find could make him rich. "I can nestle it under the neighbour's chicken," he thought. "Soon, a chick will hatch, then it will grow to be a chicken which will lay many eggs. I will sell the eggs and buy a cock. The eggs will hatch and give chicks. These will grow to be chickens and cocks and I'll be selling eggs and chickens in the market until I make enough money to buy a donkey, then a mule, then a house. Then I'll marry the most beautiful girl in the village. We will have children and I'll love them dearly but I'll bring them up well. They'll be disciplined, good children who will obey their father, but if they misbehave I shall beat them with this stick right here." At which point, our young man raised the stick with all his passion and came down on the egg. He could not have aimed more precisely!'

Rayyes Ahmed burst out laughing, threw his grey scarf over his shoulder and raised his long bamboo stick above the child sitting nearby, in the mock gesture of beating him. 'Just like the young man ... they dream just like the young man! Poor fools!' He sucked his cigarette intently and let out the smoke in small puffs, his eyes reduced to slits of sarcasm.

A muffled laughter came unexpectedly from one of the dark corners of the courtyard. 'Get going!' shouted Rayyes Ahmed not unkindly but firmly.

Huddled forms rose up – two villagers were still squatting there. 'Good night, Rayyes Ahmed,' they called as they crossed the courtyard with a sense of inevitable disappointment. They looked at the crescent moon, delicately drawn in a deep sky. 'If the moon were asked what it would like most, it would answer that the sun be veiled for ever!' mumbled the villager to his companion as they approached the gate.

The crescent moon hung translucent above the courtyard, and now it was the only companion for Rayyes Ahmed and Amm Gaber. All the villagers had left and the night settled. The newly appointed school guard, who stood in the corner holding his gun, was barely visible. Rayyes Ahmed was not bothered about the boy Mahmoud staying behind. He had taken a liking to him ever since he had known him. His mother had entrusted him to Rayyes Ahmed, hoping that he would give him a job in the excavation.

'The last time there was an excavation, they arrived early in the day,' said Rayyes Ahmed. 'I wonder what's delaying them.'

Amm Gaber's gaze was blank. His pupil-less eyes were like mirrors, or perhaps like bowls of milk – that was how Rayyes Ahmed saw them. Rayyes Ahmed did not expect an answer from Amm Gaber. He was in a way talking to himself. He respected the old man but he thought that anyone who spoke to a tree was somehow strange, perhaps even mad – Amm Gaber was often heard talking nonsense. Some believed, however, that he was a saint who saw beyond earthly logic, a guard of the unseen.

The villagers went to their mud-brick houses. The privileged few bathed in the blue light of their televisions. Programmes seemed to be set in the future. Not all people live in the same times. The gap between their reality and the world on the screen was unbridgeable. As the night advanced, some of the villagers sank into sleep. Some were wide awake. Awake or not, the villagers dreamt of the foreign diggers who would bestow riches on them. For the dead this was a nightmare. It was the belief in Wadi Hassoun that the dead dreamt. How else were they to keep connected with this world? As it could not be proven that all those who were in this world were alive, it could also not be proven that all those who were buried were dead. The old legend in the village meant that the dead could rob you of your sleep or make you fall asleep and decide whether or not to tear the curtain that veiled the world of dreams.

By this time of night, the few shops in the village were closed, except for the tobacco shop. Since people might feel the urge for a cigarette at any time, the owner of this little shop stayed awake. And like every night, his friend the tent-maker kept him company, stitching by the light of an oil lamp. Pieces of cloth told stories in colour sewn on to the designs, traced beforehand, like predestined patterns of fate.

In the school, Rayyes Ahmed despaired, thinking the team was not coming. But the old man said: 'Ya Ahmed, tonight they are coming.'

If time was very slow for Rayyes Ahmed, time did not exist for Amm Gaber. Rayyes Ahmed looked at him, at those white eyes that had no pupils, and asked: 'How did it happen old man, how did you lose your eyesight?'

'Listen,' whispered Amm Gaber. 'Listen to that sound.' Rayyes

Ahmed pricked his ears in hopeful curiosity. Could it be that the old man was able to hear the car engine while he could not? But he heard nothing. 'Listen,' whispered Amm Gaber again, his head tilted, his index finger raised. Rayyes Ahmed could hear nothing. '*Al-yamama tusabbih*,' the dove is singing the praises of God, said Amm Gaber. A baffled frown tightened on Rayyes Ahmed's brow, but the boy Mahmoud, sitting nearby, smiled quietly. The cooing of the dove took over, regular and rhythmic.

II

'I could see clearly from where I sat, straddling the windowsill, a hole in the mud-brick wall,' said Amm Gaber. 'The sill was as tough as a donkey's back, imprinting its mark both on my tender bottom and my memory. I was only five years old. Everyone knew I sat there every day, but I was not to make myself heard. The sill was a boundary between two worlds. From where I sat, I watched what happened in both realities. On one side, a white mule foal grazed, teenage girls strutted with large trays. On the other was the classroom.

'Soon I learnt the alphabet. *Alif, Ba, Ta.* The teacher would point at the letters with his stick and ask each pupil to repeat after him. As I had no right to speak, I used to repeat the letters within myself, and their silent reverberations spread within me. I never learnt to read and write but the letters as living beings never left me.'

Rayyes Ahmed lit a cigarette.

'It was the mid-afternoon of a hot day,' continued Amm Gaber. 'Hands were holding chins and eyes rolled in curiosity. The subject had caught everyone's attention. "This is what the earth is like, round from all sides, spherical in shape," said the teacher, holding a globe made of brown paper. "Here, at the North Pole, people get very cold. They rub noses to kiss to greet each other."

' "Fancy that," I mused. "Rubbing noses!" It was the first time I thought my grandfather's prominent nose could have served for anything. He would be able to give good kisses with a nose like that.'

The boy Mahmoud's eyes were wide open. His gaze was fixed on Amm Gaber's nose. He was amazed at how prominent it was. 'He must have inherited it from his grandfather,' he thought, amused.

'The teacher stood next to a large blackboard, holding the brown ball. "Here is America, that's Europe, this is Africa. We are here," he said, pointing at a specific spot on the globe. I watched as sixty eyes followed his index finger. Egypt was one dot, marked by his pen, and I was there.

'Unexpectedly, the teacher twirled the globe in the air. I wanted to scream: "Stop it!" but his hands were swift. Everything went upside-down. I looked at the ceiling and found myself looking at the ground. I was dizzy. I kicked my feet, hoping the donkey would take me out of the place, but was reminded that these were the sides of a wall, not a donkey. My scream of agony was overwhelmed by the whistle which announced the end of the session. The paper globe was snatched away from the master's hand. Pupils erupted from the classroom and started throwing and kicking the globe ball. And Africa had a large share. I stood in the middle of the square, in the tumult of dust, with no strength to compete. Some went in pursuit of the ball. Others went in pursuit of others. Gallabiyas were torn. The globe's rough skin was shredded. There was nothing left, only bits and pieces floating in the dust-filled air. The thin string which marked the Equator came off and the globe burst open.'

Mahmoud's eyes opened wider. Rayyes Ahmed had stopped listening to Amm Gaber some time ago. The old man's narrative seemed disconnected, as though he had been touched by the jinn, and his Classical Arabic was monotonous to his ears. Rayyes Ahmed did not notice the changes in Amm Gaber's voice as he told the story. While he rolled another cigarette, Rayyes Ahmed deliberated on the team's delay. He never liked waiting.

'Why they called it a square or a place, I did not know,' continued Amm Gaber. 'It was not clear whether the three roads or paths met at the heart of this place or forked out of it. People seemed to cross here but never really stop. And apart from the school, the other sides of this open space were made of the back walls of houses. The school was no more than one classroom, not to be compared with this new school. In those days, children learnt to read a book from all sides because there were not enough books and a book was shared between three or four children.

'Well now, imagine this little boy watching children playing in the square that was not much of a square. "Look," I called to those who kicked the ball, my heart eaten by the worms of jealousy. "Look!" I screamed with all my might. A whirl of dust advanced from all sides, it settled to reveal a circle of curious faces around me. "I'll show you something you can't do. Look at me," I said. "Keep looking!" and I swirled and swivelled the olive pupils in my eyes and with a will from the furthest depths within me, I sent them upwards and threw them to meet at the centre under my frowning eyebrows. The balls sprang again, diverging sideways. "Look at me, I can send my eyeballs in all directions! You try it!" I dared them. But no one could send his eyeballs flying. They tried for a long time, squinting their eyes, pulling their faces, and at last they had to give up. They stared at me bewildered. Some pulled at my gallabiya and exclaimed: "How can you do that?" Holding their attention, I went on sending my eyeballs everywhere until they started bouncing by themselves. I had lost control. The others watched in boisterous ecstasy. "Where are they?" I heard one of them shout. Then "Oh! Ya Allah! His eyes are white!" Then silence fell. They waited around me, I could feel their terror in the weight of their immobility. Then boredom dispersed some of them and fear made the others run away; they thought my condition was contagious. I heard the receding thud of their feet. Then the only sound was that of the wind's hollow cry. I was alone. Shreds of paper filled the air with their dance. I reached to them, trying to put the ball back together. My hands filled until they could hold no more and I had to let go to catch more paper. It was an endless vacuum.

'Eyes goggled. They swerved and turned. Then they were blank, an opaque ceramic white. A veil lifted. I had a feeling of going through hundreds of doors successively. My eyes had turned within and an immense desert landscape overwhelmed me. Its evenly drawn waves had the most soothing effect. A sense of nothingness with its wholeness filled me. But my sight went beyond, to the rotting carcass of a monster, itself a door to a forlorn landscape. A devastating expanse of terror. Blue, indigo and red hues abandoned. Erupted volcanoes, overthrown trees, storming seas, chipped stones. And my soul! Oh my soul, all bare in that desolate landscape where it had to start its journey of migration!'

To Rayyes Ahmed, the old man looked as though he was gazing into the void, his eyes opaque white. But before Amm Gaber was a desolate landscape, a twisting tree in the foreground. An imposing silence reigned, except for the sound of a waterwheel in the distance.

'They are coming tonight,' said Amm Gaber.

'*Inshallah*,' sighed Rayyes Ahmed. He looked at the old man intently and was surprised by his face. Amm Gaber looked sometimes a child, sometimes an adult, an old man and even a woman, as if these characters coexisted harmoniously within him without conflict. Time was not linear in his life. A shiver travelled up Rayyes Ahmed's spine. Perhaps it was due to the strange light of this long night and the growing chill in the air. He took a drag on his cigarette and gazed at the sky.

'It's a clear moon tonight, Amm Gaber,' he said.

The old man saw boredom in Rayyes Ahmed's voice but he replied without shifting his head: 'A silver, slim crescent.'

The little boy Mahmoud joined the palms of his hands in amazement. 'Who said that blindness is life without sight?' Rayyes Ahmed wondered to himself.

12

The rows of houses in the village were sculpted forms huddled together like a throng of people, crouched and snug in their cloaks. The crescent moon gave little light. As the car drove through the meandering narrow roads, and their journey drew to an end, the members of the dig felt tired, hungry and especially curious. Most of them did not know what to expect. The sound of the engine brought people out of their houses, but the vehicle did not stop. Everything seemed shut except a small tobacco shop. Its owner greeted them, waving his hand holding a packet of cigarettes. A man sitting huddled next to him did not look up.

Reaching their destination in the evening was not what had been planned, but nothing seemed to go according to schedule. The school was surrounded by a low wall with iron railings rising a further two metres. A man wearing a gallabiya, taking long steps with agile strides, met them at the entrance. He swung open the iron gate and held it in place with a stone. A dog barked and lunged to attack Alan, only its chain restrained it. 'Quiet,' snarled the man. He threw his cigarette butt to the ground and emitted quick sounds which made the dog stop barking. Then he introduced himself: 'Rayyes Ahmed.' His knowledge of English was limited to '*Helloo*', which he repeated endlessly as he shook hands with the members of the team. He was frustrated because he wanted to say so much more to welcome the newcomers. The boy Mahmoud left Amm Gaber and ran towards the gate. 'This is Mahmoud,' said Rayyes Ahmed as he ruffled the child's hair. Mahmoud smiled, his eyes gleaming, and Donatella could not believe how much he resembled a beautiful boy who sold soft drinks in Cairo and of whom she had taken a photograph.

She gave a smile of recognition which only the child noticed. 'It's almost the same child!' she thought. Zohra was somehow drawn to where the boy had emerged from. In that dark spot, a figure sat erect and still. Only his profile silhouette was lit, the details of his features erased by the darkness. The cooing of a dove marked his serene presence. An inexplicable shiver went through Zohra's body. The more she gazed at the figure, the further away it seemed. A solitary light faintly lit the courtyard, which was overcast by the shadow of the forking palm tree. In the darkness, the team was blind to the presence of the school guard and Amm Gaber.

Labour was divided quickly and the men went to make their beds. Zohra and Monia wanted to cook. Although the school was new, the large yellow room that was the kitchen was already dirty. Donatella started scrubbing the table. 'Halima and Hakima will be doing the cleaning as from tomorrow,' volunteered Rayyes Ahmed to Zohra, a hint of embarrassment in his voice. 'Halima is a Muslim and Hakima is a Copt, they'll both work hard for you.'

Once the apparent layer of dirt was removed from the table, Donatella was killing the invisible. 'I always thought of water and air as the two essentials of life which have no colour as such, but here, water does have a colour! It's a murky brown!' She was unaware that they were among the privileged few. Most of the village did not have running water.

The atmosphere was both strange and funny. The cook and his apprentice were woken up by the team's arrival. They felt deprived of their role in the kitchen. The apprentice walked as though still in his sleep. 'Do you need a sharp knife?' he offered with an incongruous giggle.

'No!' came Zohra's rejection. They had cooked lunch, he explained, but by six in the afternoon they did not think the team was coming so they had given it away. Zohra thought the apprentice's face was disconcerting. His eyes, nose and mouth were pushed together, producing a head that was almost animal. She wondered why he rushed to cover his mouth every time he laughed.

Still trying to help, the apprentice brought a pile of plates, but as he was about to place them on the table, in his somnolent state he dropped one. Zohra and Donatella watched it fall but were unable to save it. The arrow of time was going its inevitable way. The apprentice started gathering the pieces; the shock seemed to have woken him up. Glasses picked up two shards swiftly and was trying to match them. 'Work hasn't started yet!' said Donatella, who picked up the camera and snapped.

'It's not old enough,' said Alan.

'It's not blue!' said Mark.

'They're worth nothing. You should wait for the lustre shards,' countered the Professor. The apprentice cook gawped at each one of them in turn, he could not understand the reason behind the boisterous laughter. Zohra wanted to contribute her own comment to this game but didn't know what to say, although she joined in the laughter while she stirred the tomato sauce. Monia stood giggling behind the hot steam from the sieve in her hands. She had broken the spaghetti into small pieces.

The meal was not a success. It was too hot for most of them. Kodama San did not eat but he sat at the table, his little finger elegantly folded at the knuckle in the usual way. Monia, on the other hand, ate with great appetite, although she too thought it was hot. One dish, different taste buds. But for everyone, the hot food was like fire. Their involuntary laughter was perhaps due to a general feeling of weariness. By then, it was past midnight.

It was Monia who first whispered: '*Mashallah*, he's so tall!' when an Egyptian man walked into the kitchen, changed and perfumed, without a sign that he had been asleep.

'He's very thin too,' replied Zohra.

'What is it?' Donatella asked. Zohra translated and Donatella burst out laughing. 'Just like our spaghetti!' she replied.

'Before Monia cooked it!' teased Zohra.

'He is hot like the spaghetti too!' whispered Monia.

'Spaghetti's definitely the right name for him,' added Donatella.

All the women were laughing with tears now, spicy tears of exhaustion.

'What is it?' asked Mark politely.

'What's so funny?' asked Glasses, but no answer came. Donatella could hardly breathe, she was laughing so much. Laughter took hold of all of them, and after a while, they were not laughing it, it was laughing them! What they had not been able to understand when they had arrived in Cairo was now happening to them. They had caught the local disease. A strange feeling born from this whole new world suddenly brought them together as though they had known each other for a long time. The situation imposed an intimacy that was going to be lived by everyone differently.

In the kitchen, around the table, they made a list of things to buy, from doormats to napkins. The nearest town was at least two hours' drive from where they were. But Spaghetti took the list and said he would deal with it the following day. He was Mustapha's gift to the mission and was to be their practical man for the whole stay. He showed a pleasant politeness and a willingness to help. He was proud that he would be responsible for collecting the money to pay the workers every week. Every now and then, Monia lifted her long dark eyelashes slowly, sending a dagger into Spaghetti's heart. In the land of killers, however, a killer is no threat.

The three women, Donatella, Monia and Zohra, were to sleep in the same room. The light flickered, struggling to come on, and they staggered as they went into what was to be their shared space. The door slammed with a bang. Donatella knocked over her toilet bag and an avalanche cascaded onto the floor, from dental floss and facial masks to repair cream for the sensitive eye zone. Toilet bags were stuffed with products which displayed their sophisticated needs.

There was nowhere to hang their clothes. Zohra covered the chair next to her bed with a sheet of paper and put her dictionary on it. Insect repellent, cassettes and water purification tablets were piled perilously on the chair too. The pink sheets on the beds struck them as funny but they were already exhausted from giddy laughter. It had turned quite cold and blankets were needed. Tomorrow they would start digging up the past, and who knew what secrets the earth would hold for them? Monia combed her hair and gazed at the ceiling.

Her nightgown was studded with little red hearts. The black and white in her eyes were coal and snow. Her heart was ignited.

Glasses, Alan, Mark and Kodama San were also to share one room, Professor O'Brien and Spaghetti, another. Although he had expected to share, Glasses was not very comfortable. He always preferred to sleep alone and Alan's snoring came as a surprise.

In the women's room, that first night in the school, Monia slept soundly. Donatella too, as she always did, without dreaming. Zohra lay awake in the darkness of an unfamiliar place, with people she hardly knew. People of different nationalities. Monia was Egyptian, Donatella Italian. And what about the others? Glasses was German, Mark American, Alan English, Professor O'Brien Irish, Kodama San Japanese, and the one they had nicknamed Spaghetti, he was Egyptian too. And she herself? Half English, half Tunisian. And that figure. Yes, what about that figure in the dark? Would that figure emerge or remain in the folds of the night which had already become the past? This was the start of something unpredictable. This was where they were going to live together for months. Different people, of different races, cultures, and from different social backgrounds, thrown into a primal situation, the only link between them the buried past of a civilization alien to them.

Zohra was reflecting on these new people and this new place when suddenly, from the heart of the night, rose a singing voice. The voice had no particular age and was sometimes a man's, sometimes a woman's, sometimes a child's. Zohra wondered whether the others could hear it too or whether they were all asleep. The voice shaped the air that was breathed into it. It rose in a timeless, migrant spiral, filled the night and came to fill her heart with longing. And Zohra had to resist the urge to go and look for this voice which seemed to come from no specific direction.

And that night, except for Amm Gaber who sat awake throughout, the whole village dreamt the same dream. They all craved the riches that would surely bring them happiness. On the outskirts of the far side of the village, on his way towards the site of the excavation to be, Rayyes Ahmed also dreamt as he rode on his mule. He dismounted at the door of the beautiful Zineb, hoping to find it open. But the door was shut. So he rode on. He glimpsed a villager tying a ribbon to the Tree of Wishes at the edge of the cemetery. That villager too must have been dreaming the same dream of riches. Rayyes Ahmed also noticed the figure of Amm Gaber talking to the tree as usual, his lantern next to him, the light he sometimes carried so that people did not walk into him. Rayyes Ahmed shook his head in disbelief of the old man's familiar madness.

13

The truck was parked in the school courtyard. '*Allah Akbar*', God is most Great, written in white in a calligraphic hand, stood out against the red background of the vehicle. It had come at five. They had to wait for Donatella to change. The Professor disapproved of her shorts, which came to just above the knee. 'We have to be respectful to the locals,' he said. Then he insisted on a group photograph and the team arranged themselves on the steps of the school building. The Professor had even gone for his tweed jacket and posed, the proper way, before Alan took the photograph. As she stood on the edge, next to the climbing plant, Zohra was suddenly aware that she was where the silent figure had been sitting the night before. Somehow, it felt as though the figure had not moved. The daylight had simply erased his image. His presence was there, as strong as it had been the night before, and so was the rhythm of the dove's cooing, although the dove was nowhere to be heard. Zohra was struck by an untranslatable emotion.

They did not set off for the site until seven. As the members of the team climbed into the open back of the truck, the new driver greeted them with a grin, so wide it split his face in two. The driver who had brought them from Cairo had already left. The truck started with furious revving and zoomed out of the schoolyard, but was forced to wait. Cars drove dangerously at full speed in front of the school; people from all the neighbouring villages brought their sick to the new hospital.

The team sat in two rows, the same question mark mirrored on their faces. What was the site like? They were jolted as the truck swung right, following the car in front in which the Professor was being driven by the archaeology chief inspector. The truck jerked all over the place. 'He is a nutter!' said Donatella, her white-gloved hands holding on firmly. Donatella's face was almost inanimate, her lipstick and eyeshadow a frozen mask. But as she talked, her make-up began to blend with her skin and her face became full of life. In his black shirt, worn over a white T-shirt, Mark looked like a priest on a mission. He found the truck particularly uncomfortable and he was missing his customary morning shower. Mark had never been on a dig before but he behaved as though he had. He was observant and on top of things. He hummed nonchalantly, which made everyone take a liking to him. 'He's a bit of all right,' thought Donatella without words as she examined him.

The driver had to slow down at the bridge. 'This is Bahr Yussef, the River of Joseph,' said Monia. The river, a tributary of the Nile, was still and quiet. Its undulating surface had a sheen of orange which reflected the rows of palm trees on either side. The sun was beaming gently.

Past the river, the driver swerved suddenly to the left. He was forced to drive slowly again as he cut across the marketplace, crowded with people and donkeys. Mango sellers fussed over their merchandise, which filled the air with a pungent aroma. '*Manga, manga!*' they called. The village market was overflowing with crates and crates of them.

The smell of mango was to permeate the excavation season and seep into the grooves of Zohra's being, so much so that later, years later, when, in north London, a friend introduced her to a greengrocer's, she screamed: 'I've been here ... it's familiar ... but somewhere else!' Her friend was baffled and so was she by her own excitement as she strode around the shop. Her feeling intensified when she passed a box of mangoes and she understood the link and went quiet. How could she have conveyed to her friend what had unfolded years before in a faraway place intoxicated by this aroma?

The truck struggled through the throng. Some watched, immobilized by curiosity. Children waved and ran after the two vehicles, shouting: '*Khawajat, khawajat!*'

'Didn't we hear that word in Cairo?' asked Donatella.

'It's the word for "foreigners",' said Zohra, with a hint of embarrassment. People looked at Monia, a local among strangers, with

66

bewilderment. She laughed and held her head high. Monia was very proud to be an archaeology inspector.

As they crossed the heart of the village, a few women and children came out of their houses to stand and wave to the foreigners, people made of a different clay. Then the truck disappeared in its trail of dust.

They drove through the streets, shrouded in a soft yellow light, the houses more and more sparse as they went on. Some of the dirt roads were so narrow, it was as though the rows of mud-brick houses themselves were reluctant to stand apart. At one point the driver had to get out and remove a large stone from their path. At another they had to struggle under an overhanging tree. The car, and especially the truck, laboured while negotiating the roads, which were far removed from the world of motor vehicles.

Leaving the body of the village behind and approaching the site, they could see, from afar, a building on a little hill, dominated by its white naked dome. The white dome was huge. It stood out in the landscape. Some distance away, a tilted minaret stood by itself, detached. No mosque to justify its existence. Glasses cast a surveying look. The spiral-shaped minaret was about twenty metres high. It was decorated with intricate brickwork, amazingly beautiful and fragile. It stood with difficulty, amidst crumbling walls less than a metre high. The minaret looked bewildered, its voice silenced for ever. Once the landmark of a magnificent medieval residence, it had been reduced to a lonely ruin on the edge of a village with a far-removed reality. A gap separates the village from the glorious past crumbling nearby, thought Glasses. How had the link between the past and the present been severed?

Donatella was trying to find the right spot to take a photograph. Kodama San leaned to jot down something in his notebook. 'Writing does the remembering for us,' thought Zohra.

Rayyes Ahmed pointed at the minaret's finial. One side of it was missing. 'It fell during a severe storm,' he said, 'but thanks be to God, no one was hurt.'

'Wonderful design!' thought Glasses, admiring the spiral minaret.

As if he had been reading his mind, the Professor volunteered: 'Do you know, it's inspired by the minaret of the Great Mosque in the town of Samarra in Iraq, except that the minaret of Samarra is fifty-five metres high!'

'Wow!' exclaimed Mark. 'Awesome!' Mark was paying great attention, as he did not know much about Islamic art, having specialized in European art.

'But we don't know how this spiral shape came about originally,' the Professor continued.

'A bad omen,' cried Rayyes Ahmed, who had just noticed that an owl had made its home in one of the minaret's niches. A stone was already flying from his hand. Alan, passionate as he was about the preservation of the environment, had to control his anger. The Professor would not have approved of aggression against Rayyes Ahmed! The second stone missed the owl too. Alan only just contained himself.

Zohra was absorbing their surroundings. There was such a contrast with overcrowded Cairo. The site was empty – one of those places where one could see the sky every time one looked up and the earth every time one looked down. There was a sense of cleanliness about it. But the excavation team would soon raise the dust. First, the Professor had to choose the different areas where digging would start. He went around with Kodama San, poking the earth, assessing which parts would be pregnant with the past. 'You have to take Sabry with you,' said Colonel Taher. The chief inspector, Head of the Archaeology Police, was present because it was the first day. Afterwards, Monia was to report to him if they needed anything. 'Sabry knows where the Germans dug eleven years ago and where they didn't. You don't want to waste your time, Professor!'

Zohra translated. The Professor smiled, the plans of the German excavation were rolled in his hand. They looked in the direction of an old man whose dark brown face was marked by a white moustache. He stood apart from the other workers and they recognized him to be undoubtedly Sabry. The Professor ignored the advice politely. Kodama San was busy with his magnetic survey, looking for anomalies that would signal the presence of pottery kilns.

Some of the workers gathered around Monia, who was trying to make sense of what they wanted as they all talked at the same time. In his long gallabiya, Rayyes Ahmed, the foreman, paced around, master of the open space. The ground seemed to follow his wide strides. He was trying to get the workers to organize themselves. Both Muslims and Copts pulled at his sleeves. They were men, teenagers, and children who insisted they were older than they looked. In fact, it was difficult to gauge people's ages; some of the men were actually much younger than they seemed.

The Professor was flushed with enthusiasm. His long-held dream was about to come true. A mute boy would not let go of him; he so much wanted to join the excavation. The Professor had a heart big enough to take everyone but it was up to Rayyes Ahmed, the foreman, to select the workers and Mark, the project manager, to accept them. 'We need about fifteen men for each site,' said the Professor. He had mentioned the number twelve earlier but had obviously decided to stretch it a little.

A large cemetery covered a raised area, a uniform spread of hand-sculpted tombs, all painted white. On the slope of the cemetery was a strange tree. It stood steadfast in the face of time. Its ravaged, wrinkled branches, frozen in a frenzied dance of agony, suggested it had been struck by lightning. It was laden with a strange fruit. To its naked branches, colourful strips of cloth were tied, each the tongue of a wish.

'What's that tree?' asked Donatella.

'That's the tree of Jesus and Mary,' answered Rayyes Ahmed. 'It sprouted from a stick which Jesus pressed into the ground and it's honoured by Copts and Muslims alike.' Rayyes Ahmed paused to take a drag of his cigarette. 'It's the Tree of Wishes,' he concluded with a serious expression on his face. Zohra translated.

'People tie a ribbon for a wish and, with God's will, the wish comes true,' added Sabry. Donatella laughed at the story of the Tree of Wishes. As she translated, Zohra was astonished at the multitude of ribbons. They must have come from people's clothes, flowery from women's garments and all different sorts from men's, but especially light blue, which seemed to be the favourite colour for gallabiyas. The tree appeared to stand alone, but as she looked, Zohra noticed the back of someone sitting next to it and saw the boy Mahmoud run towards him.

Opposite, in the far distance, stood a mud-brick house which had orange windows. Its façade was painted with a row of figures holding hands. Their long plaits too were joined, creating an undulating motion. A woman in a deep purple dress stood at the door, watching the team. She too had long dark plaits. Even from afar, they could see she was very beautiful. 'That's Zineb!' beamed Rayyes Ahmed before he went to talk to her.

The painted façades of the few mud-brick houses in the vicinity were very attractive to the newcomers. They unfolded an enchanting narrative, their bright colours phantasmagoric in the dull surrounding. Donatella stopped to take a photograph. A throng of children gathered around her, mesmerized by her blonde hair and fair skin. She laughed and gestured to them to stand to the side while she took a picture of the fresco. There were boats, planes, men praying, and words of benediction. They learned later that these were the houses of those villagers who had made their pilgrimage to Mecca. But the façade of the beautiful woman's house had different imagery. It had nothing to do with pilgrimage. This was the woman with gifted hands who painted most of the houses in the village.

A goat, a donkey and its offspring were playing in the open space while a buffalo stood watching. A man wearing several grey gallabiyas and an indigo turban wandered aimlessly around. None of the villagers paid him much heed.

A grid was being set swiftly and the Professor explained about charting the location of artefacts within its squares. Alan was listening to him intently. Colonel Taher talked to Monia aside before he offered his best wishes to Professor O'Brien as the director of the excavation and left. The team had to stay late at the site that day. Professor O'Brien was keen to start digging as soon as possible.

The following day, near the lonely minaret, the first trench was traced, ten metres by ten metres. The first hole to be dug in the past's memory. Alan was to supervise the area of the minaret, 'Area A'. The Professor warned Alan not to get too close to the crumbling masonry. Monia was given 'Area C', forty metres to the west of Alan's site, and was enthusiastically organizing her workers. Donatella was to supervise the site on the edge of the cemetery, 'Area B', about two hundred metres to the north. As she walked towards it, she seemed strikingly out of place. Fifteen workers followed her with shovels and mattocks slung over their shoulders. Glasses watched Donatella from afar. 'She carries herself in a way which reflects the way she was brought up ... Italian women are the most beautiful women in the world and "donna", the Italian word for "woman", carries within it the voluptuousness of womanhood,' he thought.

'*Wad yanta w-hoowwe, dantu wlad el-balad khalliku wlad el-balad 'ala tool!*', You're the natives of this land, make sure you remain so, shouted Rayyes Ahmed at the fifteen men as he strutted about, pointing with his long stick, warning the workers to be well behaved with the beautiful Donatella.

Zohra accompanied Mark, the Professor and Rayyes Ahmed, translating when needed. She felt strangely at home here. Apart from his frequent sneezes, Mark was silent, but his thoughts were loud. Which spot would reveal the Blue Manuscript, he wondered. He told the Professor to take as many workers as he needed and to dig as many areas as he could. The Professor was considering other possibilities and Kodama San was in deep concentration, trying to help. Rayyes Ahmed sent the boy Mahmoud to call Sabry and the boy ran with nimble feet.

'No,' warned Sabry when he saw the spot where the Professor stood. 'The Germans have already dug there!' The Professor nodded and continued with his calculations.

The excavation had started. The sun spread, hiding the moon in defiance, one would think for ever. The mattocks cut through earth, opening trenches. The field supervisors watched attentively over the digging as it proceeded. They followed every hoe and spade. Somehow they were conscious that every site was unique, perhaps holding within its entrails a fragmented past that could be reassembled into meaning.

Outside the few mud-brick houses visible from the site, people sat and watched. There was no trace of a morning breeze. Around eleven-thirty, the team stopped for a break and headed for the building on top of the mount, between the minaret site and the cemetery. The building with its impressive white dome was the Mausoleum of Sayyida Nesima. An old woman with hair the colour of fire sat near its doorway. This was Om Omran, who prepared tea for pilgrims and who would also make tea for them. Rayyes Ahmed had thought of everything. The team sat on the mat-covered platform along the wall of the mausoleum, enjoying the exchange of words and the respite from the sun. Against the wall, a man worked in concentration, embroidering a tent. The smell of grilled meat spread from within the shrine. Visitors went in, carrying chickens. One was even struggling with a goat. 'Patience is a virtue of ears,' mumbled Om Omran as pilgrims' pleadings to the saint to lift their poverty came from within the mausoleum. The man who had been bent over his embroidery interrupted his needlework and disappeared inside. He emerged with a mat which he spread facing east and began to pray. Alan gazed at him, bewildered, as the man lifted his hands in a gesture of surrender. Glasses stood up to go back to the school. He was to set up a basic conservation laboratory for the season. In the brief moment he had sat next to Donatella, a strange feeling had come over him. The initial sense that he had seen her before returned.

Zohra saw how Glasses looked at Donatella. Unexpectedly, she thought of Donatella's birthmark, revealed the night before when she had undressed. 'A large mark and not very pretty.' Zohra was surprised by the meanness of her own thought.

'This is Haj Salem,' declared Rayyes Ahmed, introducing a man who was to guard the excavation site at night. Mark was slightly concerned that the man was too old. The house where Haj Salem lived with his son and his grandchildren was only a few metres from the mount of Sayyida Nesima. There were no pilgrimage paintings on its façade because Haj Salem was not really a haj. He had never been to Mecca. But the pious man was unanimously given the title 'Haj' by the whole village. And now he was chosen to be the guard because of the respect he commanded rather than his physical strength. Besides, he was very poor, and Rayyes Ahmed wanted to help him.

The members of the team sipped their tea and studied their surroundings. Zohra found herself gazing at the man next to the Tree of Wishes on the edge of the cemetery, waiting for him to move and reveal something. But he seemed motionless. He reminded her of the figure sitting in the darkness of the courtyard on the night of their arrival. Her attention was diverted to Rayyes Ahmed, whose figure receded as he descended the hill. Directly opposite, in the distance, the beautiful Zineb was at her door. Rayyes Ahmed's whole body seemed to talk. The door leaf hesitated for a moment then shut and Rayyes Ahmed came back.

People did not usually close their doors here. After finishing their housework, the women sat outside. There was no separation between individual and communal lives. Only Zineb closed her door. But a few minutes later the door would open and she would stand watching again.

The digging was resumed. Kodama San attached a small camera to a kite and launched it into the air. The Professor walked around thinking about other potentially lucrative areas, areas which he believed were part of the Fatimid Green Pavilion. He thought of his lustre wasters. His whole being wondered where they could be. He also thought about other ways he could generate more work for the villagers. After hours of digging, they had barely scratched the surface, they had not gone beyond the sedimentary strata, but at least they had started and that gave him a feeling of great satisfaction. Although he had made a special visit to Wadi Hassoun the year before, to explore the entire site, he had still not identified all the potential areas. A tyre careered into his leg and a throng of children picked it up. They ran after it as it turned and turned, rolling all the way down the mount. 'The mount looks promising,' thought the Professor to himself as he eyed the hill, crowned by the white-domed Mausoleum of Sayyida Nesima.

14

'It was in the steamy fever of the washroom that I first confided in my mother. She was rubbing my scalp hard, stirring the images. And I started to describe to her what I could see, incredible visions overwhelming me. "Outside that door," she yelled, "nine of your brothers are waiting to be scrubbed!" Involuntarily she slapped me. I slipped from the low chair into an abyss. In that strange moment, wrapped in darkness and haze, we silently knotted a pact with our guilt. She swore that she would never hit me again and I swore that I would never tell her about my visions.'

Amm Gaber fell silent for a moment before he went on talking to the Tree of Wishes. At the edge of the cemetery the tree stood conversing with the breeze of dawn while the old man conversed with it.

'I became notorious for my perceptive touch. Because of my blank eyes, I was surreptitiously introduced to inner worlds and with time my hands grew to touch sculpted forms, bottoms as soft as peaches, and lips with the taste of sweet grapes. Soon, I realized this was forbidden fruit.' The old man covered his face with his palms and chuckled before he went on.

'I was absorbing more and more secrets, and that was how a bottomless well began burrowing inside me. With words I made a necklace and I kept changing its stringing. The words in my rosary did not follow any order. Within every word, there was a word. A string of constantly changing meanings. My fingers read these words endlessly. My beard grew the colour of time. The beads in my rosary were words with no tongue. White is the colour of time. My beard proves that. With time, my beard did not become green, it became white. I cannot see my hands but I can see beyond this Earth. The loss of my eyesight sharpened the eye of my heart.'

The breeze brought a caress to the old man's face and, in his own way, he could see ribbons, tied to the Tree of Wishes, fluttering like wings of hope.

'Tree of trees, you are already carrying thousands of secrets, lovers' wishes, those who long for a beloved, a relative, a friend, a cure for the sick. Each of your branches forks out into other branches. Every branch tells a story; it ascends skyward with its twists. Colourful ribbons knot around your branches, phoenix wishes of desire and hope, forever imploring that you bring them to fruit. People know you never sleep. They trust in your dignity to treasure the secrets eating day and night at their hearts like worms, secrets they themselves can no longer keep. O Tree of trees, I hope your heart can bear my tales.

'There was once a man who confided in his wife and made her promise absolute discretion. Months went by, years went by, and the man suspected his wife had divulged his secrets. "Have you revealed my secrets?" he asked. "You must have emptied your heart to some-one," he reproached. "You would've wasted away, otherwise. A word that carries a secret is a dagger that pierces the heart."

' "Yes," confessed the woman, "I have told your secrets to the tree in the courtyard."

'The man went and dug at the base of the tree, only to find a wrig-gling horde of worms. "You see," he said to his wife, "had you kept the secrets in your chest, this is how your heart would be!"

'Tree of trees, my unique listener. If only you could answer back. A long, long time ago, everything but everything used to speak. It was the Prophet Solomon who put an end to this, as it would have been unbearable to humans. Just imagine, a husband comes home and the carpet says: "It's on this carpet that your wife has rolled with her lover only a short while ago," and the shoe says as he lifts it to beat her: "Have pity on me. I am weary, I have walked a long way this morning to take you to your mistress!" '

Amm Gaber laughed before he continued. 'I heard this from my father, a story-teller, descendant of a family of story-tellers. It was a time when the story-teller had many listeners.

'My father,' sighed Amm Gaber, 'my father took me on a long, long journey. My mother had been urging him to search for a cure for my eyes. She had grown impatient with what she called "crazy visions". She did not know that there was nothing to cure. As we went from country to country, Father collected many stories and told them throughout the journey. But I grew to tell my own stories. Unlike my father, my journey was in an inner landscape which imprinted itself on my words. And to my stories, no one wanted to listen. I have been labelled mad. It was the easiest option; people do not like to think. Those willing to think wanted me to be a saint. They would not allow me my mistakes.

'My tale is made from a thread as black as the night and a thread as white as the day. O old tree, tree of youths, I want to keep digging but deep within myself . . . Tree of trees, you are never tired, forever growing. From death your life has risen, your roots deeply entwined in the soil of this cemetery. O Tree of triumph of life over death, one leaf drops dead and two spring forth. Tree of renewed youth, you stand watching the seasons, your robe changing, but your core remains intact. You stand a dignified witness of truth. Your inner rings record the passage of time in silence. Unlike you, Tree of trees, I was given one childhood, one youth.

'O Tree of trees, my back is hunched . . . I have become small, lost many teeth and my memory is betraying me. I am a child again but without the hope of growth. Unlike you, there is no spring after my autumn.

'Every silver hair in my head has a story for every one of your veins. Your roots embrace and entwine with the deep earth and from death flourishes your blossom which nourishes hundreds of people with hope. If I were to take off every piece of my clothing, I would not be naked. If you hear me out I will stand in my utmost nakedness.

'Father put me on his shoulders one day and left the house. My mother said she would wait for our return. On several occasions, Father hesitated, especially when he was lost, and wondered whether we should go back, but I sensed the way and directed the journey. We had been travelling for over a year, had crossed different countries and were somewhere in Africa, when Father was told by a stranger we met on the road about the miracles of a saint in Egypt. He was surprised. He had longed all his life to visit the home of his ancestors. Many centuries back, his great, great ancestor, a renowned story-teller, was sentenced to death because he told a story about the pleasures of beautiful women and he had to flee Egypt for his life. Anyway, my father was very inspired by the idea of travelling to the land of his ancestors in search of the saint. Long dead was the saint, but her *baraka*, her blessing, was still alive in her mausoleum and the stranger's confidence convinced my father that it would restore my eyesight. Father put me down from his shoulders and listened attentively to the stranger's detailed description of the way to the auspicious mausoleum. I still remember the thin voice of that stranger. And so, tracing the reputation of the saint to its source, we crossed boundaries again and from country to country, from town to town, from village to village until we reached Wadi Hassoun and the revered shrine of Sayyida Nesima.'

15

There was no hope left for worms which had spend most of their lives underground eating their way through the soil. As the hoe hit the earth and turned it inside out, countless little creatures scuttled away in search of safety. The work had built up to a rhythm of digging and shovelling and layers of earth were being removed.

The site had an imposing openness. Only a few shrubs grew in this expanse of light brown earth. Children sprawled near their doorsteps. The man with the indigo turban wandered, leaving a trail of dust as he dragged his feet. The few mud-brick houses squatting around aroused a feeling of thirst. Opposite the Mausoleum of Sayyida Nesima, in the distance, next to Zineb's house, someone was building an extension to his home. He mixed the mud and threw it in handfuls to cover the wall. A young girl was helping him, probably his daughter. Donatella took a picture of them.

The Professor paced between the areas that were being excavated, accompanied by Mahmoud. The boy hopped everywhere like a little bird that would prefer to fly. His white turban looked like a halo around his dark face. The Professor asked Zohra to transmit his instructions to the workers, stressing the importance of stratigraphy. 'Tell them to keep the walls of the trenches straight and the floor level.' Rayyes Ahmed walked around, keeping one eye on the workers and one eye on Zineb's door. From afar, he could see it close and open, open and close, flirting with temptation.

Monia supervised the digging very closely in Area C where the first traces of brickwork were already visible. The way she dressed made her look particularly commanding. She held an umbrella and wore a scarf over her rollers. Her dress was tight, taking care of all the curves, but also long enough to satisfy the local expectation of decency. Everyone respected Monia for taking her work seriously and disregarding her appearance when supervising on site. But Monia did not mind how she looked in the mornings; it was all in anticipation of how glamorous she would look in the afternoons.

In the Cemetery area, Area B, Donatella was beset by some villagers who came to visit their relatives. 'Whose grave are you digging?' someone wanted to know.

'We're digging for other reasons.' No one understood Donatella's few words of Arabic. She might as well have been speaking Italian. Zohra came to the rescue. As she translated, crossing boundaries between worlds, Zohra felt a disconcerting lightness. From where she stood, she could see the profile of that figure who sat next to the Tree of Wishes. It was the figure she had seen the first night in the courtyard. That profile with its dignified nose was unmistakable, but the lines of the face were now visible and the young profile was that of an old man! 'That's Amm Gaber,' said Donatella.

The sun was hot. Most of the men worked in their white underwear, long-sleeved T-shirts and trousers. They had kept their brown skull-caps and their white turbans on. The trenches were already quite deep and some men half-disappeared into them. Others stood on the edge, receiving the full baskets of rubble which they emptied promptly, returning for more. Others worked with wheelbarrows. Donatella admired the men's attractive features. Their dignified stature, their long limbs and granulated skin, reminiscent of the desert, appealed to her. As she looked, however, she was conscious of the chasm that separated them from her.

The workers did not know how to excavate, except for Sabry, who had worked with the German expedition several years before. In no time, however, they all learned the secret of the job and started to recognize what was valuable and what was not, according to the criteria of archaeology. Soon they would bring the pieces which they knew were significant to the site supervisors. They even picked up the names of pottery types. 'Sgraffito!' one of the workers shouted on the seventh day of digging, brushing off the earth from a shard he had found.

'They're a quick study!' said Mark with satisfaction. Professor O'Brien, on the other hand, was not interested in Mamluk pottery. He was eager to go deeper and reach the earlier phase of Fatimid occupation, impatient for his lustre wasters. But archaeology had to read the events of history methodically, in reverse.

The team stopped for their usual break. In spite of the heat, they all climbed the mount of Sayyida Nesima cheerfully. They sat beneath a strip of canvas which had been fixed along the mausoleum wall to extend the shade. Everyone laughed at Donatella, whose face was covered with earth. In her site, the dust was even worse than in the other areas. She took off her gloves, which were no longer white, and waited for the tea which, by now, they had all agreed was effective in quenching thirst.

Om Omran sat in her usual place near the doorstep of the shrine. Folded in two, she poured the tea and shook her head as she steadied her hands. She tipped the first heaped spoon of sugar, the second, the third and the fourth into each glass; they all disappeared like white lies.

'Aren't you scared at night?' asked Zohra when she realized that Om Omran lived in the mausoleum.

'If there are no visitors, which happens very rarely,' the old woman assured her, 'the spirits keep me company. May God protect us against misfortune,' she said, gazing towards the cemetery. 'To set foot on a grave brings bad luck.' She stirred the tea, before she whispered: 'Have you seen the man who is wandering in the village? That's what happened to him ... his feet are never to find peace again! The dead have to be left to rest.' Zohra was relieved that the others did not ask for translation. The old woman lifted a glass, brought it close to her eyes and, satisfied, passed it to Rayyes Ahmed, who seemed totally absorbed in his dreams. 'And don't cross the stream without saying "*Bismillah*",' she warned, talking half to herself, half to Zohra. 'The jinn attacked someone who made the mistake of crossing without first saying "*Bismillah*". The poor man's been ill ever since. I told him he can only put things right by making amends to Sayyida Nesima. But he never did.' Om Omran slurped her tea. 'Many years ago, the jinn took revenge on a family and impregnated their beautiful daughter, who used to bathe in the river at godforsaken hours ... their only child!' She looked at Zohra. Her wizened face suddenly animated, she said, chewing her lower lip in anticipation, 'Will you come tonight? There'll be a real feast here, *inshallah*. There's nothing like fresh grilled goat's meat.' She winked at Zohra and carried on mumbling to herself...

With the first sip of tea, all four spoons of sugar rose to the surface, but Rayyes Ahmed reached for the sugar bowl and added another two spoons to his glass. As he gazed at the house opposite, Rayyes Ahmed's eyes were reduced to slits of pleasure. He gulped the tea in one go and began descending the steep mount. The beautiful Zineb stood at her door, the flowers of her headscarf in bloom. Her hair, parted in the middle, was held with a row of pins on either side before it came down in two thick plaits. Her crescent earrings glittered in the sun. The postman walked by, following a map of the village in his head; roads in Wadi Hassoun did not have names. Today he was surprised that Zineb did not call after him as usual. The beautiful Zineb, who had waited for years for him to bring news from Libya, did not even look in his direction. Her eyes were fixed on the newcomers.

'If you come tonight,' Om Omran told Zohra suddenly, 'wear orange. That's the jinn's favourite colour.' Zohra smiled as the old woman prattled on.

'And tell that *khawajiyat*,' she added, pointing to Donatella, 'to be careful not to step on a tomb. Otherwise, the dead won't just visit her dreams, they'll snatch a piece of her life.' Zohra felt a shiver crawl up her spine. Donatella had not stopped dreaming since she started digging in the cemetery site. 'Dreams come from the dead,' added the old woman, as though answering Zohra's thought. Zohra was baffled. She would have liked to see the old woman's face and seek the meaning missing from her words, but all she could see was the top of her head as she sat, folded in two. From her black scarf, unruly strands of red hair escaped, looking like translucent flames in the sunlight.

'It's time to get back to digging!' declared Mark. The Professor was already up, eyeing the saint's mount from a distance.

16

It was dark. He was in an unknown place with unknown people. He was not sure where the fear came from but it was now inflated within him like a monster and it kept him awake. 'My God,' he thought, 'I could be anywhere.' Although it was the fifteenth night he had spent here, he could not visualize the surroundings, nor could he get a sense of the room, nor where its walls stood. He managed to get up but walked into a wall, bumped into things ... and when he finally switched on the light, he was sweating. He could see his crumpled clothes bulging from the bag as if they were his own intestines. Little things scattered around – his things – were like the colour and the shape of himself and were somehow comforting. A mirror stood in front of him. He averted his eyes, afraid he would see a reflection that was not his. Kodama San's bust of Nefertiti stood on the windowsill, its eternal gaze fixed straight ahead. The others were deeply asleep, snoring. He found himself listening intently, trying to distinguish the different sounds that now fused into one monotonous tone. He could not tell who, apart from Alan, was snoring. 'People of different nationalities snore in the same language,' he thought to himself.

A smile escaped him. 'You've got to accept that you belong to the club of people who've got their roots in the sky.' The words of a friend back in Munich leapt in his memory. Glasses switched off the light and fumbled back to bed. He would be able to think more freely in the dark. Privacy was almost non-existent in the school. Only the night provided some. Darkness was a screen that separated them, and only then could one give room to one's thoughts.

The night was silent but each one of them was filled with the noises of themselves. On the site the digging stopped at two in the afternoon, but in the privacy of the night it started again within each of them, as though their nakedness was emerging from under the many layers of their existence. Old Om Omran would say: 'The world of the dead is being disturbed and the dead are never really gone.' The team's personal memories were being brought to the surface the way the personal objects of the dead were being unearthed. For the excavators these were archaeological finds, but they were once parts of people's lives. In the dark, Glasses listened to the silence, the snoring now subsided. Suddenly there was the sound of something rolling on the floor. He did not have to wonder long about what it was. Alan's after-shave permeated the air. Glasses covered his nostrils. Now he could hardly breathe. He was here in the room with the others, but in the dark it was his different world of consciousness that emerged. He lay flat on his back. The throng of monsters started manifesting themselves on the ceiling. He tried to reason with himself. He could not see the ceiling, let alone see what was on it, but he could not dispel the thoughts that tormented him. The bristly hair on his chin itched. He started having second thoughts about letting his beard grow during the excavation season.

Although he was tired, Glasses could not sleep. A fly was buzzing around, trying desperately to get out. Both door and window were closed. 'Flies come into the room through a small hole, but until they find a window or a door open, they can't find their way out,' he thought. His breath was growing tense. He became aware of the air in the room, more conscious of sharing the space. He felt confined in his loose pyjamas, his skin too felt tight, a feeling he had known throughout his childhood. It gave him the excuse to lie in the bath for hours, gazing at a world map painted on the wall, refusing to get out when his mother urged him to. 'I need to loosen my skin.' His mother's face appeared before his eyes, laughing at his childish words.

He always wanted to escape anything that defined and labelled him, but he felt that he would never be able to. Even after death, they would label his tomb. On the tombstone would be inscribed his name, his date of birth and his date of death. With this thought, a simple reality hit him with its finality. One is never to know such a personal date as one's own date of death, yet everyone else would. It would be public knowledge.

He thought he should not blame this place for his sleepless night. He was used to insomnia, though he had not suffered from it for some time, not even in Cairo. Now he could hear the regular breathing of his room-mates. He thought they were all fast asleep. This bothered him even more. The laboratory where he worked was large enough. Why should he not move his bed there? He would truly have his privacy then. The thought struck him as the perfect answer and he could not understand why he had not thought of it before. Somehow the idea brought some comfort and he started drifting off.

Mark always stripped off his clothes easily, which embarrassed the others. They did not know that he was not naked. For Mark was never naked, not even under his skin. The bed was quite uncomfortable but it was his worries that prevented him from sleeping. Yet he had not given Glasses the slightest sign that he was awake. Would they ever find the Blue Manuscript? In London, before embarking on this project, finding the Manuscript had seemed plausible. Now that he was here digging for it, the site seemed but a barren, unpromising place. But Mark was quick to nip doubt in the bud. He also had dismissed the proposal to 'solve the problem', as Mustapha had put it. There was no problem. It was early days yet. The excavation would proceed systematically and they would find the Blue Manuscript. All that was needed now was a stroke of luck. His mother had always said that he was lucky, and indeed he always had been lucky. But give credit where it was due, he had always worked hard too. Luck did not come by itself.

As the night sank, layers of memory lifted. Mark found himself almost praying, for the first time in his life, for luck to be on his side. For luck to visit him the way it had visited the art dealer to whose hands was brought an entire volume of the Blue Manuscript. He could just picture him in Istanbul. The English dealer, Winston, was something of a connoisseur, but he had no idea about the existence of the Blue Manuscript then. Mark could just imagine his excitement when he fell on what he recognized to be a masterpiece that was to bring him a fortune, and undoubtedly a substantial one in 1920. Mark certainly needed such luck. He remembered how he had acquired a single page from the known volume of the Blue Manuscript for the dealers, the two brothers who were sponsoring the excavation, how pleased they had been with him. He indulged in the memory of the auction house, the voice of the auctioneer taking the bids on the page and a close-up of the hammer striking: 'To the gentleman in the striped jacket!' But Mark could not take pleasure from this memory for very long. The sponsors were in London yet he could already feel their pressure. It would increase with every day of the dig that brought no sign of the Blue Manuscript. After all, he had convinced the dealers that it was worth investing in the dig. The only way to ignore the weight that pressed on his chest was to go to sleep. He felt the urge to pass water but could not contemplate walking on tiptoe to that disgusting lavatory. He managed to go back to the comforting thought of Mr Winston, the English dealer, and his serendipity before eventually drifting off.

The night sank deeper into oblivion. The room seemed to get shorter of breath. Everyone's expiration was inhaled by everyone else. A strip of bluish light penetrated the window unexpectedly and hit the floor. A leaden tiredness weighed. Breaths mixed within the enclosed room.

There was hardly enough air for the number of lungs in the room where Donatella, Monia and Zohra slept either. The atmosphere was contaminated with insect-killers which seemed to have more effect on humans. There were five beds in all; two bunk beds and one single, distinguished by its white net, held by two poles. Donatella wore many layers, covering herself entirely. In the dark, wanton mosquitoes were guided by the smell of blood, a fragrance of desire which sharpened their prosboces into daggers. They squeezed through the holes of the fine lace, through the protective layers, into the lascivious flesh. Because of these blood-sucking creatures, every ten seconds someone, somewhere in the world, dies of malaria. Donatella could not drive this thought from her head. She prayed that the tablets were working. Had she not read somewhere that mosquitoes played a decisive role in deterring the white man in the conquest of Africa? All of a sudden Donatella thought of Howard Carter, who discovered the Valley of the Kings. The English archaeologist died, stung by an insect, or was it Lord Carnarvon, the man who sponsored Carter . . . Donatella heard Monia say something in her sleep and was amused. The thought of the tomb of Tutankhamen came back to her. Did the dead retaliate? With insects? Donatella tried to stop herself being silly. But all she could do was toss and turn with worries. Was it a mosquito which stung the man, in fact?

The room was wrapped in darkness. Donatella finally fell asleep. Zohra was still awake. She listened to the silence of the night and wondered whether that singing voice she had heard the first night would come again. She could still hear it in her memory. Donatella twitched and sighed. A few words escaped her – a deep voice which seemed to come from another world. Zohra could not decipher anything. She was not even sure whether Donatella's words were in Italian, French or English. Zohra answered back, trying to engage in a dialogue with the other world, but to no avail. In Donatella's nightmare, mosquitoes were a hundred times larger than her.

In the courtyard of the school, the guard was asleep, his gun at his side. Had Rayyes Ahmed seen him he would have given him a kick. 'Never put your gun down even when you sleep. It must be part of you. This is your duty,' he had told the guard many times.

But Rayyes Ahmed was far away, on the other side of the village. He was going around the site on his mule, making sure everything was in order. He found the guard there asleep too and prodded him with his stick and called: 'Haj, Haj,' in frustration.

Earlier that day, Rayyes Ahmed had whispered pleadingly to the beautiful Zineb: 'Leave the door open for me tonight . . .' And she had given him one of her mysterious smiles. But tonight he had found the door closed yet again.

17

Hands shuffled large notes with confidence while other hands quivered with pleasure on receiving them. The hands that gave the money were also counting what was to come from this purchase. The hands that were receiving it were in disbelief at how lucrative an old manuscript could be. A buying and a selling hand shook.

As soon as he had pocketed the money, the Jewish vendor adjusted his fez and made an attempt to leave, as if he feared that Mr Winston would change his mind. The English dealer, however, was in a talkative mood.

In the room of the Sarayi Hotel, Mr Winston had a warm feeling. Not generated by the red Persian carpet, teeming with dragons and phoenixes among lotus flowers, which covered the spacious room, but by the gut recognition of a connoisseur, that he held a rare treasure in his hands. He had never seen a manuscript like this in all his years of dealing and he made a promise to himself that he would make a fortune out of this find. He took the monocle from his waistcoat pocket, placed it to his right eye and scrutinized a page. He had found no colophon in the manuscript but he was still hoping for a sign that would disclose its date and place of origin. The last two pages were empty. They were, in fact, a much later addition, white paper that had been annexed to the blue vellum. Why these Muslim calligraphers hardly ever signed their work was incomprehensible to him. He raised the manuscript even closer and examined the official customs stamp which stated that the volume had left Iran two years earlier. But the manuscript was not Persian, that much he knew. He trusted his trained eyes, which were familiar with the art of calligraphy even if he could not read the letters himself. And what was the implication of this line of text at the end?

'It's very clear,' repeated the vendor, now standing one step closer to the door. 'The manuscript was bequeathed to a mosque in Istanbul in the sixteenth century.'

Mr Winston traced the line with his index finger. He so much wanted to know more. This was a special manuscript. Even though he had seen nothing like it before, it was clear that this was one of two volumes of a Quran. He wondered about the fate of the rest. He turned the old vellum pages very gently but they still made a plaintive sound. The combination of gold and indigo was a guarantee in itself of a royal commission. He knew that in the Byzantine world, only official documents of significance were written in gold on blue parchment. But he had never seen such a combination in manuscripts from the Muslim world. The manuscript was unique and precious. He knew that at once, but how could he convince those in London?

The vendor stood still. 'As long as he doesn't change his mind!' The mere thought of Mr Winston changing his mind made him shrink. He was worried that he would lose the fortune he had just pocketed.

Mr Winston was absorbed in his plans. A persistent pecking on the window interrupted his thoughts. Walking towards the *mashrabiyya* and opening the little window within it, he saw a crow perched on the sill. He took a handful of nuts and kindly spread his palm.

The vendor hesitated about asking Mr Winston what was bothering him. Then he drew himself to his full height, which was still short. He had decided that even if the English collector changed his mind, he would not give him his money back. He would be very sorry to lose one of his regular clients but this was the best transaction he had ever made over a manuscript. He stood waiting for the appropriate moment to retreat. Mr Winston looked out of the window but his dense thoughts wove a screen over the view. He knew that he would have to create an identity for the manuscript, an astute marketing ploy that would guarantee the desirable fortune.

The crow picked at the nuts, hopping in ecstasy. Mr Winston gazed at its sheen and its long, stout beak as it cracked the nuts expertly.

He placed the manuscript in his suitcase, reached for his pipe and rummaged in his pocket for a box of matches. His brow puckered. 'You know,' he said to the other man who was now regarding him fearfully, 'I had great difficulties two years ago when I came to export some manuscripts I had acquired here. They were packed to be sent to London as ordinary merchandise, but when the chief of customs inspected the box, he confiscated most of them because they had the word "*waqf*" stamped in them, meaning "religious bequest" as you know, often followed by the name of the institution to which the book was bequeathed. He declared the manuscripts stolen property that should be returned to the institutions from which they had been taken. When I protested that those institutions no longer existed, he simply ignored me and had the large box taken away.'

'What did you do?'

Mr Winston drew on his pipe. 'I invoked the aid of the consul general and together we went to see the *Vali*, who told us that so many Arabic manuscripts had left the country in recent years that the Porte had completely prohibited the further exportation of old manuscripts.'

Mr Winston's brow furrowed even deeper and he bit hard on his pipe as he remembered that fear of never setting eyes on the manuscripts again.

'A Turkish friend of mine with whom I have now unfortunately lost contact revealed to me that the mayor of Istanbul was the founder of a charity which was in great need of financial assistance. My friend suggested that a donation to this charity might alleviate the authorities' scruples.'

A cunning smile escaped the vendor.

'I paid the mayor a visit and brought up the subject of his charity and he agreed to allow me to make a donation. The following day, the export permit for the manuscripts came with a note to the effect that as I had helped his invalids, it was the least he could do. I simply added my donation to the cost of the manuscripts.' Mr Winston arrested his shrugging shoulders halfway so as not to reveal that even with this addition the manuscripts were acquired very cheaply.

'If this is what's troubling you,' said the other, 'I will of course give all the help you need for the manuscript to leave the country legally. But I think that the page of religious bequest might have to be removed from the manuscript to facilitate its passage through customs.'

Mr Winston reached into his case and took out the manuscript. 'That's a consideration,' he said, his hands dallying with the *waqf* page.

'Don't worry,' said the vendor, 'everything will be arranged.' Then he seized his chance to say goodbye, promising to be in touch in the next few days.

Alone in the room, the warm feeling returned to Mr Winston as he held the manuscript. He knew it to be a medieval treasure. His hands acted almost of their own accord. They removed the *waqf* page. And it was in this very moment that a revelation dawned on him. A revelation that was to determine the fate of the volume of the Blue Manuscript in his hands. His brow cleared suddenly and his voice escaped him. 'I'll detach all the pages from the manuscript, not just the *waqf* page, and I will sell every single page for a fortune!' Mr Winston started undoing the first stitch of the binding very carefully.

Out of the window, Mr Winston could see the Jewish vendor scurrying at the end of the street. He seemed even shorter from where the Englishman stood. Mr Winston smiled as he watched him disappear in the crowd and he bent to pick up a nut that had fallen from the windowsill.

The crow gave a high-pitched, resonant 'cruk-cruk' and descended on the collector's palm with its sharp beak. Then the bird flew away with the kernel in its throat, straight to its incubating female.

18

In the school, everyone was having their siesta, except the three women. Donatella was rehanging the mosquito net above her bed. She called it her 'bridal tent'. A mesh had already been fixed to the window, the perfect prison for mosquitoes. Donatella was badly bitten and was obviously in pain, but both Monia and Zohra laughed as she twirled in the room, showing her mercilessly mosquito-bitten body and repeating in her American accent: 'My poor liddle body!'

Zohra glimpsed Monia's diary on the floor and felt tempted to read her thoughts. Monia left her diary around as if she was the only one who could read Arabic. 'She seems to think of everybody else as a foreigner,' thought Zohra.

'You know,' said Donatella, 'that Egyptian architect we visited in Cairo had thirty-three cats in his house!'

'What architect?'

'The famous Hassan Fathy,' replied Zohra

'I never hear about him,' said Monia indifferently and went back to her newspaper. She had brought a stack of newspapers with her and kept rereading old news. 'You know,' she said, 'in Singapore they have competition about public toilet, the best gets award!'

'No, I didn't!' replied Donatella. Then, looking for her slippers, which had wandered under the bed, she announced: 'Nature calls!'

It was only a few minutes later when they heard her scream and rushed out.

'Donatella! What's up? Are you all right? Is it the viper again?' shouted Zohra. A viper had given Mark a fright two days before.

Donatella was in shock, 'No, no, it's not the viper.' She blushed when she saw all the others, their siesta had been cut short. 'A peeping Tom!' she mumbled. 'I'm all right now, he just gave me a fright, that's all.'

She was not absolutely certain about what she had seen when she sprang to her feet at the sound of hushed laughter. The face seemed to be that of a child, crushed against the glass, eyes wide open. And now she did not want anything done about it. But when Rayyes Ahmed heard about the incident, he insisted on investigating the matter.

Fridays interrupted the daily cycle of digging. They stayed in the school on Fridays but there was always a great deal of work to be done. Donatella, Zohra and Monia were working on the shards. Donatella was wearing a sleeveless top and, standing nearby, Glasses could see a dark mole close to her breast, a raised mole which looked like an eye. She sat on the edge of what the team members had named 'the shard garden', a low cement platform near the climbing plant. They had it built so they could clean and sort the finds. As they emerged from their final rinsing, the shards shone like precious stones. The colours were varied and their tones beautifully deep, a myriad of green, yellow, cobalt blue and manganese purple. When wet, the colours looked particularly intense. But soon, the sun would suck the water from them and part of their beauty with it. The boy Mahmoud kept rewetting some of the shards. It was mid-afternoon, yet the sun was still strong. The Professor traced the edges of some shards with his finger. 'The clay is sometimes buff-coloured, sometimes red,' he said as though speaking to himself.

'What you mean?' the boy asked. It was his favourite English phrase and it had become an amusement with everyone.

Monia sang a popular Um Kulthum song, while she adjusted her bouffant. Her eyes twinkled and her teeth shone against her dark skin. It was her way of flirting with Spaghetti when he crossed the courtyard carrying his diplomatic case, which the others suspected to be full of money. Spaghetti glanced in her direction and smiled when she sang: 'Every fire becomes ash, however long it burns, except the fire of passion ... except the fire of passion which burns stronger day by day.' Donatella and Zohra took advantage of Monia's preoccupation and pocketed some of the pottery fragments for their colour, not their value. Although he was trying not to, Glasses found himself imagining the shape of Donatella's body. He kept looking at her mole, when suddenly he felt the mole was looking at him, so he looked away, embarrassed. Opposite, the guard was wetting the courtyard, refreshing it after all the heat it had absorbed during the day. His rifle stood in a corner, against the wall. On a line, two white hands waved in the intermittent breeze. Donatella's gloves. Across the courtyard, a beige tent had been erected for mealtimes. Near it, Hakima and Halima were scrubbing the team's clothes as they gossiped. Their dialogue buzzed randomly from the nectar of one topic to the next.

'Zineb's husband will never come back.'

'He's seeking riches in Libya!'

'He's deserted her.'

'Apparently she can't have children.'

'She's barren!'

'She's been deprived of motherly love.'

'There's nothing like a mother's love for her child.'

'There's nothing like a mother's love.'

Hakima walked towards the line. Her large breasts did the walking with her legs. She gave Mark's trousers a good shake.

'Zineb's so lucky, Rayyes Ahmed brought electricity to her house.'

'You'd think she's one of the rich few!'

Halima was spreading the Professor's trousers on the line when she glimpsed an indigo turban beyond the courtyard's iron railings. She nodded in its direction.

'The *majdhub*. His presence is a blessing to our village.'

'No one should shun him, people should feed him wherever he goes.'

Zohra's heart beat fast. For a moment she thought it was Amm Gaber. Rayyes Ahmed did say that he might come to the school today. But it was only the village wanderer. She looked at the two women who never stopped talking.

'When the benefactors of the digging come from England, I will ask them to help with my daughter's wedding expenses,' said Hakima.

'And I'll ask them to help with my father's pilgrimage.'

Hakima bent to the basket for another peg.

'Did you hear about the mirror in which you see the whole truth?'

'Impossible!'

'You can see everything inside, you see bones, heart, the whole truth.'

'Think of the courage needed to look in such a mirror.'

'Next time you go to the hospital, you'll look into it. The new doctor who trained in America is using it all the time.'

At the shard garden, Donatella, Zohra, Monia and the boy were still cleaning pieces of pottery. The apprentice cook brought them hot tea.

'It's like a rainbow,' said Donatella, trying hopelessly to reach the lizard which the boy Mahmoud had found licking drops of water from the tap. Zohra translated and the boy's eyes twinkled. The lizard was not Donatella's only adoptive pet. A grey kitten which had come to stay with them was now fast asleep near the shard garden. It was only a few weeks old. Monia had named it 'Catkoota'. Every day, Donatella gave it some of her chicken, shredding it into small pieces. The cook thought such luxury was wasted on the cat.

'*Shufti?!*' Monia exclaimed to Zohra. Glasses looked in their direction, intrigued by the Arabic word. Then a whole conversation was triggered about the word that had roots in different languages.

' "Take a *shufti*" is an English expression,' said Glasses.

'Really? I didn't know that,' said Zohra.

The Professor eyed the shards on the cement platform with some disappointment. After three weeks of digging the site had not yet yielded anything exceptional as far as he was concerned. But the Professor knew that patience was the archaeologist's best companion. 'It's early days yet,' he said. 'We will find those lustre wasters.'

Spaghetti got another of those suggestive looks from Monia when he crossed the courtyard, helping Glasses move his bed to the laboratory. Monia's behaviour, however, did not escape the Professor, who felt responsible for all the team members and their actions. 'We'd better get on with the registration,' he told Monia. All the finds were treated with great care. Paper fragments and linen textiles, wooden comb fragments, glass and a large number of pottery shards had been unearthed. The textile fragments required immediate attention. Alan photographed every find twice, once in black and white and once in colour, while the Professor and Monia worked on the registration. They gave each piece an accession number, recorded the exact location of its discovery, noted its measurements and wrote a brief description.

Near the steps to the school building, the apprentice cook was vehemently sharpening a knife on the stone he usually used as a seat. A sack of potatoes sat to the side. It was simply a cooking knife but the shimmer of its blade, as he eyed it with admiration, reflected a potential crime. 'Every spice has four or five different flavours; it depends on how you treat it,' stressed the cook with the tone of a connoisseur before he sucked on his cigarette. In the apprentice's hands, the potato skin was as shrivelled as Om Omran's face. It curled and wormed its way between his knees on to the earthen ground. On the steps, the cook stared from under his bushy eyebrows. 'Don't throw the peel in the garden!' he reproached his apprentice. 'Roots grow from the eyes of potatoes.' He took another drag on his cigarette. 'And make sure you cut the t'ships fine!' From his vantage point the cook noticed that the chickens which had been bought for the day's meal had escaped and were being chased by the guard. But this was not why the dog on the other side of the courtyard was barking. The dog barked often, perhaps protesting against the flies, the chain that tied it, or perhaps to claim the soaked bread that lay beyond its reach.

Late that afternoon Rayyes Ahmed stopped by to announce to Donatella that a number of the village children had been identified and beaten. They were forced to admit what had happened. Three of them had climbed on each other's shoulders and they were going to take it in turns. 'We wanted to check if the foreign lady peed in the same way as the rest of us,' they had confessed. Donatella laughed after Zohra translated. Everyone was amused. Zohra wanted very much to ask Rayyes Ahmed why Amm Gaber never came, but felt awkward. Rayyes Ahmed also mentioned that the rich Jamel Bey had invited them to visit his orchard.

'You should definitely go,' said Hakima to Zohra.

'You shouldn't miss the paradise of Wadi Hassoun,' added Halima.

This was the first Friday of the crescent moon, the day for renewal. Halima explained to Zohra how tradition in the village had it that on this day, young women would have their hair trimmed and would spend the day beautifying themselves, helped by the older women. Men would leave the village for the outskirts early in the morning and only return to their women at sunset. She handed Zohra and Donatella pieces of bark. 'Use this. Just look how it cleans the teeth,' she said, beaming with pride, but Donatella did not like the way it turned the lips saffron red.

That evening, after dinner, they stayed on in the tent where Kodama San was drawing everyone's portrait. He even took pleasure in drawing the cat, but he refused to draw Zohra, which upset her, though she made sure it did not show. His excuse was: 'Your face has been drawn once and cannot be drawn again!' Whatever he meant by that. Everyone sat still, waiting for their face to emerge from the paper. Green-eyed Donatella appeared in black and white as the charcoal moved across the page. It now occurred to Glasses that Donatella had the same lips as his favourite film star, Ingrid Bergman. How could he have missed it? He wished he could have Donatella's portrait but did not dare ask. The bird in his heart fluttered.

After Kodama San finished with the portraits, the cook started reading the cup for Monia. Intrigued, they all gathered round.

'For a moment I thought he was going to talk about the boat in the cup,' said Mark.

'Boat? The boat in the cup?' inquired Zohra.

'You know, the painting by Magritte!' Mark was the only one to laugh at his own joke. They were not as familiar with the painting as he was. A copy of it hung in his office in London, to where his mind often wandered.

'Ask whether he can see the Blue Manuscript,' he whispered to Zohra between breaths of laughter. During the cook's readings, Mark began to sense a seriousness rise within him which caught him by surprise, and he felt a great apprehension of the unknown. The others simply enjoyed the cook's adventure. They were totally absorbed when piercing cries suddenly reached the tent, but they remained unmoved. This was not the first time it had happened. The hospital next door was a stage where dramas unfolded.

The cup told Monia that she would soon be married. 'How soon?' she urged the cook.

'Very soon, *inshallah*,' he reported without lifting his eyes from the cup. Monia's eyes flashed in the direction of Spaghetti.

'Sleep is king,' said the apprentice, who got up, heading for bed. At that very moment, the lights went out and everyone screamed. 'Don't worry,' said the apprentice. 'It's only a power cut, I'll bring candles from the kitchen.' Zohra translated and her words had a reassuring effect. Mark had promised to project slides of the Blue Manuscript that night, but the event had to be postponed. With every candle the apprentice lit, the atmosphere in the tent was transformed. The cook continued with his cup readings. Mark took a candle and headed to the 'medicine room', a small alcove at the back of the laboratory, to bring some more beer.

'Need a hand with the medicine?' asked Donatella with a smile as she staggered after him. They referred to alcohol as 'medicine', an amusing disguise in the Muslim context. In the alcove room, Donatella helped Mark pour the beer into Coca-Cola bottles, a further disguise. But this was not the only thing that delayed them in the medicine room.

The whole village bathed in obscurity, and on the surface not much separated it from the Middle Ages. Near the site, Rayyes Ahmed passed by his beloved's house. He dismounted from his mule and knocked at her door to see if she needed any candles, but there was no answer. He glimpsed the form of Amm Gaber in the distance, next to the Tree of Wishes, where he sat every night. 'That's someone for whom it doesn't matter whether it's dark or light,' he thought. He was surprised to find the site guard fully alert. 'You've been spared my stick tonight, Haj,' teased Rayyes Ahmed. The guard greeted him warmly and offered him tea which stewed on glowing embers. Rayyes Ahmed got back on his mule and headed for the school to check if the team needed anything.

The first thing that attracted Rayyes Ahmed's attention when he entered the tent was the great number of Coca-Cola bottles around. He suddenly felt a terrible thirst and asked the cook for a bottle. 'Our visitors are coming in a few days. I hope these power cuts don't last,' the Professor said to Rayyes Ahmed.

'Don't worry Professor,' said Rayyes Ahmed via Zohra, 'the power cut doesn't happen very often and it'll be over by the morning.' Then he noticed the boy Mahmoud snug next to Donatella. 'Come on,' he urged, 'your mother must be worried about you. She'll be wondering where you are!' Mahmoud was reluctant to leave but he was smiling. Rayyes Ahmed walked out, his hand on the boy's head. He sipped his Coca-Cola with intense desire.

The team stayed up very late that night, enjoying themselves. They began to talk about their dreams and threads started to weave between them as they exchanged their intimate worlds. In this enclosed environment, it felt the most natural thing to do. Donatella looked at them with astonishment. 'But I never dream!' she said, without feeling convinced herself any more. They all laughed. It was clear she was quite drunk. The excavation members seemed to have settled down at last and the school had become a home which brought the different people together. The world out there was remote. And tonight, under the blanket of darkness, interrupted only by the hesitant flame of the candles, they got close. Some of them got even closer than they expected.

19

Glasses was busy labelling the bags. He was pleased to visit the site today. His days were usually spent in the laboratory at the school. He pressed on the cellophane bag. For a moment he feared that if he lifted his hand the label would come with it, something totally different inscribed on the other side, referring to him rather than the object he was labelling. In the distance, a little girl sat on the doorstep of her home, playing a drum, the pot held tightly between her knees. She beat it quickly and the pot reverberated with tunes of indigenous flavours. Three other girls were dancing. All four were the grand-children of the site guard, Haj Salem. They wore flowery dresses and had scarves tied around their hips, accentuating their bellies, and the dialogue between the pot and the little bodies was humorous. They performed in line, moving in twists and turns, chanting alternately: '*Halawtu hilwa*', '*el-halawani*', '*halawtu hilwa*', The sweet-maker, his sweets are sweet. Glasses watched, totally absorbed. The girls moved so fast, transforming their dresses into rainbows and perhaps into tongues of flame. They wiggled their hips and giggled with shyness. The show was given every day. By mid-morning, it was brought to a halt, when the green door was flung open and their mother claimed the pot for cooking. Glasses was still pinned to the same spot. He felt the flutter of the slightest breeze.

'It's gone!' shouted Donatella. Glasses woke up from his daze. He realized the cellophane bag had escaped and heaved a sigh. 'Polluting the landscape, eh?!' teased Donatella. 'Aren't you going to run after it?'

'*Shay, shay!*' called Mahmoud.

'Time for a break already?' Glasses teased Donatella in return. 'You call this work?!'

They sat against the wall of Sayyida Nesima, sipping the tea. Mark could not make up his mind whether he found the tea disgusting or not. Donatella tried to catch his eye but Mark's gaze was deep in his thoughts. 'I wonder how Dr Evans will react to the excavation,' he remarked.

'Well, she's visited digs before, you know!' replied Professor O'Brien.

Donatella was now absorbed with the boy Mahmoud, who was tracing her name in Arabic on the earthen ground with a twig. 'Dou ... naa ... tella'.

Om Omran served the tea and talked to Zohra, or perhaps more to herself. She squinted as the warp and weft of her words spread and looked intently at nothing in particular – well, nothing that the translator could see. Perhaps the negative aspect of the world was unfolding before her eyes, perhaps the jinn world manifested itself in the blazing sunlight.

'When night gets really dark,' said Om Omran, 'the spirits of the dead come out and sit on their tombs to talk to each other. They get very angry if anyone from this world is around. They might throw stones to drive them away.'

Zohra was gazing at the cemetery, at the Tree of Wishes and Amm Gaber next to it. 'I should talk to him some time,' she thought. But an inexplicable feeling knotted inside her and she wondered whether she could ever be anywhere near him. She barely followed what Om Omran was saying. To the others, the Arabic words were simply invisible. Glasses had thought it would be enriching to enter a new world, a world in which a totally different language was spoken. But after hearing Arabic spoken around him for a few weeks, the words seemed to build an opaque screen.

'Will you come and teach me Arabic in the afternoons?' Glasses asked Mahmoud. Zohra translated and the boy smiled and nodded. 'But we start now,' he said, tracing an Arabic letter on the ground. Zohra translated as the boy gave his first lesson. 'Just a dot can change the sound and the meaning. So the same letter is transformed into a different one when you add another dot, for example.'

'And these are called "diacritical marks",' explained Zohra as she added a few quick strokes to the letters of Donatella's name, still visible in the ground.

'*Fa*, for example,' said the boy Mahmoud, 'has only one dot above. Add another dot and it becomes *qa*, you see that?'

'*Ka*,' said Glasses, intending to repeat what his young master was trying to teach him.

'No, no, *qa*,' Zohra smiled and added: 'Close your eyes. Listen. *Qa*. It's coming from the back of the throat not from the front of the mouth.'

'*Ka*,' interjected Mark. The boy grinned and shook his head. The other members rose to the challenge. They concentrated, closed their eyes and tried to grasp the difference. They could hear *qa* but could not say it.

'What is it?' they asked the boy again.

'*Ka*,' said Mahmoud and he roared with laughter, kicking the dust with his feet and rolling on the ground. Only Zohra realized his mischief but such an energetic laughter was contagious.

Kodama San gave the boy a felt pen. On top of the lines of destiny on his palm, the boy traced the Arabic letter. '*Shufti?*' he told Zohra. To Glasses, the familiar word was an opening in that opaque screen, a window that let in some light of understanding.

The tea-break was longer than usual. Glasses and Zohra continued the conversation about Arabic. They clearly shared a passion for languages, and Donatella wondered whether Glasses' attention was shifting away from her. The Professor was anticipating the arrival of his wife and Dr Evans the following day if everything went according to plan. 'But does anything go according to plan here?' he thought. This uncertainty brought a change of mood.

The sun was out with a vengeance. The mother of the dancing girls brought water to the workers. She woke up the site guard, her uncle and father-in-law, and made him drink. Mark had stripped to his T-shirt. Still, the heat was oppressive. 'You should wear your shirt,' advised Rayyes Ahmed. 'One suffers more like that.' Zohra translated and Mark reached for his shirt. The digging proceeded systematically. The men worked hard. The site supervisors were attentive. And Mark made sure nothing interrupted the digging until two o'clock.

On the way back to the school, the still, cool river was a remote vision of impossible desire. The team members were hot, thirsty and dirty. The sun had burnt their faces. But their consolation was that now they were almost 'home'. The truck-driver slowed to a crawl to cross the wooden bridge.

'This,' said Donatella, eyeing the plastic bag in her hands, 'will reveal something significant about Area B. I can't wait!'

She held the bag carefully. 'None of us can wait,' declared Glasses with equal enthusiasm. He studied Donatella's hands. She was still wearing her gloves, again no longer white, but he was sure that underneath the layers of dust, her skin was silky. 'In fact, I'll do it right after lunch,' he said. Donatella's teeth sparkled in the sunlight. There was always a hint of mystery in the way she smiled. She handed him the bag. This was the first coin they had unearthed. 'When she sees it clean, it'll be my gift to her,' Glasses told himself. He would do it as quickly and as meticulously as possible. He did not mind sacrificing the hour of siesta; he hardly slept anyway. His hands closed in a gentle embrace around the little bag. He looked at her from under his glasses. She was excited and his own excitement doubled. 'What luck I chose to visit the site today,' he thought. 'Why wait for the siesta? I'll do it at lunchtime.'

The truck hit the earth road in a great bump that brought them closer together. 'In fact, I'll do it straight away, I am not that hungry,' he whispered to Donatella. He spoke quickly, as he always did when he was excited. A warm feeling spread within him, the kind of feeling that could kindle a fire. Donatella's eyes shone. Faces were hiding behind dust. Lips were pink. And circles had remained bare around eyes. Everyone looked as though they wore a mask. Somehow the more dust you had, the better an archaeologist you were. Zohra had helped herself to earth when no one was looking. She wiped her hands on her clothes and even on her face. She wanted so much to be really involved, although she was no archaeologist.

'What's so beautiful about a coin,' shouted the Professor from the other side of the truck, 'is that you don't have to guess its date from its style, the date'll be written on it and that'll date the strata of the trench!' Mark's nodded agreement ended in an intense sneeze.

'*Gesundheit*,' responded Glasses. Everyone laughed.

After they had showered, they sat down to lunch. But Glasses was in the laboratory and Donatella watched over his shoulder. He had arranged all the tools and chemicals brought from London neatly on a shelf. Donatella had studied chemistry at the American school in Rome, but the numerous bottles of various colours did not mean much to her. She looked at the books piled on the other side of the table. They had all brought books to read during the excavation season, but Glasses had brought many more than the rest of them.

'All these books! I am impressed by your patience,' said Donatella, reaching to the top of the pile. 'Can I?'

'Sure,' replied Glasses.

Donatella was surprised to notice a book she had always heard of but had never seen. 'How many books we feel we know because we have always heard their titles,' she thought. 'I don't know why,' she said, 'but I always imagined Dante's *Inferno* to be a big book!'

'It is in meaning!' said Glasses with a smile. His hands continued to be busy.

Donatella's eyes were fixed on the word 'Dante' along the spine. She saw in her mind's eye a pensive Dante in stone, standing over a piazza in the city of Verona, holding a book in his left hand. She reached for another book in the pile.

'How are you going to read a five-hundred-page book? Who has the time?'

'You think books don't deserve such time?' he retorted. A quiet look in his wide eyes came from behind glass. Donatella was almost embarrassed and she looked down. A flat rubber band coiled like potato peel on the floor next to the large steel box. She picked it up.

Glasses chose two containers and reached for one of the bottles. Donatella was looking at him closely. 'I wonder how much younger than me he is?' she pondered as she watched him. His hair was sleek and beautiful. She noticed the cloth bracelet around his wrist, woven of multicoloured thread. He was so precise with his hands. 'Elegant hands,' she thought.

In the tent, each excavation member worked wholeheartedly on their chicken bones, except Alan, who long ago had revealed that he was vegetarian. The conversation focused on the coin and the dating of the trench. After the others had eaten a hasty meal, they rushed to the laboratory. The door opened and Glasses' aloneness with Donatella was abruptly brought to an end.

'So?' ventured the Professor.

'Not yet,' said Glasses.

They came close to him. If only they knew that he could not concentrate when surrounded by so many people.

'Fatimid!' said the Professor. 'I'm sure it's Fatimid.'

'Mamluk,' said Monia. 'The pottery shards found in the same trench were recognizably Mamluk.'

'But,' insisted the Professor, 'that type was also produced during Fatimid times, it'll be a Fatimid coin.' He smiled then added: 'Anyway, the beauty of a coin is that it doesn't lie!'

'Will the date of the coin determine whether we're digging in the right place for the Blue Manuscript?' Mark's words were full of hope.

While they waited for the coin to reveal itself, Zohra leafed through Dante's *Inferno*. 'I thought you're not supposed to take library books out of the country!' she teased Glasses.

'I waited a long time before it was available . . . a friend will renew it for me. I had to bring it . . . now that it's finally come back from prison where someone was reading it!'

Everyone laughed. Glasses tried to change the subject. 'Saladin is mentioned here, would you believe!' he said, adjusting the marker and putting the book away. Glasses bent closer, watching the chemicals at work on the heavily corroded coin. He liked the constant challenge that conservation involved and the necessity to be meticulous, the role conservation played in preserving the identity of things. Suddenly, he lifted his spectacles to his forehead as though he wanted to see with his naked eyes, however myopic. 'What?' he exclaimed. He had failed Donatella.

Donatella held her hand over her mouth in quiet disappointment. 'Oh, no!' said the Professor as he took a closer look. 'We're digging where the Germans have dug before.' The disappointment, however, was soon followed by boisterous laughter. Even Glasses joined in. But Mark was not laughing. He was not an archaeologist and patience was not really his companion. Even when Donatella sent a few lightning looks in his direction, he did not respond. It was clear that Mark was ignoring her. His thoughts were preoccupied with what he regarded as more serious matters and their night of intimacy was obviously the decision of alcohol as far as he was concerned.

'I'm sorry it's not quite what you expected,' whispered Glasses.

'Thank you anyway,' said Donatella. 'It's even better!' she added, faking a smile.

'Well,' said the Professor, 'we'll have to check whether according to the excavation laws a Coca-Cola top belongs in the museum in Cairo or is among the few finds that are allowed to leave the country!'

20

The Professor kissed his wife, who could not believe how dark he had become. Working in the hot sun, the team seemed to have acquired a new skin. Under a layer of even powder, Mrs O'Brien's face looked particularly white in contrast. Dr Evans, the art historian, Dr Chevalier, a bone specialist, Mrs O'Brien and Mustapha were given a tour of the site. 'It's so hot!' said Mrs O'Brien. The others looked at her without much sympathy. They had become more tolerant of the heat among other things. The arrival of these new people from the outside world was curious. Dr Evans, a regular consultant to the dealers, took Mark aside to deliver a message from them. Their words washed the colour from his face for a moment. The dealers apparently had great plans for a major exhibition of the excavation finds in one of the most prestigious venues in London.

The Professor commented at length on the excavated areas and Dr Evans was particularly impressed by the scrupulously excavated foundations of the mosque in Area A. They had found Coptic carved stones embedded in the foundation walls of the mosque. Columns, capitals, tie-beams and a *mihrab*, a prayer niche, had been unearthed. And in what must have been the courtyard of the mosque, an ablution fountain had also been uncovered. As site supervisor, Alan felt quietly pleased. The bone specialist was only interested in a pre-Islamic crypt which had been discovered a few days earlier. A throng of children playing with a car tyre gathered to watch the newcomers. All action at the site had halted. But Mark made sure the digging was resumed quickly and carried on as normal. He needed luck to find the Blue Manuscript, but hard work was also necessary. So they did not stop digging until half past two in the afternoon, to compensate for the lost half-hour.

On the truck, the journey back to the school was bumpy as usual. Everyone listened to Mrs O'Brien, squeezed between Zohra and Donatella. She talked as though she was savouring every word. She pursed her lips, pronouncing every syllable; it seemed as though each word was preened and polished before it was let out into the wild world. As she spoke, she was busy removing stray hairs from her clothes with a precise flick from her immaculately painted nails. Professor O'Brien seemed overjoyed by her arrival.

The driver who had brought the visitors from Cairo had also brought the mail they had all been waiting for. Alan and Donatella sat on the stairs reading their letters. No expression could be read on Alan's face, but the disappointment was evident on Donatella's. Clearly, her father had not received the letter she had posted over seven weeks earlier. In it, she had enthused about the pharaonic art she had seen and how their delay in Cairo had also provided the opportunity to visit the Museum of Islamic Art, which had come as a marvellous surprise. Distant dialogues were out of sync already. At times, the world out there felt truly beyond reach.

The Professor emerged later in the afternoon. The others were working in the shard garden. His face was very relaxed, the bloodshot eyes were light blue again and anyone could have asked him for a favour had they wanted to.

The afternoons had always been relatively quiet in the school, but today was different because of the visitors. The team were hosts for the new arrivals. The cook had the idea of a barbecue for dinner so he was setting a fire in the middle of the courtyard and there was an atmosphere of feasting. Zohra watched, inspired. For her, fire purified everything.

'Haven't I seen you before somewhere?' Dr Chevalier, the bone specialist, asked Zohra unexpectedly.

'I don't think so!' she answered. Donatella made a remark in French which clearly embarrassed Dr Chevalier but which Zohra did not understand. Dr Chevalier looked away, still thinking that the plainness of Zohra's face was familiar.

Monia appeared in the courtyard transformed, looking even more radiant than usual. She wore a dress which squeezed around her waist, held by a zip that Donatella had helped fasten. All of Monia's dresses were so tight one could always tell whether she had eaten or not, every curve visible. Their frills and trimmings revealed they were undoubtedly the work of one master dressmaker.

Leaning against the window, the apprentice cook held a fine-meshed sieve close to his ribs and rhythmically removed debris from coriander seeds. His face was washed with tears; on the sill was a tray with a mound of finely chopped onions, his large knife lying next to it.

'He is up to something,' teased Monia. 'What's behind those onion tears? Why does he always cover his mouth to conceal his smiles? Why did he adamantly refuse to have his fortune read, even though he doesn't believe a coffee cup can know anything about destiny?'

Glasses surveyed the courtyard from the steps of the building. His lips parted, suggesting that he was about to say something, but he was simply thinking. The tree, or rather the three palm trees which stood at the centre, tall and proud, branched out from a single trunk. The trees were old yet the school building was still incomplete; the courtyard must have been built around the trees. The apprentice came out of the kitchen, carrying a tray filled with lamb. Glasses was a gourmet and found the food in the school inedible, but today the planned grill looked promising. His attention was drawn to the cook, who was on his knees, begging the fire with his breath, and the fire flared generously in response. As he watched the cook's breath become fire, Glasses thought about how much he disliked fire. For him, fire destroyed everything. There had been no letter from his parents. His mother had written to him regularly from Munich when he was in London. Perhaps she did not think it necessary to reach him in such a remote place. But oh no, not his mother! And for once he wished he had received a letter from her.

With the new visitors, a different language was added to the dialogue. People travel and carry their languages with them, and Zohra thought of how much she liked these differences. Her task was to reach for similar meanings. She crossed barriers between people of different nationalities and she felt like a ghost among them. But there was also the untranslatable. That which was unique, particular to each language and each culture, and there were many moments when she, the translator, felt trapped in that zone, the zone of the untranslatable.

21

'*As-salaamu 'alaykum,*' Peace be upon you, said Mustapha, bowing as he entered the room where the finds were kept.

'There's no one there,' exclaimed Mark.

'Angels are everywhere,' said Mustapha, 'and they see everything. Two angels record one's deeds. The one on the right shoulder records the good deeds, the one on the left, the bad.' Mustapha spoke in a matter-of-fact tone, and Mark could not tell whether he was serious or not. 'In traditional Arab architecture, doorways were always low so that when people entered a space they naturally bowed to the angels,' added Mustapha.

Professor O'Brien and Dr Evans went to the tables on which the finds were spread. 'Our restorer has hands of gold,' declared the Professor.

'Conservator!' specified Glasses with a twinkle.

Zohra stood behind Dr Evans and reflected quietly as she eyed the finds. The objects dug from the trenches of the past showed the culture's modernity, an extraordinary vision with no trace connecting it to the present reality. A sigh escaped Zohra. A lot of beauty had been unearthed among the hardship of poverty.

Professor O'Brien beamed with satisfaction as he showed Dr Evans what had been uncovered so far. There was a great deal of pottery, several complete bowls and an array of fragments. And although none of them was lustre-painted, he was excited at the prospect of what he would find, now that they had finally entered the Fatimid layer. Green-glazed and earthenware oil lamps sat in a row. The dry climate had helped the survival of textile fragments.

To one side was a selection of small finds. Among them was a tiny agate inkwell with an inscription carved on all four sides. Monia had not been able to decipher it. She tried one of the Fatimid rings and laughed; it was too large. Donatella reached for the only significant metal object, a large incense-burner which stood on the floor. It was a finely decorated cast bronze. Its hoof-shaped feet gave the impression that it was about to walk. 'Surely, you'd think metal would survive best, but there's hardly any Fatimid metalwork,' said Donatella, who was more familiar with pharaonic archaeology than Islamic.

'Let's not forget,' said the Professor, 'that most of the Fatimid treasures were dispersed, and metal objects were often melted down. Not a single gold vessel described in historical texts has survived.'

'The textual descriptions of Fatimid treasures are quite extraordinary!' said Dr Evans, her voice slightly distorted by a slender cigarette holder although her cigarette was not lit. She spoke of codicology and Zohra was relieved that she did not have to translate. She had no idea what codicology was and she winced every time the word came up.

She asked Glasses, who whispered back: 'The study of manuscripts.'

Zohra sighed. 'Is that all?!' Glasses was handling the paper fragments with gloves and tweezers. The irreplaceable evidence of the past was treated with the utmost care, examined, registered, assessed, photographed and catalogued. The work of the team was a well-organized chain. They found it so exciting to handle objects hundreds of years old. From the excavated finds, they pieced together history, or so they thought.

Leaning over an earthenware jar, Zohra and Monia were trying to decipher a band of inscription. When they did, they shouted in unison: 'From clay I'm made take care of me for so are you.' They looked at each other and exploded with laughter.

'I'm not a specialist in seals but I think this might be a talisman,' said the Professor, picking up a rock-crystal disc among a group of seals and handing it to Dr Evans.

'Sigillography is such an interesting field,' she said. 'There is a small group of rock-crystal pieces intended for use in certain rituals of petition, particularly for soliciting rain. They are therefore true talismans but it's difficult to know why their inscriptions are in negative.' As she examined some of the seals, she added: 'Different virtues were attributed to different gems as we know from mineralogical treatises. Cornelian was used against toothache. Ruby was believed to strengthen the heart. Emerald was supposed to be powerful against snake bites.'

Mustapha picked up another rock-crystal talisman. He brought it close to his eyes.

'It's a talisman against floods,' said Monia.

Dr Evans looked at her. 'Rock-crystal is supposed to prevent bad dreams,' she added.

'The date of this particular talisman corresponds to AD 1050, so it's attributable to the reign of al-Mustansir,' enthused the Professor. 'As you know, Caliph al-Mustansir had to abandon the Green Pavilion after the revolts of the Banu Hilal tribe in 1052. The pavilion was left to decay for many years.' Professor O'Brien spoke to the site supervisors as if he was in the classroom. He paused, thinking that the production of lustre pottery in Wadi Hassoun must have come to an end with the Banu Hilal revolt.

'Many historical accounts include detailed descriptions of the Fatimid Pavilion and gardens, tainted nonetheless with the usual style of exaggeration, typical of these kind of accounts ...' Dr Evans expanded on the Pavilion as she gestured to her pile of photocopies, dominated by highlights in dayglo pink. The excavation members went closer to Dr Evans and concentrated on her words.

Zohra stood outside the circle for a moment, wondering about the multiple nature of reading, before she leaned forward to study the photocopies of the historical treatise. She found herself scrutinizing the figure which stated the size of the Green Pavilion. It crossed her mind that in the Arabic text a zero was a mere dot. What if one of those benign dots were missing? That would certainly be misleading about the scale of the Green Pavilion, and consequently the site of the excavation. Zohra dismissed the absurd thought. 'Why should a zero be missing?' But from within her the absurd question was answered. 'All it takes is for the ink to fade at the dot; all it takes is for the drop of ink not to be shed by the pen.'

22

Mark was finally going to project pages from the known volume of the Blue Manuscript. Everyone was waiting for Dr Evans to stop talking. The art historian was speaking about the English collector who had sold pages of the Blue Manuscript in the 1920s. 'Frederick Winston recognized its value immediately and knew that it must have been a royal commission, which is quite remarkable on his part...'

'So that was how the known volume of the Blue Manuscript came to be mutilated, its pages separated and sold one at a time, each for a small fortune!' thought Zohra. An emotion rose within her and for a moment it felt as though it was not hers.

'Winston was right in thinking it was a royal commission, there is no doubt about that,' concluded Dr Evans. They assumed her monologue had come to an end, but Alan asked her whether they used paper as well as vellum in the Middle Ages and the floodgates opened again.

'They used paper of different colours in the Middle Ages,' said Dr Evans. 'According to the historical account, *al-Masalik wa al-Mamalik*, Salih ibn Ziyad brought paper-makers back from China to Samarkand after his victory in the battle of Talas in 751.'

There was no doubt that Dr Evans was a manuscript specialist. Only now did Zohra realize that this was *the* Dr Evans. A book Glasses had lent her referred to many of her publications in its footnotes. The art historian dealt out her facts. It was as though the question had pricked her brain and information poured out like rice from a punctured sack.

'A paper factory was established in Samarkand in the eighth century and in the early ninth century in Baghdad. Paper manufacture was introduced into Egypt about AD 900 and in Morocco and Spain in the tenth century, and from Spain, the knowledge of paper-making spread to the rest of Europe, first to Hérault in 1189, then to Fabriano in 1260 and to Nuremberg in 1389.'

'Hmm . . .' came the sound of appreciation from Professor O'Brien.

Donatella noticed that both Alan and Glasses were gazing at Dr Evans and was wondering whether Glasses was really impressed. She caught what might even have been a glimpse of that penetrating look he had sometimes sent in her direction. Surely he doesn't fancy her! she thought. 'Would you like a beer?' she whispered.

'Yes please,' Glasses whispered back, with such warmth that it touched Donatella beyond her own expectation. In reality, Glasses was no longer listening to Dr Evans. He became aware of the dense verbosity that had spread between her subject and her listeners like a wall of authority. He thought her turgid words were used precisely to counteract their primary role of communication. He found himself examining Dr Evans's face. Suddenly her features seemed more prominent than what she was talking about; the art historian had mainly drawn attention to herself. Glasses caught himself imagining her stark naked and he was shocked by his own thoughts. But his impulse was simply triggered by the sententious mask that never seemed to leave her. He was not even sure this was her naked voice. 'She must have been taught how to speak like that in one of the best schools in England,' he thought.

Alan stood near the door, his hand on the light switch, waiting for Dr Evans to finish. They were all eager to finally see pages of the Blue Manuscript, the object of their mission. The room was suddenly plunged into darkness as Dr Evans was in mid-sentence. 'Sorry, sorry!' Alan apologized. His hand had fallen on the switch accidentally.

He put the light back on, but Mark announced: 'Let's get the show on the road!'

By mistake, the first slide Mark projected was reversed. To those who did not read Arabic, the writing was nothing but squiggles. Zohra was trying to decipher the words but was unable to read them. The letters had no diacritical marks. In the case of the Blue Manuscript, however, even for those who could read Arabic the letters were not easily recognizable when Mark projected the slide correctly. But to everyone in the room, stunningly beautiful enlarged details emerged from the dark. The boy Mahmoud and Kodama San, who sat next to each other, were both in full concentration. The boy was fascinated by the images of light on the wall. The cracks in the vellum pages were like wounds.

The coated voice of Dr Evans, with its affected English accent, came with yet more information. 'The rich blue colour was achieved through an elaborate process of dyeing with lapis, though initially scholars could not believe lapis lazuli had been used.'

Mark's voice, with its American accent, intervened. 'Lapis was always reserved for the robe of the Virgin in European Renaissance painting.'

'*Mashallah!* God bless. A master indeed! Next one *blease*,' came Mustapha's cigarette voice with its smoky resonance.

The room had been transformed into a cinema with the privilege of seeing without being seen. In the back row where Monia and Spaghetti sat, a zip was being slowly unfastened. The darkness of the room accentuated by the coolness of the image was a soothing haven in contrast with the heat of the day. And Dr Evans's drone padded the blanket of darkness which was bringing lovers together.

Zohra lay on her bed, reflecting. The beauty of the Blue Manuscript had stayed with her. To her, who hardly knew anything about Islamic art, these pages came to represent it. She finally saw what all the team's efforts were directed towards and she wondered about the dark place in Wadi Hassoun where one volume of the Blue Manuscript must still be lying silently. She visualized the excavation site at night, the place they left behind in the blinding sunlight at two o'clock every day. They had been removing strata day by day and they would continue in the months to come, peeling layers away, uncovering the past. A streak of moonlight broke through a slit in the window shutters and Zohra wondered for the first time why specks of dust danced in the light.

In the courtyard, the school guard stood motionless in the corner, his gun close to his chest. Glasses sat on the steps, thinking. He wondered why the passage of time made something special, and sensed that Mark wanted the Blue Manuscript whatever the price. It was late. Mustapha and Mark had gone out for some fresh air. The others had gone to bed; even the art historian had stopped talking. Mark was beginning to feel stifled by the pressure to find the Blue Manuscript. The dog kept barking long after he and Mustapha had closed the gate behind them. Mark was expressing his worries to Mustapha. 'You know,' said Mustapha, 'a sultan gave Juha a donkey on condition that he taught it how to read, write and speak in two years. "Are you mad?" said someone to Juha. "You're going to be hanged at the end of this."

' "Oh, in two years, anything can happen," said Juha. "The donkey could die, I could die or the sultan might die. So, no worries!" '
Mustapha laughed at his own joke, which did not seem to have the desired consoling effect on Mark.

Glasses could hardly see the guard in the darkness, but he suddenly became conscious that even if he had wanted to talk to him, he had no language to do it. Yet a bond of familiarity connected them. As time passed in this remote place, the gap between the excavation members and the villagers seemed to be closing. The many layers of interaction were connecting different languages, different times, different perceptions.

Glasses wished he knew more about Arabic calligraphy. Those letters touched his being in ways he could not comprehend. He thought of Goethe, who in *West-östlicher Divan* played with the names of various styles of Arabic writing, claiming it did not matter which style the beloved used as long as it expressed their love. And he pondered how it was that the German poet was familiar with Arabic calligraphy at all.

It was an extraordinary experience to encounter the tenth-century image through the light of twentieth-century technology, and he wondered how the Blue Manuscript had been produced and about the man whose hand had traced its calligraphy. The golden letters on the deep blue background were the calligrapher's searchlight. A light that reached them across generations.

23

'I want it to be a manuscript unlike any other, a manuscript that displays the glory of the word of God,' said the mother of Caliph al-Muizz to Ibn al-Warraq, the Court Calligrapher. 'It is going to be for my burial when God's call comes.' She spoke with the gentle authority for which she was renowned, a blend of power and humility that even her son found extraordinary. When a month earlier she had told him that he was not to consider the conquest of Egypt that year, AD 962, he acquiesced. And as he was eager to fulfil the dream of his ancestors, he was disappointed, yet he showed her no sign of his feelings. The year before, when she had returned from pilgrimage she recounted to him the magnanimity of the governor of Egypt. He had provided a significant retinue to escort her on her haj, invited her to stay in the palace and ensured her safety and comfort. And this second time she forbade her son to conquer Egypt because she was about to embark on a pilgrimage to Mecca. She would not allow the conquest to take place while al-Ikhshidi, who had been so generous to her, was still in power.

'A unique copy of the sacred text for which no expense will be spared,' she declared to the Calligrapher that morning in the palace of Sabra al-Mansuriyya, near Qayrawan. She had in fact, accompanied by her handmaiden, gone to the Calligrapher's quarters herself, an exceptional occurrence. Ibn al-Warraq's gaze was caught by the maiden's beautiful face for a moment; her golden crescent earrings glittered. Before the mother of al-Muizz left, the Calligrapher thanked her and made a promise that he would dedicate himself to the task assigned to him and hoped he would be worthy of it.

He opened the window within the *mashrabiyya*, whose carving had given the opaque medium of wood a shimmering translucence. Light poured in, bathing his face as he looked out. He stood aware of the manuscript that had just been commissioned. A minaret reached to the sky. He saw it as a pen ready to write the words of God. The traditional three spheres and crescent that crowned its tip marked the cycle of the moon. Standing there reflecting, Ibn al-Warraq became free of time. 'I shall write a manuscript worthy of the Creator,' he whispered to no one in particular as he gazed beyond, into the light that would ignite the creative spark.

It was not until the intense light of midday had shifted, its edge softened, that Ibn al-Warraq returned to his thoughts. With the change of light, he remembered the letters carved on the façade of the Great Mosque in the town of Susa, where he had grown up. The letters ran as an upper band on the high wall, and from the ground, the remote inscription could not be read, not even by grown-ups. The sacredness of the Arabic letter meant that its mere presence on a building was significant. He remembered how the inscription on that wall changed as the light changed. Sometimes it was visible, sometimes not. He could still see it in his memory's eye, when as a child, he had watched the protruding letters, written in monumental Kufic script, slowly disappear. He would spend hours watching what seemed to him like a magical phenomenon, those solid, prominent letters carved in stone vanishing. His friends thought he was obsessed. They were fascinated at the beginning but soon lost interest. For him, however, this little boy who was learning how to master his hands, continuously practising calligraphy under the supervision of his father, a master calligrapher, the fascination of the carved letters which appeared and disappeared never ceased. He became enamoured of the alphabet's forms; the Arabic letter *m* resembled a mouth, the letter *'ain*, an eye, the *alif*, an upright slender youth, the *dal*, a person bent with age, and the combined letters *lam* and *alif*, a close embrace between two lovers. His father doubted whether he would ever make it as a serious calligrapher. But, to his father's surprise, the boy grew to recognize what a joyful discipline calligraphy could be.

Having acquired an outstanding reputation, Ibn al-Warraq was called to be the calligrapher of the Fatimid Court to teach the young al-Muizz. He never returned to the town of his childhood, although it was not far from Qayrawan. Yet every day he watched the shift of light carve the letters in his memory's eye, and every day it seemed as if it was for the first time. A band of calligraphy ran from the edge of the window where he stood now with the ninety-nine names of God carved in wood as a wainscot. Ibn al-Warraq's eyes rested on 'ar-Rahman, ar-Rahim ... as-Salaam' (the Compassionate, the Merciful, the Source of Peace). The Calligrapher was familiar with Arabic letters engraved in metal, sculpted in stone, painted in glaze, carved in wood, embroidered in silk thread ... And now, for the commissioned manuscript, he wanted them to shine with light.

It was that darker stage of twilight; the light had just stepped beyond the moment of hesitancy. Ibn al-Warraq was sitting in that same place, opposite the window, but the view was of a different season. It had been over two months already since the mother of al-Muizz had come to see him. On the table were leaves of paper with many calligraphic experiments which had not met with his satisfaction. The pen rested to the side. He had been applying himself completely, in search of the visual expression for the commissioned manuscript, writing and rewriting, practising constant transformations that came closest to purification. His wish was to see content and container as one in the new manuscript. But how?

He was becoming gradually effaced by the descending darkness. And the moon and stars in the inky sky gazed at him where he sat. The moon was simply a witness of time, a luminous disc of consciousness. He could see the minaret, a constant feature of the picture from his window, more in his memory than in the material reality of the moment. The voice of the muezzin pierced the obscurity of the night. Other voices reverberated from the tips of other minarets. They crossed, overlapping, one fading, one starting, in a reaching motion under the dome of the sky.

'How appropriate the human voice is for the call to the faithful,' thought Ibn al-Warraq as he pondered the origin of the call to prayer.

When the Prophet met with his companions to address this, some had suggested sounding a bell like the Christians, some suggested a horn as was the custom of the Jews. And others suggested using a gong like the Hindus. It was then that Umar, one of the companions, told them of his dream which had recommended that a man should stand in a prominent place and call the faithful to prayer with the words '*Allah Akbar*'. Umar's suggestion was being considered when Ali, the Prophet's son-in-law, joined them and said he had had a similar dream.

For Ibn al-Warraq, the purity of light was the closest to the quality of the voices now reverberating, interrupting the darkness around him. 'The prolongation of sound as in the voice of the muezzin will be traced in the new manuscript,' he thought.

He had been staring at the sky for a long time, the moon approaching the horizon. Intense indigo came to wrap his whole being in penetrating silence and he saw that it was also this silence that he must convey in his calligraphy. The night had come with inspiration and creative insight. Its depth and the brilliance of the stars would find their way into his work. It suddenly became clear what the manuscript should be like. It was to be his vision, his original expression of the sacred text. 'While basing his style on the masters of the past, a good calligrapher has to transcend their models to create his own vision,' his father had told him. Ibn al-Warraq sensed that the time had come for him to transcend what had been passed on to him, to transform the layers of ancestral knowledge, to give from himself. He thought of the famous calligrapher Ibn Muqla, who sixty years before in Baghdad had devised a cursive script that was mathematically proportioned. Writing in the Maghreb was different. Attention was directed less to the particular significance of each letter, and more to the collective harmony of the text on the page.

While the Calligrapher was absorbed by his reflections, his apprentice entered the room with a jug of water. His mute gestures simply added to the silence. He placed the jug nearby without uttering a sound, lit the oil lamp and retreated, leaving Ibn al-Warraq gazing silently out. A door had just opened before him after a long quest of creativity. Ibn al-Warraq had fasted from speech for a month now and the apprentice was taking special care not to disturb him. There was only the rhythmic wheezing of his chest. He reached for the jug and poured from it. Within its neck, he glimpsed a beautiful peacock, framed by a line of calligraphy. The delicate piercing had transformed the thick clay into lace. It was the jug's filter, cleansing the water. Grace filled his being. 'The written word marks one of the great differences between humans and animals, and unlike animals, humans have developed a sense of the beautiful,' thought Ibn al-Warraq. For a brief moment, he was intrigued that the exquisite image of a peacock had been placed where it was not conspicuous. 'Inner beauty,' he thought, 'is not for human eyes alone. Beauty comes from the Creator and returns to Him.'

In the wavering light, he gazed at his long, slim fingers. How many times had he told his right hand: 'You will trace the worthy copy of the sacred word even if it requires a lifetime.' He cast a glance at the dark blue sky, the golden moon and the luminous stars. It was a full moon. Full of mystery. A flame-coloured volcano, blazing in the depths of the sky, refusing to be extinguished. 'Has it got fire in its blood? Is it a piece of life, of hope in a dark sad night? Tomorrow, alas, the sun will put it out, but only to shine with more light, more life, perhaps more hope.' The inspiration for the Blue Manuscript was being born. 'This is how my letters must look, just like the moon and the stars in the deep indigo sky with all the mysteries of the night's silent velvet. Golden letters on deep night blue will be my searchlight in darkness.'

Ibn al-Warraq prayed that he would be able to achieve his vision. He also prayed that his life would not come to an end before the copying of the text was complete.

'*Alif, Lam, Mim,*' Ibn al-Warraq recited in his heart. '*Alif, Lam, Ra,*' ... '*Ta, Sin, Mim*' ... He went on repeating those letters which started some of the chapters in the Quran – enigmatic letters which have eluded all human attempts to decipher their meaning. Letters which held the meaning of the sacred, the unattainable.

The night became darker and the stars shone through the dome of the sky like tiny openings letting in the divine light. The universality of the night's face, this immensity of darkness and the wholeness of silence. Tonight was beautiful, like every night in Sabra al-Mansuriya. Deep darkness, the offspring of the magical light which had pervaded the town during the day. Everybody was asleep, the town was shrouded in silence, proud of its pregnancy. Mystery that would give birth to a new day and bathe it in renewed light. Now the midnight blue exhilarated the mind, raising the heart to the beyond. Blue was more than one, slate blue, cerulean blue, peacock blue, sky blue, cobalt blue, blue-green, blue-turquoise . . . and turquoise was more than one . . . all telling thousands of stories . . . but all shades deriving from one colour. 'Inner beauty is power,' thought Ibn al-Warraq. 'Magical, overwhelming. Inner beauty is the Creator. A way to Truth.'

In his heart, the Calligrapher's silent recital never ceased. '*Alif, Lam, Ra*' . . . '*Alif, Lam, Mim . . .*'

24

The kite took off and flew further and further away from the site . . . slowly it became a tiny dot in the sky which the naked eye could hardly discern. Within it, however, was an artificial eye with an extraordinarily wide vision. An eye that could see an immense expanse. The higher it went, the more it saw, always in focus. From up there, people looked like ants, and in spite of the newcomers – Mustapha, Dr Evans, Dr Chevalier, Mrs O'Brien – the site seemed empty; most of the workers had been swallowed by the trenches. Kodama San, deep in concentration, was flying the kite for aerial photographs, quietly pleased with the wind that was helping his mission. Hardly anyone talked to him and he hardly spoke – only when politeness obliged, but when was such polite conversation real exchange? Everyone saw Kodama San for his technical brilliance. No one was aware of his intuitive finesse.

In Area B, at the site on the cemetery slope, Donatella was on her knees, rummaging with a trowel confidently. Zohra envied her the expertise of archaeology. As he watched Donatella, Mustapha felt he should disapprove of the tight T-shirt which accentuated her full bosom. His hair was brushed back in tidy waves. He looked inappropriately immaculate with everyone else around covered in dust. The sweat on his forehead was desperate for the handkerchief neatly folded in his pocket. He stood at the edge of the trench and looked down at the well of treasures. Greed was digging a hole inside him, but when he saw the day's finds he was not impressed. The site was yielding more and more paper, nearly all from the Mamluk period. Most fragments had Quranic verses; that was all that people buried with the dead. Though Mustapha was careful when examining the fragile pieces of paper, he still dropped one. The numb part of his palm where he had cut himself as a child had long since lost sensation and often caused such mishaps. He also held the dusty finds with reluctance. Dr Evans accompanied Professor O'Brien to the cemetery site.

Donatella became accustomed to the sight of one young woman, a Copt, who came every morning to the Tree of Wishes to tie a new ribbon. 'How pathetic,' she said. 'People seek hope by any means.'

Zohra did not comment. She simply wondered whether it was a different wish every day. She observed the Tree of Wishes. So many colourful ribbons had been tied to its branches. Some appeared and others disappeared. People in the village had many wishes but there were always enough branches on the tree for their ribbons. 'Perhaps a new branch would grow especially for a new wish, if necessary,' thought Zohra. The branches of the Tree of Wishes seemed energetically drawn against the blue sky, like dark lightning in a storm. Their violent twists seemed to contrast with Amm Gaber's composed stance. She wanted to get closer and hear what Amm Gaber was saying, but found herself rooted to where she stood. She could see his lips moving but his words remained soundless.

'Why's that old man talking to himself?' asked Dr Evans. Zohra looked at her with blank eyes. The untranslatable emotion returned unexpectedly.

'Oh, no,' interjected Donatella. 'Amm Gaber's not talking to himself, he's talking to the Tree of Wishes.' Dr Evans was baffled but did not ask any more questions. She reached for her hair, tying it at the back, exposing a cranial expanse. The workers digging at the edge of the cemetery had been instructed to avoid the dead – not that they needed to be told. Dr Chevalier, who was a guest of the sponsors, was busy gathering bones. Zohra watched him, intrigued.

The beautiful Zineb stood at her door, watching the team at work. Her gold crescent earrings sparkled every time she tilted her head. The earrings were undoubtedly, as was the tradition for all the women in the village, her wedding dowry, her capital. Rayyes Ahmed gazed at her. His infatuation distracted him from his duty, but as soon as the door was shut he returned to the workers to bark out his orders.

Near the lonely minaret, Alan chased two plastic bags, bloated by the wind. He caught them before they settled into the earth's strata and suppressed his fury about the careless littering of the landscape. Alan organized his finds methodically, carved wood, painted glass and engraved metal. He was fascinated by the fragmented remains. For him, interaction with objects was safer than interaction with people. He saw his work as a valuable contribution to the work of other archaeologists.

'Monia!' gasped the boy Mahmoud as he approached, running towards the Professor. The Professor followed him to discover that the workers had unearthed several lustre pottery fragments in the corner of one of the rooms that were gradually being unearthed in Area C, where Monia supervised the digging.

'Fatimid!' declared Professor O'Brien with great excitement as he examined one shard which had part of a lute painted in brown lustre. His trained eye recognized the authenticity of the eleventh-century find. No mistaking the Fatimid brush stroke. He tilted the fragment to reveal metallic reflection in the sunlight. These shards were parts of one container, of high quality. They were far from being the wasters he was hoping for, but they were Fatimid lustre-painted pottery shards. The Professor's ecstasy refuelled his enthusiasm to push the search for the wasters that would prove his theory about lustreware production in Wadi Hassoun. He was absorbed in his joyful examination of the fragments, oblivious that work had stopped for the mid-morning break.

Outside the shrine of Sayyida Nesima, Mrs O'Brien spread her scarf on the mat-covered platform before she sat down. Om Omran, who served them tea every day, sat on the mud floor near the door of the shrine, squinting at the newcomers. In her youth, the old woman used to draw a precise black line to highlight her eyebrows. With time, the line had moved away. The gap between the applied eyebrows and the faint originals showed how much her vision had deteriorated. She poured the tea slowly, examining each glass closely before she passed it on. Donatella handed the Professor his glass. 'Hold your fire,' he said, 'while I do this.' He was trying to match the lustre shards.

Dr Evans had one glimpse of the shards, entirely covered in decoration, and her commentary began. 'This is typical of the *horror vacui* which is at the heart of Islamic art.'

'*Horror vacui*?' Zohra felt in need of a translation. She looked at the fragments, trying to work out what Dr Evans meant. The art historian's words seemed large containers which rang with an echo devoid of meaning.

'Fear of the void, that's what the Latin expression "*horror vacui*" means,' explained Dr Evans. 'Because these people originated in the desert, they had an innate fear of empty spaces, so they were afraid to leave any empty space within their designs. That is why Islamic art is full of ornament.'

'What a ridiculous interpretation!' thought Zohra.

Dr Evans drew on her cigarette through the slim holder and exhaled as the boy Mahmoud handed her a glass of tea. The smoke made him cough violently. She had her book open again at a relevant page. 'Look at this shard for example,' she said. In order to date the objects, she was invoking comparisons continuously. Something could only exist in relation to something else. To see the object without resorting to a parallel meant she would have to look at what was actually in front of her. Her eyes moved between the open page and the shard in her palm. 'There is absence of corroborative material,' she concluded, slamming the book shut. Zohra was intrigued. She thought the art historian was not aware that every shard was part of a container which perhaps held food and was part of a human reality.

Mahmoud was still coughing. Donatella rubbed his back and Alan reached for a glass of water. 'Oh dear,' said the art historian, only then aware of his discomfort. '*Kifkhalk?*' she asked.

Dr Evans had in fact asked the boy how he was, but it took Zohra a moment to decipher what she actually meant. '*Keef halik,*' said Zohra, translating the awkward Arabic into understandable Arabic. 'She is supposed to speak Arabic,' thought Zohra, 'a significant tool for the study of Islamic art history, but her knowledge of it seems pretty limited!' She sent the art historian an indignant look. 'She speaks Arabic with a strong accent and thinks about the culture with an even stronger accent,' Zohra's look seemed to say. The boy drank. He laughed, shaking his head, and took to his heels.

In spite of her weak vision, Om Omran could see the boy Mahmoud running. 'Be careful, my boy,' she shouted. 'Beware! Don't step on the tombs of the dead.'

The Professor stood up. 'I'd like your opinion,' he said to Dr Evans. Out of earshot, they surveyed the mount of Sayyida Nesima, talking intensely.

The digging resumed. As the project manager, Mark made sure that today the workers did not stop before two o'clock as they had the day before. To his mind, every minute counted. Pressure was building within Mark. He was more and more conscious that he would eventually have to account to his bosses. Time was passing. Would he find the Blue Manuscript?

As the team gathered their things, getting ready to leave the site for the day, the beautiful Zineb reappeared at her door and beckoned to Mahmoud, who ran towards her. 'Her husband's away in Libya, seeking riches,' said one of the workers, as he looked in Zineb's direction and reached for his gallabiya.

'If he was here,' said another worker, 'he would have a job with the *khawajat*.'

'Indeed,' answered a third worker, 'but what's seasonal doesn't last.'

The boy returned with a pink Libyan towel wrapped around a gift from Zineb to Zohra and said that Zineb would like to teach Zohra how to make bread. Rayyes Ahmed placed his stick on the ground and unravelled the towel, revealing a large round loaf, still warm. 'You see,' he told Zohra as he handed the loaf to her, 'she makes beautiful bread!'

'Delicious,' said Donatella. 'I would love to learn how to make such wonderful bread.'

Keen eyes followed the excavation team as they disappeared, fixed particularly on one member. The beautiful Zineb had watched them every day until the dust and smoke from the truck had screened everything from her sight. Today, she had not been aware of Rayyes Ahmed as he stepped closer. The moon face retreated behind the door leaf, only the right half visible to Rayyes Ahmed, who longed to quell the desire that burned within him.

25

The sun, so bold in the morning, was blissfully shy in the late afternoon, but it remained warm until the early hours of the evening. Walls cast long shadows. Catkoota stretched like a long sentence, her tail assuming the shape of a comma. Donatella's kitten had grown.

Dr Chevalier paced the courtyard, watching from behind the dark glasses he never removed, not even in the cool shade of the tent when they ate.

'No chance we see his soul!' said Monia quietly.

'He struts around like a peacock,' replied Donatella with a chuckle.

'Not so glamorous.'

'Just as pompous though.'

When in the truck, on the journey home, someone had asked Dr Chevalier what was in the bag at his feet, he had snarled: 'Nothing.' Then he had added: 'Animal bones!'

'I can't sleep with those bones in the room, I'm sure they're human bones,' Spaghetti protested. So Glasses had taken the bones to the laboratory and kept them under his own bed.

In a corner of the school courtyard, the boy Mahmoud was giving Glasses his afternoon Arabic lesson. 'You should learn some verbs,' said Dr Evans. 'Mahmoud keeps teaching you nouns, the verb is more important than the noun.'

'What are they saying?' asked the boy when he recognized his name was mentioned. Zohra, who was sitting on the edge of the shard garden, translated, crossing the boundaries of languages as usual. But the boy seemed slightly perplexed. 'What you mean?' Mahmoud asked. His favourite English phrase brought laughter. Zohra smiled and shrugged and the boy let out a giggle of complicity and announced that the Arabic lesson had come to an end.

The apprentice cook sat in his usual place. Tears filled his eyes as he peeled, as though the layers were not those of the onions but of his memory bringing emotion to the surface. Sometimes, one cannot tell the tears of sadness from the tears of joy. But onion tears are neither.

The cat was now curled at Donatella's feet. Its emerald-green eyes stood out against the grey mass of its coat. Monia and Zohra carefully spread the lustre shards which belonged together on a tray and gave them to Glasses, who tried to work out which pieces fitted together. Two shards matched perfectly at the breaking line, like two beings that spoke the same silence. The Arabic letters too were linked and the continuity of the word was restored. Glasses sighed. His hands pressed, keeping the two pieces joined. He glanced at Donatella, whose hair shone in a shaft of orange sunlight as she threw her head back, sending a warm ray in his direction. He stood still for a moment, feeling reluctant to separate the pieces. He thought: 'This is how love stories should be.' He was puzzled by his own feelings. The bird in his heart spread its wings and attempted to fly. He watched Donatella playing with the cat. Its grey fur looked so soft, its paws pale ash. He reflected how the cat's childhood lasted only a few weeks.

Glasses did his work with great precision. German glue had brought a Fatimid bowl back together and the bowl was almost complete. 'Tomorrow,' Donatella said to Glasses. 'Monia'll have them dig in that same spot, the rest of the bowl will probably be there.' The missing piece would reveal the musician's face, still buried perhaps. The Professor felt like going to the site and digging right then. Though the site was not especially far, access was only possible within strict and particular rules. The sacred past was well guarded.

The bowl was registered, given the accession number seven hundred and three for a name, and was described as 'almost complete'. It was possible that this would be replaced by 'complete' the following day, but for now they had to stick precisely to their conclusions. Just as at the end of any other day, each find had to be photographed with a scale measure next to it; a full shot of each object, one in colour, one in black and white. Alan looked at the Fatimid lustre bowl through the lens. At the centre of the split-focus screen, the bowl looked broken. He adjusted the lens, bringing the two sections together. 'If we find the missing piece tomorrow,' he thought, 'I'll have to photograph it again.'

The room was quiet. Everyone was working. Professor O'Brien was excited. He would probably not sleep tonight. It was because of lustre that he had come to this forsaken place after all. Now, a nearly complete bowl from the Fatimid period had been unearthed. Only by finding lustre wasters or a pottery kiln with traces of lustre, however, would he be able to prove his theory that in medieval times Wadi Hassoun had been a centre of production for lustre pottery. A complete bowl could have been imported, after all.

'Do you know how much a bowl like this would sell for at an auction house?' Donatella's question interrupted the Professor's thoughts.

'Well, complete,' he replied, 'it's worth over a hundred thousand pounds.'

'What's the significance of the decoration?' Zohra's question triggered a long discussion. The find had a different value for each individual. Zohra listened to the dialogue which crossed between all the members of the excavation team except Kodama San. It was a dialogue on different layers, revealing different interests.

Kodama San was in the darkroom developing the aerial photographs which showed the various excavation areas. People looked like ants, palm trees like stars and the excavated walls like the foundations of prospective buildings. Later, he and the Professor would study the photographs closely to determine the areas with the most potential. In the darkroom the images were emerging slowly, the way the past emerged as they dug. Outside, the pale blue of the sky had transformed into the deep dark blue of night.

26

'It was a great idea to come out for the day,' thought Glasses. Donatella looked happy. He jerked, trying to prevent a button that had snapped from his shirt running into the bushes. He had lost two already. 'I should stop playing with my buttons,' he thought with a smile, 'otherwise Jamel Bey will have a crop of buttons next year!'

Donatella gave him a quizzical look. 'What's so funny?'

'In two hundred years they'll be excavating buttons, not Coca-Cola tops!' he said. She laughed and the boy Mahmoud giggled, though he had not of course understood their English. Glasses wondered if he could stay on after the excavation and travel and whether he could invite Donatella to join him and whether she would accept.

Jamel Bey was showing them around his orchard. In the field nearby, men bent over, working on the land, among them the son of Haj Salem, the guard. They dressed and behaved like the workers on the site. Even the black rubber baskets were the same as those in the dig. Their work was seasonal too, except that the crops were different, yet both had roots. They farmed vegetables in the fields and harvested art objects in excavations. The workers in the orchard were better paid than workers on other farmlands. Now, however, they were envious of the workers in the excavation. But they would not dare ask Jamel Bey if they could leave.

Rayyes Ahmed looked with admiration at all the fruit trees and the luscious plantations in Jamel Bey's orchard. The land was generous. It held riches in its entrails. Trees here were laden with heavy crops. Rayyes Ahmed's little round eyes swerved like two olives and gleamed with appetite. He dreamt of having an orchard like this himself. The tree trunks were painted green and from afar they looked unreal. The orchard was nothing less than a little haven. Clean-shaven Jamel Bey had inherited it from his father and had done everything to keep it alive.

Professor O'Brien looked in every direction. He wondered silently whether the orchard would be a good area to excavate, whether his lustre wasters were not buried under the fruit trees! He quickly dismissed the frustrating thought. 'Actually, we're some distance from the location of the Green Pavilion and the palace city,' he consoled himself.

'A tree has a living soul,' said Jamel Bey. 'Whoever kills a tree takes a life.' He went around pointing at the trees and saying their names in Arabic and English, as though he were introducing members of his extended family.

'How impressive he knows all this,' said Zohra to herself. 'I have no idea how to translate those names. A tree is simply a tree for most of us.'

'Because of nature's constant renewal,' said Jamel Bey, 'the orchard will look quite different next week.' Everyone followed him and listened except Mustapha and Mark, who walked to the side and whispered together incessantly. Mark seemed quite worried.

'Remember the Juha story!' said Mustapha in consolation. 'With time, anything is possible.' Every now and then, Mustapha patted Mark on the shoulder. 'My friend!' he repeated, smiling. Mustapha's smile always came as a surprise. Those glistening bubbles released irresistible charm.

A group of five children appeared from between the trees, chasing each other in a game. 'My sons,' announced Jamel Bey with pride. They gathered around the boy Mahmoud, who was poised to catch a butterfly. It spread its wings against a green leaf. Orange, russet and ochre glowed in the sunlight.

Mahmoud made a tentative move. The wings came together and the bright colours vanished, exchanged for a velvety dark blue. 'It's praying,' whispered Mahmoud. 'We shouldn't disturb it.' He came running towards Glasses and said: 'All you need is the whole alphabet. Once you learn it, it's easy. You'll be able to write whatever you want.' Zohra translated. Glasses laughed. He went on laughing as he brushed his shiny black hair back.

'What's so funny?' asked Zohra.

'I just remembered a funny story.'

'Yes? What is it? Go on, we'd like to hear a funny story,' she nudged him.

Glasses opened his mouth to say something then paused. 'Go on then,' encouraged Donatella.

'I don't remember it very well,' said Glasses. Zohra was intrigued but said no more.

Jamel Bey led the way. He made large leaves bow to them, clearing the passage as they drew nearer. They could hear the splashing of water. The sound got louder as they advanced. Professor O'Brien paused, trying to determine its source. Jamel Bey glanced back at the intrigued faces. He swept aside a thick curtain of branches and they saw a huge waterwheel turning in the stream in front of them. It raised the water and splashed it onto the orchard, it revolved in its timeless journey, powered by the flow of what it gave.

Kodama San, who rarely showed interest, was very intrigued by the waterwheel. He realized that the feature he had failed to identify in one of his aerial photographs had in fact been this. Donatella's camera clicked. A figure stood at the waterwheel. They recognized Amm Gaber from his silhouette. Jamel Bey explained that he also had an electric pump to irrigate, but the old man used to be his father's gardener, he had been around for a long time. 'Amm Gaber is inseparable from the waterwheel!' said Jamel Bey. Zohra was surprised. She thought that Amm Gaber was inseparable from the Tree of Wishes. 'You should take him with you when you make your journey, he would enjoy it,' suggested Jamel Bey, who had heard the team discuss a trip to the desert. 'I know that Amm Gaber loves the desert.' Zohra wondered what a blind man would see in the desert but she felt uncomfortable with her own thought.

Jamel Bey continued with his tour. 'Like the root of a plant, the stream feeds into the Nile. And in this level land, water can be diverted easily.'

Dr Evans eyed the waterwheel with great interest. 'This wheel bears a great similarity to one represented in a thirteenth-century manuscript from Andalusia, "The Story of Bayad and Riyad", kept in the Vatican Library in Rome.' The Professor faked a bit of enthusiasm in response. Dr Evans asked Jamel Bey: 'How old is this waterwheel?'

'As old as the land,' replied Jamel Bey. 'As you know, waterwheels were used in pharaonic times.' Jamel Bey's face and demeanour and indeed his whole presence exuded peace and calm. 'This particular one is very old. I remember my grandfather mentioning it in his childhood accounts.'

They sat under the pergola, under the soft reflections of a warm afternoon, most of them wrapped in their own thoughts. The chirping of birds heightened the silence between them. Monia's eyes engaged in an intense dialogue with Spaghetti. Glasses was playing with the cloth bracelet around his wrist. Something in him touched Zohra. Was it his sensitivity? she wondered. Somehow she sensed that he too was an alien. And what was the story he'd refused to tell? As he looked down she felt the seriousness of his thoughts in the weight of his eyelids. She wondered whether everyone could hear his heart's flutterings for Donatella, who sat near him but who was preoccupied by the picture she was about to take.

Zohra wondered whether she would stay single for ever. Every man who showed an interest in her was in harmony with only one side of her, not the other. Her mother accused her of being 'too Arab' when emotions gushed out unexpectedly. She was 'too English' for her father when she showed reservation and planning. 'I don't know if I can fit it in,' she had said to her father when he asked her to visit her uncle on one of her work trips to Denmark.

'How can you say such a thing?' he reproached. 'You've become too English!' Her father had so much wanted her to be Arab. It was he who had named her Zohra. Her mother thought she was expecting a boy and had prepared a list of boys' names. On her mother's list were 'Adam' and 'Basil', names which could pass in both the English and the Arab worlds. She had stressed that if it turned out to be a boy it was certainly not going to be called 'Mohammad'. Her father had recounted this to her many times over the years. 'Can you believe it?' he had said. 'She insisted that it would be a disadvantage to be called "Mohammad" in the West. She said to me: "Don't be selfish, you've got to think of the boy, he is going to live in London after all." Anyway, that's your mother for you!'

'Do you still have film in your camera?' Donatella's question startled Zohra and brought her back to the present which Donatella was about to record for the future. Donatella had seen the orchard through her lens. She had not stopped taking photographs.

Zohra was reluctant to hand over her camera but she did so, saying: 'Of course, no problem.'

Donatella, raising the camera to her eye, insisted on a group photograph. Mrs O'Brien took a little mirror from her handbag and refreshed her pink lipstick before posing for a photograph with her husband. 'Smile, darling,' she nudged him. Just before Donatella pressed the shutter, other children suddenly appeared. 'More of my children,' said Jamel Bey, overflowing with contentment.

Glasses caught sight of Amm Gaber and rushed to help him. Amm Gaber smiled and Glasses thought the old man had an incredibly youthful inner aspect. The lines on his face were not the lines of age, but the map of an inner journey. Zohra followed them quietly with her eyes but her heart beat uncontrollably as she watched the figure of Amm Gaber recede. Night was falling and the patterned shadows of the pergola were a sweet lullaby. Soon, the orchard was swallowed by darkness. A man brought two lanterns and a tray of candles which he placed on the low table in the centre. *Karkadeh* was served, and as they tasted the local drink they tried to think of a similar taste to identify it, but found none.

A night full of stars, glittering seeds of time, dispersed on a seamless dark ground. The face of the moon looked bare, its naked brightness startling. Mustapha looked at it briefly. It struck him how similar to a woman's face it was and he had the fleeting thought that it should have been veiled. He was suddenly conscious of its illuminating gaze, like that of a threatening witness.

'The moon affects the weather,' said Jamel Bey, 'and consequently the growth of plants. Vegetables should be planted when the moon is bright, except potatoes, which should be planted when the moon is obscure. And wood retains its quality when cut at the very beginning of the crescent . . . Farmers have followed these rules for centuries.'

Jamel Bey sensed a perplexed silence from his guests. 'One has to plant everything that grows above ground,' he explained, 'when the moon is ascending, and anything that grows below ground when the moon is waning. Whatever you sow when the moon is red will never grow.' Then he repeated for no apparent reason: 'Whatever you sow when the moon is red will never grow.'

Mustapha drew deeply on his cigarette and held in the smoke for a moment, before he let it out in a sequence of rings. He looked at them long and steadily as though they were his thoughts. He wished he could share his grand plan with his father. The manuscript he had inherited from him would have to wait a little longer. 'The deal with Jamel Bey is what matters now,' thought Mustapha, 'I must convince Jamel Bey to pay more money. My calligrapher in Cairo has had to mobilize all his resources to carry out the work of years in a few months. Jamel Bey has to understand this is a miracle in itself.' He took another drag and hesitated, censoring the smoke rings, suddenly fearful of exposing his thoughts.

Donatella had been bitten by insects. Zohra noticed one crawling on her arm and sent it flying. The Professor flattened a few between his palms, while Mustapha brushed them off kindly. He rolled another cigarette and offered it to Glasses. It came like a temptation. Glasses had given up smoking at the start of the excavation so he politely declined.

He reflected that the only time he liked insects was the German way, when made of chocolate and eaten on the first of May every year. He smiled and inched forward towards Donatella, filled with concern for her. She had just been bitten yet again. Donatella had begun to find him appealing. Familiarity was starting to have its effect, and with it came the comfort of companionship.

When the call to prayer reached them, Mustapha took his leave and Jamel Bey led him towards his house, which remained inaccessible to the others. Mustapha's fingers worked on the rosary as he followed Jamel Bey. Mustapha prayed on time, when possible, five times a day, pressing his forehead repeatedly against the coarse prayer mat. That was how the mark on his forehead had been acquired. Mustapha and Jamel Bey stayed inside longer than expected. Following their prayer, a conversation had taken place between the two men. On their return, relief was apparent all over Mustapha's face. He sat next to Mark and began whispering to him. Jamel Bey followed the conversation between Mustapha and Mark with his eyes. Something dark rippled past the pergola and Mark instinctively jerked to avoid it. 'It's a bat,' said Jamel Bey with composure. 'They're mostly active during the first half of the night. This is the time when insects are abundant. They fly around with their mouths open on the off-chance that they'll catch something.' A smirk of disbelief appeared on Alan's face but no one noticed it in the semi-darkness.

From Mark and Mustapha's whispering, a phrase escaped. 'More time,' urged Mustapha. When the others looked in their direction the two men's faces were masked by smiles again. Donatella eyed Mark with mixed feelings. She glanced at the gold ring on his finger and turned her attention to Dr Evans, who was telling anecdotes. Everyone was laughing. They had not imagined Dr Evans could be funny, but they had been wrong.

No one had noticed the disappearance of Rayyes Ahmed until he reappeared. His eyes shone with gleams of desire. Most of the afternoon, he had been pleading with the beautiful Zineb to leave the door open for him later that night. 'Zineb sends her love,' he whispered to Zohra.

Another group of children appeared. 'My children!' announced Jamel Bey again with great pride.

Rayyes Ahmed leaned over Zohra's shoulder and whispered: 'Jamel Bey comes from a family renowned for its fertility. It is said that one of his ancestors had seventy-seven children. God has blessed Jamel Bey in more ways than one!' It struck Zohra how bountiful Jamel Bey's orchard was, an abundance of greenery in such an arid landscape.

The land overflowed with produce. She remembered the exchange she had overheard between Halima and Hakima.

'During a period of drought,' said Hakima, 'the rain fell only on Jamel Bey's land. Jamel Bey was away and a huge dark cloud covered the entire orchard. There was a terrible crack of thunder and his wives were scared. A torrent of rain fell.'

'A tailor-made cloud with *baraka*, a blessing from God,' interjected Halima with a ring of awe in her voice.

'He's destined to be the richest man in the village.'

'The orchard is the only green spot in this desert place,' was Halima's refrain.

'Farmers aren't always rich. Who can predict the rain?'

'His fortune depends on how often the sky weeps on the orchard!'

'You know, his twenty brothers-in-law are claiming their share.'

'Peace is never complete.'

'Only in the tomb.'

'And even that's not sure!' was Halima's reply.

'Those two never tire of gossip,' thought Zohra with a smile. 'They can't grasp that the orchard flourishes because Jamel Bey is rich enough to control the irrigation of his land.'

As they sat silently under the pergola in the dark, they could hear the waterwheel turning on the other side. Jamel Bey's words came back to Zohra: 'Amm Gaber is inseparable from the waterwheel.' Every now and then, Mahmoud's giggling came like a fluttering butterfly. Amm Gaber was reading the boy's features with his finger-tips. The forehead, the brow, the eyes, the cheeks, all the lines that defined the face. He smiled. His hands remained extended in the air, still holding the grace of the boy's beauty. 'It's Mahmoud!' said the old man, and the boy laughed the way he did every time they went through this game of complicity.

27

'Tree of trees, my faithful listener, what is a face but two eyes, a nose, a mouth, set in an oval, yet shaped in different ways? With the number of people on this globe it is difficult to imagine that unlimited variety. But here we are, and all this unlimited variety seems normal. Identical twins attract our attention more. They are considered a miracle. Sameness interests us more than difference. The ordinary is extraordinary but we cannot see it. The uniqueness of creation, its unlimited forms given to one same feature, is truly extraordinary. It is difference as well as uniqueness which is a miracle.' Amm Gaber moved his hands in mid-air. He could still feel Mahmoud's facial features between his fingers. He was silent, his eyes a ceramic white.

The Tree of Wishes stood steadfast, its boughs like arms forever spread towards the sky. Its branches stretched upward in an irregular yet harmonious symmetry.

'Tree of trees, this is how the story of the four people and the translator goes.' Amm Gaber lifted his head. The multicoloured ribbons on the Tree of Wishes, cut from the clothes of different people, danced in unison.

'Four men sat together talking in the market when a coin was dropped among them. They rejoiced at their good fortune. "I will buy some *'inab*," said the Arab. The Persian objected. "I don't want *'inab*," he said, "I want to buy some *angur*." The Turk protested. "I don't want either of those, I want some *uzum*," he cried. "Well, I want *stafil*," said the Greek. And a fight broke out between them. A gifted translator, fluent in all languages, would have reconciled their argument. He would be able to tell them that each had wanted the same thing – grapes.

'Tree of trees, how many people of different nationalities speak the same language and how many people from the same background are separated by their common tongue? This is my father's story. I heard it many times. Every night, people gathered to sit together in the Mausoleum of Sayyida Nesima and listen to my father's accounts unfold endlessly. I would feel the atmosphere grow warm, the threads of stories linking people. With a story-teller no place is too small, worlds expand. My father's stories grew like your branches, stories within stories.

'Every night, my father apologized to the goat from whose skin his tambourine had come. Then he mentioned that like all of us who are alive the skin became warm. So perhaps, just perhaps, it got a feel of the stories. Every now and then, he would declare: "It's thirsty!" and I could hear him wet the skin of the tambourine because it was too hot. This always brought laughter, not just from the children. Grown-ups too were amused. My father, the story-teller, tapped with two hands on both knees and asked everyone to do the same. Tree of trees, it was just like rain. Listen . . .' The sound of rain filled Amm Gaber. It was interrupted by thunder. His face was that of a child.

'All the listeners used to join him, stamping feet for thunder, tapping on the palms with two fingers for light rain, and rubbing hands to hear the wind. "Do you know," said my father to his listeners one evening. "Do you know that the moon owes its light to the sun?" Silence began to fill the space. "The moon is invisible tonight," he continued, "sleeping in the shade. Tomorrow night her edge will catch the light and she will reveal a crescent. The crescent will grow to half. Soon she will look at us full face, then gradually retreat into the shade, trailing a different crescent as she goes. Until the new moon in the shade again begins her monthly cycle."

'My father's listeners were not interested in hearing what they already knew, so he continued with one of his old accounts. My father had collected many stories on our travels. Stories are free. They do not belong to anyone, passing from tongue to tongue. We walked endlessly. At times he carried me on his shoulders. He was a big man.

'Tree of trees, another of his stories went like this. There was once a man who never confided in anyone so that his secrets were never revealed. He trusted no one's discretion fully. For safety, instead, he would go to a well and pour out his heart's secrets. After he walked away, however, an echo reverberated from the bottom of the well, and by chance someone passing by heard it. And this man repeated what he had heard. So who was responsible for the divulging of the man's secrets? Surely not the echo, surely not the passer-by but the man who first confided in the well!'

Amm Gaber laughed wholeheartedly. He took a deep breath then began to sing. His voice seemed to travel a vast desert before climbing mountains, crossing valleys, flowing with rivers then returning to the desert. His voice reflected the journey within his inner landscape.

'We had been travelling for over a year before Father and I reached this village. The reputation of the saint had brought us from far away in the hope of a cure for my eyes. Sometimes my father would write talismans for the villagers. "The twenty-eight letters of Arabic belong to four categories which correspond to the alchemical elements of fire, air, earth and water," my father explained to me. "Letters of the water group are effective against fever, while those of fire increase the intensity of war. Each letter of the alphabet has a numerical equivalent according to the *Abjad* system. The first letter *alif* equals one and is a symbol of divine unity." Father also knew the properties of stones. "Lapis strengthens the will and kindness," he once told me. He was of so much help to everyone. When he died in Wadi Hassoun, the villagers organized his funeral and cried over him like one of them. I never went back to where I came from, not because I did not know the way but because one can never go back. And here, there is nothing to cure. It is not that I cannot see them, they cannot see me.

'Tree of trees, from my father's stories I learnt a great deal. But no one ever wanted to listen when I spoke. Most of the stories I told were my own.'

There was no response from the Tree of Wishes but Amm Gaber's words found their way into the veins of every leaf.

'You probably wonder why am I telling stories . . .' The old man stopped to laugh. 'You grow, you give fruit but you never ask why.

'That house, I cannot see, beyond this earth I can. The loss of my eyesight has sharpened the eye of my heart. You stand like a rock, you do not utter a word. Your silence, the witness of truth. Secrets wriggle and gnaw at my heart like worms. Every silver hair in my head has a story for every one of your veins. Your roots embrace and entwine with the deep earth. From the earth of death flourishes the blossom. Hundreds of your youths are nourished. My great-grand-father was a storyteller, so was his great-grandfather before him and the one before. You, Tree of trees, are my only listener. Throughout the years I have dug into the layers of myself and now that I am old and approaching the end of my season, I still have not reached the final layer. O Tree of youths, I want to dig but deep within myself. One life is not enough to excavate everywhere within ourselves.

'I want to walk the road in the desert of my soul . . . Truth lies behind countless layers. Removing thousands does not mean uncovering it. It took me years to see beauty in ugliness. Your skin is ravaged but your youth is forever renewable. Tree of trees, you have been standing for hundreds of years. Within you the rings of time tell of truth.

'I lived a thousand years, died a thousand times, the ash of my bones is the fire of time . . .'

Amm Gaber's mutterings were like threads gently sewing together the day and the night. The site was empty. Haj Salem, the guard, was asleep, leaning on his gun. Rayyes Ahmed walked stealthily. There was no sound to be heard, not even the murmur of Amm Gaber's voice, whispering to the Tree of Wishes. 'Some disconnected madness, no doubt!' thought Rayyes Ahmed as he glanced in his direction, advancing with nimble steps towards the house of the beautiful Zineb, but already from afar the door seemed shut. He walked a few steps further to be certain before he went back to wake up the guard with a prod from his stick. Then he mounted his mule and headed towards the school, although he thought everyone there would be asleep by now.

28

Deep down, when the light went off and everyone was asleep, he knew who he was.

He had told his father: 'It has nothing to do with me, your concentration camp, your holocaust! I don't want to carry your pain.' In fact he had grown to know that concentration camps also contained other races. But here, in Wadi Hassoun, he was far away from Germany, far away from his father. Since his departure for boarding school – his parents had insisted that he went to school in Tel Aviv – his father had not been there to repeat the story to him. But he himself, the Rosen part, who was the carrier of that story, had never stopped telling it to himself.

In the pit of the night, he had entered a deeper recess of his mind. Impulsively, he dug even deeper into the trenches which reveal that we are not just ourselves but those people we carry within us too. In the enclosed space of this excavation season, everyone's inner world was emerging. As the layers lifted, they brought his father's history to the surface. A history he had rejected as not his own. He did not inherit any of his mother's superstition but fear had a strong hold on him.

He had crossed half of Marienplatz, in Munich, before he folded the piece of paper and secured it in his wallet. He had buried the Rosen part of him in that courtroom, or so he thought. He quite liked the name Daniel, so did all his friends, but it remained fundamentally a Jewish name. He had thought long and hard before changing it. He had had enough. He had wanted to live his life as himself. But who was that? He felt the gossamer touch of fear as it curved up his spine.

Glasses remembered how his father had remained submerged in a cold pond for hours, breathing through a reed, to escape the Gestapo. His father had described his fear in detail to him. A suffocating pounding of his heart filling his head. The cold gnawing at his body. An inhuman control to prevent that natural shivering reflex which would betray his living presence. That fear, he himself had inherited. Cockroaches shrieked, cutting through his thoughts. He had no doubt what was said about cockroaches being able to survive a nuclear war was true. He lay down wondering whether it was true too that cockroaches could carry up to twenty times their own weight. Rayyes Ahmed's voice saying 'Goodnight' to the guard in the school courtyard came into the room. Rayyes Ahmed never went to sleep before the early hours of the morning, and during the day he went around dreaming.

Glasses could not understand his father's wish to be cremated. Was burial not much better than cremation, especially with his history? Glasses pushed the thought of death away and tried to go to sleep, but the thought rose again and persisted like an itch beyond his reach. Tossing and turning, he tried to think of something pleasant. He struggled to imagine Donatella's body, but could not sustain the image for long. Glasses, who had been fascinated by geography as well as mathematics, especially when he was a child, never imagined that the woman of his dreams would come from the 'boot of the world map'! That was what he had called Italy throughout his childhood. And from Rome, the eternal city, a city of so many layers, a city where trees hang sometimes unexpectedly from the sky. As he lay on his back, gazing at the ceiling, he thought about how it felt to experience 'the other'. Glasses' thoughts raced. All this was formulated in German, although he spoke Hebrew equally well. He was very happy to be German and loved German people. The Germany of his generation was a place he was very attached to. In Wadi Hassoun he only spoke English. Some of the others, too, held their mother tongue within themselves.

The tick-tock of the clock was beginning to get on his nerves. He thought of getting up and having a beer from the back alcove. The so-called medicine room, where alcohol was stored. The thought that he would not have to conceal the true identity of the alcohol in a Coca-Cola bottle as usual appealed to him. He was about to get up when he realized that he did not really feel like a drink. He watched mechanically the luminous green tips of the clock's hands going round in a regular motion, then looked to the window. It was three minutes past three when he looked back. He always got a sense of magic when this happened. Ten past ten, two past two, four past four ... He never understood why. Perhaps time was simply a game played on us by the hands of the clock.

Suddenly, he heard a sound in the room; something had fallen ... it must have been his diary, loaded with fiery dreams about Donatella. Why did these things keep happening as though moved by an invisible hand operating in the dark? The tick-tock continued. Nothing interrupted its relentless cycle. Glasses' tortured thoughts would not go away, like a trapped fly that was trying desperately to leave the room but was unable to find the hole by which it had entered. In his childhood, what he had loved most was to think. Thoughts travelled without boundaries. They gave him freedom. Sometimes, though, the lack of discipline in his thoughts made him their prisoner. Worry rode an unbridled horse and he had to think of ways to overcome it.

Now he was repeating to himself Hebrew words similar to the Arabic words he had heard during the day. His Jewishness, which he submerged during daylight, emerged persistently in the dark. He had never felt so Jewish in his entire life. The more he hid it, the more Jewish he felt. 'What you hide digs a hole inside you,' his grandmother used to say.

A shimmer of light came through and a little bright lozenge settled on the wall. Since mosquitoes had no effect on him he got up and opened the window. There was a full moon. He felt the craving for a cigarette but had none, he had hoped this expedition would be his chance to give up smoking completely. He gazed at the courtyard but was not seeing it. The window had become a hole into his past. Scenes from his childhood unfolded before him.

The moon had been their only connection for seven years, and it was a strong bond. When, at the age of five, he was taken away by his father, his mother took him outside to the garden and told him as she held him firmly: 'Look at the moon wherever you are and know in your heart of hearts that you're looking at the same moon as Mummy.' And for seven years that was their link, before his father remarried his mother!

Glasses remembered how upset his father had been when he refused to concede to his father's request that he attend a religious celebration that took place with the first full moon of spring. He had not wanted to miss a film starring his favourite actress, Ingrid Bergman. Oh how passionately in love he had been! Those seven years of his childhood were filled with stories. His father used to enjoy reading to him. The story he had refused to tell Zohra in the orchard for fear of revealing too much about himself had been read to him then. Having suppressed it during the day it had surged now vividly in his father's voice from under the many layers of memory. Glasses listened just as he had as a child. 'A villager was on his way home on the eve of the Day of Atonement. He knew that one was required to have a festive meal before the start of the fast, but he said to himself: "I can indulge in the feast here and still make it to the town for the Yom Kippur service. I'll even have time to change into my best clothes." When he finally jumped on his horse and headed back, he took a wrong turning and got lost in the woods. The sun was setting, bringing the hour for the Kol Nidre prayer. The villager was distraught. He realized that he was doomed to spend the holy night and day isolated in the woods, without the prayer book. "Dear God," he cried, "there's only one thing I can do now, I'll recite the letters of the alphabet and you, Master of the Universe, can make them into the prayers!" '

Glasses laughed with the same freshness now as he had on hearing this story as a child from his father for the first time. He wished he had shared it with Zohra earlier that day. All the things he had wanted to say to her in his discussions about languages came to him now.

'Modern Arabic letters evolved from Phoenician letters via Aramaic script,' said Glasses in a low voice alone in the laboratory room, 'as did modern Hebrew. Vowels are not directly marked in Hebrew or Arabic. Vowels are marked by using three basic signs above and below the line. In Arabic, there are also extra consonants, twenty-eight in all, while in Hebrew only twenty-two consonants are marked.' He traced the Arabic letters with his index finger in the dark void as he thought about the similarity between Hebrew and Arabic. He played with the three letters in Hebrew which indicate *ktb* or *ktv* and watched them take different meanings: *kotav* (I write), *katoov* (written), *mikhtav* (letter), and even *kitovet* (address), *kitoobah* (marriage certificate), *katban* (scribe). Just like Arabic, various additional signs were used to help with the pronunciation of the vowels. The voice of his teacher in Tel Aviv came to him. 'The system of dots which are placed above or below the letter is called *matres lectionis*.' 'Just like Arabic!' Glasses' voice rang out in the laboratory room. Why did he not tell Zohra about all those similarities between Arabic and Hebrew? 'Yet there are also differences,' he thought. 'Arabic letters look completely different from Hebrew.' In the darkness of the laboratory, the golden letters of the Blue Manuscript appeared to him as though they were projected on the wall just as on the evening of Mark's presentation. And Glasses wondered again about the master calligrapher who had written them.

29

The window was open. Its leaves tapped repeatedly against the wall. Ibn al-Warraq's hands, firm and steady, stilled them for a moment. He stepped back and took a breath. 'Stay still!' the deep look in his eyes seemed to say. The window leaves did not budge, but as the Calligrapher settled in his seat, the leaves rapped against the walls again and he was obliged to respond to their persistence. His breath had become even shorter and his chest released a continuous wheezing. He held each trembling leaf aside and looked out. The trees were in flame, the trunks that supported them steady, standing like the poles of beacons. Autumn had arrived. The picture was changing. Time was doing its work.

The Calligrapher washed his hands and perfumed them with musk. He sat down, cross-legged, straightened his back and took as deep a breath as he could. He picked up the bamboo pen, dipped it in the agate inkwell and proceeded with his writing in silence. The sacred text was constantly being repeated within him. He knew it by heart. The simple geometric forms of Kufic script dictated the harmonious proportions. His hands traced the horizontal and vertical strokes, building the internal rhythm, elongating some letters, shortening others. He gave the letters life from his personal vision.

He reached for the oil lamp and brought it closer. The night was letting its velvet curtain unfurl rapidly. A sense of the infinite overwhelmed him. It was cool and the air was damp. The dedicated work of the whole day had produced only a few words. He had all the patience in the world, but he was getting old. He looked forward to the day he would see the manuscript bound and the day he would make his pilgrimage to Mecca. His respiratory ailment was creating delay and he hoped that his life would not come to an end before he completed both volumes.

After many experiments, Ibn al-Warraq had decided to omit the diacritical marks. Traditionally, these were often added in colour to give the manuscript a festive look. No diacritical marks, no enunciation signs in the Blue Manuscript. It was as though the text was not intended to be read aloud. It was an omission that was meaningful for him. 'When one knows the Quran by heart, recognizing one word suffices; as tasting a single drop suffices to recognize the sea,' was Ibn al-Warraq's thought. He reflected how his calligraphy was now a direct reflection of the text's spirit on to the page, as though the meaning and the sacredness of the text were translated into the aesthetic structure of its expression. The traced words were not images. They were not sound. They became rhythm which was not that of the reading of the text but that of its internal structure, which could neither be explained nor interpreted. Like those enigmatic letters preceding some chapters in the Quran, their meaning remaining enclosed within them. A sublime meaning that no one can penetrate. '*Alif, Lam, Mim* . . .' Ibn al-Warraq recited in his heart as he traced the letters.

After having worked and worked for months, Ibn al-Warraq had completed a few pages which he judged to be satisfactory. They held his vision and hope that his copy of the Quran would contain the silence of the night, that the letters would shine like stars in a dark sky, that they would have light distilled by the moon from the sun.

'The Caliph's mother is back from her trip,' said the apprentice with as soft a voice as he could.

The Calligrapher did not utter a word. By now he had been fasting from speech for over a year. He stood by the open window again. The autumn picture he had seen earlier had disappeared. 'Tomorrow, the mother of al-Muizz will see the first few pages of the manuscript,' he thought. He felt the cool breeze on his eyelids, conscious of the night's seamless sheet of deepest blue. He held a page in the light of the full moon. The golden letters floated. Light and silence filled his being. The apprentice stood close by, timidly, in admiration, thinking in disbelief: 'The fate of this magnificent work is to be buried with the Caliph's mother!' He wondered what the lady of the Court would think of what his master had so far accomplished. He was surprised that Ibn al-Warraq himself did not seem worried in any way about her return. The floating letters shimmered and the Calligrapher's hands trembled. 'It's time to rest,' thought Ibn al-Warraq. His fatigue was apparent.

'I respect your commitment to silence,' said al-Muizz's mother to Ibn al-Warraq. She did not wait for a reply but started telling him about her journey with great enthusiasm. She praised the generosity of the governor of Egypt, his hospitality as she crossed on her way to pilgrimage. Then she brought up the subject of the commissioned manuscript. And to his surprise, she told him to discard everything he had done so far. Instead, she would like him to write a manuscript the way she was about to describe, as she now knew exactly what she wanted. The Calligrapher flinched. For the first time, his fast from speech was truly tested. All the efforts of his experiments, all his hard work, his trials and perseverance appeared before his eyes. He felt a terrible tension. 'It was in the pious city of Jerusalem,' the mother of al-Muizz continued, without noticing any change in the Calligrapher's state, 'that I saw a vision of what the manuscript should be like.' She did not know how to convey to the Calligrapher what she had seen. Al-Muizz's mother was silent for a moment, grappling with words.

Eventually she spoke. 'I do not know how this could be achieved in a manuscript but the image captured my heart,' she said. It was in the mosque of the Dome of the Rock that the mother of al-Muizz had seen inscriptions running on the outer and inner faces of the octagonal arcade. 'There were golden letters sparkling against a deep blue background,' she finally revealed.

Silently, without a sign of astonishment, the Calligrapher opened the wooden box next to him and handed her the first pages of the promised manuscript. Al-Muizz's mother closed her eyes. That was the most a princess would do to express her emotion.

30

Zohra felt uneasy while translating. At the time she could not understand why. In a strange way, she felt as though she was betraying something, but she could not identify what it was. She was finding it difficult to remain neutral as a translator. For a moment she felt that there were two tongues in her mouth, superimposed in synchronized motion like a pair of scissors editing what came out.

'The workers will not dig at the new site. They have already decided,' said Rayyes Ahmed.

'What?' cried Professor O'Brien after Zohra had translated. Because of the use of two languages, reactions in the dialogue were delayed. And today Zohra stood at the junction of conflicts. She was the one who experienced the raw emotions of the speakers. Tempers simmered in the heat. The Professor's nostrils widened and his eyelashes twitched in anger. They moved in a similar way when he was happily excited, but not so intensely. He gesticulated demonstratively. Becoming angry was out of character for the Professor. He cast a glance in the direction of the few houses around and wished none of them were there. By the time he descended the slope of the cemetery site, anger had formed a knot inside him. He would dig every inch of this land for his lustre wasters.

Mark was adamant. 'If it's important to dig there then that's where we'll dig,' he said, in a tone that matched the redness of his ears.

Professor O'Brien knew that the mount of Sayyida Nesima was important. Part of it had not been formed naturally but was an accumulation of sediment. 'This could be the most promising area of all,' he stressed. He could tell when earth was fertile in archaeological matters. Besides, both Kodama San and Dr Evans had reinforced his assessment. His nostrils flared. Trouble. He knew it would come sooner or later. And now, how was he going to handle it? He would have to adopt a role of authority. He was a kind man and always disliked the unpleasantness of confrontation. But he had no choice. He quickened his steps. The others followed. They all walked without talking but there was no silence. The air tightened. Professor O'Brien was thinking what he should and should not say and do. He hummed Puccini, lines from *La Bohème*, to try to calm himself a little.

> *Your tiny hand is frozen*
> *Let me warm it into life.*
> *What's the use of searching?*
> *We'll never find it in the dark.*

They reached Area A, the site of the lonely minaret. Alan was securing a glass shard in a plastic bag. Workers stopped their work and followed. At Area C, Monia was bent studiously, writing labels. Here too, action came to a halt. 'They won't dig in Area D,' announced the Professor in answer to all the questioning eyes, the knot of anger tightening inside him. His steps seemed to speed even more at the sound of his own declaration. The two site supervisors followed. It was clear that the Professor was gathering support. Monia felt that her policing skills were about to be tested. The workers acted instinctively. They did not know what was really happening. Nevertheless, they put their tools aside and followed. All walked in solemn force now. Only Mahmoud was missing. The boy had not yet come to the site that day. Every morning, Mahmoud walked to the edge of the village to help his mother gather firewood so she could bake bread. On some days this delayed him.

On their way to the mount of Sayyida Nesima, they saw the beautiful Zineb, who waved and urged Zohra: 'Come in, come and see my house.' Zohra promised her she would, another time. The longing smile in Zineb's eyes was like silent lightning or perhaps dancing snakes. Rayyes Ahmed walked behind everyone else and glanced back intermittently, admiring Zineb's curves as she stood, one hand on her hip, as sinuous as the Sayyida Nesima mount itself.

From afar, the workers looked like statues, immobilized in the blazing sun. The Professor walked faster and his shoulders seemed even broader. The others could hardly keep up with him. They were getting closer to the shrine of Sayyida Nesima, its overshadowing dome a milky white breast, the nipple still generously offered to the sky. Three teenage boys stood gesticulating. Their fingers moved forward and backward. One of the boys was dumb, but which one? In the eyes of the mute boy was a deep well. If they were to dig there, they would find only stone. Trapped, his voice was a scream without sound. Zohra could not understand what they were discussing but there seemed undoubtedly to be a heated urgency to their exchange. She noticed that a strip had been removed from the sleeve of the mute boy's gallabiya. 'He must have tied the strip to the Tree of Wishes,' she thought. A villager stood at the top of the hill, watching them as they advanced, a blank look on his face. He was carrying a cock, a sacrificial offering to the saint. The cock struggled, flailing its wings. Its fury seemed to reflect the mood climbing the mount.

Hand prints, the colour of fire, covered the walls of the saint's building. 'What's all that?' Alan asked Zohra.

'I don't know,' she answered. 'Probably henna.' Instinctively, Zohra knew they were blood prints made from the sacrificial offerings, but she felt that her translation of the image would be a kind of betrayal, letting the others in. She was losing her neutrality.

'Aaah,' said Alan, 'for a good omen!'

'That's right,' Zohra agreed. 'It must be.'

Men and boys rested their chins on the handles of their hoes. Their faces set like flints, unyielding. The look in their eyes, like daggers, sharpened by anger.

'We won't dig in the mount of Sayyida Nesima,' said Sabry.

'We won't dig in the mount of Sayyida Nesima,' repeated all the others after him. Their voices came clear and forceful, their timing precise. Zohra translated. Om Omran sat in her usual place on the threshold of the mausoleum, squinting as she watched the scene.

'The saint will take revenge,' said one worker. 'Anyone who digs in the saint's mount will turn to stone. We can't touch the soil where her soul rests.' His words sent shivers of fear into the souls of all his comrades.

The Professor suppressed his rage. His voice came gentle but persuasive: 'We will keep far away from the saint's tomb and dig near the base of the mount.' The workers from all the other areas gathered around the scene. They looked like extras in a film. One wore a red sweatshirt with the English word 'GO' written on it in thick white letters. It was large enough to be read from the other side of the circle, but he himself did not know what his chest declared. For him, the letters were mute squiggles. The Professor and the rest of the team stood to one side, the workers were on the shrine's side. A wall of silence stood between them.

Looks wandered everywhere. Several of the workers were cross-eyed. The blessed Nile was also the carrier of diseases. One worker started shouting. He spoke quickly. Monia answered back in the same style. Zohra could not unravel a word. Only Monia's tone of authority was clear. The atmosphere among the workers had already boiled and was starting to overflow. Sabry wiped his face with the palm of his hand. He reached for a cigarette in the pocket of his striped waist-coat and looked up. His eyes narrowed, only the shiny olive pupils visible. He had particularly large hands. '*Yabni, hut fi-batnik battikha sifi*, we won't dig,' he said to one of the angry workers.

When Mark gave her an inquiring look, Zohra felt like translating the words literally: 'Put a watermelon in your belly, my son.' Instead, she translated the meaning of the metaphor. 'He told him to calm down,' she said. Zohra was not faithful in her translation.

'*Ashhadu an la ilaha illa Allah Muhammad rasul Allah*' – I testify there is no God but God; I testify Mohammad is the messenger of God – said the worker to deflate his own rage. The *Shahada* brought him to his senses and he stopped shouting; the other workers did the same.

The overflow had ceased but the atmosphere was brimful with anger. The stubborn silence was finally broken by a young worker whose eyes were shadowed by a baseball cap. His wet tongue drew lips on the dusty face, then the lips spoke. 'We have to receive the order from our Omda. If he says we dig, then we'll dig, otherwise no.' Mumblings from the workers brought apprehension.

When Zohra was asked to translate, she felt her tongue fork again. All the workers who had been allocated for the new area chorused in agreement: '*Allahu Akbar!*' God is most Great! The rest of the workers, all those who had come from the other areas, repeated with ardent spontaneity: '*Allahu Akbar!*'

Professor O'Brien, Mark, Donatella and Alan looked at each other. Their eyes filled with the familiar fear of incomprehension. 'God is most Great,' Zohra translated. It was unnecessary. A tense politeness began to regulate the conversation.

'Then we'll get the Omda!' announced Monia.

'I'll go and get him,' said Spaghetti as he hurried towards the truck. In Monia's eyes he was definitely nearer to the sky than the others, his strides had an ascending quality to them. Thanks to her man, the problem would be solved. She volunteered to accompany him.

The engine of the truck chugged, fuelled by the tension of the moment. The heavy vehicle swerved with a defiant screech. The exhaust released a cloud of trailing satisfaction that enveloped Spaghetti, Monia and the truck. 'The town is a long way away,' said Rayyes Ahmed. 'They won't be back for a while.'

'OK,' declared Professor O'Brien to everybody, 'we'd better get back to work ... each to his site!'

Each supervisor stood at their area, perplexed. An hour went by. The mount of Sayyida Nesima was visible from all the excavation areas and everyone looked in its direction. Complications had started. It felt as though the air was suspended. The Professor was striding back and forth between areas. The boy Mahmoud ran in small spurts behind him. 'Need something, need *mayya?*' His questions were lost on the Professor in his own mutterings.

The whistle call resounded. Each group of workers gathered the bags of their findings into the rubber baskets and handed them to the supervisor in charge. Rayyes Ahmed had arranged an alternative truck to take the team back to the school. It was smaller and certainly more dilapidated. They sat squashed in two rows. Their faces were masks of dust, their lips dry. Donatella's straw hat gave her a veil of lace, patterned in light and shade. 'Not great,' she remarked, looking at the basket of finds on her knees.

The shaking truck rocked them home, a rough lullaby. Their brains dulled, they could hardly think. The sun was beating down on them. They were hot and sticky and they all longed for a shower. They gazed at each other during what felt like a long ride. In the enclosed world of the excavation, emotions seemed to race. Mrs O'Brien did not know what to say to console her husband. He rarely got angry, and she knew, on these occasions, she had to leave him alone as he always insisted.

They crossed the village. Cactus and hemp sprang from the mud-brick walls, casting grotesque shadows. Mud-brick houses had many lifetimes to bake. One house looked as if it had coarse skin. The mud surface had cracked from the intense heat. Mud-brick walls had their flaws. They were somehow human and they felt and breathed like everyone. They probably groaned in the heat too and whistled in the wind. Life unfolded between living walls. On the bridge, the driver had to be careful to avoid a small boy nonchalantly peeing in the river.

At the school they were disappointed to find the water had been cut off. Lunch had been delayed again. The apprentice cook was leaning against the kitchen window, slicing onions. In his eyes, two swollen tears were transfixed in hesitation.

'Potatoes go green if you expose them to the light,' shouted the cook as he moved the sack of potatoes which Spaghetti had bought the day before. The apprentice ignored him and continued with his onions, his eyes fixed on his long knife. He paused to remove the delicate skin of one onion, the way one would lift the protective page of a precious manuscript. He wore his usual lack of concern. A comb that stuck out of his pocket was in constant use, making sure his hair reached from temple to temple. His baldness would only show on a windy day.

When the team finally sat around the table, the atmosphere was still opaque with tension, perhaps too thick even for the apprentice's knife. As she shovelled vegetables on to his plate, Mrs O'Brien encouraged her husband: 'Daaaaarling . . . it's gooooood for you.' The others suppressed their laughter. Mrs O'Brien's tender coaxing did not help the Professor's frustration. In fact, matters worsened as the evening wore on. Coincidentally, it was this night of all nights that an entrepreneur came from the nearest town, looking for the director of the excavation to sell a number of antiques. Professor O'Brien's fury emerged for the second time that day. The visitor could not have known the extent to which the Professor would find this offensive to his integrity.

Professor O'Brien lay awake thinking for a long time. He heard the words of his grandmother from within himself. He remembered how she had a profound fear of flying. One day, she had declared unexpectedly that she was going on a pilgrimage to Lourdes. 'But surely,' his father had said, astonished, 'you'll have to fly there! Won't you be afraid?' To this, his grandmother had retorted: 'Oh no! Sure nothing'll happen on the way to Lourdes!' Such was his grandmother's faith. Now he could somehow understand what the saint meant for the people of Wadi Hassoun. He felt sympathy for the villagers rise within him unexpectedly. Perhaps it would be better to forget about excavating the mount of Sayyida Nesima and to concentrate on the other new areas. Surely one of them would provide his lustre wasters. Contemplating this reassuring thought, Professor O'Brien fell asleep. In addition to finding wasters, he dreamt of finding a kiln which proved that lustre-painted pottery was produced in Wadi Hassoun, and how the theory made him renowned as a distinguished scholar. This pleasant dream brought a smile to his face. Lying by his side, Mrs O'Brien watched over him and wondered why he looked so complacent after such a terrible day of tension.

It was a night of dejection in the school. Donatella and Glasses, sipping beer, sat in the courtyard with Zohra. Glasses reflected, intrigued by the villagers' strong reaction to digging in the mount of Sayyida Nesima.

Now that nearly all the guests had left, they felt some satisfaction at having the place to themselves again. The cooing of doves softened the atmosphere. They all felt tired. For the first time, Zohra wondered why yawning was contagious and how it worked. There was an emptiness, against which little things stood out, as though experienced for the first time. It had been a charged day.

'I thought some time in Egypt would do me good,' said Zohra. 'The weather would be nice and it would be a kind of holiday. Besides, being on an excavation should be exciting.' She turned to Glasses. 'You know, in my job I find myself translating all sorts of subjects and hearing information I wouldn't usually come across. I thought this time I'd get to know a bit about a culture I'm supposed to belong to, partly, but about which I know very little.'

Glasses was listening, his chin in his hand. 'What language do you think in?' he asked.

'I think in two languages.'

'Which one do you like speaking most?'

'Certain words in Arabic express some things better and certain English words express other things. The ideal would be to speak in a language that combines both.'

Then Zohra thought to herself how the zone of the untranslatable was made of those very aspects that were particular to each culture. The untranslatable created her sense of isolation.

'I've always thought that it's only when the whole world is racially mixed,' said Glasses, 'there will be peace in the world.'

Zohra laughed. She had a little laugh and a small voice. 'I'm not so sure, because with the mixed marriage of my parents, I was brought up in a war zone. My mother the West, my father the East. I grew up in the chasm that separated them.' There was a moment of silence before Zohra continued. 'When I was three – so I was told – I started to recognize the existence of two languages. I would point at bread, look at my father and say *khubz*, and then I would look at my mother and say *bread*.'

Glasses was suddenly aware of a faraway look in Zohra's eyes.

'They quarrelled all the time until they separated. In my upbringing, each side was conditioned to cancel the other side. I so much wanted each half to be whole.'

She was constantly moving, like a train, on parallel tracks. The two tracks going on a similar journey, taking the same turnings, breathing the same fumes. They seemed to join in the distance, but in fact they never met.

'One evening, when I was a teenager, at an Indian concert in London,' reminisced Zohra, 'the woman introducing it said: "East and West have become like hand in glove." At which point, a sarcastic remark escaped me. "Which is the hand and which is the glove?" Afterwards, I thought: "How cynical! Was that my mother or my father speaking?!" I knew deep down who it was but I didn't really want to know.'

'It must be very interesting to work as an interpreter,' said Donatella, changing the subject.

'No, I have no right to interpret. I don't expound meanings. They go through my ears into one container and come out of my mouth into a different container. I translate. I transmit. I transfer the meaning from one container into another.'

Only the moon in the dark sky above the courtyard was present. It went round in an endless journey, and wherever they were the moon was there too. The moon, a sickle or a feminine eyebrow, or perhaps, tonight, more of an incomplete question mark, suspended over their heads. Both Glasses and Donatella were intrigued but silent. Zohra was immersed in her thoughts. 'The word is of tinted glass. In my profession, I strive to match the tints, to sharpen my sensitivity to nuance. To be a good translator, it's essential to have honest precision.' For a moment, she became aware of the cooing of doves above her. 'Language developed for communication. The word was created because of the other. But the word is also used to alienate the other. A translator is the conduit. The more transparent I am, the better I am doing my job. My challenge is to not leave any personal mark on what I translate. I have constantly tried to connect worlds, I am constantly facing that fear of the other, never running away from it. At the site, today, I was more visible than ever, more conscious of the gap that separates the two cultures of my parents.'

'The nights are getting longer, *quelle belle lune!*' said Donatella.

Glasses listened quietly. He loved Donatella's rasping voice.

'I always wanted to learn French, it sounds so beautiful,' said Zohra.

'It sounds so romantic!' remarked Donatella.

'I was impressed when I heard you speak French to Hassan Fathy in Cairo.'

'That architect spoke perfect French, didn't he!' exclaimed Donatella.

They were all silent but the three of them shared the same memory. They were in the architect's house in Cairo. A wooden bench ran around the sides of an alcove. The walls of the room were covered with books. Every now and then, cats appeared from nowhere, coming and going, peacefully. An elderly maid brought a tray of tea and took her leave. The architect, they discovered, lived alone except for his thirty-three cats. 'Was he lonely?' Zohra reflected on the fate of such a special man. He had been designing houses in a faraway village, with the hope of helping people help themselves. He wanted to return the human dimension to modern architecture, writing poetry with his walls, creating light and shade which danced gracefully. Beautiful poetry and poor people's needs merged. The new village was to house many people. It was built with mud-brick, the cheapest local material. The lines, forms, spaces, all played a music that was pure and simple, the kind of simplicity that came from a distilled complexity, not readily understood. He had wanted to build for the poor. Ironically, in the end it was the rich who commissioned his buildings, not the poor.

They were silent in front of the black and white photographs which the architect had showed them of his work. Donatella had taken photographs of the photographs.

'Where's Mark?' Donatella brought them back to the courtyard of the school in Wadi Hassoun.

'He went to sleep early.'

'I asked him to show us the slides of the Blue Manuscript again but he changed the subject.'

'He's obviously in a bad mood.'

'Well, would you blame him, with all the aggravation of today . . .'

They spoke in English. To the ears of the school guard who stood in the corner, almost invisible behind the night's curtain, and the cook who crouched smoking nearby, their discussion was incoherent sound. The boy Mahmoud, who snuggled close to Donatella, followed the dialogue with his eyes, naturally wide open.

About an hour later, Zohra was sitting in the courtyard alone except for the cook. She was submerged in sadness and somehow she longed for that anonymous voice, the voice she had heard once, the first night in Wadi Hassoun. That first night seemed suddenly very far away. Where was that luminous voice in this bleak night that refused to wipe away the events of the day? What was the story behind the saint? Zohra wished she could know who Sayyida Nesima was. 'Sayyida Nesima.' She murmured the name of the saint to no one in particular. 'Sayyida Nesima.' The name wanted to be uttered. Zohra hoped the cook did not hear her. The cook was waiting for Monia. He was not going to go to sleep before she came back, although he had been up since dawn when Dr Evans, Dr Chevalier and Mustapha had left for Cairo. The cook did not approve of Monia's behaviour and neither did Rayyes Ahmed, who had passed by the school after checking on the site.

Spaghetti and Monia did not come back until the early hours of the morning. The cook was furious. They said the Omda was not to be found in his home. He was in another town where his daughter had just given birth. Spaghetti would drive first thing the following day to get him. Monia explained that on the way to the Omda's house they had been misled and then they had had a flat tyre. That was why the trip had taken much longer than expected. Everyone they had asked on the road had given them the wrong directions which took them further out of their way. No one had wanted to say that they could not help. The generosity of the people mingled with their well-meaning lies. The cook knew better, he was suspicious. Besides, that truck was so high, anything could have happened there between the two without anyone seeing it! The cook was right.

31

'A long time ago,' said Amm Gaber to the Tree of Wishes, 'perhaps a few hundred years ago, a man was travelling in the desert with his pregnant wife. It was in the middle of nowhere, with no living soul in sight, that this young woman unexpectedly went into labour...'

Amm Gaber reached for the trunk of the Tree of Wishes. Its rough bark felt reassuringly present. With his index finger, Amm Gaber traced its sinuous veins and continued with his narrative.

'The man carried her to the only shelter around, a hollow in a rocky outcrop where she suddenly gave birth to a boy and died. The man was at a loss about what to do. He would have to journey across a vast expanse of desert to reach his tribe. He knew that if he took the newborn it would have no chance of survival. The baby would soon die for lack of milk. To his deep sorrow, the man realized that he would have to leave mother and baby behind and cross the desert alone. Reluctant to remove the baby from his mother, he laid it on her right breast, with her right arm around it. Then he sealed the entrance to the hollow with a wall of stones and rode away.'

Rayyes Ahmed, who was going round the site, walked surreptitiously and planted himself in front of Haj Salem like an apparition. The site guard was startled. 'Are you *ins* or jinn?' Are you human or spirit? he asked when speech returned to him.

Rayyes Ahmed laughed demonically. 'It's only me!' he reassured the guard and crouched next to him. He pointed to Amm Gaber in the distance, sitting in his usual place, talking to the Tree of Wishes. 'You should ask him,' he said, 'whether he is *ins* or jinn, not me!' Then he added: 'Who wants to hear what he has to say anyway?' and let out another demonic guffaw. The guard joined in his laughter and offered him a glass of tea.

Near the Tree of Wishes, Amm Gaber was continuing his account. 'A year and a half later, a party of the same tribe was crossing the desert and happened to pass by the same spot where woman and baby had been entombed. Knowing the story, they went to see if the wall was intact. To their amazement, they found a hole in the wall. Outside, on the sand, they saw the tracks of a child's feet running all over the ground. In great fear, and filled with superstition, they quickly rode away from the haunted place. On hearing what had happened, the father hurried to the desert, where he found the hole in the wall and the small footprints. Looking inside, he saw a boy sitting and prattling beside the mummified form of his dead wife. The mother's body was all dried up, except her watchful right eye and her right breast, which was full of milk, as round as a dome. These were similar to those of a living woman. Awestruck, the man took away the child and rode off. Before departing, he carefully buried the remains of his dead wife, this time in a sand grave.

'It was around this tomb that the tribe went back to build the Mausoleum of Sayyida Nesima. From them came the saying: "There's nothing like a mother's love".'

Amm Gaber's tale came to an end and he withdrew his hand from the Tree of Wishes.

32

They were still waiting for the Omda. Digging continued in all the areas except the newly chosen spot on the mount of Sayyida Nesima. Some of the new workers waited, wondering whether they would be paid for the last couple of days. The general atmosphere was still tense, charged by the controversy. When the excavation members gathered for their tea-break near the mausoleum, the boy Mahmoud came running with a message. 'She wants you,' he gasped out of breath to Zohra, pointing to the beautiful Zineb.

The room was bare, its nakedness thousands of hands that pulled at Zohra's clothes. The patterns marked on the earthen floor by the swift motions of the palm-tree branch were still visible. A firm hand must have persisted, sparing only the grains that would not separate from the ground. It was very clean and there was an inviting, cool breeze. The room still smelled of damp earth. Soon she would hold her tight. She had a feeling the beautiful Zineb had a firm grip. She would get close, perhaps too close. The look in Zineb's eyes was naked. The pupils in those eyelashless eyes were distinct, no shadow cast on their gaze. That penetrating gaze which did not seem to come from Zineb's eyes, but from behind them. Her face was only a mask through which she was peeping. The kohl outline accentuated the effect. Her arms, voluptuous and dangerously smooth, would draw Zohra into the far corner of the room, where she would have no escape.

Zineb advanced towards the cupboard that stood in one corner of the room. Her henna-decorated feet made no sound. The floor was uneven and the cupboard sloped uncertainly. Zohra's imagination leapt before her. Zineb pulled at the door, which squeaked in complaint before it surrendered. It was big enough for two. Zohra saw Zineb's arm stretch towards her from within the cupboard, grab her hand and draw her in. The door shut, leaving the handle out of reach. In the pitch-dark within, one could only feel. Zohra's heart throbbed loudly and she wondered if Zineb could hear it.

But the cupboard was not empty. It was stuffed to the brim. The beautiful Zineb knew what she was looking for. She thrust her hand inside and brought out a very bright pink mass. It was one of the best towels her husband had sent from Libya. 'For you,' she declared. Zohra's whole body was under a strange influence and the colour might have shown in her cheeks. 'It's for you,' stressed Zineb. She had enough assertiveness for both of them. Zohra took the fluorescent towel. She could not say that she had no use for it, that in fact she would not have anywhere to put it without attracting everybody's attention.

Zineb reached for a sprinkler and shook it over Zohra's head. Zohra stepped backwards, making involuntary acknowledgements to the room, its cupboard, its earthen floor and its low ceiling. The beautiful Zineb followed her. On her lips, the suggestive smile of a mute person, the look still peeping from behind the mask, piercing through Zohra's. The harsh brightness of the courtyard came as a surprise. From a shady corner, a buffalo and a goat who seemed totally at home looked at Zohra with recognizant eyes. In a corner, a water jar stood awkwardly on sticks. The dancing figures painted all along the walls, echoing the figures on the house façade, were suddenly reassuring. She was no longer alone with the beautiful Zineb. But soon, Zohra felt she was bathing in the same light as Zineb, who stood close by, too close. Her scarf, rimmed with glittering flowers, was tied in such a way as to bring a cluster of them to the crown of her head. She gazed at Zohra while she fiddled playfully with the ends of her plaits below the waist. Zohra became aware of Zineb's almond-shaped hazel eyes, her honey skin and the odour of a beast of desire growing within her. Her crescent gold earrings flashed in the light. 'Nice earrings,' said Zohra. It was her way to interrupt the long moment.

The large number of colourful bracelets on Zineb's wrist tinkled as she reached to the earrings. 'They're yours,' she said and handed them over, insisting that Zohra take them.

Reluctant to take them, Zohra swore that she had an identical pair and quickened her steps towards the front door, tripping on the way as she mumbled: 'Thanks for everything!'

'I can teach you how to make bread,' came Zineb's invitation with a smile as she pointed to the shady corner in the courtyard. To Zohra, the clay oven looked as though it had its mouth wide open, hungry. Its skin was flaking. The clay oven must have been baked every time fire was lit within it to cook bread. Zohra looked away. The eyes of the figures on the walls seemed to be watching them.

A few steps led Zohra outside, back into the world. She walked, glancing back. The towel, a mass of the brightest pink, covered her head and heightened her feeling of nakedness. The villager who was building an extension to his house was throwing handfuls of mud on to the wall. But the busy scene could not distract her attention from Zineb's door. The look smouldered behind the mask. From those pale eyes, two shafts of light shone right through Zohra.

She joined the others who were at the end of their tea-break. There was a considerable distance between the top of the mount where Zohra stood and Zineb's house, yet Zineb's gaze seemed to reach and pull with invisible filaments. The whole scene of which Zohra was part was the beautiful Zineb's theatre, over which no curtain could be drawn. Zohra stood there, trying to protect her being with a thick wall. She felt sure that if the wall revealed a hole, however tiny, Zineb would get in!

The sky was clear and still. The Tree of Wishes stood patient. A bird perched on one of its branches, someone's deep purple wish curled around its neck. It was one-twenty when they finally heard the sound of Spaghetti's engine, bringing the Omda. Mahmoud called Zohra, who was at the cemetery site. She was needed for translation. It was amazing how this little boy related to everyone around. He had picked up a few English words already. But when Zohra's services were required, all he needed as a signal was her name.

The Omda sat down and the wooden chair disappeared behind him. He was rather upset to be dragged away from the feast. Contempt left his mouth and infiltrated every line in his face, even the lines of wisdom. He wore an orange embroidered scarf and an elegant white turban. They handed him a bowl of buffalo's milk. His face disappeared behind the bowl as he drank. Everybody waited. Men and boys rested their chins on the tip of their hoes. The Omda would not cancel the new site without suggesting a replacement, so they would be able to dig somewhere else. Surely he would not cut the source of their bread. If not, better to dig at the feet of the saint and let the saint turn them into stone than for hunger to turn them into dust. Workers waited for the verdict, so did the Professor, Mark and the site supervisors. Professor O'Brien was willing to let go of the auspicious site. There was none of the frustration he had felt two days earlier. The memories of his grandmother had untied the knot of his anger. Deep down, he was still dreaming of lustre wasters that might be buried in the bosom of the mount. He had, however, regretted revealing the mount's potential. But Mark was still adamant. The Blue Manuscript might be there. Although out of worry and to himself, Mark had started considering Mustapha's proposition.

The Omda lifted his head and cleared his throat. Everyone looked up. The length of his face was accentuated by the heavy earlobes that dangled from his turban. He caressed his bushy moustache. His scarf fell over his substantial belly and added to his presence. He leaned forward, his hands tightly closed over the silver handle of his cane.

The Omda had a glass eye and its fixed gaze was more intimidating than his good eye. 'The saint would have given us a sign,' he said when he finally spoke. 'It is perfectly within her power to give us a sign, had she wanted to prevent us from digging.' Many of the workers heaved a deep sigh. Some started intoning under their breath. Mark and the others looked at Zohra with questioning eyes as she translated. The boy Mahmoud watched the English words come from her mouth with a desire to catch them the way he did butterflies.

There were different reactions to the Omda's decision. Triumph from some, relief and defeat from a few, but acceptance from everybody.

Monia looked at Spaghetti. He was taller than ever. Having conquered an Omda, he was at least an inch nearer to the divine sky. She gazed at him with ardent admiration and felt the ache in her heart when he avoided her. They all respected the Omda for his clear decision, but the relief brought by this verdict lasted only for a moment. The words of the worker, from two days before, rang in everyone's head including the Professor's. 'Anyone who digs in the saint's mount will turn to stone.'

But Sabry took his hoe and held his arms high, ready to strike. Mouths went dry and tongues went stiff with apprehension. Everyone froze beyond the burning heat. Pores shed their tears, thick and swollen. Men and boys rested their tools. Bent over, it looked as if they had shrunk. Lips twitched in anticipation. The only sound was the buzzing of flies, their message amplified by the overwhelming silence. At this very moment, the whistle blew for the end of the day. The decision to dig was postponed.

The Omda was loaded with chickens, eggs and other gifts and everyone kissed his hand. He left to visit Jamal Bey before returning to the celebration marking the arrival of his grandson.

In the truck, they sat watching the site recede into the distance. To those with their backs to the front, it felt as though they were going backwards. They were travelling in time, looking at the past. The beautiful Zineb waved Zohra goodbye. Zohra could hardly swallow.

They were at the end of one day's work which had made them advance another step deeper into the past. Inside the swelling heat wave, a cool breeze was waiting impatiently for the late afternoon to emerge. The Professor was feeling a strange sense of relief and thought that it would be best to start digging at the new site the following day. That night, however, inexplicable apprehension reigned.

33

Breath was held back by the slowness of Sabry's motion, his own fear and unspoken anticipation. They stood at the foot of the mount, expecting it to move at any moment, to take a step backwards, away from the workman's hoe. It began its arc through the air. '*Bismillah*,' intoned Sabry as it pierced the earth. Sabry struck hard. He struck again, joined now by all the other workers.

'Hold it,' shouted Professor O'Brien, who seemed to have regained his authority within seconds. 'We have to outline the trench precisely first.' Just five metres by five metres. That was what all the fuss was about. But within the trench lay stories beyond its size.

Zohra stood at the top of the mount and watched the story unfold. There was not much to translate this morning. She noticed that the Professor's shirt was not bright green any more. Its colour had faded. In fact all their clothes had faded, both with the sun and with Hakima and Halima's earnest scrubbing. They were gradually blending with the bleached landscape. The Professor felt pleased that work had returned to normal. He was keeping an observant eye, making sure that every site was carefully penetrated. Once disturbed, there was no going back. He wanted to circulate and thought that if he had another supervisor he would be able to follow the progress in all the areas more easily. Mark stood wondering whether the new site would yield the Blue Manuscript and put an end to the anxiety over which he was beginning to have little control. It was strange for Zohra when Professor O'Brien asked her to supervise the new site of Sayyida Nesima. She felt privileged but she had no idea what she was supposed to do. 'Just separate the finds from each stratum according to the medium. Pottery in one bag, metal in another, and so on,' said the Professor.

Zohra had known nothing about archaeology, and the objects they excavated were a real discovery. As she sat there, supervising the workers, her reflections unfolded. She had already learnt a great deal but she found many of the theories of art history strange. Some were intriguing but not very convincing. Her own misconception that no figurative representation was permitted in Islamic art had been shattered and Dr Evans's interpretation of *horror vacui* was absurd. Surely it was an act of devotion, not of fear, to fill the spaces in a design with a potentially infinite pattern.

More pottery shards and some coins were unearthed. Zohra placed every find in the appropriate bag and added the corresponding label. Her gestures were weighed down by a fixed stare. Zineb stood at the door, as stiff as that tilted cupboard in her room, one hand toying with her plait. What were that placid look and that slow saffron-red smile about? What made them so disturbing and made Zohra feel so vulnerable? She realized, now that she had become the supervisor at Sayyida Nesima, she was to become the object of the beautiful Zineb's gaze constantly, not just at tea-breaks.

The workers removed layer after layer, as though scraping the inside of memory. They sieved the earth as though wanting to make the silent grains speak. The boy Mahmoud came running up the mount, holding one of those fluorescent pink towels. 'She gave you this,' he panted.

'For me?' Zohra was more shocked than curious. She struggled to unknot the corner of the towel, her fingers unsteady under Zineb's piercing gaze. Within the pink towel were Zineb's earrings, shining gold. And they came as a disconcerting surprise. The boy Mahmoud took to his heels. He wanted to see Donatella to tell her that the following day, Friday, he would come early to the school and take her to his mother, who would show her how to make bread.

There were a lot of visitors to the shrine that morning. Om Omran called Zohra and gave her a piece of grilled meat, fresh from that morning's sacrifice. Zohra sat and ate with the visitors, whose simplicity and generosity of spirit were overwhelming. As usual, the tent-maker sat leaning against the wall of the mausoleum. It suddenly occurred to Zohra that some of the bedspreads they had seen in the markets of Cairo, on sale mainly for tourists, were made in places like this. There was a huge gap between where they were made and their final home. She watched the tent-maker at work. He was telling stories with no sound, just pieces of cloth stitched by hand. Even without language, there was no mistaking the Egyptian spirit. He meticulously sewed the coloured pieces to fit the design already traced on the canvas base. The colours were only following their fate, and only when they were laid out did the pattern manifest itself.

On the façade of the mausoleum, the hands of blood were the colour of chocolate. That morning, flies swarmed in hand shapes on the newly marked prints. Different sounds echoed from within. They had brought a young woman with a baby. 'Her breasts are dry,' Zohra heard one of the women whisper. The woman's breasts swelled and the nipples hardened when the child cried in the adjacent room. The baby was brought to the mother, who held the tiny creature against her milky breast with deep faith in Sayyida Nesima. Joyful shrill cries emanated from the mausoleum. Om Omran watched them spiral upwards. The fresh whiteness of the shrine's dome glowed even brighter against an immense blue sky.

'Milk is like blood,' said Om Omran. 'If a woman suckles two children of opposite sexes, one her own and the other the child of another, those children become brother and sister and they can never marry . . . milk is like blood.' Zohra did not understand what she meant. The old woman turned to a visitor and advised: 'Go and tie a ribbon to the Tree of Wishes, our sacred tree will also help fulfil your heart's desires.' The visitor ripped a strip from her flowery scarf. Zohra followed her to the cemetery with her eyes. Amm Gaber was in his usual position and she wondered whether he was talking to the Tree of Wishes.

'Where's my share of the grill?' shouted Rayyes Ahmed as he ascended the hill.

'What did he say?' inquired Om Omran.

'He wants a piece of meat,' explained Zohra. The old woman laughed and held out the meat as Rayyes Ahmed approached.

'Thank you,' he said, then leaned to whisper to Zohra. 'The old woman is over a hundred years old you know, that's why she has her new milk-teeth.'

Zohra studied Om Omran's face, which was full of wrinkles. 'Its layers call for excavation,' she thought, smiling to herself. She was already thinking like an archaeologist after just one morning of supervising.

Rayyes Ahmed looked in the direction of Zineb, who stood at the door. 'Hasn't she got the face of the moon on the fourteenth night!' he marvelled. In a sweeping gesture, he threw his grey scarf over his shoulder. 'I'm getting married,' he whispered, looking suddenly younger, his twirled moustache darker.

'I thought you're already married,' retorted Zohra.

'Oh, she'll be my second wife. Don't tell anyone yet.' He talked in a daze, totally oblivious of the piece of meat in his hands, now covered in flies.

'She sent me her gold earrings,' Zohra told him.

'She what?!'

'She sent me her gold earrings as a present,' repeated Zohra, unravelling the pink towel.

Rayyes Ahmed caressed the earrings as though he was touching his beloved's ear lobes. 'How generous!' he exclaimed.

'I told her they are beautiful but I didn't expect her to give them to me. Such an expensive gift! What am I going to do?'

'Well, she'll never take them back,' said Rayyes Ahmed. 'A gift is a gift, and besides, you know, it's tradition in Wadi Hassoun that if a guest likes something, you must give it to them.'

'I wish I hadn't said anything.' said Zohra.

'What's done is done,' replied Rayyes Ahmed. 'Don't worry. That's her old dowry. I'll be buying her new earrings as well as adding gold to her anklets. A new dowry for when I marry her.'

Rayyes Ahmed smiled and gestured to the village wanderer, approaching the shrine. A loose end of his indigo turban dangled over his shoulder like a long strand of hair. 'The earth's his bed and the sky's his cover,' said Rayyes Ahmed. The wanderer came close. In spite of his many gallabiyas, he seemed impervious to the scorching heat of the day. Rayyes Ahmed gave him his piece of meat. The wanderer ate and dragged his feet, leaving a trail of dust. Soon he was far away, a moving speck on the horizon.

At a quarter past two, the supervisors, dirty and hot, were on their way to the school, wondering what had been prepared for lunch. Probably chicken as always, and again Alan would be frustrated with the vegetarian alternative, eggs.

They were pleasantly surprised when the apprentice cook brought out a crate of green-faced mangoes with deep red cheeks. The team gorged themselves. They sat on the steps, lethargic, drinking beer. 'The archaeologist's favourite drink,' Professor O'Brien had commented. Only Zohra was drinking real Coca-Cola, but then Zohra was no archaeologist. Every now and then they tried to remove the mango threads that clung fanatically to their teeth, the aroma of mangoes filling their nostrils.

'I wish we still had some chewing gum,' said Donatella.

Glasses smiled and flicked his straight hair. 'Some chocolate would be nice too,' he echoed.

Donatella glanced at him for a moment and wondered quietly to herself when the next batch of letters would arrive from Cairo.

The apprentice cook squatted on his usual stone. His face was washed with streams of tears. He was peeling onions again. From within the kitchen, hot as a furnace, the cook roared the apprentice's name and warned: 'Don't go on peeling until nothing is left as you always do!' But the apprentice grinned below his comb-moustache, his hand suppressing his laughter. And he continued peeling away, his tears mixing with his sweat, his eyes, nose and mouth brought even closer together in concentration.

Zohra could not remember what the effect of onion tears was like and wondered whether they brought any relief. 'The onions grown in the soil of this land certainly have a strong flavour and bring tears more easily,' she reflected. The apprentice removed the thick layers and reached the delicate muslin skin. He peeled it off smoothly, with the gentle hand of a lover, before he cut the onion into small pieces. Near him, the cat was chasing its tail and Donatella laughed as she watched.

Halima and Hakima were proud they had managed to finish the washing that morning before the water was cut off. The light breeze of the afternoon was pink; bed sheets filled one line, clothes were stretched on the other. The relationship between people went from formal to intimate. Kevin's striped shirt billowed next to Donatella's black bra, while the Professor's underpants danced gently next to them. Professor O'Brien, a respected academic and a revered scholar in London, had become a familiar companion. The relationship with him had begun to change from the first days of the excavation. Seeing him in the early hours of the morning came as a surprise, especially to his student Alan. The protective layers of formality had dropped. And the inevitable shifts, the outcome of living together in Wadi Hassoun, were creating a kind of family closeness.

Rayyes Ahmed came to inform them that it would not be long before water would run again. 'How does he know?' sneered the cook.

'Oh Rayyes Ahmed knows everything that goes on in the village,' said Halima.

'He does indeed!' confirmed Hakima. Rayyes Ahmed pretended not to hear.

Zohra asked if he could help with some shopping. She wanted to buy gold earrings like Zineb's. Rayyes Ahmed said he would happily take them to the right shop. Zohra translated for Donatella. 'The nearest town is two hours' drive,' added Rayyes Ahmed.

'Provided there are no nails on the road!' said Donatella.

Everyone knew that the beautiful Zineb had given her gold earrings, her capital, to Zohra as a present. Although the boy Mahmoud had not said anything to anyone, it had not been possible to keep the incident a secret.

Hakima and Halima started dispensing information with abundant meanness about the beautiful Zineb, their arms crossed under chests of drawers of bosoms. As they spoke to Zohra, Donatella understood nothing.

'Her husband left his mother with her and never came back, not even when his mother died.'

'He's seeking riches in Libya.'

'Before he left, he swore that he wouldn't return until he had enough money to buy an orchard like Jamel Bey's. That's where he used to work.'

'She's barren.'

'There'll be no children.'

'She's waiting,' said Hakima with a sigh, the implication of which was not clear.

'Yes,' thought Zohra, 'the beautiful Zineb is waiting, bursting at the seams with desire, like the cupboard in her room, bursting at the seams with the substitute goods that her husband has sent from Libya.'

The beautiful Zineb was also considered an outsider. Halima raised her crescent eyebrows. 'She has no family, you know,' she said, her eyebrows still arched for effect. 'She's not one of us.'

'She's a foreigner,' said Hakima. Zohra looked at her, intrigued.

'She comes from another village,' explained Halima.

'Her husband promised her the moon before he left.'

'That was over six years ago!'

'He sent her a lot of things from Libya though.'

'That was some time ago. It's been over four years now since she's heard from him.'

'Rayyes Ahmed's helping her get a divorce.'

'Such a kind man!'

'He also brought the electricity to her house!'

The ashy cat stretched in a little pool of sunshine. A few of its hairs shone golden. It was not totally grey after all. 'Catkoota,' Donatella called and the cat answered back with a happy mew and came to curl on her lap. Rayyes Ahmed called the boy Mahmoud and told him to go back to his mother. The boy wanted so much to accompany the party to the town, but Rayyes Ahmed insisted that he did as he was told, otherwise his mother would be cross yet again.

'*Bokra, bokra*,' announced the boy, gesturing to Donatella with a beaming smile.

'He's reminding you of your bread-making lesson with his mother tomorrow morning,' said Zohra.

In the central wall of the Coptic shop, behind the counter, there was a colourful picture of St George and the Dragon. The breeze from the fan in the ceiling was almost too cold. Zohra knew what she wanted or rather what she needed. She spoke Arabic, but a different language was required in the transaction. She left it to Rayyes Ahmed to haggle over the price. The Coptic shop sold all kinds of jewellery. Donatella and Zohra decided on having chains with their names in Arabic calligraphy as pendants. When he saw Donatella's enthusiastic exuberance, Glasses declared that he too would like a pendant. The shopkeeper provided a piece of paper on which Zohra wrote the names 'Donatella' and 'Hans' in Arabic. The man insisted that they pay for the gold chains in advance. 'Such foreign names will be of no use to me if they decide to change their minds,' he said. Donatella teased Glasses that his chain should have 'Glasses' not 'Hans'. Glasses laughed. Donatella's affectionate teasing filled him with hope.

It was very late when they got back to the village. Yet Rayyes Ahmed insisted that they go to see the beautiful Zineb. In the little courtyard, the naked bulb had a harsh, awakening effect. Zohra presented Zineb with the identical earrings she had bought. Rayyes Ahmed whispered in Zineb's ear, behind Zohra's back. He was begging his impervious beloved to leave the door open for him that night. He would come back after accompanying Zohra, and the others waiting in the car, to the school. But the beautiful Zineb ignored him. She was enjoying Zohra's closeness as she adjusted the earrings for her. Her breasts, each like a full moon, brushed against Zohra's flat chest. She stared at Rayyes Ahmed with those eyes that had no lashes, no shadow of doubt cast on their gaze. And on her lips, she had that smile which revealed nothing more than the beautiful dimples in her cheeks. It was almost early morning when they left Zineb's house.

The moon-shaped loaf rose and fell. Donatella was learning how to make the traditional bread she liked so much. In the clay oven, the tongues of fire spread upwards and retreated before they spread upwards again. The boy came close to the fire and his mother rebuked him. Donatella was not worried about burning her hands. 'You can learn how to make this bread in no time, *inshallah*,' Mahmoud's mother gesticulated to her.

Donatella did not understand a thing, but laughed and repeated: '*Shukran, shukran.*' By now all the members of the excavation had learnt how to say 'Thank you'.

'*Esh-shukru lillah*,' Thanks be to God, answered Mahmoud's mother. The large loaf came out from the oven, very thin but risen. Grains of clay clung to its back. It was unavoidable. They were eating clay with bread. The earth of the place was finding its way inside them.

34

'It looks fine,' Zohra reassured Donatella, who kept brushing her blonde hair, trying to hide the dark roots without success. The three women were taking their time beautifying themselves. Donatella had given Monia a hand with her rollers, and now Monia was proud of her elegant curls. Zohra noticed that both Monia and Donatella had brushed their hair in a similar way. 'Bonds have grown in this enclosed world,' she thought with an inexplicable concern.

In the courtyard, the others waited for them. Mrs O'Brien adjusted her husband's tie. 'Daaaaaarling, it's not straight . . .' But soon after she finished tightening it, the Professor eased his collar and took a deep breath. Professor O'Brien was not keen on weddings but he wanted to fulfil his duty towards the locals. Alan stood to the side, perfumed, his hair glistening. He said to Glasses that he had used Sellotape at the back of his neck to guarantee a straight line when cutting his own hair and that was his tip to anyone who lived alone. Glasses acquiesced with half a smile and went on reading his book. He read quickly, turning each page eagerly as though he was removing a layer that concealed the truth from him.

Mark was filled with a feeling of anticipation. He was curious about the wedding. 'I presume there won't be any alcohol at this wedding?' he asked.

'I very much doubt it!' was the Professor's ironic reply.

'Marriage,' declared Alan unexpectedly, 'a few months of passion and a lifetime of ashes!'

Mark burst out laughing. 'Marry in haste, repent at leisure!' he commented before taking a generous gulp of the beer he had brought from the laboratory.

'How cynical!' remarked Mrs O'Brien.

'When will we make the promised trip to the desert?' Alan changed the subject.

They looked at Rayyes Ahmed, who did not understand the question. There was no one to translate.

Monia, Donatella and Zohra finally emerged into the courtyard. 'Three brides!' beamed Rayyes Ahmed. Hakima took a good look at Monia in the full glory of her dress and started her wishful invocations. Monia giggled and looked at Spaghetti, who avoided her gaze and dangled the keys to his portable bank. He behaved as if he owned it. Monia giggled again. The cook sent a stare of disapproval in her direction.

Glasses thought that Zohra looked different. She had kohl on her eyes and her lips were saffron-red with the bark that Halima and Hakima had brought.

'The earrings suit you,' he said warmly.

Zohra smiled and tilted her head shyly. 'Really? Thanks!'

Donatella stared at Zohra. 'It's true,' she thought, 'the gold earrings have brought some life to that dull brown hair, but plain is plain.' Zohra returned Donatella's stare.

Monia glanced at the gold earrings, the traditional wedding dowry in the village, then glanced in Spaghetti's direction, but he busied himself lighting a cigarette.

Rayyes Ahmed had brought them presents of scarves. He seemed particularly happy to take them to his nephew's wedding. His twirled moustache had a different shine, as though he had dipped its two halves in oil before moulding them into crescents. The four women liked their white scarves, sprinkled with embroidered flowers also in white, and wore them around their shoulders.

'*Yalla bina*,' urged Rayyes Ahmed, he did not want them to be late.

'Are you coming as well?' he teased the boy Mahmoud, who sat on the steps. He had been helping in the shard garden all afternoon as usual, after giving Glasses his Arabic lesson.

'Of course he is coming! We don't go anywhere without him!' said Donatella in response to Zohra's translation.

Everyone was in a jolly mood. They were ready to go when the phone rang. The corroded phone rang very rarely. It was Mustapha's voice accompanied by a lot of crackling. Then the line went dead. Mark put the receiver down, looking disappointed. His worry about not finding the Blue Manuscript had been increasing in the last few days. Like gods of some kind, the sponsors were present, absent. He could feel their pressure from thousands of miles away.

'He's not going to ring again,' said Rayyes Ahmed, 'he won't be able to get through.' To Rayyes Ahmed's disappointment, Mark decided not to go to the wedding, preferring to wait for Mustapha's call. So he and the guard were left behind. They had forgotten Kodama San was in the darkroom, developing photographs.

As she crossed the courtyard, Zohra heard a singing voice, that voice she had heard the first night in Wadi Hassoun and which had never left her. By the time she turned back to ask whose it was, there was no singing to be heard. Zohra stood perplexed. The voice was not in the courtyard. It was within her. Unexpectedly, Kodama San emerged from his darkroom in a light-grey suit, complete with bow tie, ready to go. '*Yalla bina,*' urged Rayyes Ahmed again as he threw his white silk scarf, which matched his turban, over his shoulder and walked towards the gate, proud of his guests.

They reached Rayyes Ahmed's house, where the celebration was being held. The nephew was marrying the cousin. On the façade of the mud-brick house hung green flags, each decorated with a crescent and three stars. It was a large house and they had to cross a courtyard full of curious eyes before they were taken into a separate room to eat. They were surprised by the golden chairs with flowery red velvet. The chairs were still covered with transparent plastic and made an embarrassing noise when they sat down. The women must have been busy with the food preparations since dawn. The number of dishes alone was enough to make them feel full. But to Alan's dismay, every dish was made with some kind of meat. Meat was a measure of a host's generosity. Rayyes Ahmed urged his guests to eat. By now, they were used to people constantly giving them food. This was the way people expressed their love.

Donatella insisted on a group photograph. Actually she did not have to insist. They were all very happy to pose. They stood or knelt in front of the wall where Rayyes Ahmed's primary school certificate was displayed. Rayyes Ahmed's wife adjusted the frilled collar of her dress. She was a large woman and Rayyes Ahmed was so slim. One thing was sure, he could never give her a full hug. And all wore their best smiles, ready for the click. But then Rayyes Ahmed intervened. 'Just a moment!' he said, reaching for a large wedding photograph of one of his brothers who lived in the Gulf. Rayyes Ahmed knelt in the front row and held the photograph so that the couple could be included in this memorable occasion.

After the meal, Rayyes Ahmed and his wife insisted on showing them around the house. The next room was bare except for a few triangular mirrors on the wall, between openwork niches and a large television which stood as the centrepiece. Rayyes Ahmed's wife switched it on, flicking to all the channels with great pride. The mud-brick room was invaded by the outside world. Scenes from an American soap appeared on the screen and other realities that were shocking fiction in the context. She kept flicking until the screen filled with incandescent dots. But she did not seem bothered by the interference. Then they were shown the room where the couple would be spending the night. The groom's mother had decorated it with bright colours and made it look joyful. 'How nice,' Monia congratulated her.

'There's nothing like a mother's love,' commented one of the relatives.

They went back to the courtyard, which was teeming with guests, women and children – the men sat separately outside as convention dictated. As privileged guests, the team were allowed to move freely in both the men's and women's quarters. The bride was sitting on a platform, high enough for everyone to admire her beauty and her costume, while everyone else sat on the mat-covered floor. Women sang and danced. Monia joined in and revealed herself to be as good as a professional dancer. Because of her height, she stood out among all the women. Her satin dress shimmered as she turned her hips, accentuated by the scarf, Rayyes Ahmed's gift. Her teeth gleamed against her dark skin every time she smiled and looked discreetly in the team's direction. Monia appeared to be in control of every muscle in her body but she was certainly not in control of her heart. Spaghetti was ignoring her and her heart felt broken. The Professor and his wife, and Alan too, joined in with the clapping. As he watched the women dance, and Monia flash her large eyes, the Professor remembered his carnal encounter with that stranger as a student in the ruins of Fatimid Cairo. For a moment he was self-conscious, perhaps worried that his wife would discover his buried secret. He reached for his bottle of Mirinda and sucked at the straw. Spaghetti tapped on his knees and concentrated on his cigarette. But none of Monia's subtle moves escaped him. Zohra insisted that she did not know how to dance, in spite of everybody's encouragements. The translator always wanted to pass unnoticed, to remain neutral; her mousy hair, her bland face, her small voice, all helped. But tonight, the team competed with the bride as the focus of everyone's attention. This was the first time they had been invited to a wedding in the village and they all felt they were sharing in the locals' happiness. Zohra, however, was disturbed by the thought that her own wedding might never take place because she would not compromise by settling only for one side of herself.

Donatella joined in the dance and the women accompanied her with clapping and ululation. She tied the embroidered scarf around her hips, following Monia, and discovered that it was a helpful device. The infectious rhythm of the music carried everyone beyond their differences. Glasses watched, mesmerized by the contours of Donatella's body, and he wondered again whether he would be able to ask her to stay and travel with him once the excavation season had come to an end. And Donatella danced, controlling every move and its effect on Glasses, without a sign that she was doing so.

They watched the bridegroom's mother when she performed the ritual of throwing salt into the nuptial room – salt against the jinn. As she scattered the handfuls of salt, she called out: 'If you are in the body move to the bones, if you are in the bones move to the hair, if you are in the hair move to the air.' She closed the door on the bride and bridegroom and let out a piercing ululation.

At the school, Mark was still waiting for Mustapha to call. He drank beer in the hope of drowning his sorrows, but with every bottle he only managed to whet his appetite for the next. In the silence of the night, the waiting fuelled his worries. They had been digging for months now. Unearthing the buried volume of the Blue Manuscript was starting to look like a cry for the moon.

35

Ibn al-Warraq had been working for hours, as he had every day for years now. But immersed in his work, the Calligrapher's only sense of time was eternity. His hand moved in a musical rhythm, its steadiness drawing from an extraordinary inner calmness and silent serenity, the rhythm shaping the thickness, the thinness of the line, giving it form. The point was extending, extending, becoming a letter. Like a flute, the musical instrument of breath, the pen was made of reed. 'This is the pen that will be at my side when I am laid to rest after my last breath,' the Calligrapher reflected peacefully. With this stiff plant stem, he traced the simple geometric shapes of the letters gracefully. This was pure Kufic script, before leaves and flowers had sprung from it for decorative effect.

The imprint of a deeply rooted practice was passed on through the Calligrapher's hand. But in this manuscript, something was different. Ibn al-Warraq went beyond the tradition of copying the sacred text. He allowed his hand and mind to find their own direction. He aspired to a dynamic perfection. Sometimes, his hand trembled almost imperceptibly, marking the personal touch that would make each page unique. He worked in silence. His contemplation and abstinence from speech were being channelled into the letters. He wrote. There was a constant repetition of the text in his heart. The words were being shaped by his silent recital.

He grew up with the advice of his father: 'Single-minded practice is the way to seek perfection and letters should be copied over and over again. A perpetual transformation, in search of purification and attainment of the essence.'

'It is important to stay focused,' his father had stressed. 'A slight divergence can lead one a long way astray!'

Ibn al-Warraq had learned how to sit, how to behave, how to live in order to trace the Arabic letters properly. His whole life revolved around those letters.

On the oblong page, he extended the stroke of the letter, reaching outward with an awareness of an eternal present, in which his being and inner stillness were at work. A muscular control of rhythm. The parchment was dense yet fine, strong yet smooth, just as he had wanted it, so that there would be no impediment to the sweep of the pen. 'A man's calligraphy and his character are interconnected. Cracks in his character will lead to the loss of his spirit. Everyone has two angels sitting on his shoulders recording his deeds and thoughts, the one on the right shoulder records the good deeds and the one on the left the bad,' his father would reiterate while supervising him, insisting on a slow and dignified pace. Ibn al-Warraq dipped his pen in the agate inkwell, itself decorated with a Quranic inscription: '*Qul law kana albahru midadan likalimati rabbee lanafida albahru qabla an tanfada kalimatu rabbee walaw ji'na bimithlihi madadan*', If the ocean were ink to write out the words of God, the ocean would be exhausted sooner than would the words even if we added another ocean like it.

The visual form of the manuscript which had already taken shape in his mind was being manifested through his hands. From the well of the inkpot, from the sole and infinite substance of silent ink, the letters were emerging, individual beings of changing form, drawn out with an immaculate precision. From nothingness, the letters grew, bringing light to the dark blue pages. The strokes of the pen were immortalizing the word in a space with a dramatic duality, created by a palette distilled to two colours only, a harmony of contrasts. A manuscript that held the secret darkness of the night and the luminous light of the sun. The sacred text spoke of itself as radiant with light. For the Calligrapher, gold, however precious a material, was nothing but light. Gold brought light to the silent night of indigo. 'Oh Creator of all things,' Ibn al-Warraq had prayed, 'take your light from these eyes and spread it on the page, let the letters radiate with divine light.'

And for him, gold was the most abstract of all colours. Gold leaf had been powdered to mix the ink. The blue and its impenetrable depth came from the gold-veined precious stone of lapis lazuli. Ground into the finest dust, it had been used to dye the vellum. A deep tone extracted from the blue stone. Stone-silent. It was of the best quality, brought from the depths of the Afghan mountains.

The Calligrapher had been applying himself to his task for years. He worked alone, with a sense of remoteness from the rest of the world. Rarely did his apprentice help him. And al-Muizz's mother had not checked on him for some time.

Sun and moon regulated his hours of work. His breathing had grown more laboured. His life was running out. It would not matter how many suns had risen and how many moons had set by the time he finished tracing the whole of the text. As long as he accomplished it before he passed away. Only when he had completed the last letter would he be able to rest. He looked at his pen, the tip bright with golden ink, awash in light. As he gazed at it, he thought of his wish to be buried in the desert, this pen buried with him. He dipped the pen into the inkwell, a small container from which infinite letters were to emerge.

Ibn al-Warraq looked intently at one page. As he finished writing the words, the letters seemed to acquire a life of their own in addition to their meaning. The joy of having accomplished his objective of structural potency and beautiful elegance filled his being. He had sought the aesthetic balance of the words on the page. The vertical strokes of the letters were short. The horizontal lines emphasized the page's horizontality. Repeated words were of diverse lengths, some very compact, others legato. Some words were segmented, unconventionally, to accommodate a wholeness of design. At times, legibility was surrendered to visual rhythm. He hoped that the beauty of the manuscript, the space he had created within these pages, would express the sacredness of the text.

For Ibn al-Warraq, Arabic calligraphy was in essence an art of movement. With the letters he created patterns, a nonconformist ordering of space. He paused to gaze at the musical rhythm of the traced letters. Calligraphy was not simply writing. Around every word an empty space echoed its silence with the grace of his hand and the rhythm of his own pulse. But he knew that the passion channelled into this manuscript was beyond his ephemeral life.

When still young and under the supervision of his father, he wrote his letters with brown ink on white pages. His father had told him: 'One day you will copy the sacred text in your way. You will write your manuscript and it will be unique. I don't know how. You must dream with honesty, that's all . . .' Ibn al-Warraq knew that dreaming was not enough but he trusted his father and later, much later, he understood what he meant. Next to the diligent study of tradition, creative transformation was essential. Ibn al-Warraq found his own style in the compositional structure of characters. He aspired to achieve a state of balance between extremes, and inspiration came. He saw the letters shine in a dark night. He knew then that he could start working on his manuscript. His vellum would be the night and his letters would bring light to it. Somehow, the impossible combination would express the sacred.

Ibn al-Warraq reflected on the silent power of beauty. A sacred immensity opened within the limited space of the page, written in gold on blue vellum, in elongated, unvocalized Kufic script. The diacritical marks remained in the swollen tear of ink at the tip of the pen, never shed. They remained in the invisible world and words became silent. The diacritical marks were omitted deliberately. The line of letters went on in its continuous search. Letters transmitted by the sweeps of the pen. The elongation of their being, not evoking sound but in themselves a vision of silence. In the infinite depth of the night blue, the manuscript a crescendo of silence. The dark blue, a sea of depth, a night that called for immersion, a space of contemplation. A deep blue silence which evoked *Azal*, eternity without beginning. A stillness removed from the clamour of acoustics. Silence of the sacred and the power of the written word manifest. He took a deep breath. 'How strange,' he thought, 'that someone who so deeply longs for silence expresses it through this arrangement of words on the page.'

The pages completed so far were spread around him like autumn leaves. Ibn al-Warraq studied them.

'Arabic in its sublime form speaking even to those who do not speak it, opening finer perception beyond language. The experience of silence in its wholeness. To speak without a need for grammar. When the line is mute, its voice is deeper than the letters and those whose life cannot be expressed by literature can relate to it. The silence of this manuscript is the silence of the whole world. Silence like that imposed by an immense landscape that lifts our being into a state of grace, purifying it ... and to which human beings of any race, creed or religion can relate. Ineffable. A sacredness for all. A sacredness for all.'

He arranged the pages carefully together, positioned the lion paper-weight to guard the pile, and thought of the assembling of the loose pages. The binding of a manuscript was a very significant occasion. He so much longed for all those pages to be joined for ever. There was still a great deal of work to be done. His asthma was worsening. Would he complete the two volumes of the manuscript? Or would his ephemeral body fail him? Would the shell break and spill the meaning? He took a deep breath. An attack took hold of him, throwing him into convulsions. It did not release him for some time.

36

Mattocks, shovels, hoes and spades had not known rest for some months now. Men dug continuously. Covered in dust, their feet looked as though they had been modelled in clay. Zohra felt that if it were to rain, the workers' feet would melt and mix with the earth. Rain? What rain? The scorching sun highlighted the absurdity of the thought. She glanced at the searing sky. 'It's difficult to imagine now,' she thought, 'that the sky holds the rain!'

The burning sun came to bake the mud village every day. Now, the site supervisors looked almost as brown as the locals. Even Mrs O'Brien's face had acquired a dark layer. Yet, at another level, as time passed, people's masks had started to drop.

The rhythm of the work-chain was marked by chanting. The basket of rubble passed from shoulder to shoulder, until emptied on the growing mound. Sabry sieved every load. He grew to recognize the pieces that were sought after, old objects which he accepted were valuable, without knowing why.

Professor O'Brien had been advised by Monia to have every bit of the rubble sieved. 'You never know,' she had stressed, 'one can easily overlook things such as beads and even coins.' The site supervisors thought it was rather tedious, but the Professor was conscious of how important it was to keep an archaeology inspector satisfied. Although Monia was away, visiting her family, he still made sure the workers followed her instructions.

'All I want,' said the Professor, 'is a lustre waster, then I can prove that lustre-painted pottery was produced here. I am convinced that sooner or later we will find one.' Zohra tried to describe to the workers as best she could, never having seen one herself, what a waster would look like.

'We'll find it, Professor!' said Alan. He turned to Sabry with a large lustre pottery shard in his hand, 'It would look like this . . . but ruined, something that would have been thrown away, because it was damaged during firing, you see . . .' Zohra translated and was surprised to find that Sabry had already understood.

'We'll find it *inshallah, bi-iznillah,*' he reiterated.

Alan smiled and thought to himself: 'We're trying to find something that was thrown away because it was damaged and for us it's very important!' Alan was eager to find a waster for his Professor.

Sabry laughed innocently as he watched the grains of earth separate and rush hurriedly through the tiny holes. He put the sieve to rest on his lap, one leg folded, one stretched amidst the rubble. Several heaps had accumulated during the morning. He adjusted the cap on his head before reaching for the jug which the guard's daughter-in-law had brought and took a gulp. With his wet tongue, he drew a distinct outline of his lips and reached for his cigarettes. There was something magical about all this sieving, a kind of separation between earth and time. A deep turquoise peeped through the grey mass. The ceramic shard was as large as his palm. Sabry spat and wiped the granulated surface with the hem of his sleeve. The colour bloomed. He had seen that colour earlier, a number of similar shards had been found that same morning. He turned it over and looked at the stroke painted in black. Then he rotated it. 'It might fit with the other pieces,' he thought. 'Mahmoud,' he called the boy who was playing with some children. Mahmoud grabbed the shard, ran up the mount and handed it to Zohra.

Over the sound of earth shaking in the sieve and the workers' humming, came Zohra's enthusiastic reaction: 'It fits!' She waved to Sabry. Quiet joy filled his heart. He flicked off half of the cigarette which had turned into ash and took a drag, watching with narrowed eyes the grains of ash disintegrate, dance a little in the air and embrace the earth. Then he glanced at the children playing nearby.

'A butterfly!' screamed Mahmoud. A throng of children gathered around it, their eyes wide open. They were mesmerized by its bright colours and its size. They tiptoed in pursuit until they caught it.

'Look at its wing,' marvelled one boy. The butterfly's colours came off, so he dropped it and wiped his orange and purple fingers on his gallabiya.

'Look at this!' cried another child, holding the butterfly between index finger and thumb.

'That's its head,' shouted another.

And it went on, until a puzzled child cried: 'Where is the butterfly?!'

Broken fragments of wing fluttered in the dust at their feet. Mahmoud stood silent, in a state of shock. Sabry croaked with dry laughter and picked up his sieve.

The workers dug. Their vertical journey was methodically planned. It proceeded in layers. 'What if we dug until there was no ground to dig into? What would there be?' asked a teenage worker.

'You're not here to talk!' shouted Rayyes Ahmed. '*Yallah, yallah,*' he urged as he strode past the site. His bamboo stick flexed to accommodate his posture, his moony face fixed on his beloved's door. Rayyes Ahmed walked with his head held high, a dignified look, his chest inflated with a sigh so long it could not be drawn.

The digging raised raging swirls of dust. Zohra felt that by the end of the season dust would penetrate into her very soul and permeate her being. Specks danced in the air and settled, forming a thin screen on everything. She was filthy. Zohra was used to clean and formal circumstances, working mainly in Switzerland or America. This was the first time she had taken a job in such an environment. The other excavation members, too, felt stripped of the comforts of their existence.

The workers had just finished removing yet another layer at the site, but what they were looking for was resting under many layers. The earth displayed some of its many colours, sometimes red, sometimes grey, sometimes brown, sometimes a warm ochre. The little girls danced in front of their home. They twirled and twisted in a frenzied performance, a shyness in the daring way their bodies moved. '*Yallah, yallah, yallah,*' pressed one who stood to the side, clapping rhythmically. Zohra watched, smiling. Both the Professor and Alan watched as well.

From a distance, Donatella too was trying to follow the girls' performance. Mark hardly noticed it. He was buried under the rubble of his worries. The pressure from the sponsors of the excavation was mounting, fuelled by his own burning ambition. The cemetery site was yielding a lot of paper but nothing related to the Blue Manuscript. The Professor's comments echoed in his thoughts. 'Saladin burnt books, the renowned libraries of the Fatimids. Now, we're willing to comb the earth for one manuscript.' So much digging had not taken them closer to the key find. Among his fragmented thoughts came a flash of London, where time was money.

He stretched his arms and looked at his dirty hands. The dry earth had cracked, echoing the branching lines of his palms. A desire to decipher the mysteries of the future crept over him. He shuddered. What was it about the unknown that was so frightening? The muscles in his legs tightened and flinched, driving him down, all the way down to Sabry. 'Water, water please!' cried Mark, pointing to the jug. Sabry poured the languid water, exposing the nakedness of Mark's hands.

'*Mayya, mayya*, water, water,' said the old man with a knowing smirk. 'You can't bear dirt, mister; it's only earth, mother earth!' Mark did not understand Sabry's comment. He sneezed then smiled, lifting a whitened lip on nervous teeth.

'*Ma – ya, ma–ya*,' he repeated.

'*Mayya, mayya*,' stressed Sabry and shook hands with Mark. They had just crossed boundaries with a word and for a moment, Mark almost felt comfortable with it.

Rayyes Ahmed's whistle announced the tea-break and they headed for the mount. Om Omran bent over her spinning wheel, drew out the wool, winding on. Her flaming hair contrasted with the whiteness of the slub. In the heat, it was difficult to imagine the need for wool. Everyone knew, however, that the winters were bitterly cold in Wadi Hassoun and that Om Omran's blanket would be most welcome. A woman sat on the ground, breast-feeding her baby. The air filled with the rich smell of mangoes as the guard's daughter-in-law came with an armful that her husband had brought from Jamel Bey's orchard. He had taken the opportunity to profit from one of Jamel Bey's regular trips to Cairo. She asked whether the team would honour the wedding of her cousin by their presence. 'I'll be very happy to take you,' said Rayyes Ahmed before he walked towards the door upon which his eyes were always riveted. His passion was ripening.

'It's a distant cousin of mine. She is marrying old,' said the guard's daughter-in-law. Zohra translated.

'Old!' exclaimed Donatella. 'How old is she?'

'Nineteen,' replied the guard's daughter-in-law. 'But we thank the Tree of Wishes. Who would have said that cousin Ibrahim would come back from Libya and marry her! He was away for eleven years.' As she translated, Zohra thought Donatella looked forlorn. A conversation about age followed. Mark was shocked when he realized that Sabry was only forty-eight years old, the same age as himself. He acted as though life was in front of him while Sabry behaved as though life was behind him.

The team needed translation constantly. Listening to conversations in Arabic was sometimes frustrating for those who could not understand. Glasses, however, who had come to visit the site that day, was more curious than anything else. He was able to decipher some Arabic words thanks to his young master, and was asking Zohra about a particular word when Donatella sent a stern look in his direction.

'Of course, women grow old while men get more distinguished,' Donatella heard Zohra say to Glasses. 'That's why a woman should never bother with a younger man,' added Zohra. Glasses laughed.

'Not quite!' said Donatella. In the bright sunshine, the colour of her eyes disappeared. 'Only a cynic would agree with that.' Zohra saw the thorny words as green. They reeked with jealousy. Perhaps the words were yellow and the container was blue but the meaning was green. That was more like it! She dismissed the thought. Was she going mad? Donatella was starting to dislike needing Zohra for translation.

The guard's daughter-in-law talked to Zohra. Her hand rested on her seven-months-pregnant belly as she sought information about everyone with such daring forwardness, as though there were no boundaries between people. She was stunned that Zohra was in her mid-thirties and not married. Her face beamed with curiosity. All of a sudden she giggled. Her attention had been taken elsewhere, in the direction of the site guard. Haj Salem, her father-in-law, was fast asleep against the wall of the mausoleum. 'The Haj looks like a corpse!' she commented as she slapped the back of her hands and laughed wholeheartedly. The hardship of life in the village was evident. Yet people's faces glowed with optimism. 'I'd better go and look after those rascals!' she added before she waddled towards her house to claim the cooking pot from her children, who were still singing and dancing.

Zohra glanced in the direction of the beautiful Zineb, who seemed to be listening to Rayyes Ahmed. Zohra's indiscreet nature meant that she had to tell Donatella and the others about Rayyes Ahmed's plans. 'Rayyes Ahmed told me his dowry to Zineb will also be the traditional pair of crescent gold earrings. He boasted that more gold will be added to her anklets, claiming it would bring even more poise and pride to her walk!' Zohra was surprised by her own nervous laughter.

'How romantic,' said Donatella with dreaming eyes.

'What's romantic about a second wife?' Zohra was indignant.

Just at that moment, cries reached them from afar. Flowing robes were moving in a slow line. At the head, two people carried a stretcher on their shoulders. It was a funeral. They recognized only the village wanderer who was walking behind, a strip dangling from his indigo turban. The mourners crossing on the other side seemed far away. Death was remote. 'The poor man died leaving five young children!' said Rayyes Ahmed, out of breath. He had just run up the hill.

The wailing was getting closer. A turban hanging from a pole meant that the deceased was a man. Men were taking turns to shoulder the bier. 'One gains great merit from carrying the bier,' said Rayyes Ahmed to Zohra.

Om Omran adjusted her black headgear and murmured: 'In death, all people are equal. A hundred years from now we'll all have returned to the belly of our mother earth. To the mud.' No one could hear what she was saying and no one would have wanted to. No one liked to encounter death, not even in speech, but the old woman was well acquainted with it. She had been the washer of the dead for thirty years, her profession only brought to an end by old age, and for more than thirty years the dead had visited her regularly in her sleep.

'We should get on,' said the Professor, urging everyone to resume work.

In the cemetery, the mourners came close to Donatella. The tomb they dug for the new arrival was not unlike the trenches of the excavation. Zohra watched from afar. The cemetery seemed populated with anonymous figures. For the first time she thought about the dead lying peacefully and the hectic activity nearby. The proximity between living and dead, part of the reality of the village, was very tangible, as a villager was digging the grave, and an excavation worker a trench. The body, wrapped in no more than a simple piece of white cotton, was lowered into the hole. Like most people in the village, the man was poor. Even if he had been rich, he would still have been buried with an identical piece of cloth, like all Muslims. The tomb was filled. The land to which man belonged but which never belonged to anyone was his final resting place. The mourners retreated, their long gallabiyas brushing the ground in sorrow. A life extinguished.

Professor O'Brien was humming his favourite Puccini while he outlined a new trench after discarding one as a useless cesspit. Everyone was intrigued and wondered how the Professor had reached his decision. After all, there was no sign of what past was buried under their feet. It was obvious that what was not apparent did not necessarily not exist. They also wondered how he could bear those thick corduroy trousers in such heat.

From the site of Sayyida Nesima, where she was supervising the digging, Zohra could discern the figure of Amm Gaber in his usual place, next to the Tree of Wishes. He seemed particularly remote. Even in her visits to the cemetery site, she was never able to approach him. Something kept him far away. Now, it felt as though the figure had never stirred from that dark corner where she had seen him the first night in the school. She wondered without words why that untranslatable emotion kept coming back.

The work had started to feel as monotonous as the surrounding landscape. Time was taking time. Nothing worthwhile had been unearthed in hours. The sun invaded the surroundings, swallowing every single shadow. There was still another hour to go. A white goat watched the digging. Girls walked by with large jars of water from the river. A little girl ran wildly. She had hair like hay; either it had not been brushed for some time or this was its nature. She wore a glowing green dress with orange flowers. Colourful dresses brightened the grey, barren landscape.

Kodama San handled the large portfolio and the tripod as though they were a feather, although he was not a large man. The boy Mahmoud followed him with the tape measure. He never understood what Kodama San was doing when he looked into his theodolite, nor what made him act immediately afterwards. But the child never asked. The theodolite, that thing, like many other things, including the team itself, were all from the other world. The boy jumped in his playful manner and disappeared into the trench. Kodama San adjusted his hat and requested that the boy be still.

'What you mean?' asked Mahmoud, a steady hand holding the tape measure against the edge of the trench. Kodama San did not answer but the boy stood motionless. They had grown used to working together.

Zohra noticed the beautiful Zineb beckoning Mahmoud. 'She probably needs you for an errand,' she said. 'Go and see her.' Zohra removed her sunglasses and stared into the overwhelming brightness until it became dark and everything around flattened. The lissom boy ran down in a straight line, at full speed. She watched his figure recede. A trail of dust followed him as he ran. He was at Zineb's door for a split second before he suddenly took a turning around a sharp corner and disappeared. It was as if she had imagined it all. It was so sudden. Now he was, now he was not.

The sun stood still. It seemed to have reached its peak and would not budge. The men continued to dig, their gestures sluggish, their sweat running in thick drops. But they still did their work conscientiously. They handed over every small thing they found. If the supervisor's face revealed satisfaction, they too felt pleased. The site supervisors too were playing their part and had to remain steadfast. The past was in a seminal state, waiting to be discovered. A civilization in its glory lay buried under their feet. They were treading on it. And they were all expecting something special in the finds from the site of Sayyida Nesima.

37

The Tree of Wishes was changing. Renewal regulated its life but it remained a faithful listener to Amm Gaber. The digging progressed continuously into a remote time. Objects emerged, speaking a language that had to be deciphered. The excavation was unfolding history. It was not only possible to measure distance with time, but also to measure time with distance, removing layers to reach back centuries. The rays of sun pressed hard and with confrontation, squeezing the moisture from earth in no time, a part of earth that had not breathed nor seen the sun for hundreds of years.

'It's as hot as hell!' spluttered Rayyes Ahmed as he splashed water on his face. Everyone at the site felt a great thirst, made worse by the dust and the parched landscape. Mustapha, who had arrived the night before, was clearly burning. Sweat trickled from his armpits but he showed no sign of discomfort, although he did admit that it was much hotter than Cairo.

Water cascaded down Alan's throat like a refreshing spring and he felt its soothing effect like the thrill of a first-time experience. Mark waited for his turn eagerly. The plastic bottles of mineral water were undrinkable by this time of the day. They resorted to the water from the river, kept in the earthenware jug, brought by the guard's daughter-in-law. They had stepped outside the boundaries of their precautions.

'Guess which animal enjoys drinking most?' Alan asked Mark unexpectedly as he passed the jug to Zohra.

'Humans?' was Mark's guess.

'No, which *animal*.'

'Man is an animal.'

'Come on . . . I mean animal!'

'OK! Cow?'

Mark thought intently but was unable to focus on anything except the water jug.

'OK,' said Alan with a smile of satisfaction. 'You're not going to guess. What's the most enjoyable part of drinking? Not when it reaches your stomach, when it's coming down your throat, right?' The others looked puzzled. 'So the animal which enjoys drinking the most is the giraffe.' Alan burst with laughter. Zohra had to translate for Rayyes Ahmed. By the time it reached the others, it was not funny. Zohra thought her timing was probably wrong.

Kodama San was flying his kite. The boy Mahmoud followed his every move. The kite was distant and silent and yet it brought images close and made the site speak to the archaeologists in a different way. The kite descended limply and Kodama San received it with open arms. That was his most affectionate gesture throughout the time they had known him. The boy Mahmoud imitated his gesture spontaneously. He was in love with the kite.

Not far from the trench, the mute worker spread his prayer rug and began praying. He was filthy with dust but he had used a stone for his ablution. 'The prayers of the mute are silent,' said Rayyes Ahmed, half-teasingly. 'But they too must reach their destination.' His remark hung lonely in the air. The broiling heat seemed to have silenced tongues. The workers were not singing any more, as though they had sensed instinctively the danger of voicing joy to the sun. In the heat and dust, time languished.

From her site, Zohra could distinguish the figure of the Professor among the workers of the cemetery site. He was doing the supervision. Donatella had her period, so she stayed in the school where the apprentice cook provided various infusions to alleviate what he took to be the consequence of the previous night's meal. She always felt quite unwell on the first day of her cycle and the heat had made it worse.

The sieve in Sabry's hands came to a standstill. He surveyed the unbroken blue of the sky. 'The weather'll change soon,' he said with conviction.

Shadows were getting shorter and shorter and there was a sense of being prisoners of the sun. They could not wait to leave the inferno. At tea-break, Professor O'Brien announced his decision to change the times of digging to five in the morning until one in the afternoon, instead of six until two. He had a look at the lustre shards decorated in light blues and purples which had been unearthed in the site of Sayyida Nesima and declared: 'They're all Fatimid!'

Zohra was impressed. 'How does he know that from one glance,' she thought. For Zohra, who relied mainly on her ears in her profession, it was extraordinary how art historians relied on their eyes to recognize authenticity. 'This peacock eye motif and the contour line in reserve have a connection with Abbasid wares,' said the Professor. 'Within the Fatimid period, this style precedes the trend of naturalism, the revival of the Greco-Roman style.' Zohra studied the shard in the Professor's hands. It was a large fragment with a face drawn in bold strokes. 'You see, the three-quarter face rather than the full face is typical of Fatimid lustreware.' He traced the lines on the smooth surface with his thick index finger and continued: 'Ruby lustre could simply be an accident, the result of misfiring.' Professor O'Brien's eyes twinkled when he mentioned kiln accidents. His heartbeat quickened with the hope of finding a lustre waster. 'With the fall of the Fatimids in 1171, the production of lustre in Egypt came to an end. The pottery centres of Fustat burnt for sixty days. It was Saladin's attempt to eradicate all trace of the Fatimids.' The Professor seemed confident about his facts and Zohra was an attentive student. 'Many potters emigrated to Iran and Syria and the production of lustre continued there,' added the Professor. He wiped his hands over his corduroy trousers. The ridges of the fabric were almost totally worn down by now. As he examined other pottery fragments, he was in his element. He singled out one large shard and declared that it was linked to other shards unearthed earlier.

'Another complete lustre dish,' exclaimed Zohra. 'The dealers will be pleased.'

'Oh, no,' said Mark. 'These kinds of finds go to the museum, not to the collectors, and besides,' he added with a frown, 'they're only interested in the Blue Manuscript.' With the back of his hand, Mark wiped the sweat on his brow. Reluctantly, Professor O'Brien left the lustre shards and went to check what the other areas had yielded.

Kodama San was keeping an eye on Area C because Monia was away. Excavations in this site had revealed three distinct phases of building. A four-room unit had been excavated and today, in one of the rooms, they had uncovered an oven which identified it as a kitchen. The Professor became aware of that feeling which sometimes emerged when he excavated spaces where daily life had once unfolded. A strange link with the people of those remote times. 'These are clearly the foundations of one of the wings of the pavilion,' he thought excitedly. Kodama San was using a compass to determine the entrance to the building. The boy Mahmoud repeated playfully: 'Now I'm inside, now I'm outside, inside, outside,' all the time skipping over the excavated remains of the walls.

The Professor, who was trying to focus, felt irritated by the boy's frivolity. 'Stop that,' he barked. The boy retreated but quietly continued his amused recital.

Stones had collapsed in the middle of what used to be another room. With time, a roof had become a floor. Now, the collected debris had been amassed in a huge mound. The foundations of the room had preserved the footprint of a builder from the late tenth century. It was the same as the footprint of any of them.

Among the finds that intrigued the Professor was a wooden mould in the shape of a winged fish. He put it aside and picked up a small earthenware piece which he readily identified as a jug filter. It was decorated with the pierced image of a peacock, framed by a line of calligraphy, but it was considered a relatively insignificant find. Once upon a time, that little filter had cleansed the water that people drank, thought Zohra. And no doubt water had the same quenching effect on human thirst then as now. Alan was very pleased with the finds, but it was as though these objects had been made just to be dug up and they had always existed as pieces of archaeology. He was excited by relics.

The most fascinating find always seemed to turn up at the end of the day's dig. The beginning of a pebbled alleyway was unearthed in Monia's site and thrilled them all.

The hooting from the truck was so brusque and loud that it seemed to raise dust itself, but under the narrow strip of canvas the thanatoid body of the guard stirred only briefly. Within minutes of the truck's arrival the whistle went off, marking the end of digging for the day and announcing the time to go home. Spaghetti did not even get out. He was in a strange mood, perhaps a state of nostalgia that he could not acknowledge himself. The truck was covered in cuts and bruises from its haphazard journeys. It struggled to adjust itself to people's needs. Under the weight, the bridge too strained to maintain its grip on both banks of the river, reminding itself of many years of survival. The intense colour of the river seemed to disappear in the gulping heat. Haziness fused it with the sky. One could see the languorous air. An impenetrable shield was given to the water by the sun. The truck jolted. Zohra asked Mark if he could project the slides of the Blue Manuscript again. It was the third time she had raised the question. Mark said that there was a problem with the projector and flicked his hair which, originally brown, had become almost blond with the sun. He was trying nebulously to change the subject when they all had to duck and avoid an overgrown tree. Mustapha turned his back to the sun and narrowed his naturally kohl-lined eyes. Sweat had left a streak of salt down his back. Professor O'Brien sat quietly on the other side of the truck. In fact, no one said anything more for the rest of the bumpy journey home. A sweltering silence seemed to weigh. Somehow, everything had started to feel absurd – the sweat, the digging, the notes, the recording and thorough documentation of every detail, all the data about the exact location of every find . . . Whatever was lying there, hidden in the ground, lay peacefully, unconcerned whether they dug it out or not.

The excavation had gone on, overriding everything. And as they removed each stratum, deeper in the trenches, it became clear that these were layers of time. But as these layers lifted, the layers of daily experience settled . . . and the site supervisors were starting to forget that patience was the archaeologist's best companion. Every day died with exhaustion and every day was born with less curiosity for the unknown.

38

Because of yet another water cut, Hakima and Halima were cleaning the women's room in the afternoon. Donatella sat on the bed, Catkoota curled peacefully on her lap. Behind her, the yellow paint of the walls had already begun to flake. Zohra was cutting her nails. The growth was defined by the edge of her nail polish. It was not long before all archaeologists had dirty nails. No one bothered now with a thorough cleaning the way they had in the beginning. As she talked, Hakima cupped her hand to sweep the little pile of nail clippings into a bag with the rest of the dust. Little bits of themselves were joining the locals' refuse. All of a sudden, the cat jumped from Donatella's lap as though it had sensed something imperceptible to the rest of them. Halima made a face, pointing at the hair protruding from Hakima's scarf. 'You see her hair?' she whispered.

'Yes?' said Zohra, looking at Hakima, who was adding the final touches to the sweeping of the floor.

'Bluish-white hair is a sign that she'll go to hell!'

'Is it?' replied Zohra, startled. There might be only one letter different in their names, she thought, but there was a staggering difference between the two women!

The moment Halima had left the room, Hakima came close to Donatella. She so much wanted to talk to her, as she knew she too was Christian, but there was no language. She folded back the sleeves of her dress and proudly displayed the tattoos on her arms. A cross on the inner side of each wrist, Christ in glory on the upper part of one arm. On the other, a resurrection scene, Christ rising from a tomb with two angels above his head. Hakima was proud of being a Copt.

She pointed to the images as though she was showing her undying faith in the very indestructibility of tattoos. Unexpectedly, she leaned even closer and whispered: '*Aspereeen!*' Medicine was magic in Wadi Hassoun and Donatella played doctor in the village. The team had used most of what they had brought with them on the locals.

In the late afternoon, the team worked in the shard garden as usual. Rayyes Ahmed appeared with soft drinks for no particular occasion. The sweetness of Mirinda had become nauseating by now. Donatella gave her bottle to Mahmoud and the boy was happy to drink more. Alan had to control himself not to spit it out. They had run out of beer. The medicine room was empty and they hoped it would be replenished soon.

In a corner, the apprentice cook was dreamily slicing tomatoes. The blade of his large knife had gone deep into the flesh when he raised his head to answer the cook who had shouted at him from the kitchen. It was getting late for dinner. The cook emerged to announce: 'I'm cooking *bamiya* for you.' By now, all the members of the excavation knew this was chicken with okra and rice. Blue flies buzzed around the dog but it did not bother to chase them. The cat jumped on the dog's back and settled comfortably as if this was the most natural thing in the world. The apprentice covered his mouth to muffle a laugh. Spaghetti paced restlessly in the courtyard. He was obviously in a bad mood but he himself could not understand why.

Because Monia was still away, the Professor worked with Alan on the registration of the finds. The irreplaceable evidence of a past was treated very carefully. Those objects in danger of disintegrating were dealt with first. 'The science of archaeology starts its fight against time immediately!' said the Professor. In the laboratory, Glasses had just finished treating the surface of a Fatimid bowl. It was intact, decorated with two dancers, painted in honey-coloured lustre. 'Just look at the fine body!' said Professor O'Brien as he examined the bowl. He was so agitated, Glasses was concerned he might drop it. He stood hesitating but did not dare interrupt him. 'Around AD 1100 a new body material, fritware or stonepaste, was made in Egypt. It was probably developed in response to the quality of porcelain imported from China.

In Egypt, fritware was a revival of an old technology which goes back to the second millennium BC.' Glasses was relieved when the Professor went to see the others, leaving him to work in peace.

They had excavated more lustreware than the Professor could have dreamed of. The tables in the room of finds were now filled. Surprisingly, many of the bowls and dishes were in remarkably good condition. There were also many fragments which had been reassembled to form large parts of various containers. And the Fatimid lustre displayed a majestic array of wonderful decoration, lively figurative scenes, intricate arabesques and magnificent calligraphic inscriptions. The Professor surveyed the field of colour, an endless harvest of undulating hues, beauty and refinement reflecting the vision of a civilization. He glanced in Zohra's direction. She was concentrating hard, trying to decipher the fragmentary inscription that ran along the rim of a small dish. He was aware that fluency in Arabic was not enough for such a task. Monia's training meant that she was more capable than Zohra when it came to reading inscriptions. The Professor wondered why Monia had still not returned. He thought that if she was not back by the following day or two, he should perhaps send Spaghetti to collect her.

Kodama San was drawing pottery profiles from a large number of shards spread in front of him. The Professor thought his drawings showed great dexterity. Each one of those shards was originally part of a container, and on the graph paper the Fatimid lustre bowls and dishes emerged, complete. 'The work's going well.' The Professor's voice rang with satisfaction, but Mrs O'Brien knew that deep down he was disappointed. All these impressive lustre finds, yet not one of them was proof that they were made in Wadi Hassoun, simply that they were used here. Only finding a waster, something damaged in the firing, would prove that lustre was produced in Wadi Hassoun – no one would bother to import such a damaged item. Mrs O'Brien felt sympathy for her husband.

As on most evenings, they all sat with the Professor and discussed the finds. They tried to answer many of the questions raised by each day's digging. What was the function of the wooden mould in the shape of a winged fish? Professor O'Brien was a great speculator, but no one could match Dr Evans, who had excelled in this skill. Tonight, the members of the excavation seemed to go through the motion of speculation with less enthusiasm. Alan retreated to bed early. He quietly disliked the company of people and was feeling the season had gone on too long already. Confinement was beginning to tighten its grip. Glasses announced that Dr Chevalier had forgotten to take his bones with him when he left. Everyone laughed. 'Serves him right!' said Donatella.

'Just imagine Dr Chevalier somewhere in the world trying to walk without his skeleton!' said Glasses and the laughter increased.

They had been discussing excavation laws with Mustapha for some time: what finds were allowed to leave the country and which were to be kept in the museum in Cairo. Mark focused intently on this. The boy Mahmoud was mesmerized when Zohra translated part of the conversation. He could not imagine what a museum would be like. Mustapha bit his lip when he remembered the guard in the museum. It would have probably made a difference if he had believed him or had pretended to believe him. On the other hand, perhaps not. It was too far-fetched! He could not have pretended to believe the guard had been woken up by the moans and groans of the objects in the museum! The guard did not confide in anyone else apart from Mustapha what he was experiencing in the museum during the night. 'Everybody would think I'm mad,' he had told Mustapha.

Mustapha himself had thought he was deranged. The man was useless. He was not man enough, he concluded. Had he collaborated, we would have made a fortune and I would have had my Mercedes.

'Idiot!' The word escaped him. Zohra looked straight at Mustapha but he averted his eyes. She thought he was ashamed at being caught calling Mark an idiot but he simply found it hard to look a woman in the eyes. Besides, he had not called Mark an idiot, it was the museum guard who had refused to collaborate in retrieving some pieces from the museum and making an easy fortune who was the idiot.

The archaeologists returned to their speculation, trying to

reconstruct history. 'History doesn't exist,' was Zohra's provocative remark, 'only the interpretation of it.'

'Some interpretations can be fascinating though,' retorted Donatella.

Zohra turned the page in her spiral-bound notebook and busied herself scribbling. She was intrigued by everyone else's theories, by the archaeologists' complacency in inventing stories about the past. She thought there was nothing wrong with that, except that they seemed to be so confident they were reconstructing history while in fact they were sometimes piecing together suppositions. But who was she to know. She had to remind herself that she was a translator not an archaeologist.

That night Zohra found it difficult to sleep. For her, these old objects were carriers of history and her ancestors kept her awake. The present mediocrity of her father's mundane reality juxtaposed with the sophistication of his culture's past. She felt him unworthy of his heritage. She lay awake, thinking. As the dig went on, Zohra felt that they were digging within her as much as in the earth. The window was wide open. Heat was worse than mosquitoes. Her eyes fixed on the moon that swam in an expanse of darkness behind the veil of the window mesh. The moon which not long ago had exceeded the stars in brightness had reappeared as a slim crescent, on its way to becoming a full moon yet again. The following day, as was the custom in the village on the first Friday after the new crescent moon, the ritual of women cutting their hair would take place. But time had slowed down and a day felt like a week now and the reality of this remote place had begun to seem the only reality. The world of Wadi Hassoun had become self-contained, its well-established customs the norm, as though no other way of living could be imagined.

By dawn, voices came from all over the village and joined like the threads of a collective memory. In their singing the villagers lamented their sorrows. Their song included the story of the fever that had killed many of their men, a fever they believed was brought upon them by the German *khawajas* who came to dig. It was the same song that welcomed every new crescent, the myth-song of the village. Amm Gaber, silently awake, leaning against the Tree of Wishes, smiled in recognition of the story of Sayyida Nesima and many other truths about real historical facts and happenings in the village across centuries, woven into the mythical song that was chanted once a month.

At this unearthly hour, Zohra found herself trying to imagine the people who had walked down the alley, which had now been excavated completely. Perhaps the Caliph al-Muizz himself once walked down it, she mused. She reflected how walking down the Fatimid street brought a strange sensation to all of them. She remembered a game-slab, still embedded in a stone seat. In this alleyway, people had walked and played many centuries before. As Zohra had walked down it, she felt her own steps were tracing the tenth-century steps, connecting their stories, a humanness that cut across time and space. Humanness is indivisible, she thought.

39

Interlacing spirals spread, framing a field of arabesque in the reddish-brown leather.

The mother of al-Muizz traced the spine with her finger, admiring the embossed design that filled the surface of the binding. The craftsman was truly a master. The warm leather made a beautiful binding, a second skin for the manuscript. Each volume had a *lisan*, a tongue, a flap, to give it further protection. Al-Muizz's mother opened the volume in front of her. The wide expanse of the cool night sky was complemented by the contrasting earthy cover. She admired the balance of the words within the page, glowing with light on the deep blue background. Words that had gone beyond sound. Between those leaves of binding, the Calligrapher's expression of beauty was nothing less than a silent prayer. And al-Muizz's mother noticed that this sublime work was not signed. Like many calligraphers of his time, Umar Ibn al-Warraq never signed his manuscripts. And although she knew this about him, she was surprised that he had abstained from signing even this, his masterpiece and perhaps his last major work. She was aware that the Calligrapher had grown very old and that his health had deteriorated.

In the life of a manuscript, the making of its spine and the binding of its pages was a day of great celebration and festivity. For this manuscript the ritual was taking place at Sabra al-Mansuriya, its birthplace. Younes, the palace confectioner, had spent two whole days preparing sumptuous cakes and sweetmeats. But he did not make any sugar figurines. This was the year AD 969, a full three years before that moment of creative inspiration in the new Eastern Palace in Cairo when he reached the peak of his sugar-making artistry.

The Calligrapher observed those present, joy filling his being. The long-awaited day had finally arrived when all those loose pages were being bound together for life, united in one coherent world. The Calligrapher recognized that he had accomplished his task but reflected that the nature of the beauty of the manuscript remained a mystery.

Al-Muizz's mother revealed to Ibn al-Warraq that his wish to go on pilgrimage to Mecca was now granted. She announced to the assembled guests that one volume of the manuscript was to be buried with her. When in due course death would visit the Calligrapher, the other volume would be buried with him. Some of the guests were aghast. 'How could such a valuable masterpiece be fated to burial? How could lapis and gold be a meal for worms?' whispered a Christian guest.

'The word of God,' replied his Muslim companion, 'is more precious than gold and lapis.' In any case, the manuscript will be in her burial place not in her coffin.' The Calligrapher himself had only wished to be buried in the desert, with no more than his pen, as was traditional.

Today was the day the Calligrapher broke his vow of silence after almost seven years. He was uncertain whether any sound would pass his throat. And the first words he uttered felt broken. He took a deep breath and recited a verse from the Quran: 'All that dwells upon the earth is perishing, yet still abides the face of thy Lord, majestic, splendid.'

The first volume of the manuscript was being bound, the second awaiting its turn. Every stitch was carefully sewn by the craftsman, with such earnest dedication. He was securing the final stitch almost in slow motion when a messenger entered the ceremonial hall. This was in fact the very first stitch to be undone centuries later by the hands of the English dealer Frederick Winston in Istanbul in 1920.

The news was first whispered in the ear of the guard. Then it was passed from one attendant to another like a precious rose before it was finally unfurled gently in the ear of al-Muizz's mother. The news brought sadness then joy into the princess's heart. Al-Ikhshidi, the generous governor of Egypt, had passed away. She could finally give her son, al-Muizz, leader of Ifriqiya, permission to conquer Egypt, the long-awaited mission for which the general Jawhar had been carefully groomed. Egypt would now be her final resting-place, with the first volume of this magnificent manuscript at her side for eternity.

40

A brief golden glow preceded sunrise. Then the surface of the still water became a mirror of light. The line between sky and water was obliterated and with it all perspective and space disappeared. Spaghetti drove the team to the site at five o'clock and immediately left for the nearest town on a mission.

That morning the truck was full. Glasses had decided to visit the site, Mustapha had not returned to Cairo and Monia had at last come back. Something about her was fundamentally different, but the others were unable to pinpoint what it was. Monia's mannerisms had changed. She had always covered herself as much as she could when she went to the site as a precaution against the sun. For some reason, however, she seemed even more covered up than usual. Her scarf drooped over her forehead and there were no rollers in her hair.

It was the Prophet's birthday, but Mark had managed to negotiate a bonus rather than interrupting the digging. The workers welcomed the deal. It was an unusually busy morning at the shrine. The sacred space served many needs. The saint was a source of benediction and prosperity. A man's pleading voice could be heard from within the mausoleum. He was begging the saint to alleviate his poverty. Om Omran went inside and found him pacing endlessly around the Saint's tomb.

'My son,' she interjected, 'if Sayyida Nesima did not answer you after the first round, she's just not going to. There's no need to make the other visitors dizzy!' The old woman came back, murmuring to herself. 'The walls have ears, that's why they listen. Had they tongues they would protest! Go and tie a ribbon to the Tree of Wishes.'

Some of the visitors to the shrine walked over to the tree and tied a ribbon each. The visitors lingered whispering about the fair woman on the edge of the cemetery. Fifteen men worked under her supervision. Donatella was in a dreamy state. Earlier that morning she had found small stones arranged in threes and fours on the tombs as if someone had sat there the night before, playing a game. But Haj Salem, the guard, had stressed that no one had been near the site since the excavation team had left the previous day, although he did agree that things looked different. 'Perhaps it was the jinn,' he added, and intoned protective incantations. The presence of jinn was a matter of fact. Although Zohra had not translated everything, Donatella felt uneasy and did not ask further questions.

Other visitors sat in front of the mausoleum and gazed down on Zohra and her workers. As he did every day, the tent-maker sat against the wall of the mausoleum and worked with his needle. A salesman loaded with merchandise roamed around offering beads, in effect selling happiness, luck and protection. The site guard who slept along the mausoleum wall woke up as if he had heard the salesman's cry in his dreams. He bought a charm and pinned it to his gallabiya. 'Against poverty,' he mumbled before resuming his sleep. Several people bought charms. Even Glasses got a string of beads. He was about to ask Zohra to tie it around his wrist when Donatella offered to help. As she was securing the beads, Glasses felt self-conscious when he noticed that the colours of his old cloth bracelet had, after all these months, blended with dirt. Donatella's own hands, however, were filthy, as she no longer used gloves on the site.

Not much had been excavated in the site of Sayyida Nesima that morning. Zohra had been watching ants at work, as they meticulously arranged the precious grains of earth into a perfect hill, when Mahmoud put a large shiny fragment in her hand. Zohra ran to the Professor with an excitement she did not recognize as her own. 'This is not lustre!' came the Professor's deflating comment. 'Salts in the earth react with the glaze and produce iridescence.' Zohra tried to explain to Sabry, who chuckled.

'Not everything that shines is gold!' said Sabry, reaching for his cigarettes.

The Professor smoothed back his hair and smiled. 'Actually,' he added, on closer examination of the shard, 'this is Chinese.'

'Chinese?' Zohra was surprised.

'Oh yes,' said the Professor, 'it'll be an import, we are on the Silk Route after all.'

His thoughts quickly shifted to lustre and he said: 'You know, lustreware is one of the great innovations of the Muslim world. The Chinese never made lustre!'

'A Japanese potter has recently revived Islamic lustre pottery,' said Kodama San, his little finger elegantly folded at the knuckle. They both looked at him, surprised. Kodama San had never revealed the extent of his knowledge beyond the field of his technical expertise.

The Professor was still considering new areas to dig. As she watched Kodama San and the boy measure a trench, Zohra suddenly realized that half of Kodama San's little finger was in fact missing, and that for all these months they had misread the reality. Zohra ambled back to her seat. 'The boy must have known about Kodama San's little finger all along!' she thought. Despite her tendency to indiscretion, Zohra did not tell the others.

As the excavation continued, there was a sense that a miracle could occur at any moment. Everything seemed to be in a state of anticipation. In some trenches, the workers had reached the Roman layer. In others they had reached the pharaonic. Zohra reflected on how the strata of different civilizations stood, one supporting the next, and soil told the human story. The division in strata was the scientific archaeological method, but a clear continuity could be seen.

Donatella showed them a pharaonic slab that was found at the cemetery site and everyone examined it with great curiosity. 'I wonder what it says,' said Zohra, intrigued. Donatella, who had been trained as an Egyptologist, wanted to say something. But all looked silently at the hieroglyphs, at this magical language where the word was the image.

'On every pharaonic tomb is written, "Know thyself",' Donatella volunteered. She knew this from her father, long before she studied in the Institute of Archaeology in London. As a child she had grown familiar with the hieroglyphs on the obelisks of Rome, but this was the real thing. She wondered what her father's excitement would be like if he were here.

'How were the hieroglyphs read?' Zohra asked.

'They were read from right to left and left to right. It depends where the figures are facing.'

Zohra wondered what the Ancient Egyptians sounded like. Glasses studied the writing intently and pondered over what he had once read about *The Book of the Dead* of which many copies were stored in the tombs. Of all the wealth that the Ancient Egyptians accumulated for their afterlife, it was the word which had most significance and was to ensure happiness in the other world.

An ochre, muddy light enveloped the village for a moment. A sudden wind made the wishes on the branches unfurl and dance, impregnated with premonitory hope. 'It's the *Khamaseen*,' shouted one of the young workers.

'Keep your mouth shut,' said Sabry. 'It's just a light wind. It'll pass. Nothing more, nothing less.' Others were also angry at the young worker's words and whispered reprimands. His mere utterance of those words might attract the dreaded *Khamaseen*, the scorching desert wind.

The boy Mahmoud ran after Kodama San's hat and almost caught it but the wind snatched it. As he ran, the boy inadvertently stepped on the carefully shaped anthill. Zohra was startled. As for the ants, a gigantic creature had crushed their world. Laughter tickled the boy as he ran in pursuit of the hat. Every time he thought it was within his grasp, the wind snatched it again and he laughed and rolled in the dust like a zebra. The wind blew the hat into one of the trenches and the boy disappeared after it.

Monia was busy with the large number of finds from her site. She gripped a translucent disc between her thumb and forefinger. She could see the engraved Arabic inscription but could not decipher it. 'It's a seal or maybe a talisman,' said the Professor. 'The inscription is in negative. We'll have to use a mirror to read it.' The boy was fascinated. He held the seal in the sunlight, trying to read it; his wide-open eyes a pool of curiosity.

'*Un beau regard*,' said Donatella, with a smile.

Zohra, who had always wanted to learn French, remembered what her mother had often said about it. Such a sensuous language! Perhaps that was what her father had used to charm her mother, she thought, though she could only remember them speaking English at home. Zohra wished she had learnt more languages. By learning a new language, the boundaries between worlds are more easily crossed. Could I have spoken a third language as fluently as English and Arabic? she wondered. Could I have held another language as closely to my heart? I would have been like a train travelling on three tracks! But she understood what Donatella had said in French.

'This is another word for my special collection,' said Zohra. '*Regard*. It has something unique. A directness about it that's significant for the meaning it carries. Somehow, the word "look" doesn't quite have that.'

'There are a lot of differences between English and French,' said Donatella with a purr.

'Well, yes,' said Zohra. 'The English talk with their mouths shut. The French move their lips!' Glasses laughed his heart out.

Zohra was deep in her thoughts about '*regard*' when the truck drew near the site. Spaghetti emerged with a large package of sugar figurines, a magnet that attracted children from every direction. Time being linked to the moon in the Islamic calendar means that the birthday of the Prophet rotates through the seasons. It was lucky for the children that it came now. They gathered and jumped playfully around Spaghetti and Rayyes Ahmed, who distributed the figurines. Spaghetti was laughing but Rayyes Ahmed told the children off playfully, clearing the space around him with his long bamboo stick. Spaghetti kept seeking Monia's gaze but she was looking elsewhere.

Rayyes Ahmed went to see Zineb, who watched with eagerness from behind her door. He told her he had wanted to buy a magnificent sugar figurine for her but had to restrain himself because of the need for discretion. He smiled and added: 'I will be making a trip to the desert with the excavation team soon. You could come with us?'

Zineb twiddled the ends of her plaits and sent elusive looks which, though charged, never seemed to disclose anything.

The figurines' vibrant colours were the colours of life. The joy of the children in this desert village with the sugar dolls was effervescent. One small child skipped in ecstasy. She talked to her figurine, asking all sorts of questions. Contrary to the people who had originally made it, the figurine had forgotten its lineage. Otherwise it would have told the child about its history, tracing its journey all the way back to the skilful hands of Younes, the confectioner of the Fatimid Court. The sweet-maker himself was unaware that he had, with his creative stroke, marked the start of a new phenomenon. He never imagined that his creation would eventually live outside the palace as a popular tradition and that long, long after the tenth century, it would bring joy to many a child. And now, it did not cross the minds of the excavation members that there was a link between these figurines and the Fatimids. It would have seemed far-fetched to read history in such a simple, popular event.

Donatella handed the boy Mahmoud a purple and orange winged horse. His eyes lit up and he threw his arms around her in a joyful embrace. She felt the tremor of his excitement and was suddenly aware that he was a tiny child, not the reliable messenger that they had come to know throughout the excavation.

The children posed to have their photograph taken, each holding a sugar doll. It was a colourful sight. They stood static, waiting for the magic click of the camera, and did not even bother to wave away the flies. The village wanderer passed near by, a glimmer in his half-closed eyes. He did not even pause out of curiosity. Donatella gestured to a child standing to the side to pose with the group, but she refused. 'My father wouldn't approve!' insisted the little girl.

'Who is going to tell him?' Donatella reluctantly asked Zohra to translate.

'I will,' replied the girl, in a matter-of-fact tone, as though this was an inevitable consequence. Everyone laughed at her candid answer.

The workers put on their gallabiyas at the end of the digging and suddenly appeared dramatically taller. They waited for Rayyes

Ahmed, their faces lit with today's happy prospect. It was Sunday and Sunday was pay-day. They would be able to buy meat for their families. Besides, they were receiving a bonus. Rayyes Ahmed called each worker in turn by his name and Spaghetti handed him the notes. The tired banknotes were larger than their worth.

It was at lunchtime, when they expected her to turn up in one of her sexy dresses, that the dramatic change in Monia was fully revealed. Monia was wearing a wide dress that covered her from neck to toe and a scarf which ensured that not a single hair escaped. The cream-coloured veil contrasted with her dark complexion. The hijab made her face look slimmer. 'It's no less than an inexpensive facelift!' thought Zohra. The headgear and dress still had matching frills and confirmed that the same dressmaker had continued to fashion Monia's clothes. Monia was concentrating on her chicken and ignored everyone else's baffled incredulity. Her religious attire was surprising even for the Cairene cook. This was long before the hijab had become fashionable, its popularity at times diluting its religious message. Monia's change of dress was clearly a statement about a change in moral direction, and the cook could not believe it possible. He was nonetheless very proud of her, as if she were his own daughter. 'More chicken?' he offered generously.

'*El-hamdulillah*,' Thanks be to God, said Monia.

Alan looked fixedly at the large eyes which gazed at him from the plate, the all too familiar two eggs fried in a bit of oil, that the cook had prepared for him.

'Would you like some more Zahra?' said the cook when he noticed Zohra looking at him. She laughed.

'The diacritical marks in Arabic change the sound and therefore the meaning,' said Zohra. 'He calls me "Zahra" which means flower, while "Zohra" means beauty.'

'How extraordinary!' gushed Glasses, fascinated.

'In Arabic, people's names have meanings,' continued Zohra. 'Sometimes, the name doesn't correspond to the person at all, and it might even be funny.'

'Really?!' said Donatella with a veiled sneer.

As poor as they were, people in the village went out of their way when they named their children. Names did not cost anything. And names that meant 'precious', Ghali, or Nabil, 'noble', were frequent. Donatella was watching Zohra and Glasses as they got closer and closer with laughter. She intervened occasionally but could not contribute much to the conversation. The boy Mahmoud wanted to understand everything and Zohra was doing her best to explain.

After the siesta, they worked hard on the finds as usual. Monia held the seal to the mirror to read the inscription. There was a magical aspect to the mirroring in the seals. Two worlds, the visible and invisible, a world of reality and that of reflection. The boy was so fascinated that he resisted when Rayyes Ahmed came to take him home. 'Your mother must be waiting for you and she'll be furious with you again!' insisted Rayyes Ahmed. Donatella reassured the boy that he would come the following day and help with the shard garden as usual.

The boy giggled when Donatella repeated: '*Bokra, bokra!*' with a heavy foreign accent. He hugged his winged horse as Rayyes Ahmed ushered him to the door.

Zohra admired the ease with which Monia was reading the inscriptions on the ceramics. 'Good wishes to its owner as long as there is moon and sun,' said Monia with confidence.

'*Baraka lisahibihi.* Blessings to the owner *ma nahat hamamatun*,' she read from another bowl.

'As long as the dove coos,' translated Zohra.

Spaghetti stood at the door. Monia kept her gaze low and continued with her work. Spaghetti was even more shocked than the others that Monia had returned as *muhajjaba*, covered from top to toe. The change had shaken his judgement of her. Now it was he who could not take his eyes off her.

41

With the passage of time, Donatella's net, intended for mosquitoes, had become a prison for her too. She was being bitten in broad daylight and she realized that flies and mosquitoes could get to her quicker than she could get away. This was long before she discovered that she was in fact being bitten by fleas in Wadi Hassoun, not mosquitoes. She sat on the bed caressing Catkoota, who seemed so peaceful. There was an ashen fragility to the cat. One would think that it would crumble into powder at any moment. No one could imagine that only the day before, such a delicate creature had brought a bird fluttering for its life into the room. Suddenly the cat sat up, cocked its ears and remained motionless. It had sensed what was happening long before anyone had heard or seen anything. Soon after, screams penetrated the room and brought everything to a standstill. A howling of owls. A shriek of agony. The land of emptiness. The voice of loss was recognizably the same everywhere. Even when compressed to silence within, it was the same. There was no mistaking it. Monia interrupted her prayers. Zohra's hand froze in mid-air, strands of hair dangling from her brush. The door burst open. 'They brought a boy from the hospital!' said Halima. Nobody spoke. She stood in the doorway, light pouring from behind her. They could not see her face.

Hakima's silhouette appeared behind Halima. 'It's too late. Not even the doctor trained in America could do anything!' They all rushed out except Monia, who would not respond to the urge of curiosity before securing her veil. It had become an indispensable layer.

In the courtyard, women beat their heads as they wailed. The colourful blossoms of their dresses heaved in waves of gathered folds which would soon be engulfed by the black of bereavement. A man stood in the middle of what had become a courtyard of grief, a limp child in his arms. He made a hundred steps to move two metres. His arms stretched forward. On one side, the child's emaciated legs dangled. On the other, his head seemed to weigh heavily. He laid the child on the earthen ground and stood up. His arms remained stretched out, as if still carrying his burden.

The inanimate body drew all the people around it. Huddled together in a circle, they kept a restrained distance. The doctor (who was in reality a nurse who did a doctor's job) stood to the side, watching. The team could see only her back and recognized her chignon, held by an unmistakable miniature hatpin. Only one woman advanced toward the centre and sat on the ground, next to the body. She pulled away the violet band around her forehead and her crimson headscarf fell. Her face seemed even longer. She stretched her legs and shook her head restlessly, releasing an extended tirade. All of what had happened immediately preceding the child's death, every single detail, was endowed with an immortal sacredness.

'He woke up before all his brothers and said: "I'll go and fetch firewood for the oven."

'I said: "Go to sleep! I'll wake you up when the bread's ready," but he sprang to his feet and followed me. "Wait there, wait for the cars to pass!" I shouted. But he rushed to cross the road. He thought I was urging him to cross – my voice was drowned by the noise. He thought he could go faster than the cars but he never made it to the other side. Instead, he made it to the other world . . . oh, light of my eyes . . .' She slapped her chest with hard blows marking the rhythm of her cries as she lamented her child.

'God takes first whoever He cherishes. My sweet daughter was only three years old when the Almighty claimed her,' was one of the women's response.

A torrent of blackness gushed from the gate and spread in the open courtyard. 'Oh no, the wailers . . .' Whatever Rayyes Ahmed was going to say was swept away by a shrieking flood of uniform anonymity:

'Wa wa wa ...' Women slapped their faces, uncovered their heads, and pulled their hair upwards. Every hair keened before the Creator from its very root to its split ends.

Mustapha raged with disapproval. Anger spread, staining his face. He frowned and the mark on his forehead seemed darker. He felt like reaching for a long stick and driving the unwelcome herd out of the courtyard. 'What undignified behaviour in the face of death!' he muttered. He worked his fingers on his rosary and his anger began to subside.

The wailers acted as though they were calling the dead back from the other world. Their haunting shrieks could be heard by Amm Gaber sitting quietly, whispering to the Tree of Wishes on the other side of the village. Zohra could hardly discern the wailers' words but their meaning was unmistakable. The women beat their chests and tore at their dresses. The amount of displayed grief was impressive to the onlookers. But Mustapha could not bear them wailing like this. 'Let the boy die,' he muttered.

Among the group of wailers they noticed Om Omran when she started spreading her hennaed hair, raising it towards the sky. In the middle of the pool of blackness, it truly looked like fire.

'There's nothing like a mother's love,' she chanted, and some of the women repeated after her: 'There's nothing like a mother's love.' 'There's nothing like Sayyida Nesima's love for her child,' added Om Omran.

The boy's premature death had stunned everybody. They found it difficult to believe that Mahmoud, their energetic, lively messenger, was dead. Who would have thought that the ten-year-old would die?

Mustapha consoled the mother. He patted her on the shoulder, repeating the *Shahada*: '*La ilaha illa Allah, la ilaha illa Allah.*' There is no God but God. Then he stood solemn for a moment, still muttering to himself. He wrapped his rosary around his wrist, leaned on his knees and with a precise and sure hand closed the boy's eyelids respect-fully. Then he picked him up swiftly and walked with dignity towards the gate. The crowd dispersed.

That night, Zohra lay awake in the face of death. Words burst and meanings spread like splinters within her. The night was deeply silent. Only Donatella tossed and turned in her dreams. And the morning took a long time to come. Donatella was too dejected to work. She was still affected by the dream in which the boy had paid her a visit. A strange feeling surged within her, a regret for not having prevented Rayyes Ahmed punishing the little children who had played peeping Tom on her. She could not understand where the feeling had come from and why it was so strong. Glasses did not know how to console her. He searched within himself for a way to alleviate her dejection. But his tongue remained locked in sadness. Only Shakespeare's words emerged to fill the void within him, but he could not speak them. 'Give sorrow words; the grief, that does not speak, whispers the o'er-fraught heart and bids it break.' Donatella's eyes narrowed, the green pupils seemed particularly green. Tears swelled and Glasses expected them to be emerald when they ran down her cheeks. The whole team was in low spirits. They could not shake off the impact of the event. This death had brought them together and their silence spoke the same language. The boy had followed the work's daily rhythm earnestly. He was so involved in the excavation. No one imagined that he would not be with them until the very end of the season. His enthusiasm and excitement was inspiring to them all. And now, none of them felt like going to the site. But Mark insisted on proceeding with the digging. 'La di da ...' he hummed as he climbed into the truck. And Donatella wished he would not.

It was clear that the villagers were only too familiar with death. For them, death was the most natural thing. Only a few days after Mahmoud's burial, his father said: 'It doesn't matter, we'll have another child, inshallah!' Donatella was furious when Zohra translated. She found it strange that this culture lived so easily with death.

It had been very difficult for Donatella to take that last photograph of the boy, but she had done so at his mother's request. After the boy's death, Zohra had avoided the mother's gaze. It was all she could do in the face of what had happened. Strangely, Monia's attitude was the exact opposite. She kept over-acknowledging the incident to show her sympathy. The mother's grief was not comfortable with either attitude. She had sunk into silence, had looked death in the eyes and could not give sorrow words. And her unuttered words journeyed far away ... perhaps to the well of silence.

42

Zohra shaded her eyes, trying to make out the Professor and the teenage worker from a distance. She had been waiting impatiently for the whole of twenty minutes. The teenager obviously could not explain anything to the Professor. But she now thought it would be irresponsible to go herself and leave her team by themselves at the site. She thought of how agile the boy Mahmoud had been, how rapidly he had delivered messages and carried out errands. She heaved a deep sigh. From afar, Donatella and her workers at the cemetery site were moving shadows. Only the Tree of Wishes was prominent, the figure of Amm Gaber next to it. Zohra had begun to wonder whether she should send someone else to get the Professor when she spotted two figures walking towards them.

A worker's hoe had struck a solid surface. 'Go gently, follow the object . . . easy,' said Zohra, not knowing what to do. It just seemed like common sense.

Sabry ordered the man to leave the trowel aside and he started removing the rubble with his bare hands. 'I saw how the Germans did it,' he said. Others stopped digging and stood watching the birth of a large find. 'It seems to be a stone. But it's refusing to budge!' Sabry worked meticulously, brushing away the earth. 'No, it's a container of some kind!' he declared. The workers got closer. It was then that Zohra had asked Sabry to stop and sent the teenage boy for the Professor. Sabry continued to remove the earth almost stealthily as though he could not control his curiosity.

'We have to see what the Professor has to say first,' Zohra warned gently.

Professor O'Brien hurried his steps when he saw that the workers were not digging. Most of them were leaning on their hoes and looking fixedly in his direction. He approached with apprehension. He felt a stabbing in his guts and a premonition rise within him. The workers at the site stood upright.

A red and yellow strip of cloth brushed over the ground. Near Zineb's door, Rayyes Ahmed watched it from the corner of his eye. 'That's someone's wish come true,' he insinuated with a smile. In the distance he noticed the Professor hurrying towards the mount of Sayyida Nesima and the workers standing around, apparently idle. His heart sank with the thought of further complications but his steps were assured and unhurried towards Area D.

Professor O'Brien worked carefully with Sabry. All the workers fixed their gaze on the two men's hands. The Professor was excited. The surface of the jar shone in the light. 'A lustre find, maybe even a waster,' his mind rushed to conclude, but he was soon able to recognize that the shine was mere iridescence caused by burial. Reaching it from the side, they could see the full outline of the jar. It was complete and of a common type, monochrome-glazed. An earthenware lid sat on top of it, seemingly too large. They were still working around the jar methodically when all the other site supervisors except Donatella had reached the mount of Sayyida Nesima, followed by their workers. They gathered around, as curious as the rest. This was the second time that all the workers and the members of the excavation had been together at this site. The first time, it had been the day the workers had refused to dig. The Professor and Sabry continued removing the earth around the jar, working with nimble hands. The trowel remained unused, its green handle contrasting with the reddish soil from the earth's belly. Monia stood over Sabry and the Professor, watching closely.

The sun was scorching the ground and they were all thirsty, but no one was even conscious of their thirst, so preoccupied were they with what was happening. No one was interested in the tea-break. When the Professor finally got the jar out, it seemed simply filled with earth. And for a moment, people looked at each other with empty eyes. But from under the rubble, from under the dirt, shone a find within the find. Gold. The round pieces were as new as the day they were struck. The coins came free of any earth that had clung to them, and there was no mistaking the precious non-rusting metal. The workers began to dance. Boys jumped and called. Some of the men clapped as Sabry cantillated a happy song, throwing his sieve in the air, the way he would a tambourine. Every one rejoiced as they wove a song that was the child of this magical moment.

One group sang: '*Baraka*, blessing is what our saint bestows … Sayyida Nesima! Sayyida Nesima!'

The rest answered: 'The Earth gives! The Earth gives to its children!' Their words overflowed with joy and Zohra felt like joining them. The mute worker jumped higher than all the others, his eyes glistening. His chest released a hoarse sound which echoed as though coming from a deep well. Monia gestured to the crowd to step back a little.

It was then that Donatella joined them. She had been with the Tree of Wishes. Amm Gaber had not stirred as she tied a ribbon to one of its branches and spoke to it in Italian.

The Professor examined one of the coins and recognized an eleventh-century type. The calligraphy was in good mint. He was still on his knees, not sure what he should do. 'What a find!' he beamed excitedly. Mark was not that excited. He knew that such a find would not leave the country. Archaeology rules had become tighter and tighter. Gone were the days when one could come and dig in the heart of a foreign land and fly away with its treasures. Mark was doing his best not to appear dismissive but could not help looking indifferent. He was filled with the urgency of finding the Blue Manuscript. The excavation season was drawing to a close. Mustapha knelt and touched the coins with reverence. His eyes shone with their glitter.

Professor O'Brien restrained himself from digging his hand deep in the jar to get a sense of the overall number of coins. He wore a stern look on his face. He had been getting more and more out of character recently. The gold find was a strange reminder of the failure to find his lustre wasters. He looked at the jar. The film of earth that covered it was already losing its moisture and thirst tightened his throat. He rubbed some of the dry earth and was on the verge of calling Mahmoud for a glass of water when he remembered that the boy was dead.

43

The cook, the apprentice and the cleaners whispered incessantly. With all the excitement, they could not do their work. The Professor, Monia and Zohra leaned over the magnifying glass to read the concentric lines of inscription. The shining coins dug out from beneath the rubble carried the name of Caliph al-Mustansir. Zohra remembered Professor O'Brien talking about this Fatimid caliph. She had scribbled his name in her notebook in Cairo. They deciphered 'There is No God but God'. And on the other side 'The year 439'.

'This corresponds to AD 1047,' said Professor O'Brien.

The Professor summoned all the members of the team, including Rayyes Ahmed, who stood all eyes, twirling his moustache. The Professor also made sure that Monia was present in her official capacity before he emptied the jar on the white scarf Rayyes Ahmed had given her on the night of his nephew's wedding. He counted the coins three times in a loud voice. 'One thousand two hundred and two coins in all. Again, one thousand two hundred and two coins.' And again. One thousand two hundred and one coins were identical. And one coin was slightly smaller.

It was a magical day, the day they found the treasure. Though the telephone hardly ever worked, to the surprise of all, Monia got through to Cairo at the first attempt – these things have their ways. Still, she had to battle against the usual crackling which interfered with the conversation. Arrangements had to be made promptly for the gold to be dispatched to the capital. Spaghetti was to drive Monia and Colonel Taher, who had wasted no time in reaching Wadi Hassoun, thrilled at the news of such a magnificent find, a hoard of gold. Rayyes Ahmed also took permission to get a lift to Cairo for a short visit. They were to leave at the crack of dawn.

For now, the responsibility of guarding the find was given to Spaghetti, who looked at Monia as though the treasure was hers. Rayyes Ahmed stopped twirling his moustache when he heard the school guard's voice accompanied by consecutive knocks on the door. 'Rayyes Ahmed! Rayyes Ahmed! *Iju, iju!*' were the guard's alarmed cries.

'Who?' inquired Rayyes Ahmed, as did the eyes of everybody in the room.

'Who's here?' asked Zohra. Mark found it hard to swallow. His heart raced uncontrollably. It would not be out of character if they decided to surprise him after all. As precisely scheduled as their life was, the collectors also liked catching people off their guard. It gave them a sense of total control.

Instead of following Rayyes Ahmed, who had vanished after the guard, Mark found himself rooted to the ground, his eyes fixed on Zohra. The translator put the guard's last words into English: 'He said the villagers are here.'

'The villagers?' exclaimed the Professor. Underneath the tone of astonishment in his words, he recognized that strange feeling which had risen within him the day before. The intuitive knot that had tightened inside him then was now tightening even further.

Rayyes Ahmed gesticulated with his stick to force the villagers to retreat, to keep outside the courtyard of the school. It was only with the help of the school guard that he finally managed to close the gate. From behind the railings of the courtyard, the villagers looked as though they were imprisoned. They were happy to stand there and get a whiff of the saint's golden blessing, eager to be close to the treasure. Halima resumed her half-hearted sweeping of the courtyard.

'Stupid beast!' Rayyes Ahmed spat the words and just about managed to restrain himself from hitting the dog which had not reacted to what was happening. It was flopped nonchalantly in the corner, watching with an indolent air. Nearby, the cat curled upon itself, deeply asleep, both eyes covered with its paws, desperately seeking peace. From afar, it looked just like a heap of ash. If she was not careful, Halima might sweep it away.

Mark watched what was going on and understood without the need for translation. He crouched on the ground of the courtyard, his heavy head in his hands. The stabbing needles of a migraine had begun. He stared. His eyes followed Halima. It suddenly occurred to him that the broom swept with its head. Somehow, the discovery of the gold brought with it the inexplicable feeling that whatever everyone was hoping for would not happen. Finding the Blue Manuscript now seemed very improbable. With that thought, fear erupted inside him. Deep down, Mark felt like a puppet in the hands of his paymasters. He was manipulated by invisible hands.

Deserted at night, the site was like an entirely different place. The dark sky was studded with stars. The question was still hanging whether beneath the undisturbed layers of earth there was a manuscript that reflected the dimension of that beauty. It was a strange night. Rayyes Ahmed and the guard watched over those layers that had not yet been removed. Rayyes Ahmed hoped that the team would find the object of their search. He had heard about the 'Blue Book' and he knew it was important and Mark had promised him a substantial bonus if it was found. Rayyes Ahmed was going to have the best wedding the village had ever seen. The gold treasure was a good omen. The thought filled his heart with nostalgia for the desired future as he gazed at the door that was still closed. He drew on his cigarette and sighed. Rayyes Ahmed felt that he did not know the village that well after all. Something had escaped him. He took another drag on his cigarette. His eyes narrowed and he made a pact with himself that Zineb's dowry would be even more substantial than he had envisaged. Haj Salem, the guard, was wide awake, still in a state of disbelief. His wide-open eyes were fixed on the site of Sayyida Nesima. He wondered what other treasures lay beneath the earth. Soon, the edge of the sacred mount acquired a golden halo in his haggard eyes.

44

The Court scribe looked at the tip of his pen, stained with the ink of death, and leaned forward. He was about to write, 'The Nile's low level has led to prolonged drought, which has brought devastating famine to the country, God's wrath on his people. The famine has been very severe and in this year of 443, the calamity is worse. It has devoured people's reason, driving them to despair. In the month of *Sha'ban*, a group of people in Cairo killed and ate the mule of Vizier al-Yazuri. The perpetrators were hanged in a public place. But driven by rapacious hunger, other people ate those who had been hanged. Caliph al-Mustansir left for the Green Pavilion in the region of Wadi Hassoun where he received news of further unrest in the province of Ifriqiya.'

But the scribe changed his mind and these events were never recorded. He looked up. His eyes met the haggard look in the face of his young apprentice. He glanced at the blank paper in front of him and wondered about the events that would unfold and fill his empty pages if he did not censor them. He was aware that history was being made in the great hall, where the Caliph had summoned his minister, al-Yazuri. Their meeting was to decide the next course of action.

Deep down, the scribe knew that even if he did record what was happening, his words would disclose only one layer of history. There were other layers he would never know and therefore, as much as history existed in his recordings, history did not really exist. As he replaced the lid on the inkwell, the scribe reflected how everything had become so precious, even the ink which he had refrained from using to record the macabre events. Only time had a different quality to it. There seemed to be more of it on his hands.

In the great hall, Caliph al-Mustansir was deep in the abyss of worry for his people. The distance that separated him from the capital could not keep the troubles away. For the first time, retreat to the Green Pavilion was failing to provide peace and serenity. The severe measures taken by some of his advisors to control social unrest in the capital had simply increased people's rage. And now, he had to address the situation in Ifriqiya. The weight of silence interspersed the few words exchanged between Caliph and minister. Their silence, however, was busy planning. The minister had just proposed his great political strategy, the means by which Egypt could be rid of the curse of the infamous Banu Hilal. And now he awaited the Caliph's verdict.

The paintings on the central wall of the great hall had lost their brilliance. Their vibrant colours had grown dull. On the upper-right corner, the top layer of paint had started to peel, revealing a blue layer. They were sitting in what was once the blue-domed hall with gold calligraphy. It was originally commissioned by Caliph al-Muizz, completed by his son, al-Aziz, and its calligraphy was devised by Ibn al-Warraq. When, many decades later, Caliph al-Mustansir took the decision to have the great hall painted, nothing could dissuade him, not even his advisors, who indicated that the blue dome was precious to the Caliph's great-great-grandfather, al-Muizz, long dead, buried in the soil of his beloved Cairo, within the Eastern Palace with all the Caliph's ancestors. But al-Mustansir would not heed this argument. He was determined that the space be transformed into a glittering jewel. So two painters were summoned for a competition. They were each to paint a dancer and interpret the lightness of her movements with a trompe l'oeil effect. This very much pleased the young Caliph. The hall was transformed from a silent into a festive space with an abundance of reds and yellows. Even the bands of calligraphy carved in wood which ran as wainscot in the room were turned over, the wood reused and scenes of courtly entertainment, of dancers, musicians, hunters, were carved on the back and painted in bright colours.

'Time is not to be trusted,' thought al-Yazuri. The frescoes were a reminder of times gone, of laughter, dance and merriment. Now, the painted dancers were no more than ghosts of a glorious past. Built on an extraordinarily large scale, the Green Pavilion was enclosed within orchards that ran for miles. Its gardens had, at the time of al-Muizz, transformed the desert into paradise on Earth. But now, less than a hundred years later, the orchards were slowly dying. Even the sturdy trees were about to surrender. No water meant death was slowly seeping into this joyful haven. Foreseeing hardship ahead, the wealthy had hidden hoards of gold coins, hoping to secure their future. But in the famine gold was of no use and its glow faded when death came to extinguish the life of its owner.

Caliph al-Mustansir too was looking at those paintings in the great hall. But to him, the dancers in the paintings brought vividness to his dreams. The theme of the redecoration of the pavilion, which had been undertaken a few years earlier, had been inspired by popular songs, songs that praised the beauty and fiery dancing of the woman he wished to marry. In his eyes, the hall was still the glittering jewel that reflected his dreams about the woman of his desire – a desire that al-Yazuri knew nothing about. The Caliph was aware of the dangers that would follow if his feeling for this woman was to be divulged and so he guarded his secret with utmost discretion. Yet nothing would have surprised al-Yazuri. He had been initially surprised, however, and greatly amused by the contrast between the carefree al-Mustansir and his strict grandfather, Caliph al-Hakim, whose fanaticism it was said pushed him so far as to forbid cobblers from making shoes for women to ensure that they never left their houses. He was also believed to have forbidden the making of the dish of *mulukhiyya* simply because it was a creation of his rivals in Iraq, the Abbasids. And was it he or was it someone else who sentenced the Court storyteller to death for telling the story of *Leila and Majnoon?* The same night, the storyteller had to flee the country for his life. 'Truly,' thought the minister, 'the values of a civilization are not impervious to corrosion. One individual leader can make or break a vision of a civilization.' But if the minister had had any idea of Caliph al-Mustansir's feeling for this particular woman, he would have strongly advised him against pursuing it, not for moral but for political reasons.

While still waiting for the Caliph to speak, the minister stole a look at his face, but there was no sign of what the Caliph was thinking. Only his lips quivered reciting the Quran.

'Very clever!' were the Caliph's words when he finally spoke. It was shrewd of the minister to think of dispatching another expedition of the Bedouin tribe of Banu Hilal, a fierce force, to Ifriqiya, where the local governor, Ibn Badis, was persisting in disobeying the Caliph's instructions. He was seeking independence and had even pledged allegiance to Sunni Iraq rather than to him, the Ismaili imam in the Fatimid central government of Cairo. Ibn Badis had gone beyond the bounds of acceptable conduct. Al-Yazuri's plan was a clever way to rid the country of the Bedouin tribe and the disloyal governor at the same time. But what the Caliph did not reveal, and what the minister did not know, was that the plan would serve the Caliph in even more ways. While the men of the Banu Hilal would be away, he would marry the woman he so much desired, a woman already betrothed to one of the leaders of the infamous tribe. Al-Mustansir flew in his dreams and the dancers in the paintings of the great hall came back to life. It was neither the dancer coming out of the wall nor the dancer disappearing into it that was performing before his eyes, but the woman of his dreams who had now leapt out of his imagination. The hall regained its bright colours, its glory and merriment. Caliph al-Mustansir had no idea that less than a year later he would be forced to leave the pavilion, never to return to the region, and that the glory of that palace was to find ruin in a much shorter time than it took to build it.

It was not in Wadi Hassoun but in the Eastern Palace in Cairo that the Court scribe continued his recording of events, because he too had had to leave the Green Pavilion, never to return. He dipped his pen in the same inkwell and wrote, filling the space. 'Another wave of Banu Hilal descended on Ifriqiya, with a letter from al-Yazuri to Ibn Badis with a message of inevitable destruction. But destruction brings destruction. Within months, the youngest son of Caliph al-Mustansir was killed by the Banu Hilal. This was their retribution for what they considered a humiliation brought upon one of the tribe's most distinguished men.' The breath of the scribe's pen was weakening. The last few words on the page were a faded brown and the last dot invisible. The scribe immersed the tip of the pen in the dark ink and continued. 'And it was with this terrible wound and under siege from the Banu Hilal that al-Mustansir fled the Green Pavilion, which had been his favourite retreat. The pavilion was ransacked and reduced to ruin. This was but a faint echo of what has been inflicted on the province of Ifriqiya and its inhabitants.' It was not only contemporary chroniclers who recorded the destructive force of the Banu Hilal. Centuries later, the historian Ibn Khaldun described their destruction of Ifriqiya as devastation by a plague of locusts. Only the head gardener, who was a local, had stayed behind in Wadi Hassoun, together with all of his seventy-seven children. He was determined to die with the trees. But he survived the hard years, and eventually he managed to rescue a small part of the orchard. The Nile level eventually rose and the waterwheel turned again. The orchard blossomed. Its trees outlived its owners. And the rule of al-Mustansir once again saw prosperity, although he never returned to the Green Pavilion. Al-Yazuri, however, with the intention of consoling the Caliph, brought part of the Green Pavilion to Cairo by orchestrating another painting competition to recreate the hall of the dancers in the Eastern Palace.

The buildings of the Green Pavilion and the whole desert palace complex remained in ruins for many years and were a suitable dwelling only for lonely owls until the next caliph, al-Musta'li, restored some of its buildings and the Green Pavilion once again enjoyed royal patronage. But Fatimid rule eventually came to an end. And although some Mamluk rulers took an interest in the desert palace, the Mamluk dynasty did not stay forever. The cycle of civilization turned again. The place seemed doomed to ruin and the Green Pavilion was once again deserted.

45

Multiple forms moved with agility and surreptitious lightness. Each figure had a head the size of a large pumpkin sprouting with horns of all shapes. From a bundle slung on the shoulder grew the head of an axe, the tip of a trowel, a spade, a shovel, a mattock, a stick, a metal rod, the greedy teeth of a rake . . . People carried all the tools they could lay their hands on. Men, women and children in flux, advancing from different directions. No one recognized nor acknowledged the other. They were united by an implicit conspiracy. Everyone had slunk silently from their doorstep, feeling their way before they found themselves conjoined in their mission. They would split the earth wide open, turn it inside out, hitting where it could not hold its scream. They emerged as the ghosts of themselves. Monsters of fury. Exploding rage taking visible form. Their hands and legs multiplied. Animal or human, the creatures advanced, their sharp tools extensions of their limbs. They moved in the obscure expanse of a night that seemed to have no morrow.

The irony of fate was unbearable. The contradictions of torment tore their peace to shreds. Their hard reality of misery had been mocked by the shining riches of the past, dug out from under their feet. Time had done them wrong!

They proceeded. Shadow puppets with no strings attached. They advanced, shapes blotted together, one huge monstrous ghost which leaned forward, opened its mouth with its fangs of axes, mattocks and other tools, ready to attack. They will strike until the earth reveals what it had hidden from them all those years. Gold. A treasure, a few metres from Haj Salem's door. Shining gold.

People in the village had been heedlessly crooning a popular song since time immemorial: 'Have you ever heard of gold going rusty even after being buried in the earth for centuries?' A dazzling glimpse of the gold brought the meaning of the words to the fore.

A background noise of laughter and chatter rose from the cemetery. But louder were the mingled thoughts of the digging creatures mingling at the base of the hill. The moon's faint light had painted shadows of what they had become – monsters of themselves, ever ready to strike. The figures on the façades of the houses too seemed to come to life. Arms became maces, nails grew into claws, hair into thorns, noses into sickles, teeth into saws, thrust forward piercing the thickness of the night. In the eyes of the monstrous ghost, each archaeology site was surrounded by a halo of gold. Limbs moved with the unison of a haunting obsession ready to tear to shreds the veil of the invisible. The villagers ground the same echoing thoughts over and over again.

'Gold at the feet of our saint. Those foreigners! They must have divided the treasure amongst themselves by now. How much would everyone's share be? It's all her *baraka*, her blessing. Would she not give us, her children, what she's bestowed on those foreigners? Our saint's head must rest on jewels, precious stones. Don't they say that she was capable of miracles? That her hands made water freeze? For hundreds of years our saint must have been sleeping on treasures. Her body, sealed off by gold, could not have been spoilt by worms. Our saint must remain untouched. But nothing will harm her even when we dig and take what's around her. More gold and jewels will come and replace what we take. Our saint's *baraka* has no end. And next year, we can dig again, there'll be a harvest of gold for us every year. This barren earth, that refuses to give fruit or vegetables or even grass to our goats, can give gold. But you, saint, how could you bestow the gold on unbelievers before us?

'If only one could lift her head slightly, only for a moment, so the jewels can be gently removed. Sold in the capital, their price will feed the whole village for years to come. Our village is the chosen one. It is blessed. Who would have said that a treasure was buried so close to Haj Salem's door? He who has wished to make the pilgrimage journey to Mecca for so long and could never afford it.'

They dug united by fever. Their unison was the unison of anger and frustration. Their stomachs sank with fear and anticipation. They were a mighty swarm of locusts.

They had started with the hill, ascending until reaching the mausoleum itself. All their lives, Haj Salem's sons had walked barefoot on the soil of this village. They could not afford sandals. Yet a stone's throw from the Haj's house, a treasure lay under those same bare feet. The barrier of time had isolated them from the gifts of the past. The people of the village had never thought that a treasure could be buried at the foot of the hill crowned by the very saint they had unremittingly implored to alleviate their poverty.

'That director decided where to dig. He must've known where the treasures were hidden. Remember how much he insisted on opening the mount? Didn't that Tunisian explain his words: "This is the most important site." He knew it was. These *khawajat* come and dig holes in the heart of our land! The gold is in our village. We are the ones who have been blessed but we don't know where the blessing is. That Professor knows, he's got brains. How can he come from the other end of the world and recognize that a few metres away from Haj Salem's door lay a treasure, waiting to shine in the light. How could a treasure hide from them in the dark for hundreds of years without anyone of us knowing about it? The Haj's family has lived here for generations. They were born in poverty and they died in poverty.

'Who could have known that gold was held in the belly of this earth? One would have to die, disintegrate to dust, mix with its grains before one can know what it holds – just when it's too late!

'This earth will be turned inside out. We'll find all the treasures left for us by our ancestors. We'll get a good price for them and our misery'll come to an end. What's under the earth we walk on is ours and belongs to us.'

They dug everything, unable to stop at the door slabs. The treasure could be in the courtyard. But it was not in the courtyard. It could be in this room, that room, the other ... and the frenzy spread ...

until the room lost its ground. Then, the tumult of hands attacked the walls, demolishing them. The palms of blood that had been stained by these same hands on to the walls of the shrine for its protection could not hold them back.

When they had finished with the shrine of Sayyida Nesima, the villagers moved to the cemetery site. They dug around the Tree of Wishes, and wrenched its roots from the earth. From within the bleak heart of its trunk, white worms, almost colourless in the dark, crawled out everywhere. The villagers continued with their digging fury. Dazzled by the gold, they lost the line of reason. Reality was suspended. Then, a violent wind whirled suddenly from nowhere, took over, pulling at their robes, tightening their grip.

It was in the middle of this chaos that they halted, stunned by the sting of stones on their backs. The stones came from the cemetery, hailed by the dead. The Tree of Wishes lay on the ground, a lifeless log, food for fire. Only the ribbons danced in the wind. Every ribbon was a wish, a longing dream. From under the Tree of Wishes, the worms continued to creep stealthily into the world. An army of white worms writhing in the blackness of night, befuddled. Each worm a secret in stupor, that had never seen the light. For them even the night was brighter than the obscurity of their subterranean life. The sky was dark, the moon had set. Only the light of a few stars still floated there. Light that had taken millions of years to reach Wadi Hassoun.

Amm Gaber was not telling stories. When words fail, silence is the only way.

46

The site was the ghost town of a nightmare. Disbelief spread among
the excavation members as they gazed in shock at the scar left by the
monstrous ghost. Daylight had revealed the full extent of its fury.
'The site is ruined!' cried Professor O'Brien, distraught. 'Irreplaceable
objects destroyed, history reduced to powder!'

Mark expressed his anger with composure. He was surprisingly
calm, reluctant to involve any authority. Between violent sneezes he
insisted: 'It's important we wait for the dust to settle. The digging
should carry on as normal.' The Professor was outraged. At a distance,
the villagers stood watching in silent dismay. They had of course
denied everything. As she translated, Zohra felt her tongue break into
splinters. She was unable to transmit any meaning. She could not
extract any sense from the villagers who were themselves trying to
fathom what had happened. The sight of what they had done to their
revered shrine brought desolate tears to their eyes.

Mustapha sat on a stone next to Haj Salem, and worked continuously on his rosary. 'Fa'in sa'alta Allah fas'alhu al-lutf', everything is
written. We don't ask God to take back fate but simply to temper it,'
he said, trying to console the guard, and told him a story. 'One of the
companions of the Prophet knew it was his fate that a rock would
fall on him. But what happened after the companion had prayed and
prayed for God's mercy was slightly different. The rock still fell on
him.' The guard looked at Mustapha with awe, question marks in his
eyes. 'It's inevitable,' explained Mustapha, 'but an eagle had nibbled
at the rock and broken it into small pieces which fell bit by bit. So
what was written did happen.' The guard's eyes widened and the

question marks enlarged. Mustapha's gaze spread over the site, his fingers still working continuously on his rosary. 'This whole thing is inevitable,' he said. 'They couldn't help themselves. We thank God no one was harmed, that it only came to this.'

That night, the site lay deserted, forsaken. Not even the guard was present. In the orchard, near the waterwheel, Amm Gaber began telling a story. It was a story which was seven centuries old and which he had heard as a child from his father in the shrine of Sayyida Nesima itself. It was a story called '*When in Baghdad*'. Baghdad, '*Madinat as-Salaam*', 'The Abode of Peace' – that was how the glorious city was called in the Middle Ages. Amm Gaber was murmuring and his words could only be deciphered by those who come close.

' "*Kan ma kan* – there was, there was not." These were my father's special opening words of each one of his stories,' said Amm Gaber. 'There was and there was not a man who lived in an old mansion in Baghdad – a mansion that had been stripped of everything. Only a solitary old fig-tree stood at the centre of a once grand, desolate courtyard. He had lost all the riches inherited from his ancestors and all he was able to do was weep and lament over his losses. And every night, he had the same dream with the same persistent voice: "Go seek riches. Your wealth is in Cairo, in the old part of the city, within the back streets, among the ruins. In the *iwan* of an old house, dig and you'll find treasure." He grew weary of the dream but the sameness of the voice built a credibility that eventually managed to convince him. Such is the persuasive influence of repetition. One day, he decided to leave Baghdad on a long journey which would take him to Cairo, the capital of the Mother of the World.

'When he finally reached that great city, he felt lost and distraught. The city was immense, and bursting with sumptuous buildings, so how was he going to find the *iwan* of an old house? After weeks if not months of searching for the place he had seen in his dreams he was in a destitute state. He had spent whatever little money he had on caravanserais and had nothing left to live on, and so began roaming the streets every night, and that was how he was noticed by the night-watchman. Night was the time thieves did their dirty work, and here was a man whose foreign attire, or what remained of it, aroused suspicion. The night patrol jumped on him and seized him by the neck. "Please," pleaded the man, "I am not a criminal. I came from Baghdad because of a dream ..." And he told the nightwatchman his story.

'At the end of the foreign man's account, the nightwatchman burst with explosive laughter which gradually transformed into heavy sobbing. It was as though he was pounded by the echoes of his own guffaws. "I have reason to believe you!" uttered the guard. "What a fool you are! I myself have had that dream. How many times, I heard a voice telling me in my dream: 'Go seek riches in Baghdad. In the old district, in "River Street", in a house in the courtyard of which grows an old fig-tree, a treasure is buried.' But I didn't follow what the dream told me. It was only a dream. Look what's become of you, wandering the streets in a foreign country, eaten away by hunger and weariness!" The man listened in disbelief to the nightwatchman's words and started a frenzied dance. He had not lost his mind. He had simply recognized his street and his house and the fig-tree planted by his grandfather. He sighed with joy and realized that he had undertaken this long journey from Baghdad all the way to Cairo to find out what was already in his own home.'

A few drops of water wet Amm Gaber's face and it glistened like a mirror. The waterwheel went round with a regular splashing. The moon was split in the middle, half in the light, half in the dark. Eventually, the invisible half would manifest itself.

246

47

The figure could hardly see as he stumbled surreptitiously over the uneven ground. It was the perfect night, only partly lit. The moon glowed red. It had turned half of its face away, embarrassed. Dispersed clouds occasionally drifted before it. The site was an empty blackness and the muted voice of a flute seemed to rise from the darkest depths of the night. He muffled another sneeze and trod carefully. The trenches were now just gaping holes. And although the conditions were perfect for his mission, they made it more precarious. He had already identified the inconspicuous cavity in which he would plant the seed of his greed.

A cloud fortuitously drifted away from the moon, which watched him with its half face, its dim light inadvertently guiding his hands, although the figure did not need guidance. He could have accomplished the deed in total darkness. He had rehearsed the plan in his mind so many times over the last two nights, lying in his bed while the others slept. Although he doubted that Mark had slept at all, having considered the plan 'a big risk', as he had put it. The figure groped forward, wary only of the danger of being swallowed by one of the many holes. Planting the find was not so much of a risk. The guard who had become his friend would probably do anything for him or for the right sum of money. But it had been a wise move to get rid of him. Discretion was the key to this operation. It was important that no other living soul should be party to it. He was not worried about what the experts would think of the manuscript.

The master calligrapher in Cairo had grasped the general intent of the original from beginning to end. He ruminated on the overall appearance, examined the pen method and even the way individual strokes were finished. He did this as if he were witnessing the authentic master at work. He deliberated the nature of the task for some time before he set pen to vellum. An exact likeness of style was sought. He had worked for months, copying letter for letter. He and his assistants had worked day and night to duplicate authenticity with all the traces of time: soiled edges, slight fraying, oxidization, creasing, some discolouration and staining, a few worm-holes ... 'The worm-holes', thought the figure as he lowered the manuscript into the gaping mouth of the deepest hole torn into the trenches by the monstrous ghost two nights before, 'are particularly convincing.' The Cairene calligrapher and his assistants had truly mastered the art of deception. A sense of achievement filled him with satisfaction. When he looked up, he felt the urge to draw the veil over the visible side of the red moon's face. A line of smoke snaked upwards from his last cigarette and he absent-mindedly flicked the ash on to the ground.

From between the tombs, the breath of the flute came faint and languid. The figure crept tentatively away, withdrawing from the chaotic site, and crouched on a stone in self-gratified relief. 'Everything has gone according to plan. It's done, and I've done it. My hands have sealed the final touches.' A quiet smile spread on his face as he caressed his moustache. His patience was at last about to bear fruit. Soon he could truly savour the dreams he had indulged in for years. But the words of Jamel Bey came to him from nowhere: 'Whatever you sow when the moon is red will never grow.' He felt the craving for a cigarette devour him. The guard seemed to be taking far too long. Slowly, the sound of the flute died. Silence wrapped around him. All he could hear were the incantations on his lips as he worked on his rosary. The realization that he was totally alone seized him. The darkness grew darker and the cold colder. The guard was taking for ever. He sat still. Somehow, he thought it was not wise to move. To find comfort, he reached for the feeling of satisfaction deep within himself again. 'The Cairene calligrapher really is a master,' he thought.

He had refused to reveal to him how he had achieved the ageing process on vellum and would only reveal how it could be done to paper. 'Leave the page in hot water and tea for two minutes and that will give you ten years. Four minutes give you twenty years.'

'For other marks like acid-reaction to atmosphere,' an assistant had volunteered generously, 'sprinkle instant coffee on the page and hold it in the steam of a tea pot. The more you steam it, the more the stain spreads.' Although in the darkness now, the figure had doubted whether he had been told the truth.

His longing for another cigarette and a glass of tea gushed to the surface again. There was still no sign of the guard whom he had dispatched to the local shop. He was motionless. Only his lips quivered, striving to ward off fear with incantations.

In the tobacco shop, like every night, the owner was still awake. The tent-maker still kept him company, continuing his stitching under the light of an oil lamp. Haj Salem gratefully sipped the tea which had been offered to him.

'So will the workers be paid for the days they didn't dig?'

Haj Salem chuckled. 'It won't affect me. I'm paid to guard holes in the ground!'

As the point of the needle pierced his canvas for the next stitch, the tent-maker remarked without lifting his head: 'So you've deserted your post tonight, Haj?'

'Ah, I've kept Mustapha Bey waiting!' interjected Haj Salem. 'A packet of cigarettes before I go.'

The Tree of Wishes lay somewhere between life and death, in a fluttering dialogue with the breeze which seemed to be growing stronger. Its roots wrenched from their birthplace, clutching in a last desperate gasp, its ribbons robbed of their lively colours by the viscous darkness which had now veiled almost everything.

48

In the desert, the flamboyant minibus swayed across the sun-coloured expanse. With its bright hues, this was a bus one could never miss. It was furnished with colourful bulbs and fetishes and fringed with coins that brushed the ground, reeling and swaying like tassels vibrated by a belly dancer. And as the bus staggered along, somehow it was more human than machine.

Their footprints had already disappeared and the wind, drawing such regularly patterned waves, soon erased the last tracks of the minibus that had brought them. There was no sign now of how they had reached where they stood. Ripples of sand. The desert has no memory. There was only the presence of the moment. Their shadows were getting longer, Glasses' shadow longest of all. It was late afternoon but the desert was still hot. The sand dunes changed colours magically. The uniform waves stretched beyond the boundaries of vision, a burning ochre red, a rich mustard. The sky was pierced with bold strokes, red, orange and yellow. A patch of mauve completed the spectacular picture. 'If this was a painting, it would look affected,' thought Zohra.

Donatella's curls hesitated timidly in the heat wave, the light green of her eyes a fountain of freshness. Under Glasses' eyelashes, Donatella's image was transformed. He had always dreamt of meeting Ingrid Bergman in the flesh, of kissing her perfect lips. And for a moment he felt chilled.

From her canvas bag, Donatella retrieved a flask of juice which she had made from a mixture of pawpaw, mangoes and peaches. She gave some to everyone. As she sipped her drink, Zohra attempted to look at Amm Gaber's eyes. Her thoughts about '*regard*' came vividly to her. What was the '*regard*' in Amm Gaber's eyes? Zohra found it difficult to meet it. Amm Gaber's white '*regard*' was disturbing.

'That's the way it goes,' said Amm Gaber, after emptying his glass. 'Once the juices have been mixed there is no distinguishing one fruit from the other. It is all but one species.' Zohra avoided Amm Gaber's gaze as she translated. And the members of the team looked at each other, bewildered. Why was he stating the obvious and what did he mean by 'one species'?

Rayyes Ahmed laughed and rolled his eyes to imply: 'Here we go again! Don't worry about it, he's mad!'

'What's the meaning of his words?' thought Zohra, gazing ahead reflectively. The sand was so fine, so clean, its colour golden. The desert was a nothingness that was not empty. A word came to her suddenly and she turned towards Glasses to share it. 'The word *ténéré* is a name given to this kind of desert landscape by the Tuareg. It also means "nothing" in their language.'

Donatella produced a meticulously folded plastic bag and started filling it. 'Are you going to catalogue it?' teased Glasses, with a twinkle. She laughed. 'I want to keep a token of this incredible scenery,' she said. It seemed appropriate, along with the camera snaps, to gather a bit of everything to preserve the moment. She glanced at Glasses and thought how attractive he looked when he smiled.

Zohra attempted to look at Amm Gaber again. She felt like describing the atmosphere to share the experience with him and wondered what to say. Amm Gaber sat with his hands stretched out as though he were trying to caress the breeze. There was nothing to impede its journey in the open space. As she looked at his dignified face and studied the multitude of its layers, Zohra felt as though the texture of his skin wove a world between them. And all of a sudden, she felt the urge to scrutinize his empty white eyes. Her mind turned away and wondered of what use were eyelids for someone who had lost their sight and why eyelashes never turned white with age.

'There's nothing,' said Zohra. 'It's completely empty.' A smile travelled across Amm Gaber's face as he listened to Zohra's tentative descriptions of the desert. Her Tunisian accent was a bemusing difference. He visualized the landscape that was at the start of his inner journey, the grains which formed a broad belt around the world. 'Purity and perfection,' came Zohra's words. But Amm Gaber was aware that not far from the horizon lay a camel's putrid carcass. Amm Gaber's nose was particularly pronounced. It was a family trait he had been told when he was a child.

'You are the translator?' Amm Gaber's words surprised Zohra and she had no answer.

'What meaning do you look after?' he asked. And Zohra wanted to think him mad and dismiss his comment but could not. She stared. She was still staring when the boundaries of Amm Gaber's eyes suddenly disappeared and their whiteness spread out. A strange impulse took hold of Zohra. The impulse to reach towards his hands, which she saw stretching towards her. Amm Gaber's fingers trembled and Zohra's heart trembled. She felt her hands were not her own any more. And the desire to hold Amm Gaber's overwhelmed her but her hands burrowed into the sand. Desire knotted at the root of her heart, unable to unfurl like a flower that cannot grow in the desert. And her heart turned to stone and weighed heavily.

The breeze was growing. The edge between sand and sky blurred as grains were lifted, a veil of lace. The wind was giving the desert wings. The colours of the sand were changing swiftly, modulated by the dust. Slowly, mounds and ridges gathered to build dunes. The waves near the wind's face were one colour, the waves away from it another. 'The desert is the place where Arabs originated as nomads,' stated Alan for no reason. The others looked at him, puzzled. The sky changed colour and shades of deep pink appeared from nowhere. It was now surprisingly chilly and the atmosphere almost wet with dew. They wrapped up and waited for the minibus to return. It was already over an hour late.

The heat that had been absorbed during the day had been radiated into the sky. A deep dark blue highlighted the luminous crescent and stars. A night of glowing embers, tiny apertures, neatly cut into a dark drape of velvet. Centuries ago, a twin night gave birth to Ibn al-Warraq's inspiration and he transmitted its light into the silence of the Blue Manuscript.

A sense of sadness filled them all, except for Rayyes Ahmed, who was dreaming of the pleasures of darkness. The Professor was particularly dejected at what had befallen the excavation and all that had become of the team's meticulous work. It had been six days since the ill-fated night when the villagers had raped the site and the daily routine of the dig had come to a halt. There was palpable tension between the Professor and Mark. He had not wanted to touch the site after the villagers' attack, while Mark was eager to see the digging continue.

It was getting late. The moon drew nearer and in the silence, Zohra felt like reaching out for it. It was closer than Amm Gaber's hands.

'I want to fill myself with this emptiness. Our life springs from mystery and goes back to mystery. It is not even sure it is the same mystery.' Only Zohra heard Amm Gaber's murmurings but was not confident she understood his words. The others hardly noticed that he was speaking.

The night was imposing its silence. Only Mustapha's lips quivered, reciting the Quran. The darkness erased their distinguishing features. No one saw Donatella's hand snuggle into Glasses'. They were far away from everything and everyone. Only the moon and the stars were present. And even those might have disappeared long ago.

It was then that Amm Gaber started singing. The unique prints of his voice filled the night, and in the desert of darkness, before Zohra's eyes, all those ruins in Cairo came to life, their delicate stucco carvings traced in a pattern of light. The prints of Amm Gaber's voice penetrated Zohra like a torrent of joy and sadness which broke and flowed with an overwhelming current. And Zohra recognized the voice that had mysteriously captured her heart that first night in the school, the voice that had filled her with longing or perhaps love – an impossible love, perhaps a doomed love. Zohra's tears remained invisible to the others. To Amm Gaber, who sang with his eyes closed, the tears cleansed the limpid air as he shaped it into a higher level. It was as though the body had been emptied. Only the voice rang from within, intensely purifying. The voice traced the expanse of the landscape, stretching beyond boundaries. The words extended, shedding their diacritical marks. They swam in the desert waves with exhilarating freedom, their contours extending to the infinite, taking the wholeness of silence further.

49

The beautiful Zineb looked wistfully at the site, empty, deserted. She could just about make out Haj Salem, crouched on the slope of the hill. The excavation team had not come for seven days now. She had not seen Zohra during all that time. And the unbearable absence brought the scent of the desolation that would pervade her world once the foreigners had gone for good. Dejection permeated Zineb's body; her desire would remain unfulfilled.

She stood forlornly, waiting for something she knew would not come. It was already late afternoon and she had not moved from her door since the morning. For days, only Rayyes Ahmed had been, and on each day he had declared: 'They're not coming to dig!' And then immediately changed the subject. 'Will the door be open tonight? We will talk about our wedding plans.' Zineb had always laughed when he threw this question at her, but on the previous day she had not. For the first time, she had become aware of something she had perhaps always known – that Rayyes Ahmed was serious in his proposal. 'Where is Rayyes Ahmed today? Even he has not shown up.' Today, for the first time in months, the beautiful Zineb had not felt his desire devour her through his gaze. And, for days, she had not been able to devour the translator through her own.

As she had stood watching from behind her door in the last few weeks, the whole world had seemed covered in glass. She could reach it with her gaze but could never touch it. And now, even the glass had become frosted. The beautiful Zineb felt locked out, rejected, and for the first time, she missed the presence of Rayyes Ahmed. Today she waited, stifled by the beast of desire that inhabited her,

her brown skin taut and smooth, her body a volcano, burning with longing for another woman. Nurturing that beast, she had prepared another gift for Zohra. She could have sent it with Rayyes Ahmed if only he had come. Will they ever come back to dig again? It was getting dark. The villagers had retreated into their houses and closed their doors. Only the beautiful Zineb stood, gazing into the darkness. She did not feel the urge to retreat to her aloneness, to her ghost companions. She waited motionless, wondering where Rayyes Ahmed could be. No answer came except the howling of the wind which stirred her confusion even more.

The Tree of Wishes lay on its side, a corpse waiting to be buried, the ribbons on its branches now mere shreds of meaningless cloth that had simply wounded the garments from which they had been ripped. Amm Gaber sat in the dark, listening to silence. The whole site, a cemetery. A series of dug-up tombs. 'This is the last time you will hear my words, O Tree of trees,' said the old man, 'you, my one and only listener.

'Tonight, Tree of trees, there are as many stars as there are white hairs on my head. Old age has brought white hairs as messengers of death. When half of the moon is night, the other half is day. Such is the duality of our reality. The Earth is turning even if I cannot feel it. Its firmness under my feet is but an illusion. Everything is moving but the turn is so slow it is invisible.

'Fire can protect you from the cold. It can also burn you. Fire can cook your food. Memory knows that it was the rubbing of two cold stones which produced a spark that gave birth to fire.

'Tree of trees, as a boy I used to spend my time between listening to my father, the story-teller, and helping a man in the village, who sculpted soapstone. He would pick stones, of similar shape and size, and would ask me to choose before he sculpted them. "This one is a bird," I would tell him as I felt the pieces. "This one a fish, this one a beetle . . ."

'The world is different from a different angle. People dig for different things, for water, for oil, for the past, for themselves . . . and the Earth moves in its cycle.'

The night's darkness thickened. In the far distance, directly opposite Amm Gaber, the tip of Jamel Bey's orchard could only be seen in the old man's mind.

On the edge of the cemetery, he whispered to the Tree of Wishes. 'Imagine,' he said, 'just imagine, if you take away the unknown, what a terrible life it would be!' The old man's words were soaked in sadness. Blotted by grief, their meaning was hardly decipherable.

50

At about eleven, a wild wind rose and danced around, devilishly teasing their hats, their pens, paper and any weightless objects it found. Kodama San's hat scurried towards a trench and, as he chased it, he thought vividly of the boy Mahmoud. The wind insisted on lifting Mrs O'Brien's skirt, exposing the white of her thighs. It relentlessly refilled the trenches with rubble. And the team struggled to carry on with their work. Professor O'Brien stood at the site of Sayyida Nesima, wondering whether to end the digging for the day. In reality, his enthusiasm had dwindled after the site had been turned upside down. But Mark was adamant that the work continued without interruption. He was still optimistic. To lift the Professor's morale, he even offered to convince the dealers to extend the duration of the excavation. But the season had already gone on for too long, and Professor O'Brien could already sense the team's listlessness.

'We've got three more weeks, Professor,' said Mark. 'We should at least make sure we finish exploring the main trenches, you could even open a new one.' Then he added with a voice coated with enthusiasm: 'We might still find the Blue Manuscript.'

The Professor thought Mark was even more obsessed than he had realized. How could he insist on digging in these conditions, with the site in such chaos? 'How scientific!' he exclaimed to himself.

'Look,' added Mark unexpectedly, 'you might still find your lustre wasters. It's worth persevering in Areas A, B and C.' The Professor was in shock. Mark was now directing the excavation! He stood perplexed, not knowing what to say, when he was saved by the hat, or rather by the wind which had hurled his hat down the hill and he had to run after it. By the time the Professor returned, Mark had ordered the workers to proceed.

'He'll pay you double from now until the end of the season,' Zohra had translated. The news had spread in no time and the wind brought reverberations of cheering among all the areas. At the site of Sayyida Nesima, workers sang as they dug. They woke up Haj Salem, who lay stretched against the wall of the shrine. They continued to dig with astonishing fortitude in spite of the wind. But it was clear within an hour or so that they had to leave the site. Some of the team were frustrated. Some were rather relieved. As she watched them, the beautiful Zineb held her door, a hesitating leaf.

By the following morning the wind had abated slightly. The Professor was trying to contain himself as he kept his hands busy with a new trench on the side of the hill. He was aware that he should not upset Mark. It could ruin his chances of ever returning for another season and even finding his lustre wasters, which he was still confident were buried somewhere in Wadi Hassoun – but where? He had traced the new trench and changed his mind about it several times. Kodama San had been non-committal.

Zohra lowered the peak of her cap to protect her eyes further from the dust. She had not imagined that being an archaeologist could mean working in such conditions. She glanced in the direction of the cemetery and could not distinguish Donatella. The workers were tiny slow-moving figures.

On the edge of the cemetery, the Tree of Wishes lay lifeless. As she searched for her pen to label a bag, Donatella noticed that Amm Gaber was nowhere to be seen. She wondered whether he kept away because he had lost his usual place under the shade of the tree or simply because of the blustery weather. She gestured to the workers, asking them to look for her pen in the trench, but they had no idea what she was trying to tell them. Frustrated, she thought of the boy Mahmoud and how quickly he would have run against the wind to bring her another pen. Her heart sank in sadness. But a look at the bag of coins brought a smile. She remembered her very first coin which turned out to be a Coca-Cola top! Glasses had paid careful attention, he so much wanted to do a good job for her. His dedication to his conservation work, his meticulous approach, was remarkable. She could visualize him now, bent over an object, giving it his utmost care. He and Mustapha were lucky, staying indoors at the school, away from the wind.

The workers had barely removed the first layer of the new trench. Professor O'Brien stood near the edge singing *La Bohème* to himself again:

> *What's the use of searching?*
> *We'll never find it in the dark.*

He was wondering about his lustre wasters when, suddenly, animated shouts resounded from Area A. The Professor abandoned his trowel and rushed towards the screams. Instinctively, the workers threw down their mattocks, hoes and baskets and followed. The few children in the distance ran after them. Those who were playing with a car tyre left it rolling on its journey. Zohra and Donatella too left their sites. All could sense ending, a suggestion of death in the urgency of the screams. They hurried, engulfed by the dust, a flock moving against the wind, drawn by the uproar which was becoming louder and louder as they approached. Now, they could see Area A from a distance. Figures jumping frantically. Professor O'Brien was breathless, perspiring, though not just from the heat of the sun. Now, he could distinguish Alan, Monia and Mark among the workers. He recognized some of the sounds in the middle of the screams and was trying hard to decipher what they meant. He could not trust his ears and his heart pounded with disbelief when a few steps unveiled the words fully: 'The Blue Manuscript! We've found the Blue Manuscript!'

'It is unreal,' Zohra thought. 'The object which has brought us to this remote place, the object for which we have been searching, working every day in the heat for months, the object which has become familiar through descriptions, photographs, accounts, is now manifest, and for the first time it seems somehow fictitious.' There, as she stood among the rubble, in Monia's hands, was the manuscript. Damp, fragile, it had to be handled with the utmost care. Zohra watched, perplexed, and Mark's first mention of the Blue Manuscript in that strange café during their first night in Cairo came to her for no apparent reason.

In the school, the telephone worked and for the first time was surprisingly clear. From the other side of the world, the dealers were close. Mark could hear the voice ringing with pleasure and visualize white teeth flashing, naked in response, as he heard: 'Excellent, Mark. Well done!'

He put down the receiver and turned to Professor O'Brien and the others, waiting to hear what he had to say. 'One of the collectors is coming,' announced Mark, 'to see our wonderful find.'

The manuscript was put in the laboratory for safe-keeping. Glasses had to attend to the immediate conservation measures to stabilize it. He was slightly nervous as he handled such a precious find and could not help feeling privileged. What a gift it was to touch this tenth-century work, produced by the hands of a great calligrapher. The authenticity of the moment overwhelmed him. He felt the power of this unique creative work pass through his protective gloves. He could almost feel the heartbeat of the calligrapher as he gazed at the lines of the golden letters on the deep blue of the vellum, so permeated were they with the spirit of a great master.

Glasses found it difficult to leave the manuscript. He was still in the laboratory when Donatella put her head through the door and insisted that he joined them. 'Come on, we're having a real party!' she said enticingly. Her blond curls were neatly arranged into a chignon worthy of the celebration. He smiled. He could see that she was already quite tipsy. The bird in his heart was ready to fly. 'I'll only be a minute,' he replied, when he finally spoke.

It was a merry feast. The room where the team usually worked and where topographical drawings were pinned to the ochre-painted walls had been transformed for the occasion. Kodama San's desk became a buffet loaded with Coke and Mirinda bottles. As in all parties, not all people were enjoying themselves for the same reason. No one had seen Mark quite so excited. The dealer's phrase was still resounding in his head: 'Excellent, Mark. Well done!' And now, with all the beer he had consumed, he had begun to indulge his pleasure at the success of his mission. Mustapha did not approve of the drink but no one mentioned alcohol. As usual, beer was consumed from Coca-Cola bottles but its effects spread with noticeable speed. Mustapha's bottle, however, really was filled with Coca-Cola. In the case of some people, such as the cook and his apprentice, who were particularly frolicsome, no one was sure what they were drinking. The apprentice unexpectedly went wild, dancing with the guard's gun, a red fez on his head, Alan's sunglasses and a grin on his face. A missing front tooth was an integral feature of the smile he had managed to suppress for months. In fact, this was the first time a full smile had escaped the apprentice cook. Hakima and Halima whispered and giggled as they watched everyone's demonic side venture into the open. Outside, the wind too was stirred by the wild energies of celebration. It rose to a round of frenzied dance, putting the hinges of doors and windows, the weight of objects and the roots of plants to the test. Zohra's thoughts went to the Tree of Wishes and to Amm Gaber next to it. She wondered whether, by this time, he would be sitting in Jamel Bey's orchard near the waterwheel.

'My friend,' Mark kept saying to Mustapha, 'we'll organize an even bigger party when the collector arrives!' And Mustapha responded with a coy smile, glistening with charm. The cigarette between his fingers coiled in smoke. Absent-mindedly he flicked the ash on to the floor.

Donatella looked happy. She even wanted Glasses to dance and kept pulling at him until he got up. How would he ask her to travel with him after the dig? The question tortured him as he moved gently, as though he were doing his best to avoid bumping into invisible things. The alien nature of the music did not help. He was trying hard to find the rhythms which came naturally to those who grew up with them. Monia sat in one corner next to Mustapha, watching the dancing with downcast eyes. Spaghetti ambled across to join them. Monia sang the words of Um Kulthum in her heart but would not allow her lips to go beyond a benign expression. In her green satin dress with a matching head veil, she moved discreetly, on the seam of provocation. She so much wanted to dance, but she was not going to destroy the image she had carefully nurtured for Spaghetti. Now that she had finally got him.

The party went on until the early hours of the morning. Spaghetti's attempts to seduce Monia led only to disappointment, which was, in a way, the kind of reassurance he had wanted – it proved to him that she was not loose after all. Her recitations of the Quran came to him as a shock and had a sobering effect. By the time he drank the strong coffee she had made for him, he was listening intently to her instructions about how to behave when meeting her family. Mark and Professor O'Brien gave their permission and Spaghetti and Monia set off before dawn for her hometown. The cook had accompanied them to the gate, wishing them luck, reiterating his best wishes, and Rayyes Ahmed shouted as he mounted his mule: 'Don't forget to invite me to the wedding!'

The mule struggled against the wind and Rayyes Ahmed slapped it with his stick while dreaming of his own wedding to the beautiful Zineb. 'One day, *inshallah!*' he sighed as he urged on his mule, impatient to check on the door of his beloved.

In the school everyone else was asleep, including Glasses, whose exhaustion had defeated his usual insomnia. His dreams were crammed with images from the party, people dancing like phantoms, including himself, in his striped gallabiya. The wind which had started late in the afternoon had grown stronger and stronger. But their deep sleep was not disturbed by doors slamming angrily nor by the dog's barking, made louder by the wind. The few containers in the courtyard and the sieve which the apprentice used for spices had been hurled to one end. By mid-morning, however, everything had calmed down as though nothing had happened. The dog was once again lying nonchalantly asleep and the cat curled peacefully next to it. There were no other signs that the night had been so violent. And the wind's true nature remained invisible, its devilish mischief not apparent.

51

It was already early afternoon when they emerged from their sleep, still tired and deflated from the events of the previous day. Everything felt strange. There was never any question of going to the dig. It was all over. Whatever they had expected and anticipated all these months and beyond . . . even before getting here, was over. And now, the anti-climax had already begun to seep in. It was surprising to feel the absence of Monia and Spaghetti. Towards the end of the afternoon, Glasses was sitting next to Zohra on the steps of the school building. She talked to Halima and Hakima, who still laughed at her Tunisian accent. Intermittently, Zohra translated to Glasses the different nuances between Egyptian and Tunisian dialects which often led to humorous misunderstandings. They were laughing wholeheartedly, when Donatella came and whisked him away.

The apprentice stood at the doorstep of the kitchen sharpening his knife. The blade twinkled. 'At the end of every knife there is a potential crime!' he reminded himself. A wide smile revealed the gap in his teeth. He turned his back to the sun and started whistling a love song. The cook was reclining on a mat. He took a drag from his cigarette, a sip of his concentrated tea, and cast a gaze. His horizon ended at the far wall of the courtyard. The apprentice muttered something about the presence of jinn as he ran after an empty plastic crate which refused to stay still in the corner. The wind had sent the crate to the other end of the courtyard and was adamant it would reveal the apprentice's baldness. His hair kept flapping up and down and every time he stopped to rearrange it, the crate took the opportunity to scamper off again.

'We've run out of onions!' he called to the cook.

The evening meal was chicken yet again, but for the first time without onions. After dinner, they all dispersed as the after-party atmosphere lingered. Glasses had a headache and went to rest. He had moved back in with the others. For some reason, Mark wanted to keep the manuscript separate and the laboratory became the room of *the* find. Mustapha and Mark had retreated there and closed the door.

Zohra sat on the steps, conscious that her assignment was coming to an end. She reflected on all the events she had lived in Wadi Hassoun. The night was getting colder and she wondered whether she should go in when she realized that she was sitting in the very spot she had noticed that figure the night of her arrival. That figure was Amm Gaber, but Amm Gaber still seemed an anonymous presence after all this time.

Mustapha sat on the bed and sank into the soft mattress, talking to Mark. 'Where did Glasses find all this soft bedding?' he wondered. 'My bed's not as fleshy!' Mustapha did not feel the urge to smoke as much as usual. He was about to reach for the cigarette he had placed on the ashtray when he felt the heaviness of his eyelids like an iron curtain. He could hardly keep his eyes open. And he could not understand where this sense of overwhelming exhaustion came from. 'I'm going to sleep,' he said to Mark, as he stood up, holding his rosary. '*A'udhu billah,*' he mumbled, cursing the devil, when a yawn escaped him. The room was stuffy. Both men had been in there for hours with the window shut.

'Goodnight.'

As he tiptoed in the corridor, Mustapha tripped, stepping on the cat, which screeched before it escaped. Donatella heard the scream and turned and tossed in her dream.

'Goodnight,' Mark whispered back as he double-locked the door of the laboratory on his way out. But a good night it was not going to be.

Rayyes Ahmed was patrolling the site when he glimpsed the guard asleep, stretched against the wall of the shrine. Pulling on the reins of his mule, he walked on to check the door of his beloved before he would come back to give him the usual wake-up prod. The moon was absent. He walked down the mount slowly and carefully as he had done every night, desire smouldering inside him. No light came from the house of the beautiful Zineb. The house was bathed in darkness. But the door ... The reins fell from Rayyes Ahmed's hands. He rubbed his eyes. He went closer. No, he had not imagined it. The door, that door so firmly closed against him, was open. Rayyes Ahmed was in disbelief. Part of him preceded the rest of him and he tripped. He stood still for a moment to regain equilibrium. His heart raced so loudly, it seemed to have woken up the wind. He folded his arms around himself and bit his lower lip, as though to prevent his heart from leaping out.

Rayyes Ahmed advanced slowly towards the door, slightly ajar, discreetly inviting. From the other side, the beast of desire waited impatiently to be released. The house could not contain it any more. When Rayyes Ahmed finally reached the door, after only a few paces which had seemed like miles, he found it was stuck. He was struggling to ease it, when it suddenly flew open and felt surprisingly light. He closed it. Then, into the enticing darkness within, he proceeded ...

Rayyes Ahmed and the beautiful Zineb did not talk about their wedding plans. In fact they did not talk at all. In a room wrapped in silent obscurity, passion ignited and flesh was consumed, starting with a taste of the saffron-red lips. There was no room for words, only a sweetness in the air which Rayyes Ahmed had never known, and in the dark, his hands were his eyes. They passed over hills and valleys. They spread slaking caresses, his fingers opening channels for the desire which had been filling the beautiful Zineb to the brim, the way Libyan goods filled the stiff cupboard in the corner of the room. The rows of hairpins fell scattered. Darkness held the shape of the beloved that was desired and before Zineb's eyes was Zohra's body, the body she had so intensely craved for so many months. While in the gush of the moment, Rayyes Ahmed was overwhelmed by the taste of honey from the source he had conquered. If walls had tongues they would speak, they would be best telling the story, but they had only ears. Rayyes Ahmed's hands were now spreading ripples of fire over the skin of the beautiful Zineb. The heat stored in their baked bodies was being raked. Taut skin was loosening. And the silence that had taken over was shattering into groans.

Outside, the wind was beginning to moan. Windows and doors rattled, trying perhaps to say something . . . The figures on the court-yard walls seemed to lean towards the room, wanting to hear more. The figures on the façades of houses danced and Haj Salem the guard had fallen into the abyss of sleep. And how much he would have preferred to have been kicked awake by Rayyes Ahmed and wrenched from his nightmare. He was dreaming of a strange beast, the like of which he had never seen. It was half woman, half man, escaping from one of the houses in the village. The beast's many breasts bounced as he ran after it, aiming to shoot it, but the bullets from his gun were totally ineffective. He chased the beast, which ran with such speed, spreading such huge feet, that at times he felt it was hovering above him, not galloping ahead. One foot was on the ground, the other in sheets of cloud. The beast of passion. The more it ate, the hungrier it became. The more and more inflated beast was immersed in the clouds and the guard fell from exhaustion and fear into an even deeper sleep, to an even lower ring of the abyss. The clouds became darker and darker and a deafening thunder exploded . . . but no one could hear it.

The honey of male conquest had a stale aftertaste. The room was fusty. Kohl tears stained the pillow. Rayyes Ahmed had already started hating the woman who lay beside him, like a lifeless sheet. The fruit of Rayyes Ahmed's desire had started rotting prematurely. Perhaps Rayyes Ahmed had known all along, unconsciously, that the night she left open the door, the dreams of his wedding plans would corrode. Zineb will not see the gold crescent earrings. Her feet will feel heavier but not from the gold added to her anklets. Under the darkness that covered them, the ripples that Rayyes Ahmed's hands had drawn over the beautiful Zineb's body were already turning into wrinkles.

Suddenly, a sharp noise, the roaring of a fierce lion, so far yet so close, piercing. Its mouth so wide, its darkness blotted out the space.

Rarely did this mouth open but the village lived in apprehension of it. That lion might swallow a house or two, the whole village perhaps. On the other hand, the lion might simply be yawning. When the lion opened its mouth, the earth shook, houses trembled, people lost their senses. Yet no one had ever set eyes on this lion. All they ever saw was the back of its throat. Its voice spoke the language of terror.

Death's grip tightened, choking the light. In no time the air blackened, an explosive summer storm. The roof trembled, rattling its bones in a fit of apprehension. The sky burst open and the tent was inundated with a torrent of stinging silver. Water gushed everywhere. Everyone fled to the kitchen, the warmest room of all. The team members, the cook, his apprentice, Halima and Hakima and even the school guard. Egyptian, American, English, Tunisian-English, Japanese, Italian, Irish, German ... all were united in fear. The cat sprang in. The miserable rat dangling from its mouth seemed heavy for its tail.

The wind swept away whatever was in its path. It performed its spiral dance before it wrenched everything and spat it out, lifeless. It stripped everything naked, to the bone, then there was no bone left. A cotton cloud, dark, as though drawn in charcoal, advanced slowly, swaying its huge belly. It roared and howled, pregnant with a beast. The wind carried its howl to reverberate in the furthest corners of unconsciousness before it began to wail. The charcoal cloud ignited. A windstorm erupted. Possessions were seized feloniously into the air, whirled around and dropped ... lifeless corpses. There was another brief moment as if pausing for breath, before the leaden sky poured torrents of water again, cleansing everything. Water was bliss, unimaginable in the heat that had reigned for months, and now nothing could prevent such a powerful torrent, not even a rock-crystal talisman. Mustapha, eager to quench his thirst, opened his mouth towards the sky. But water fell only on to his hands, on to the pages of the Blue Manuscript, and the fierce rain made the writing on the pages run. The water diluted the albumen glue used to fix the golden ink to the vellum and letters ran in golden tears. The dye from the pages meandered. Deep indigo streams of lapis lazuli joined the mud that was running into the gutter. The sky sobbed, consciously erasing the calligraphy of the manuscript in Mustapha's hands. Mustapha was distraught. The wind dispersed the bemired shreds of the pages. Mustapha stood in the torrential rain, trying to rub clean his indigo-stained hands. He rubbed obsessively but the dye would not come off. As he rubbed, Mustapha realized that he had recovered feeling in the heart of his palm, numbed by the accident in his childhood. But it was also the very moment the pain of his being spread everywhere – even to his hands.

Now he was in the courtyard, now he was in the kitchen, but rain streamed through the roof. He was talking to the Professor whose face became that of Mark and he could not understand his own words which tumbled like empty containers in the hurricane. And Mustapha was at once in the village and in Cairo. Such is the fluidity of dreams. It allows for a mysterious geography defying the laws of concrete reality. No separation between places, times or substances, no boundaries. Dust became mud. Mud ran everywhere from Cairo to the mud-brick houses in Wadi Hassoun, themselves reduced to mud. But trees regained their original colour and manifested themselves in their full glory. The trees that blossomed only in spring when there was no rain to wash their dust were now, for once, blissfully mauve. These were the trees in Cairo. Yet among them was the Tree of Wishes, bright like no one had ever seen it, recognizable only by its ribbons, their wet colours intensified. Turned upside down, its roots were its branches. Mark tied a blue ribbon to one of those branches which forked like lightning. The ribbon was for the Blue Manuscript and Mustapha thought this was ludicrously superstitious. But Mark turned back, smiled and said: 'My friend!'

'His desire for success has overtaken his reason,' thought Mustapha.

Mark's gestures were so slow and everything, the whole scene, was saturated by blue. Mustapha was not sure whether he was alive or dead. He tried desperately to shut his eyes and failed. He was forced to watch what seemed even more incredible. One of the figures in the pilgrimage painting on the façade of Haj Salem's house left the wall to tie a ribbon to the Tree of Wishes. But with the torrential rain, the paint ran as the figure ran, dissolving in the currents of slurry, dying in this way for an impossible wish. What was this wish? To go on pilgrimage, perhaps? And from the tower of ruin, the owl shrieked a long, harrowing shriek. Mustapha looked at himself and saw the clay dissolve, starting from his own hands ... only his eyes remained wide open, watching every bit of himself dissolve into mud that ran everywhere around him.

Mustapha's eyelids fluttered rapidly, trying to shut in the dream or to open in wakefulness. He could feel something on his face, like the sky's eyelashes tickling him. Swollen drops of sweat trickled down his cheeks, a desperate expression of his inescapable torture. Jamel Bey's face appeared before him, for once without composure. Jamel Bey was furious at the loss of his fortune. 'You said I could trust your judgement!' he screamed at Mustapha. The more Mustapha tossed on the pillow, banging his head against the veil that separated him from the material world, the more that wall thickened and solidified, becoming impossible to break. Only the voice of the muezzin managed to penetrate that veil, when it reverberated at dawn, reminding people that prayer was better than sleep and urging them to get up and pray. Mustapha woke up alarmed by his worst nightmare. Waking put an end to the fluidity of dreams. He felt relief, but had he known what he was waking up to, he might have preferred his sleep. Mustapha reached for his little book of *Dalail al-Khayrat* tucked under his pillow. A timorous light crept through the closed window. He was deciphering the comforting prayers with great difficulty when a terrified, startled voice rang out: 'Fire! Fire!'

52

The tongues of fire twirled and twisted in a wild folly. Just like a mirage, the wavering haze of the heat robbed everything of its edge. The flames whiffled with the delectation of a feast, growing taller and taller, devouring everything. The whole team had been awakened. They stood at a distance, yet the flames felt close, filling their eyes. The fire had given the dawn the heat of midday. If the walls of the laboratory had tongues they would speak. They would be best telling the story, but they only had ears. In the darkroom, behind the double-locked door, an invisible hand had advanced. Ash had grown at one end of the cigarette placed on the ashtray. The hand had held the cigarette from the ash end and the cigarette had fallen to be smoked by the room. The back alcove, the medicine room, stacked with alcohol, had provided fuel. Fire had spread in no time.

The flames were united, determined to consume the building with appetite. The wind gave fire its breath and nothing would stand in the way of its resolute temper. The wings of fire had tongues that circled and swallowed everything they licked. The tongues of fire, a thousand dancing snakes, sucked life from everything.

The team members were bewildered. Wrenched from their dreams, they were not sure where they were. Mustapha worked uncontrollably on his rosary, and for a moment he had the impression that the beads jumped backwards, away from him. Suddenly his rosary dangled helplessly from his wrist. The tear mole on his cheek seemed lower, as though it had run down. His jaw had simply dropped. His facial features somehow collapsed like plasticine.

Glasses stared at the flames, numbed by the realization that only

271

a few nights earlier the laboratory was where he had slept. He wanted to look away but could not. Memories of his father began to surface.

The tongues of fire spoke one language, a silence of complicity broken only by vehement spitting. Fear seized Alan's heart as he gazed at the smoke building up in acrid malignant clouds and felt appalled at the devastation of the environment. Unexpectedly, the dog attacked him and would not let go of his trousers. Only with the apprentice's persistent slaps did the dog finally release him. The cook dragged the enraged beast and secured the chain.

They stood motionless. The feeling of helplessness was unbearable. The loss of the Blue Manuscript sent a wave of devastation through everyone. For some it was a copy of the sacred Quran. For others it was treasure, a useful item to realize a career promotion, or a valuable piece of historical evidence.

The guard clung to his gun the way one would hug a friend for comfort. Of what other use could it be? The apprentice walked as though still in his sleep, carrying buckets of water from the kitchen and throwing them at the fire. He gritted his teeth and wondered where Rayyes Ahmed was, now that he was needed. Water trickled down his back and chest. Soon he was drenched. 'Thank God!' he mumbled. 'Thank God the gold has been taken to Cairo.' Glasses was filled with the impulse to help him in his task. But when his legs moved, they took him to the steps where he sat and covered his face with his hands, murmuring to himself.

Mustapha's face was awash with tears. Thick drops covered his cheeks like a sprinkle of colourless moles before they disappeared into his ashy stubble. The dark stain around his eyes seemed to spill over his face and the usually prominent prayer mark on his forehead disappeared.

The wind whistled, blowing at the tongues of fire. On the other side of the village, in the cemetery, the same wind was rustling the ribbons on the Tree of Wishes, coaxing them into some kind of dialogue. The wind brought life to the Tree of Wishes but the tree was also dead. And in the ruin of the lonely minaret, the owl shrieked.

In the school, the wind relentlessly teased the flames which spread and flared. Its hoarse voice was that of a beast that woke up the embers. Donatella gazed intently into the fire. For a moment, she was not conscious of what was really happening. She stood closer to it, bewitched by the sight. Through her white nightgown, fire drew the warm outline of her body. But Glasses' attention was locked on the flames which gnawed in his guts, his hands still covering his face. 'My name is Daniel,' he mumbled.

Mark paced frantically, his hair in disarray. 'There's not much we can do,' cried Professor O'Brien as he helped the cook and his apprentice with the buckets of water. 'We just have to make sure it doesn't spread to the rest of the building, then it'll die of its own will. Thank God the room of finds is on the other side.'

'Be careful dear.' Mrs O'Brien's cry pulled Zohra from her trance.

'Where's Glasses?' Zohra wondered, searching in all directions until she saw him on the steps. 'Are you all right?' she called softly as she went to him.

Mark could not think straight. His mind was crowded with fire extinguishers. Wars, accidents, earthquakes, fires and other disasters are what happen to others and are reported in the news. Not what happen to us.

'*Ani Yahudi*,' whispered Glasses as he looked up at Zohra. She looked back at him perplexed.

'I'm Jewish ... I am Jewish, my name's Daniel Rosen, Rosen.' Although she understood the words, Zohra did not comprehend their significance. He was upset, that was clear. Glasses had surprised only himself.

'I'm all right,' he said to Zohra, 'I just need a few moments.'

The link he had been trying to sever all his life suddenly took hold of him. He breathed deeply. It had taken a journey to Wadi Hassoun and the events leading to this moment for him to realize. He looked at the others as they grappled with what was happening. A recognition of his own complexity and the need for self-acceptance came to the fore. The realization was an instant insight. It was as though the fly that had been trying desperately to leave the room had just found the hole by which it had entered. Silence.

Professor O'Brien sighed with relief, suddenly conscious that if Glasses had still been sleeping in the laboratory he too would have been consumed by the flames. He turned to Zohra and asked: 'Is he OK?'

She glanced back at Glasses. 'I think so, he just needs to be alone for a while.'

Zohra remembered how some terrible things against Jews had been said in front of Glasses. No one knew he was Jewish. His Jewish self had been well concealed, confined within him. They all thought he was Christian. He talked about Christianity as though he were on the defensive, yet he was not even religious. In fact Zohra only made these connections much later. The fire was a central monster that swallowed everybody's attention. Its glow flared on Mustapha's glistening face. His lips moved without sound.

The dog was howling and running in unruly circles within the courtyard and the cook chased after it, wondering how it had managed to escape.

Donatella drifted towards Glasses. He was curled up on himself, his head between his knees, and seemed submerged in his gallabiya. His glasses fell dangling from the black thread, the large eyes had also fallen with them. He looked up at her. Fire was in his eyes and the rest of his face was ash. Donatella sensed his pain. Glasses was distraught. He was trembling and felt ice-cold. She reached to him involuntarily and took him in her arms. His head nestled in her bosom. She had not realized just how fond of him she had grown. With the edge of her nightgown, she started wiping the perspiration from his face. His beard was wet. She held him tight and the icy fear started to melt slowly . . . It was a long time before Glasses was able to speak again. All he could think of was his father.

Donatella held his glasses carefully and tried to console him. She came closer. His eyes seemed deeper and the look in them – the 'regard' – was different. She felt as though she was seeing the person for the first time. For Glasses, Donatella's eyes were a pool of comfort.

The wind was becoming fire, the ferocious flames roaring with arrogance. As they watched, it was hard to imagine such power would ever beget fragile ash. Rayyes Ahmed was still nowhere to be seen. He had always been the one who would fix things when they went wrong. He would always appear at the school whether he was needed or not. But tonight, Rayyes Ahmed was having his wedding night at no expense. The sight of fire was beyond the horizon of his dilated pupils. He was being consumed by another fire. And he ... he was himself fire.

The window of the laboratory collapsed and the room took in a breath then exhaled an explosion. Everything was being reduced to charred blackness. Eventually, the hole that was once the window looked like the mouth of a grotto. Inside, the wicked tongues of fire flickered and wagged. Mustapha gazed at the grotto. One flame looked like a golden tooth in a wretched mouth. The flame consumed the debris in his chest, creating an unbearable vacuum. There was an ashen taste in his mouth. A sudden and overwhelming sense of help-lessness made his muscles go limp. No one could undo a stitch in the embroidery of destiny. When he was finally able to call on what remained of his voice, Mustapha spoke, addressing himself to no one in particular. That shard of a voice echoed in his chest, but to the outside world it was a mere whisper. His words had been stripped naked.

'I am being punished ...' Mustapha mumbled. 'It was a fake ... I had the sacred text faked ... this is the fire of hell which will burn me on the Day of Judgement ... it's a fake ... I had it made and I buried it when no one could see me ... but the eye of God sees all. He sees the tiny worms that crawl in the dark ...'

Mustapha's head was invaded by the sound of a scribbling pen. 'The angel is writing ...' he mumbled, 'recording the perfidy I've committed.'

Mustapha had uttered his confession in Arabic, his voice a tremor. Zohra was in a state of disbelief. Mustapha's words had a greater devastation on her than the fire. Mark did not know what to do. He did not understand a word but he sensed danger, the risks that the incontinence of Mustapha's tongue could bring. He tried to calm him with a cigarette and usher him to the side. But Mustapha would not budge, his confession seemed to have woven a web around him and pinned him to the ground, separating him from the immediate events. And all of a sudden he began howling, crying his heart out.

Mark was beginning to feel the panic take over within him. His hand lost its grip on the lid that had always kept the pressure under control. 'Calm down! For God's sake calm down!' he exploded. Mustapha fell silent. Saliva solidified in his mouth. His pear-shaped cheeks, usually full of charming words, suggested more a feeling of weight and unbearable emptiness. Words had deserted him. Now they were too far away to be reached.

53

It was a long time before the fire died out. The flames had refused to be quenched. Now the iron bed stood naked on its thin legs in the middle of the smouldering rubble, its fleshy covers consumed. Underneath, and blending into a charred background, the bones which Dr Chevalier had forgotten to take with him were reduced to ashen powder. The aftermath of the fire was nothing but pungent death. Not just death of what had been destroyed. It was more than that. Destruction was only a symptom and death had been summoned. Silence weighed in their tenebrous state.

The apprentice was attempting to sweep the floor. Mustapha stood in the middle of the courtyard, motionless. There was no sign of his rosary. His hands were buried in his pockets. Zohra was silently confused. Glasses rummaged in the debris with the help of the Professor. He excavated his clock. Its hands had interrupted their cycle. The time four minutes past four was frozen on it, but Glasses did not even notice. He managed to retrieve his large, blackened metal box and holding it with a canvas sack, he tried to open it with his knife but to no avail. '*Scheisse!*' Frustration escaped from his lips in German. The others stood around him, not knowing what to expect. They were not sure what he was doing. The box was distorted and so would have to be levered open. The apprentice cook appeared with his large knife from the kitchen and proceeded to struggle with the box, grasping it with his bare hands, impervious to its heat, but without success. Glasses took over. Donatella observed attentively, her lips parted, inviting hope. The dog barked violently, refusing the bone the cook had thrown to him. The guard paced around the courtyard restlessly, still hugging his gun. Halima and Hakima stood united by shock, their hands crossed in front.

It was some time before Glasses had any success. The box opened and the tip of the big knife snapped on the debris. The apprentice was heartbroken.

From the ashes came the phoenix that would haunt them. From within the box, Glasses took out the manuscript, slightly singed. It was intact except for the markings of artificial time. Donatella's face lit up. She felt so proud. Glasses had saved the mission of the excavation. Both the cook and his apprentice fell on the floor, praying. Halima walked away from Hakima, came to join them and began ululating joyfully. 'The fire did not destroy the Holy Quran and our saint, Sayyida Nesima, has been generous with her protection.' At the sound of a car engine, the team turned in the direction of the gate. Mustapha had disappeared.

Mark held the manuscript and took charge of the situation once again. A firm hand went back on the lid, controlling the pressure. He reached for the telephone but there was not even the usual crackling noise. The line was dead. 'Now,' thought Mark, 'we're totally cut off. And the collector's on his way from London.' There was nothing Mark could do to stop that.

Mark had declared the season over and that everyone was free to leave. It was time for the excavation members to return to their lives, but they were not the same people who had arrived in Wadi Hassoun, after all the digging they had undertaken. Glasses went to gather his things. By the time Donatella joined him in the room, he had already finished packing. There was hardly anything left of Glasses' belongings. He only had with him what he had brought from the laboratory the night before. His diary with all his ardent fantasies about Donatella had perished in the fire. Donatella stood at the door with the light behind her and Glasses could not see her face. This was the perfect time to ask. But his words evaporated. He simply did not know how.

'Shall we go to Alexandria?' Donatella's invitation came as a surprise. Glasses dropped his bag. His arms wrapped around Donatella, who was already close. He wanted to say something but words left his lips free to reach silently for Donatella's. The words of his favourite actress, the words of Ingrid Bergman, came to him: 'A kiss is a lovely trick designed by nature to stop speech when words become super-fluous.' And the trick lasted for a long time. Long enough now for the bird in Glasses' heart to take off. And he wished this now would last for ever, the way he felt when he joined pottery shards together. The words 'THE END' came before his eyes, marking the start of living his fantasies. His mother's voice whispered just below the music: 'But Daniel, she's not Jewish!'

As she gathered her things, Donatella looked at the mosquito net and sighed with relief. She was leaving mosquitoes behind. 'Surely the mosquitoes in Alexandria won't be as vicious as the mosquitoes of Wadi Hassoun,' she thought. She glanced at Zohra, sitting by the window, and was surprised to see beauty emerge in her face . . . The sun shone through Zohra's dun hair, giving it a fringe of light, and the excitement that filled Donatella's heart made her see things differently.

'I'll send you the photos,' said Donatella with an unexpectedly friendly voice as she emptied the contents of her canvas bag. The sand she had brought from the desert had seeped out, soiling every-thing. 'How can sand be so heavy when it's made of such small grains!' chuckled Donatella. Zohra did not say anything.

Alan too was ready in no time. He waited with the rucksack on his back, eager to return to the outside world. Halima and Hakima stood dejected. Hakima had tears running down her cheeks. Donatella was dismayed to discover that Alan had decided to join them on their trip. She emerged into the courtyard and looked at Mark before she threw her arms around Glasses. There was a brief commotion of embraces and goodbyes. '*Ma'a as-salaama*,' said Glasses warmly, and everyone was impressed by his pronunciation of the Arabic words. He smiled. 'I had a good teacher,' he said humbly.

'Catkoota,' Donatella called, searching the courtyard, but the cat did not appear. The smell of fire was still in the air. The driver tooted his horn at the gate. He was to give Glasses, Donatella and Alan a lift to the nearest town. Everyone accompanied them to the gate. With blank eyes, Zohra watched them walk away, dumbfounded by their sudden departure.

54

A long car pulled into the courtyard of the school, its metallic silver skin a multiplicity of reflections. Only the driver and someone sitting next to him were visible through the open windows. The dark glass of the windows at the rear screened the back seats. Professor O'Brien, Mrs O'Brien, Mark and Zohra stood on the steps, watching. None of them dared exchange looks. Zohra could hear the grinding of Mark's jaw.

The smoke from the fire had long died out but the stench was viscous, as was the silence between the four of them. They were the only members of the team still in Wadi Hassoun. Kodama San had left a few hours after Donatella, Glasses and Alan. He had shaken hands with everyone and surprised them when he declared that he was going to hitch-hike. It was otherwise an uneventful exit, as though he had simply gone to the darkroom where images would continue to emerge.

Mark came down two steps. Everyone's eyes were fixed on the car. Rayyes Ahmed walked towards it with his usual long strides. Hakima and Halima stood to one side of the entrance, their heads tilted, hoping to catch the first glimpse. The mysterious influence that had been talked about during all these months, the influence which had weighed with its absence, was about to step into the reality it had controlled from afar. The apprentice cook held the door for the driver who rushed to open the rear door.

Brown, lustrous shoes came to touch the earthen ground. The dog awoke from its slumber and opened its eyes wide. A man drew himself to his full height, an immaculate beige suit free even from the usual creases of a long journey. His scrutinizing gaze could be felt from behind his dark glasses. From the other side of the car, his double suddenly emerged like a reflection. The appearance of both dealers surprised Mark and his anxiety began to mount. But he reminded himself that the collectors were fond of surprises, and so he managed to keep the lid on the pressure. He hurried, Professor O'Brien and Mrs O'Brien behind him. They shook hands with the dealers, who seemed to look beyond them, at the derelict, blackened part of the school building. Zohra went to greet the driver and his companion, who seemed to be a bodyguard. She kept aloof, not knowing what to do, feeling out of place and insignificant. Neither of the dealers seemed to notice her presence. Mark had hinted that there was no need for her translation services any more, that she could leave. But she did not want to leave. She felt compelled to transmit what she had heard and understood. It was vitally important.

Professor O'Brien's back seemed larger than ever and Mark seemed taller. The four men walked towards the building and Zohra followed tentatively. They were about to enter the room, when the Professor turned and introduced her: 'Gentlemen, our translator!' His voice was surprisingly warm, almost with a hint of pride. The dealers shook hands with Zohra without a sign of interest.

'There's something I must tell you,' she ventured.

'Later!' interjected Mark, closing the door in her face.

From the steps, Zohra surveyed the courtyard in absent-minded dismay. There was no sign of Mrs O'Brien, who must have retreated to her room. The cook carried a tray filled with glasses of tea which wobbled as he crossed the courtyard, towards the driver and the body-guard. His apprentice walked behind with lumbering steps, two wooden chairs upturned over his head. Hakima and Halima, the cook and his apprentice, even the guard, would listen if she talked, but none of them would understand what she had to say even if they understood the Arabic. Never had Zohra felt so helpless in transmitting a meaning. It was an area of the untranslatable that was alien even to her.

'Did you see the rings on their fingers?!' whispered Halima to Hakima.

'Did you see the gold watches on their wrists?!'

'May God be praised for his creation!' exclaimed Hakima. 'You wouldn't tell who is who, so much alike they are!'

Zohra remembered Mark saying that the dealers were brothers, but he had never mentioned that they were identical twins. Both Hakima and Halima were still shaking their heads in awe and disbelief. The fact that the brothers were identical seemed to double the effect of their visit. All had waited eagerly to see the dealers in person, the power that had made possible the exploration of the village's riches. The replication in the dealers' appearance created an impersonal impact with a lack of authenticity ... Who was a copy of whom? Were they really exactly the same? One was older than the other by a few minutes and was nicknamed 'the elder'. That was how he was known in London. This was perhaps the only private information the dealers had ever disclosed about themselves.

Despair was digging a pit in Zohra's stomach. It was quite clear now. She was not going to get a chance to talk to the dealers. Mark had dismissed everything she had said, and when she had told the Professor her story he had evidently felt uneasy. He was not sure what to think and would have preferred she had not told him anything.

The team's driver would return by the afternoon and the car would be at her disposal to leave. It would be a few days in all and she would fly to London. But what she wanted most of all was to speak to Mustapha once she got to Cairo. A sigh escaped her. To Hakima and Halima, sitting on the other side of the steps, the sigh signalled serious worry.

'May it be the fate of your enemy,' said Hakima with care in her voice.

'What's Mustapha's family name?' asked Zohra.

Both Halima and Hakima looked at her, intrigued. The same thought occupied both their minds: Could Zohra be enamoured of Mustapha?

'God knows what Mustapha's name is!' they blurted in unison.

It suddenly dawned on Zohra that she had spent months with these people, months which seemed like years, so eventful and uneventful were they. And yet she did not know the full name of most of them. At that very moment the name 'Daniel Rosen' reverberated in her head for no apparent reason, and she wondered why Glasses had bothered to conceal his Jewishness. She would, most likely, never see Mustapha again. A flash of bustling Cairo came to her, with people rushing, each on their way somewhere. Mustapha? Mustapha would be in the opaque crowd of Cairo. The noise of the city in which they had been stranded for days, waiting for the permit before they could come to Wadi Hassoun, took over her fragmented thoughts, making her dizzy. It was a long moment before the rowdy image faded away.

There was no need for packing as such. Only a few bits and pieces to be slung into the bag and that would be that. All those cosmetic products brought from London had been long consumed. The bag would be lighter than when they had arrived. But within her, a dramatic change had occurred. The experience of these months had the weight of centuries. And the information about the manuscript in the dealers' hands was too much to bear. She would have to carry that truth with her, perhaps for the rest of her life.

'You look pale.' The apprentice cook startled Zohra. 'Shall I prepare some tea for you?'

'Yes, thank you,' she replied.

'Light as always . . .' he mumbled, grinning on his way to the kitchen.

Zohra felt a ball rise from the pit of her stomach and lodge in her throat. She did not know whether this was summoned by what felt like the last glass of tea in Wadi Hassoun, a sense of ending, or whether it was the unbearable information that weighed on her heart. It was then that Hakima brought sweets and offered a generous handful to everyone cheerfully. 'It's the Coptic New Year,' she announced with a broad smile. This came as a surprise to Zohra, who was totally ignorant of the Coptic calendar. In fact she was not aware of the date at all, although some of the team had been counting the days to leave Wadi Hassoun. 'Time in this place seems to have a totally different nature from anywhere else,' she thought. The daily digging had established a cycle which it seemed would go on for ever, but now, everything had come to an end.

55

The climbing plant in the corner against the steps seemed in desperate need of water. The last few windy days had also robbed it of many of its leaves. Zohra was still waiting for her glass of tea to cool down when the Professor appeared. 'The collectors want to talk to you,' he said.

In the room, all the men were standing up, and it felt as though she had walked into a tense moment. One of the dealers shook hands with her again, as if they had not met before.

'You said that you have something to say?' probed the other. She looked at one and then at the other with disbelief. The two clean-shaven faces were indeed identical. Zohra did her best to act as a mirror of events while telling them what had happened. First, she described the fire and the awe and fear it brought to those who lived it. She thought it was an important factor that would give meaning to Mustapha's confession. But one of the dealers urged her on. 'And then?' he kept saying as he fidgeted around the room. She started losing her words, something that rarely happened to her. She wished Mustapha was there, confessing, and she would simply translate.

Zohra was trying to describe how Mustapha broke down but the ball bounced back into her throat. She would usually choose the most appropriate word that would best express the meaning. She would dip into the containers, select the naked meanings and offer them as honestly as she knew how. But at this moment, the containers broke within her into perilous shards and meanings were lost in the jagged chaos.

While recounting what Mustapha had said, Zohra sensed the

collectors' impatience. As she concluded, she was deeply worried that her account would be followed by one of the brothers' recurrent interventions: 'And then?' But there was only the regular wheezing of the fan, which was hardly effective, simply turning hot air in the room. The curtain hanging over the window was coming and going with the warm intermittent breeze as though it were part of the conversation. The fetid smell of the long-dead fire was still beating. A silence of throbbing death reigned in the room. But the dealers were not to allow their dreams to be extinguished so gratuitously.

'You said, "he mumbled",' declared one of them when he finally spoke.

'Mumbled to himself?' repeated the other, taking off his dark glasses to reveal a quizzical look. The dealers' gestures were swift and brief, almost abrupt. They communicated with each other in a private shorthand.

'Yes . . . to himself . . .' said Zohra.

'Nonsense!' said Mark without a trace of anger in his voice, although his face was red.

One of the dealers gestured to Mark to be quiet and repeated: 'He *mumbled* to himself.' This time, there was a pause after the word 'mumbled' and no intonation of a question.

Zohra felt the ball swell in her throat again and blood rush to her face. She did not understand. What were they trying to imply? When the dealer spoke again, it was not to provide her with an explanation but to ask her a question. 'Are you sure you heard him correctly?'

'Of course I am sure,' she replied. 'I was standing right next to him.' The twins exchanged a decisive look before directing their eyes towards Zohra. Their indignation at the impertinence of her frankness fell accusingly over her.

'Look,' she said in a last defiance to the intimidating presence in the room and the ball in her throat and everything else, 'I heard Mustapha say he had the manuscript forged and he planted it. I heard him confess his crime and cry out his guilt. That was the reason why he was so distraught. I'm not imagining things.'

Everyone avoided Zohra's gaze now. Only Nefertiti looked at her with unwavering eyes. Kodama San had forgotten the soapstone bust he had bought in Cairo. To end the uneasy moment, Mark came to the rescue. 'You're not imagining anything,' he said. 'Distraught he was and that is why he was mumbling all sorts of nonsense. I'm surprised you took any of it seriously.' Mark's voice was on the edge of sarcasm, the tone of indignation now pronounced. Zohra's gaze fixed on the tears in the wall where the yellow paint must have come away with the Blu-tack when pictures were removed.

'That'll be all,' she heard one of the twins declare. 'We'll speak with you again later.'

'Could you please ask the Professor to come in,' requested the other. Zohra's hand was already on the doorknob when she heard the dealer add: 'Thank you.'

The Professor read Zohra's disappointment from the way she walked towards him.

'I am no manuscript specialist,' he said. 'But the scientific analysis will certainly reveal the truth.'

'They asked for you,' said Zohra.

She sat down on the steps again. Her tea was still waiting for her. She reached for the glass and poured its cold content onto the bottom of the plant climbing in the corner, aspiring hopelessly to reach for the sky. The dog's barking startled her. Car doors slammed. The engine roared and the car disappeared in the dust.

'They went to visit Jamel Bey's orchard.' The Professor's smile did not comfort Zohra.

56

Zohra glanced at the glazed pottery shards, carefully arranged on the shelf. Their attractive colours, which had originally enticed her and Donatella to retrieve them from the shard garden, had been dulled by an even film of ashy dust. The memory of that remarkable night would not be extinguished. The fiery image flared before her eyes. Soon, flames filled the space, reaching feverishly for everything in sight. It suddenly occurred to her that among Glasses' things that were burnt in the laboratory room was Dante's *Inferno*! And the absurd thought gnawed at her again, why had Glasses waited for the book to be returned to the library? Couldn't he simply have bought a copy? She felt the flames consume her body. Her thoughts were overtaken by Mustapha's confession: 'It's a fake ... I had it made and I buried it when no one could see me ...' She had been consumed in the same way for two years now, the confession burning in her memory. But tonight was the night she was going to confront them all. Tonight was the opening of the grand exhibition the dealers had been orchestrating with great finesse. 'Treasures of the Green Pavilion', the exhibition of the Wadi Hassoun excavation finds. Would Mustapha be at the reception tonight? In all likelihood he would have simply disappeared from the face of the Earth, taking his remorse with him, and that would suit everybody. But they were not going to get away with it. The moment of truth had finally arrived.

Ever since she had returned to London, Zohra had been obsessively reading about Islamic art. She learnt a great deal about its variety and wondered why it was called 'Islamic Art'. The name denied its rich diversity. Zohra read more specifically about manuscripts, about 'codicology', as Dr Evans would call it. She thought it was rather strange that the Professor seemed unaware that scientific analysis of a manuscript would not always prove it was fake or authentic. One eminent codicologist had stressed that carbon dating was not categorically decisive. 'So that means the only basis for determining the authenticity of the Wadi Hassoun manuscript is style,' she concluded confidently. 'I know it's a fake, Mustapha's confession proves it.'

A box full of photographs from the excavation season had been waiting to be put into albums for over eighteen months now. She had often delved in it and picked pictures at random, and by now they had lost their chronological sequence. She grabbed a handful. The images provoked erratic flashbacks. Here was a photograph of the Professor and his wife in the orchard of Jamel Bey. A wispy branch had screened part of Mrs O'Brien's face. Her effort at the time to refresh her lipstick had been a waste. And here, a view of Cairo at night from the Muqattam Hills. She had come to interpret their experiences in Egypt in a different way. Details acquired new meanings. Suddenly, it dawned on her that Mark had stayed behind with Mustapha on the Muqattam that night while she and the others headed back to the hotel. Perhaps the plotting between Mark and Mustapha had already started even then. She gazed at the photograph before her eyes, part of the scene they had all lived, and was seeing more than what was included within it. A realization kept cropping up, that she had lived a continuous, pervasive lie.

A close-up photograph showed a detail of a stucco pattern, an intricate pattern which could spread infinitely if not interrupted. This was the arabesque, which Professor O'Brien had explained to them in Cairo and which she had read about since. She could still hear him now after all this time. 'Islamic art's all about pattern,' the Professor had said, 'pattern as an expression of the infinite and its relation to the divine. With repetition and symmetry you get a sense of order that can go on for ever.' She remembered him pausing, almost as if he had begun that journey for himself. Then he added: 'The concept of "tawheed", the unity of the divine principle.' Zohra was struck by the eloquence of his explanation, and she remembered Glasses making a comment about the theory of fractals, but she could not remember what he had said. She was in fact not sure if she had even understood him at the time. She inspected the pattern which transformed a hard medium into lace, opening space to the infinite and making material transcend into light. The harmony of the pattern in the photograph was admirable. But, right in the middle of the wall, the infinite lines were broken by the cracks of time. As she ran her finger on the fracture which made the photograph look as though it was torn in the middle, she remembered the Fatimid ruins in Cairo and wondered what it would be like if every wound in those neglected buildings bled. The fracture was like the one in her heart. Amm Gaber came from that world which had encompassed a civilization that was doomed. It was the first time that Zohra was able to formulate that untranslatable emotion which had inhabited her since Wadi Hassoun. But even now, as she looked at the shape of the feeling she was not sure she understood its meaning.

The portrait of that seventeen-year-old woman in the cemetery in Cairo was surprisingly vivid. She had a broad smile. Her nail polish was chipped but she had vibrant red nails nonetheless! In the picture, there was no sign of the shrine where she lived with her family, in the cemetery. The picture could have been taken anywhere. Zohra remembered how they laughed at her Tunisian accent, those optimistic people who thought that they had been blessed with patience.

In one of the photographs, the workers posed. In the centre, Sabry leaned on his hoe, his face declaring a dignified air. A dark spot on the horizon caught Zohra's attention. After close scrutiny, she realized it was the village wanderer. What was his story? In all the photographs of the site there was no sign of Amm Gaber. Amm Gaber who was always with the Tree of Wishes in the cemetery. Zohra never understood how she managed to have no photograph of the tree or of Amm Gaber. Yet it was one of the most fixed images in her mind. The tree with its colourful ribbons, each ribbon a wish, a dream. Zohra dismissed the memory of the Tree lying dead. Only the words of Jamel Bey persisted: 'A tree has a living soul. Whoever kills a tree takes a life.' The villagers killed the Tree of Wishes and with it their dreams. And Amm Gaber? She could only see Amm Gaber as a figure. She could never remember his face. His white *'regard'* enveloped her. His undulate voice filled her and sometimes it felt that every grain in the desert of that voice embraced every grain in her being.

And this photograph, out of focus. Donatella was laughing when she took it. This was the boy who sold soft drinks in Cairo. He offered Mirinda, which was a discovery for all of them and which they found sweet and tasty then. The boy lived on the few boxes which formed his drink store. They were his bed during the few hours he slept. In spite of the hardship of his life, his face beamed with joy, and as he served them he sang a jolly song. The team looked surprised. The boy smiled and with laughter reverberating in the silver twinkling of the bottle-tops flying from his hand, he explained: *'Hiyya kharbana, kharbana!'* – It's all going into ruins anyway. Zohra remembered the team laughing wholeheartedly when they heard her translation.

Zohra now looked at events captured by the photographs in a totally different way, perhaps without the innocence with which she had lived them. She felt an incomprehensible impulse to take the photographs apart, to disintegrate the specks of which they were made, to make them reveal the real events. Every picture seemed to bring awareness of what was beyond its frame.

Another photograph, taken in Jamel Bey's orchard, showed Professor O'Brien, Mustapha and Mark. In the background the waterwheel seemed small, yet in real life it was huge. Mustapha and Mark stood very close, perhaps plotting the manufacture of the fake. Mark looked sweaty while Mustapha looked as though he had been dropped in oil when he was a baby. This must have helped him to be as slippery as he needed to be. But one never really knows how people turn out to be the way they are. She could still hear Mustapha's voice, that deep, cigarette voice she had heard unexpectedly many a night in the last two years. The voice that had been interrupting her sleep. He always used 'B' for 'P' when he spoke English.

Her father would love a copy of this photograph. She was wearing Zineb's crescent earrings and looked almost like one of the locals. 'When we arrived in Wadi Hassoun, we were total strangers,' thought

Zohra. 'Were we still strangers by the time we left?' She wondered about the beautiful Zineb. Was the intense desire she had sensed from her purely a paranoia on her part? And did Rayyes Ahmed marry Zineb eventually? He certainly wouldn't have married her if she had succumbed to his temptations out of wedlock. 'That kind of man is unable to embrace his dreams, if they become reality,' concluded Zohra.

And this picture which recorded the apprentice dancing in the party had also caught Monia's buttocks in shiny green satin, as she reached across the table for a Coca-Cola bottle.

And here, the school guard, like a statue, hugging his gun, caught by the flash in the dark, the wretched dog in the background, its eyes like two holes of red light, staring.

Zohra delved in the memory box again, for another pile of photographs, and shuffled through them as though looking for some meaningful sequence. The pictures were in disarray, just like her memories of the events she had lived in that remote place. This photograph revealed a sheep and a toilet bowl on one of the roofs near the Hakim Mosque in Cairo, the minaret prominent in the foreground. She remembered how they climbed the stairs, holding their cameras tight, proceeding slowly in their ascent, their only interest the view at the top. She recalled Donatella's scream when she banged the delicate vaccination spot in her arm and the tenderness on Glasses' face when he stood wondering what to do to comfort her.

She wished Donatella had not sent this photograph to her, the boy Mahmoud with his eyes closed. It was the last picture Donatella had taken for his mother. They had arranged him to look as though he was asleep so that he would be remembered that way. As she gazed at it involuntarily, Mahmoud's favourite phrase rang out in the room: 'What you mean?' and it brought sadness rather than the usual laughter. Zohra sighed. Why did Mahmoud have to die? Why such a gratuitous death? Something in Zohra had never accepted the boy's death. Perhaps such beautiful fragility was not made for this world, she pondered.

Zohra reflected on how during those months the team's lives became enmeshed with the villagers' realities, how they had shared the locals' sorrows and joys and how by the end of the excavation the people of Wadi Hassoun were sad to see them leave. She thought how, in spite of their differences of nationality, culture, education, understanding, bonds grew between people. The team had landed in the country with many preconceptions, ideas that were like holes in their heads, and they went around cutting reality into pieces that would fit those holes neatly. The villagers too tried to paste their pictures on to the team. But they soon had to relinquish the convenience of that game as life surprised them all constantly. Zohra thought of how their time in Wadi Hassoun fluctuated constantly across layers. At the surface there was no sense of the deeper level, and at the deeper level the surface did not exist.

Zohra closed the box and wished she could do the same with her indelible memories about that faraway place that had not ceased to haunt her since her return to London, torn bits of a reality that was starting to feel fictitious.

Night had fallen. No moon was present. Around her, everything was absorbed by the dark. Persian music filled the room, drawing from the farthest depths, before time, beyond existence. Words penetrated her being without literal understanding. Something in the Blue Manuscript resonated with that timeless quality. The Arabic letters, without diacritical marks to assist comprehension, were living beings which transcended language.

A page from the Blue Manuscript came before her eyes. The image was of Mark's slide projection of one of the authentic pages. Those pages from the volume which was split, its spine broken so as to sell the pages for maximum profit. As she visualized this, she felt a chill in her own spine, perhaps the chill the manuscript had felt when it was dismembered.

Silence filled her. The record had ended some time ago. Only the relentless click of the needle marked a continuous heartbeat. A singing voice emerged from nowhere; perhaps from the depth of memory, from within her, the voice of Amm Gaber, that voice which had no gender, which was at once the desert and the garden, the mountain and the river, the sun and the moon, the earth and the sky, fire and water, one and the other, sound and silence, filled the space. One half of her wanted to tell the other half that she carried the ancestors' history, their culture, not just their genes. As she discovered Islamic civilization through its visual expression, it was as though the Eastern side of her had come to know itself, and at the same time the Western side came to see the Eastern. She felt she had bridged the gap between the two. Her father was not really aware of his cultural heritage himself because a breach in history had interrupted life's continuum. The excavation had changed her own vision of her roots, of what her Arabic name was linked to. It led her to discover what was part of her but which she had never known. Somehow, she felt directly connected to the Blue Manuscript. Was it not produced in Ifriqiya, the country of her father, Tunisia? But it was clear to Zohra that this was not the reason why she felt the way she did about it.

Speaking more than one language, Zohra had learnt to use her tongue. Within this tongue was the passage from one language to another, one country to another, from one culture to another across boundaries. It moved between differences and meanings which linked everyone. And tonight she had a very important story to tell the world. Never had words played such a significant role in her life as they were about to.

Zohra left her flat with an angered determination that had been fuming within her for a long time. The padded shoulders of her jacket seemed to augment the confidence she needed. They had ignored her all this time and for once she would not pass unnoticed. Her mind crowded with the different ways she would confront them tonight. The excavation members had continued working on the finds for publication, while her role was completely finished at the end of the digging. They had not contacted her nor had anything to do with her since they parted ways in Wadi Hassoun. Only Donatella had sent her some photographs. And the bitterness of feeling rejected had been eating away at her self-worth. Tonight, she was going to the exhibition opening not because they had remembered to invite her but because she was translating for a Japanese news company who were covering the event.

The upper section of the window of the tube carriage was a myriad of reflections. Images from the box of photographs insisted on pursuing her. Memories poured forth, a thread tying her to that faraway place. The team had been thrown together in Wadi Hassoun as though it was a decisive intersection in the complex map of their destinies. Just like in this tube carriage, bodies were close, sweats and smells mixed. Her head was against someone's shoulder. Her nose under someone's armpit. The doors hissed shut. People braced themselves as the train lurched forward. The stale underground air hung stagnant in the overheated carriage. In spite of being squeezed together almost to the point of physically merging, the other still remained a stranger. In Wadi Hassoun, that remote and isolated place, the other seemed to be sometimes an angel, sometimes a horrible devil.

The rocking of the carriage echoed the racing of her heart as she journeyed towards the moment for which she had steeled herself. She was on her way to the moment of truth, to rid herself of the weight of the confession she had carried all this time. She was on her way to face them. She was on her way to create a scandal, something out of character for someone who had always wanted to be neutral. But there was no other way. The archaeologists had tried to construct history but in fact had fabricated a lie which they believed. And now, on her way to their glorious exhibition, she was imagining the look on their faces when she would drop the bomb that would shatter the meticulously fabricated illusion.

57

Rococo angels looked down with their cracked faces from on high –
an ornate, gilded dome, a sharp contrast to the naked sky that had
inspired Ibn al-Warraq. But there was no sign from here of the main
object of the exhibition. The display cabinets standing in the middle
of the grand room were lost in the hubbub. The space was flooded
with guests, filled with chit-chat, a shower of words, the fluffy noises
of socializing. Men and women mostly dressed in dark suits. The
guest of honour, a politician, a charismatic figure who had prompted
media interest in the reception, stood with the dealers and Dr Evans.
They were discussing the art historian's publication of the manuscript
– a coffee-table book which was also on display.

The exhibition and this scholarly publication were part of the meticulous process to enhance the prestige and inevitably increase the
value of the finds excavated in Wadi Hassoun. These had already
become art objects. In late twentieth-century London, these objects
were worth a fortune on the art market. The gap between this newly
constructed reality and their original context was beyond comprehension. More than symbols, witnesses of time, actual carriers of
civilization, now they had somehow acquired an entirely different
kind of value.

Yet again, Zohra was speaking someone else's words instead of her
own. She had just finished translating an interview with one of the
Arab dignitaries, for the Japanese. How strange it was to be a link in
a longer chain. Her translation of the Arabic words into English was
only half a step in the journey of communication between Arabic and
Japanese. Across the room, she glimpsed Mrs O'Brien talking to Mark.

Then she noticed the double image of the dealers, a double identity. The last time she saw them was in a faraway place that had apparently no connection with this grand nineteenth-century hall. She had left them in one of the rooms of the school and walked away from it all. The dealers had spent no more than two hours in Wadi Hassoun. There was never any question of them staying longer in those primitive conditions. Perhaps the dealers believed Zohra. They had sensed Professor O'Brien's implicit trust in her veracity. But there was too much at stake. They were not going to lose the manuscript in which they had invested so much for such a long time. It sickened them to even contemplate the possibility that their magnificent manuscript could be taken away from them by the words of a weak go-between. Before they left Wadi Hassoun, the dealers gave generously to Rayyes Ahmed – not only the bonus that Mark had promised him but also more than would be necessary to renovate the school. Spaghetti was to manage the finances. Rayyes Ahmed was very pleased with this plan. Early the following morning, Zohra left with the Professor and Mrs O'Brien, Mark stayed behind to supervise the final packing and shipping arrangements. During the long journey to Cairo, neither the Professor nor Zohra spoke about the manuscript. Zohra did not want to speak at all. It was as though she did not want to have anything to do with words. Mrs O'Brien sat between them, providing her husband with the protective buffer she thought he needed. It was a muted journey in which Zohra could feel the pain in the unspoken words on her twisted lips, her throat dry and barren. Actually, the Professor was thinking about the expedition report he would have to submit to the dealers. Deep down, he was very excited but he kept his excitement to himself. Only his eyes twitched uncontrollably. The dealers had promised him another season to further his search, but he had no intention of asking the translator to join him for it.

Zohra leaned forward to read the labels behind the glass of the display cabinets. Her name in gold Arabic letters dangled from her chain, almost brushing against the glass. She thought how the Coptic jeweller in that little shop was right. Glasses did change his mind and leave his chain behind. He did not even care about the money. The labels in the cabinets only situated the object from the point of view of art history and Zohra was not actually reading them. She was seizing the momentum within herself. She would have to handle words with eloquence and dexterity. The word was a container, a fragile one – a shell that could break into sharp slivers and spill the meaning. The translator had learnt how to handle that container carefully by profession. But tonight, she was about to speak out her own words. She was about to cry out at the top of her voice.

'The manuscript can be dated to the tenth century on the basis of the script but it can't be situated precisely in geographical terms. Qayrawan, one of the leading cities in medieval Islam, and a centre of learning and calligraphy, is a possible place where it could have been copied.' Zohra overheard the unmistakable drone of Dr Evans, who did not acknowledge her even though she looked in her direction.

Dr Evans was enthusiastically proffering an array of information while standing beside the cabinet in which the fake was exhibited. Something was what it was not. If original work provides personal contact with the source of its creation, thought Zohra, the fake can only provide contact with technical abilities. If the creative act provides contact with the real being, the fake can only provide contact with the external surface. In that meticulous copy, stroke by stroke, the distance from the source of creation stretches stroke by stroke even further. Such imitation can never be faithful. The similarity is simply an unearned sentiment. The manuscript volume behind the glass of the display cabinet is naked, wide open, yet it reveals nothing of its true identity. It carries the illusion of meaning in creasing and oxidization. The momentum of Zohra's confrontation had reached its peak when she noticed a microphone in the room and wondered whether she would speak her words into it. To discharge her duty well, her thin voice would need amplification, but her words did not. She had been choosing her words carefully, stringing them together into the most effective sentences, building up to the moment when she would create a scandal and say everything. And that moment had just arrived. She would not betray those words that were to be words of her own, those words which she had to declare because she carried the responsibility of being a witness, not just to Mustapha's confession but as the guardian of what she had come to see. Unlike her father, she would be worthy of her cultural heritage.

'Hiya!' cried Donatella. Both she and Glasses embraced Zohra. So did the Professor, with great warmth. Alan's handshake was almost firm. Kodama San's smile carried a comforting quietness. Everyone, even Mark, was friendly to her.

'Awesome that you could make it!' he said. Zohra's anger melted in an instant and everything was lost in her confusion.

There was no trace of rejection, not even from the dealers, who surprised her with an energetic, cheerful welcome. 'Our translator!' said one of them, reintroducing Zohra to Dr Evans. 'You know Professor Evans?!' Of course Zohra knew her, but she did not know until then that she had been garnished with the title of 'Professor'.

'This is what we hoped for,' said the other dealer, pointing to the Blue Manuscript, 'but never imagined we would be so successful.' Everyone murmured praise as they leaned towards the case. Mark had a wide smile, underlying his self-importance. And still, wearing the same smile, he stepped forward for a publicity photograph.

There were more than two hundred guests. Trade was operating on multiple levels in the exhibition hall. People moved with difficulty as they circulated, networking the way people do in these kinds of functions, a drink in hand, looking for the person who could be useful. Swept by the glitter and glamour of this new moment, and keeping up with the steps of her companions, Zohra found herself following the pattern of self-promotion.

And the words of protest about the fake which the translator had been intending to declare never emerged. Contrary to her habit, she did not ask which part of herself, the Arab or the English, had let her down.

Where had all those words gone? All those words she had been choosing carefully, precise words to reveal everything in the most effective way? The words of truth had migrated to the well of silence. What could she do with Mustapha's confession anyway? Everything that had happened in Wadi Hassoun started to appear more like fiction than reality. Was it all a figment of her imagination? With time, Mustapha's mumblings did not make sense. He was *mumbling* after all. His voice faded. Its smoky resonance evaporated. Did he ever say anything? Had she ever been to Wadi Hassoun? Was she ever witness to anything?

58

In the sky dome of Wadi Hassoun, a slender crescent was elegantly drawn, a new moon, but the moon did not change. Only the Earth moved and events turned. By dawn, the slender crescent had surrendered its place to the sun. A cock crowed and was answered from the other side of the village. It was the start of the first Friday of the crescent moon, the ritual day, the day men left the village and young women had their hair trimmed so that it would grow healthier. On the mount of Sayyida Nesima, scissors worked incessantly. It was a mesmerizing sight. Young women lined up, their hair loose, ready to be trimmed. The end of each hair split, forking out like the branch of a tree, not as a sign of life and growth but of death, each branching hair paler in colour and weaker than its root. It was Om Omran who cut about the thickness of two fingers from each woman's hair. Her own hair, usually the colour of fire, had become as white as snow. It had not seen henna for a long time. For Om Omran who had never seen snow, it was as white as flour. She used a *misht*, a wooden lice comb, and took her time, combing every woman's hair thoroughly. The heap of trimmings grew higher, its colour contrasting with the women's dresses, whose flowers were bright, in full bloom.

There were no men around except for the tent-maker. Leaning against the wall of the mausoleum, he was distracted from his needle-work by the scene. He pulled at the silk thread, trying to undo a stitch, but the stitch remained stubborn.

Throughout this day-long ritual, the usual songs were sung, weaving a narrative that lulled hearts. Melody and words were both joyful and sad. They told of a sacred book dug up, a crop from Mother

Earth, saved, thanks to the blessings of Sayyida Nesima, from the fire ignited by malevolent jinn. The mythical song had memorized every detail. It included the boy Mahmoud's death, the warning of stepping on the tombs of the dead, the Omda's wise guidance, the impregnation of the beautiful Zineb by the jinn, the gift of gold treasure, bestowed by the saint on the village and stolen by the foreigners ... All to the rhythm they intoned every month. They sang different words, stitching the echoes of the last events into the fateful tapestry of the myth that helped explain them. Myth was perhaps what came closest to truth. The villagers remained trapped in their reality, the gap between worlds immense. Dust had long settled and events of the excavation were more myth than reality.

The door of Zineb's house and its orange windows were closed. With her gifted hands, the beautiful Zineb, in her deep purple dress, painted and repainted the walls of her courtyard with layers of fantasy. And the colourful figures she created kept her company in her inner world.

The indigo-turbaned wanderer was sometimes here, sometimes there. Earth was his bed and sky his cover and bed was where night found him. He dragged his feet and dust followed him wherever he went. A witness outside time. One day had died but another was on its way to being born. This was the first night that Mahmoud's mother did not hear the voice of grief whisper in her fraught heart, the first time since she had looked death in the eyes that she slept peacefully. And she saw her beloved child in her dreams.

In the orchard, the waterwheel turned, lifting water, splashing. The grey cat sat next to Amm Gaber, its ears pricked and its emerald eyes wide open. Its four kittens, golden, curled up asleep. Amm Gaber reflected silently.

'The well of silence is filled with words, the serrated words of anger, distended frustration, frozen sadness ... There also reside the soft, fragrant words of love, the palpitating words of passion, words of secrets, words strangled at a tender age, words that never see the light, words oppressed at the age of thought, words with clipped wings, words which never go beyond the shape of a sigh, the swollen word, the choked word. The well of silence brings together the silences of all times. The well, dark, a dry throat, a tunnel leading beyond the abyss of nothingness. The well of silence gathers all unspoken words, stretching past the farthest future, beyond the farthest past, for there are always more unspoken words. With words, rosaries are strung; my rosary does not follow any order. No air, no sound, the nothingness of absorbent darkness, a sluiced memory and a repose from noisy thoughts, the well of silence, a well with no echo. Words dig, reaching beyond the beginning of time, until there is no number to measure time, no line to define space. There are lazy words, words that have not been used for too long, dormant words, some even sadly dead. In the well of silence words belong to different languages, from different parts of the world, from different people, young and old, male and female, rich and poor, from every religion ... The words in the well of silence are all united but their silence is not the same.

'When people swallow words, they think they are simply quashed, but these words fall into forgetfulness and from there travel to the well of silence. A journey in time is different from a journey in space. Coming from all over the world, they do not need to learn one road, to know one path. Many different ways lead to the well of silence. Some words travel through the past, others through the present and others through the future, but all meet in the well of silence.

'Wheel of water, wheel of life, I have lived in the well of silence for many years. Among the inhabitants of the well of silence are meanings that have escaped the prison of words, prisons that have unjustly distorted them. In the well of silence, words are written in white on white, the depth, a mirror of time, reflecting thousands of centuries, those gone and those to come, truth digging in a spiral. The mirror of time is found in a forgotten hour; in its depths, the meanings of words that cannot be heard.

'I want to be the wind that directs the sail towards the harbour of the beloved, the water that quenches the thirst of growth, the manure that nourishes the scent of the rose. I want to be silent.

'I do not take refuge in a comfortable perspective. We fear a vision that has no horizon, the sacred beyond definition. I search for the void. I do not fear it. I yearn to empty myself. I long to speak to you with words from the well of silence.

'They came to dig but only brushed the path of truth, close to the Blue Manuscript. Yet they could not be further away. Some were busy plotting the manufacture of the fake. All were busy plotting the manufacture of their lives.'

Drops of water wet Amm Gaber's face. The waterwheel endlessly turning, lifting the water, splashing. His white eyes were wide open, reading his own silent reflections.

'Not all silence is the same. Not all emptiness is the same. Not all simplicity is the same. A silence can be charged. An emptiness, replete. A simplicity, complex.

'The word holds unlimited power. Words open the pores of our skin, make our hair stand on end, inflict wounds deeper than the sword, heal our pain, melt our hearts . . . A word changes every time it takes a new companion. Some words are pierced, they have been worn out; people use them every time they string a sentence. The ugliness of a word does not originate from its letters just as the saltiness of the sea does not originate from the Earth that holds it. Some words cannot be saved. With mouldy tails wrapped around them, their bellies swollen, they have been distorted, lost them-selves. Some words keep away from others, hollow shells; they fear being crushed.

'When you feel speechless because you are touched by beauty, by passion, by sadness, by joy, by grief, when meanings are ineffable, perhaps the words have migrated to the well of silence.

'The roots of words from different languages interlace like living beings. Just as in every child there are all children. In every woman there are all women. In every man there are all men. Resonances are not only between different places, they are between different times, different eras. Humanity is linked in time, in space. A hand has different fingers but it is one hand.

'The well of silence, a throat that is all the silent throats of the world, with all the unuttered words. The word aching, so swollen, it cannot emerge. Words of protest, words of love, words of anger, words of justice. All the silence of the word, eager to be uttered, yet does not or cannot find a way.

'And all those words with the face of a newly born, all those words which are lost by the time the tongue can speak, all those words that hold truth, all those words go to the well of silence. Words trapped in the throat of the dumb, all the words that cannot penetrate deaf ears, words that would not take shape, words that have been censored, especially words that have been censored. The well of silence is the well of truth.'

The night had descended swiftly, unfurling. Near Amm Gaber was a butterfly. Motionless, its wings together, their backs a velvety dark blue, blending into the night's curtain. Amm Gaber's lips did not stir, only his fingers arranged and rearranged date kernels to the rhythm of the silent invocation in his heart.

'If you give me riches, do not take away my happiness.

'If you give me strength, do not take away my mind.

'If you give me fame, do not take away my modesty.

'If you give me modesty, do not take away my dignity.

'And if you give me power, do not take away my ability to forgive.'

There was a long moment of nothingness before the old man continued his silent reflection.

'Life is a moment. A king once demanded a cure which would balance his unstable moods. After much deliberation, the royal physician concluded words would be the best solution. So they made him a ring engraved with "This too will pass". When he was overwhelmed by sadness, one glance at the ring would remind the king that his sadness would not be permanent. And when he was intoxicated with joy he was reminded to remain sober because this too will pass.'

Amm Gaber chuckled. The crescent moon had grown more luminous than the night before but was tiny in the silent inky expanse of the sky. An absorbent darkness enveloped him. The sound of a flute rose from the cemetery.

'In the river, ripples flow east, west, downhill, never taking a rest. The river has a bed but never sleeps, a mouth but never speaks. O wheel of water, wheel of life, that which is covered with the days is naked. Time always passes and its layers always lift. Days are like wind in a wheel.'

For a moment, the flute filled the night with joy. Mahmoud's giggling fluttered, mixing with its voice. 'Would he still be laughing so if he were here?' Amm Gaber's question was silent. His hands stretched in the breeze; his fingertips were reading the boy's features the way they had always done. The butterfly spread its wings. Its colours were invisible behind the screen of darkness. But within Amm Gaber the colours of orange, purple and green unfurled, and in that vast expanse of the inner desert the butterfly was a miraculous flower.

'Wheel of life, the sound of that flute is flame not wind. I swim in the well of silence between the waves of meanings.

'A tear is at the end of laughter and at the beginning of crying. Wheel of life, I speak to you without sound because the well of silence needs no tongue to speak, just as you need no ears to hear. And perhaps, just perhaps, Umar Ibn al-Warraq too can hear me. Or did I lose my last listener when the Tree of Wishes was killed? I was told that my great great ancestor, story-teller to the Fatimid Court during the prosperous and tolerant rule of Caliph al-Muizz, used to say; "Without his listeners, a story-teller is nothing." I disagree with my great great ancestor. His faithfulness was to his listeners. My faith-fulness is to my stories. This was the same ancestor who handed down the story of Ibn al-Warraq's Manuscript. He related how the Callig-rapher's health had improved greatly in Wadi Hassoun. The dry climate was beneficial and a few years passed before death came to claim him. One volume of the Manuscript was buried with the Callig-rapher near the waterwheel. His pen lay beside him, its tongue dipped in the well of silence for ever. His wish to make pilgrimage was accomplished but his wish to be buried in the desert was only partially fulfilled because the desert had already been transformed into the orchards of the Green Pavilion. As a child, I visited the pavilion and its magnificent orchards in my father's accounts. But of those magnif-icent orchards only this part has remained alive. Jamel Bey himself doesn't know what treasure lies in his orchard. He runs constantly from Wadi Hassoun to Cairo and from Cairo to Wadi Hassoun, obsessed with increasing his riches.'

'I have collected words over the years, even those words that attempt to express silence: "*Samata, samt, sumut, sumaat, saamit, samut, simmeet...*" but the most sacred thing of all is silence itself. Throughout the years I have dug the layers within myself. I am approaching the end of season, still I have not reached the beginning.' Amm Gaber wiped a drop that had run down his face. And suddenly, for no apparent reason, he burst out laughing, exposing his charcoal teeth which contrasted with the glistening whiteness of his eyes.